ULTIMATE **STARZ**

by OWEN KEEHNEN

Herndon, VA

Cover photography credits:
Tyler Saint (front) photo courtesy Titan Media
Francesco D'Macho (back) photo courtesy of Hot House Entertainment
All photos used by permission.

Published in the United States
Printed in Canada

STARbooks Press
PO Box 711612
Herndon VA 20171

Cover and book design by: John Nail

ISBN: 978-1-934187-364

THE CAST OF **CHARACTERS:**

FOREWORD

When I first began this series with *STARZ,* I didn't anticipate the success of the book or that it would even be a series. Initially, I wanted to provide a voyeuristic window onto the lives of the men who star in gay XXX films. Almost from the start, these men surprised me, revealing themselves as so much more than simply sex objects and fantasy figures. From the start, it was apparent that there was no such thing as a "typical porn star." These men were individuals who entered the industry for a variety of reasons – everything from paying child support to college loans to boosting escort asking price to treating a partner to the vacation of his dreams to paying for rehab. The reasons oftentimes were not financial. Some already had very lucrative day jobs but entered XXX out of a need to be desired, acknowledgement, a quest for fame, a strong exhibitionist streak, to "shake things up," or out of a pure love of sex. Oftentimes, it was a combination of factors.

I guess my reasons for undertaking the project were perhaps to "shake things up" a bit, too. Sure, I was a fan of porn, but my background prior to the *STARZ* book had been as a journalist for magazines as well as a syndicate of gay and lesbian papers. Primarily, I was an interviewer of gay and lesbian celebrities – authors, activists, artists, musicians, and such. Among the over 300 interviews I conducted were those with such varied and historically significant folk as Paul Monette, Quentin Crisp, David Wojanrowicz, Dick Sargent, Sapphire, Camille Paglia, Joan Nestle, John Preston, Jewelle Gomez, Samuel Steward, Harry Hay, David B. Feinberg, Edmund White, Ethan Mordden, Robert Ford, Joe Steffan, Greg Louganis, James Earl Hardy, Charles Busch, Scott O'Hara, Jerry Herman, David Leavitt, Dennis Cooper, Jack Nichols, Leslea Newman, Michael Cunningham, Dorothy Allison, Sasha Alyson, Rupert Everett, Janis Ian, etc.

A decade later, the historical significance in documenting the gay and lesbian culture of that era is apparent to me. I was fortunate enough to bring light and add clarity to many of those community voices and pioneers whose lives were cut short by HIV / AIDS or other illnesses. Now these voices and can be accessed, quoted, and understood more fully through those interviews (most are on the Internet somewhere). I continue to be very proud of that body of work.

Sometime between the first and second *STARZ* book, I began to see these interviews with gay porn stars in a somewhat similar light. Some say it's just sex, but "just sex" is the basis of what defines us as homosexuals. Granted, we are more than porn, but porn is a part of who we are. You can choose not to watch it, but every gay newspaper or magazine will carry some reference to it. Porn shapes gay advertising and marketing, floods the Internet, dominates DVD sales and rentals, and has even generated a lot of money for charity. These men are the faces (bodies, dicks, and asses) of a multibillion dollar international industry that has helped shape, for better or for worse, those desires and thus our community. Seeing that light, capturing these voices, went from a voyeuristic hobby to a significant exploration of gay sex and sexual mores, gay sex work, gay sexual iconography and representation, and the mainstreaming of porn. Sure it's a fun fan guide that's frisky, hot, and filled with cock and ass shots, but hopefully it's something more as well.

The importance of these books has been further enhanced by the untimely passing of several of the interview subjects. From *STARZ* both Austin Black and Andy Dill have since passed away and from *MORE STARZ* Johnny Rey died between the time of our interview and the book's eventual publication. *ULTIMATE STARZ* is dedicated to them and to all the others who have enriched our fantasies, gotten us off while getting it on, and sometimes even redefined the ways we have sex. Enjoy.

– Owen Keehnen

ULTIMATE **STARZ**

BEN ANDREWS

So what did you first realize you had a "larger than life" endowment?

There was no one specific moment where I realized I was bigger than the rest. I just gradually noticed after being told by each guy I messed around with that I was the biggest they'd had, and that I wasn't seeing anyone bigger than me. I'm still waiting to.

How did your XXX career come about?

Back in February 2006, I was a month into living in a "model house" in Orlando, Florida, with other guys my age who were working in porn. They settled for small, crappy studios and websites, but I wouldn't settle for anything but the best. Someone online advised me that I should send in my pictures to Lucas Entertainment and I did. The very next day I got an email from them letting me know that Michael happened to be in Florida for an appearance and if I wanted, we could set up an interview. I jumped at it. He was in West Palm Beach, an hour from where I was staying, so I ended up paying a total stranger to drive me there since none of the guys I lived with would do it because they didn't

STATS

BIRTH DATE: June 19, 1985

SIGN: Gemini

HOMETOWN: Cleveland, OH

HEIGHT: 6'2"

WEIGHT: 170 lbs

TWO BEST CHARACTER TRAITS: My down to earth personality and great sense of humor.

TWO WORST CHARACTER TRAITS: An unbreakable love of fast food and a bad habit of sleeping in until the afternoon!

FAVORITE MUSIC: Christina Aguilera, Gwen Stefani, Nelly Furtado (Top 40)

FAVORITE MOVIES: *The Sweetest Thing, Mean Girls, BioDome.*

FAVORITE MOVIES I'VE BEEN IN: *La Dolce Vita, The Bigger the Better, The Intern.*

XXX COSTAR I'D DO AGAIN IN A MINUTE: Francois Sagat or Brent Corrigan.

IF I COULD MAKE ONE REQUEST ON A PORN SET IT WOULD BE: A shower! Can you believe we don't have one at the Lucas Entertainment Studios! We wash off with butt wipes!

AS A TEEN I ALWAYS FANTASIZED ABOUT SEX WITH: My older cousin and Antonio Sabato, Jr.

CURRENT FANTASY MAN: Still Antonio!

SEXIEST PART OF A MAN: Face is numero uno.

THREE INGREDIENTS OF MY HOTTEST SEX FANTASY: An abundance of foreskin, a full, natural bush and big low hanger balls.

FAVORITE ITEM IN MY SEXUAL TOYBOX: Just my trusty bottle of Pjur lube and a Magnum XL.

MOST PRIZED POSSESSION: My larger-than-life penis.

HOBBIES: Chatting online, hitting NYC night spots, and sleeping in.

PETS: My white Chihuahua, Pierre.

PET PEEVES: Smokers, snoring, and people who cut in line!

like that I was meeting with a major studio, especially Lucas. My interview went amazingly, and I was basically signed on the spot and flown to NYC a month later to begin my new life as Ben Andrews.

What were you looking for when you got into it?

I wanted fame. Living in that house with those guys made me wanna rise above them and be among the best out there, and the checks definitely aren't hurting me.

So Ben, how has making adult movies differed from your expectations?

I knew what I was getting into when I started for the most part. The only thing I wasn't anticipating was how much you sweat being under those bright lights!

Speaking sexually, very few guys are as skilled as me when it comes to ...

Giving head. It's all about technique.

What things do you usually do to prepare for a film shoot?

Sleep is definitely the most important thing. In addition to getting my zzzs, I generally don't shoot a load for two or three days prior, and I watch what I eat so I don't have a belly full of food.

And how do you usually spend the night after a day of filming?

Usually sleeping. I get headaches from the Viagra, so I take some Tylenol and call it a night.

What is the most aroused you have ever been on screen?

I think the most aroused I've been on screen so far was my scene for Encounters 3. I hadn't gotten off in days and the setup was just so hot that I had a hard time controlling myself!

Have you ever developed a crush on any of your costars? Care to name names?

I had a big crush on Ray Star back in the day. We haven't had a scene together or anything, but we both had our first photo shoots with the company on the same day and we helped each other out in making sure the blood stayed flowing to the right places for the shoot.

If you were making a movie called Ben Andrews' Orgy who would you want as your four costars?

Easy! François Sagat of Raging Stallion, Brent Corrigan, Ray Star of Lucas Entertainment, and Roman Heart.

That's interesting. It's rarely an easy question for you guys. Do you have some amazing fantasy you are just waiting for some director to ask you to film?

My fantasies are very Guys Gone Wild style, very voyeuristic. So to film a scene with a strong voyeuristic undertone would be the hottest thing to me.

Where is the wildest place you've ever had sex off screen?

There are a few! The teachers' bathroom in high school, the roof of my apartment building in the rain, and church parking lot.

How do you consider yourself a typical Gemini?

According to Wikipedia, Gemini's are "associated with youth and versa-

"I wasn't anticipating how much you sweat being under those bright lights!"

Ben Andrews [PHOTO COURTESY LUCASENTERTAINMENT.COM]

tility. Individuals born under this sign are thought to have a sociable, fun-loving, versatile, lively, communicative, liberal, intelligent, mentally active and friendly character but one which is also prone to moodiness, inconsistency, superficiality, restlessness and laziness."

That's hitting the nail on the head!

Describe your ideal romantic evening.

I'm a pretty easy date. Dinner and a funny movie is my favorite way to spend an evening on a date.

BUCK **ANGEL**

How did you get started in the business?

For years I worked behind the camera making fetish films, and MTF porn. I realized that there was no one like me in the entire adult industry, so I decided to start making my own movies and websites, and the rest is history!

What were you looking for when you got into it?

I was looking for a way to represent a form of sexuality that had never been seen in the adult world before. I was very excited to be a pioneer at the time. But now, looking back, I had no idea how hard this was going to be. Being a pioneer is not for the weak, that's for sure! It turns out the adult industry was not nearly as open to something new and different as I thought they would be! It took a lot of breaking down of doors and barriers – and surprisingly closed minds.

Do you recall the first movie you made and the first bit of direction you were given?

Well the first movie I made was my own production. It was The Adventures of Buck Naked and I basically directed myself. It was a very POV type of film. I actually had a scene in it featuring another FTM, who I got to direct. He was a natural performer, which is always good because you can just concentrate on shooting the film. I did shoot a movie with Titan and got direction from Brian Mills, the director. He was so easy to work with and made me feel very welcome and sexy. Cirque Noir was a very historical film for the gay porn world, as I was the first FTM to ever be in a mainstream gay porn film.

As a transsexual performer do you think you feel a lot of sexual role model pressure?

That is a good question! I would say I don't feel pressure because I am who I am and do what I do naturally. I'm aware that some people will appreciate what I'm doing, and others won't. But I also know that many FTMs and MTFs look up to me, and I feel very honored to have people feel that way about me and my work. I also try to be clear that I'm only representing myself, and not all FTMs.

How would you describe your acceptance within the gay XXX world?

At first they were totally freaked out by me. No one would even talk to me, let alone watch my films. But I was persistent and kept at it. Now I would say that I am pretty much accepted with very few exceptions. There are always going to be those guys who think of me as a woman

STATS

BIRTH DATE: June 5, 1972

SIGN: Gemini

HOMETOWN: Los Angeles, CA.

HEIGHT: 5'8"

WEIGHT: 165 lbs

TWO BEST CHARACTER TRAITS: My pussy and my sense of humor.

WORST CHARACTER TRAIT: A bad memory.

FAVORITE MUSIC: House, Tribal, Classical

FAVORITE MOVIES: *Raging Bull, Taxi Driver*

FAVORITE MOVIES I'VE BEEN IN: *Buckback Mountain, Cirque Noir*

XXX COSTAR I'D DO AGAIN IN A MINUTE: Lobo

IF I COULD MAKE ONE DEMAND ON A PORN SET IT WOULD BE: For it to be cleaned up after we're through using it.

AS A TEEN I ALWAYS FANTASIZED ABOUT SEX WITH: Muscled up older men.

CURRENT FANTASY MAN: GI Joe

SEXIEST PART OF A MAN: The Chest

THREE INGREDIENTS OF MY HOTTEST SEX FANTASY: Sweat, condoms, lots of lube.

FAVORITE ITEM IN MY SEXUAL TOY BOX: Double dildo, black gloves, suction pump

MOST PRIZED POSSESSION: My pussy

HOBBIES: Gym, photography, hiking the Mayan Ruins.

PETS: Four dogs and one cat.

PET PEEVES: Angry people, ignorant people, and judgmental people.

because of my pussy. They just cannot seem to get their heads around the fact that I am a man. They have so much focus on the cock – as though that is the only thing that makes you a man.

What is the biggest misconception people have about you when you meet them?

Many people are under the misconception that I am not friendly because of my hardcore macho appearance. They are always surprised, and end up saying what a really nice, down-to-earth guy I really am.

What was the best advice you were given starting out in the business?

"Keep doing what your doing!" That made me feel so good, like they understood what Buck Angel is all about! They saw the importance of my porn work, and not just for the porn world, but the whole world in general.

What do you usually do to prepare for a XXX shoot?

Shave my pussy, workout extra hard at the gym, and get some good rest! It is tons of work shooting a movie. Not that it isn't fun, too – it is! But shooting does require a lot of energy. Also, I usually travel to shoot, so it can be a long couple of days.

And how do you usually unwind after a long day of filming?

I am always super hungry after shooting a film, so I like to go out to eat with some of my co-stars, and hang out and get to know them a bit more on a personal level. I have become good friends with many of the guys I have shot films with. That is always a great perk of this job.

What is the most aroused you have ever been on screen?

During the shooting of Buckback Mountain my costar Lobo and I had

Buck Angel [PHOTO COURTESY BUCK ANGEL]

such great energy and chemistry together. He was totally into fucking my pussy and it shows! He has no hang ups at all. We did a scene where I sat on his face while I sucked his cock. It totally turned us both on that I came in his face. It was hot!

Porn sets are often the place of some surreal and hilarious incidents. Do you have any personal tale you would care to share?

Yes they are – especially with me! I remember when I was shooting one of my scenes in Titan's Cirque Noir, and I was getting my pussy licked by one of my co-stars. He looked up at me and said, "Wow, Buck, they did such a great job on your pussy. It looks so real!" I couldn't believe he said this after I had been shooting with him for the whole day having my pussy fucked and everything. I looked back at him and said, "It is real" his eyes completely bugged out. He thought that I was a biological man who had his cock surgically removed and a pussy put in its place.

That's brilliant. So does your "cock" have a nickname and if so how did it come about?

I used to call my favorite dildo "Chet" after Chet Baker, but that was many years ago before I became so comfortable with my pussy. And now I have too many cocks to name!

Do you think the industry has a responsibility regarding the use of condoms and/or promoting safe sex?

Of course! I am a huge safe-sex advocate. I don't understand people in the adult industry who feel like it is OK to promote unsafe sex. We, as pornographers, have an obligation to show safe sex. I have been offered lots of money to do unsafe scenes. That will never happen. I don't understand why it is such a big deal to promote something that is so important!

If you could change one thing about the way the industry is currently run what would it be?

Morals and ethics! I think there are way too many people who just don't care about anything but making money. They are not looking at the future of this business, they are self-interested and unprofessional. The more we police ourselves and show that we have some ethics, I think people who are not necessarily into porn might look at us differently. Porn is a business, and all aspects should be handled accordingly.

Do you have some best example of bad behavior on a XXX set you would care to share?

Actually no I don't. I usually work with my own company, Buck Angel Entertainment, so I am in control of the environment, the talent, and what is taking place. I have also worked with Titan Media, and they are super professional. I am very picky about who I work with because of what I said previously about ethics and safer sex.

Did Buck Angel Entertainment in any way come about as a reaction to your treatment in the industry or was it merely a business decision?

Actually I have always produced my own films from the start. I was producing under another business name when I got signed to the twelve picture deal at Robert Hill Releasing. But that experience was so awful for me that is when I started Buck Angel Entertainment. I have always wanted to maintain creative control over my product because I knew that if I let that go the "industry" would want to make me freak porn. That was sort of where Robert Hill Releasing was headed and also they have very horrible business practices. Now with my company I can expand to bring in more of the kind of porn that I have started in a positive way.

And what was the most difficult or challenging part about setting up your own company?

It's always about money. I bankroll everything in my business and when you start something as new and groundbreaking as what Buck Angel Entertainment does that can be quite a strain on the bank account. But a good business person always knows that to make money you have to spend money.

When you speak about the ethics portion of your company – can you give me some concrete examples of what is and isn't acceptable in a Buck Angel Production and/or set?

Thanks for asking that! I am all about running a safe and respectable company. I love porn and love making it. I want this to be a positive thing. Porn has such a bad reputation and there are many companies out there who make this happen. I want to change that and make this a really great industry. I want to have people say, "Wow working with Buck's company was so amazing." It is so important that we always show safe sex. That we never make people feel like assholes or used when coming off my sets. Just because its porn it does not have to be sleazy.

If you had to compare yourself to an

animal what species do you think best captures your essence and why?

A dog! Can't you see it? I think because on one side I am very loyal and would do anything for you but, on the other, I just love to sniff other dog's asses!

"Just because its porn it does not have to be sleazy."

If your life had a theme song what would it be?

"I Wish I Was an Oscar Meyer Wiener," or maybe, "I'm Popeye the Sailor Man."

Do you have any childhood or adolescent memory that you can look back upon and say, "Oh yeah, that kid was destined to grow up to be a porn star"?

Most definitely not! I was so uncomfortable being in a female body that I wasn't sexual at all for much of my early life. What a shame. Oh well, at least I've gotten to make up for lost time! I had one boyfriend when I was a teenager and we had sex a time or two, and it was awful. Too bad I couldn't appreciate his monster cock back then. The interesting thing is, I was attracted to men, but I didn't want to have sex with them as a female. I wanted to have sex with them as a man. Since my sex change, that has been able to happen, which has made life amazing.

If you had to choose between sex and love which would you choose and what are your thoughts about fidelity?

Well I think sex is a big part of love, so that is a very hard question. Of course love is amazing, and if you live long enough, it probably lasts longer than sex! I feel that fidelity is extremely important, and I have a strong relationship that is built on very deep trust. As a sex worker I think that is vital. I believe cheating on your partner is not at all acceptable, though I also believe it is possible to have "arrangements" or agreements that make sure each partner's needs get met. For example, maybe you agree you want to have sex with an added partner, but only when you are together. If you aren't willing to stick to the rules – the ones you develop by mutual agreement – then don't get into that relationship.

Describe your ideal romantic evening.

There is this amazing beach resort near my home in Mexico. It is so romantic and peaceful. I love to take my partner there and just relax on the beach, go swimming in the crystal clear, warm water, have great sex, and then lay in bed together reading a book.

TRENT **ATKINS**

Trent, how did you get started in the business?

I was just coming out of a crystal meth addiction and was going through bankruptcy proceedings. The agent of my ex Zane West had always told me if I ever wanted to work in the industry he would set me up. I was never interested until I needed money during those times to get back on my feet. So, I gave him a call and the rest is history.

I find it so interesting that you got into this business following recovery from a crystal problem. I think it's interesting primarily because a lot of folks view the industry the other way around – as the avenue to addiction. Have you encountered much drug use in the industry?

Drug use is everywhere. I think it's easy for people to pinpoint usage within porn just so they have something to talk about. I have done many movies and have never encountered drug use on any set. Of course some of my partners do like to have fun and go to parties and such, but they never were involved in drugs on the set. What they do outside of the shoot is their business.

STATS

BIRTH DATE: December 27, 1978

SIGN: Capricorn

HOMETOWN: Lompoc, California

HEIGHT: 5'6"

WEIGHT: 160 lbs

TWO BEST CHARACTER TRAITS: I'm loyal and honest.

TWO WORST CHARACTER TRAITS: I'm opinionated and bossy.

FAVORITE MUSIC: Rock/Pop

FAVORITE MOVIES: *Cleopatra, Quills, Texas Chainsaw Massacre*

FAVORITE MOVIES I'VE BEEN IN: *HotWired 2, The Velvet Mafia*, and *Resurrection*

XXX COSTAR I'D DO AGAIN IN A MINUTE: Johnny Hazzard, Brock Penn, and Brad Patton

IF I COULD MAKE ONE REQUEST ON A PORN SET IT WOULD BE: No breaks until the shoot is finished.

AS A TEEN I ALWAYS FANTASIZED ABOUT SEX WITH: The Marlboro man

CURRENT FANTASY MAN: David Beckam

SEXIEST PART OF A MAN: Eyes

THREE INGREDIENTS OF MY HOTTEST SEX FANTASY: Champagne, candles and lots of cum.

FAVORITE ITEM IN MY SEXUAL TOY BOX: Believe it or not, I don't own a toy box

MOST PRIZED POSSESSION: My friends and brother

HOBBIES: Snorkeling, travel, hiking, barbequing with friends, and sex with hot men

PETS: One cat named Caesar. I'm normally a dog person, but since I travel around so much right now I have a cat.

PET PEEVES: Dirty fingernails and dishonest people

What do you think you were looking for emotionally when you got into the business?

Initially it was all about the money. But then I started getting more curious about different parts of sex and sex acts. I was getting to perform things that I don't think I would have done in my own personal life.

So what are some things you've learned and explored that you've been overjoyed to discover?

Leather, slings, water sports, orgies. Still waiting for a boy on all girl orgy though where the women tie me up, gag me, and fuck me with strap-ons.

It's only a matter of time. Were the people who knew you surprised with this career development?

People were very surprised. I am extremely shy and I think everyone thought it would change me as a person.

Do you think it has changed you at all and if so in what ways?

The videos changed me in a sense that they opened my mind to fantasy and sexual behavior I would never have tried on my own, but I have not become jaded like many thought I would.

When people recognize you from your films do they tend to treat you differently and if so, how?

I wouldn't say they treat me differently. However, I tend to get thrown off a bit. I hardly ever do personal appearances so when people approach me sometimes I forget that Trent is me. I get really nervous.

Trent, what is the biggest misconception people have about you when you meet them?

People have an idea that all porn stars do drugs and are going to be a complete mess. They already have it in their heads that you are going to be less of a person than they are because you have done porn. Of course there are people in the industry who do drugs, etc. However, it's no different than in any other circle of life. Porn is taboo and people will always have preconceived notions about you if they find out you were in a movie or two. Have I done drugs? Yes I have. Do I now? Not at all and have been clean for awhile. Porn has been a way to get me to places in my life financially that I would not have had the opportunity to get to without.

So what differences if any are there personality-wise between your XXX persona Trent Atkins and yourself? Do you consciously shift into another mode when the camera begins to roll?

Trent would try anything in bed. I get to be a character so it's easy to let your guard down for certain things. Jason however is shy and sometimes a bit too self conscious so I am very critical. I would definitely try anything but would have to do it in a comfortable setting with someone I knew for awhile. I wouldn't just let some stranger piss on me like Trent would.

Do you recall your first film and the first bit of direction you were given?

I don't remember the name of my first film but it was for Director Paul Barresi. I had this stupid Jimmy Neutron haircut and was extremely un-

Trent Atkins [PHOTO COURTESY HOT HOUSE ENTERTAINMENT]

derpaid. I would have liked better direction with my name choice and with some of my movie choices, but at the time I needed money so I took all the work I could.

How do you think you are a typical Capricorn?

I always like things done my way. I may smile and say, "Sure that's fine." but, in my head I'm always thinking, "I'm the boss and I want it done this way."

What is the first thing you do when you get home from shooting a movie?

Shower and eat.

If you were making a movie called Trent Atkins' Orgy who would you demand as your four costars?

Chad Hunt, Ken Ryker, Erik Rhodes, Brad Patton.

Sounds like a very b-i-g orgy. What is the most turned on you have ever been when filming a scene?

Back in 2002 I shot a movie called *Hot Wired 2* with Brad Patton in Sydney during gay games. He was the most kind and respectful person I have ever met in the industry. His personality was enough to get me hard.

If someone were to come to you for advice about getting into the business what would you tell him?

I would say to think about everyone it might affect. Movies and pictures will be around forever. It's not just a short-term decision.

What things do you do to help prepare yourself for a film shoot?

I workout, don't eat a lot, and try and watch videos of my partner to see what they have done and like to do.

How would you describe yourself in a personals ad?

5'6", blonde hair, green eyes, tan, smooth, 7 inches, cut, versatile bottom. No drama, Laid back guy looking for someone who likes more than the newest beat or the latest designer drug to keep them up all night.

Where is he wildest place you've ever had sex?

A tanning bed

Speaking sexually, very few guys are as skilled as me when it comes to ...

Sitting on a cucumber. Damn those military boys.

When you pass a hot looking guy on the street what gets you to turn around and do a double take every time?

He looks straight as an arrow, has a little facial hair, tattoos, and a chiseled chin. I swear I'm not picky.

Describe your ideal romantic evening.

It would definitely have to be something spontaneous. No red roses or anything like that. I'd want the guy to think about who I am and what makes me smile and then come up with something that fits my personality. If I told everyone my perfect ideal night I'd get a thousand responses of the same old thing. It would be repetitive and boring.

I see your point. Then let's skip the romance. How do we get you in the sack and what do we do with you once we get you there?

Hmmmm. That would first start with a first great kiss. I have to be able to connect with someone through kissing for it to go any further. Once we are in the sack I don't have too many rules.

If you had to choose between sex and love which would you choose and what are your thoughts about fidelity?

I would definitely choose love. You can have great sex with anyone. But you can't fall in love with everyone. Define fidelity ... in gay male relationships fidelity is a tough issue. I think more couples could be monogamous but just don't put in the effort to do so. If you look around, there is so much precedence put into beauty and outer appearance and as such, it makes monogamy seem a far reach for most. Human nature is to seek the best mate. When we do not have marriage or other social constructs to define our relationships, there is no reason to be monogamous and nothing to hold us back from seeking out other sexual partners when we already have someone great standing right by our side. I have been in both types of relationships, open and closed. They both had their issues. But, if you can maintain stability and honesty either can work.

When it comes to seducing a man I've found that nothing works better than ...

Eye contact, kissing, and dirty talk.

Is it tough, interesting, or hot to watch yourself in a movie?

I have actually never watched myself in a movie. I would probably throw popcorn at it and wish I had looked better or twisted a different way.

What is the most drama you've ever encountered on a XXX set?

Drama? There isn't drama on a porn set, is there? I would have to say when I worked for a straight company that was producing a gay film. They wouldn't put anyone up in a hotel and tried to shoot four scenes in one day. Of course it was a mess and I didn't get done shooting until 1:00 a.m. and still had to drive back down to San Diego from Los Angeles. Something that should have taken a couple hours took twelve.

Porn sets are often the place of some surreal and hilarious incidents. Do you have any personal tale you would care to share?

I was waiting in the wings for a scene to finish before my scene started. You could hear what was going on in the other room. All of a sudden you hear someone scream "Cut! Cut! Cut! Get some towels." The poor guy who was getting fucked didn't do a proper plumbing job and got himself, his partner, and the camera man all muddy. I'd say that's pretty bad. Just glad it wasn't me.

Trent Atkins [PHOTO COURTESY HOT HOUSE ENTERTAINMENT]

Do you think the industry has a responsibility regarding the use of condoms and/or promoting safe sex?

The industry is not there to police everyone in their households about the use of condoms and safe sex. Most of the mainstream companies forbid unsafe sex and would never show unsafe scenes in their movies. They do all they can already to promote safe sex. Of course there are companies out there that refuse to use condoms and that is their choice. At the end of the day, we are all adults with our own brains to decide what is right and wrong.

If you could change one thing about the way the industry is currently run what would it be?

I would make the companies who produce these movies more accountable for their models! There have already been a number of deaths in the industry this year of models by drugs or STDs. They have a responsibility to ensure the safety of their product as well as the lives of the people they use in their films.

If your life had a theme song what would it be?

You take the good, you take the bad, you take me all and there you have the facts of life ... the facts of life ...

Let's go out with a bang Trent. What is the kinkiest thing you have ever done?

I was in Hawaii and I met this guy from Phoenix. He was in his mid thirties, sexy as hell, and beefy. We had chatted before he came to Hawaii and saw each other in the bar. He was doing his thing as was I. Finally I went over, grabbed him, excused ourselves to his friends and we left. We had both drank a lot and on the walk home had to pee. There is this canal in Waikiki called the Ala Way Canal. We both walked down the steps to piss in the water. I had always wanted to try water sports but never had. I kneeled down and just started drinking his piss. It was hot hot hot. He returned the favor and the rest of the night was one of the best sexual experiences I have ever had.

"Once we are in the sack I don't have too many rules."

Do you have any childhood or adolescent memory that you can look back upon and say, "Oh yeah, that kid was destined to grow up to be a porn star"?

I don't know about a porn star but I always loved the camera and for people to talk about me. Every time an article would come out in the paper about me for my gymnastics and diving competitions I would grab two or three copies and make sure everyone saw them. Porn isn't exactly the same, but it's an ego boost when people recognize you or say things to you about your work.

Describe your dream vacation.

Africa!

JESSIE **BALBOA**

How did you get started in the business?

It was always a fantasy and I came to the USA to make it true. I talked to my friends here in Fort Lauderdale and said I wanted to be in a porn movie and they encouraged me.

What were you looking for when you got into it?

To make my fantasies come true, and for sure to have some fun.

Do you recall the first bit of direction you were given?

Always, just spread your legs, enjoy and have fun ... Thank you!

What have been your usual experiences on XXX sets?

All my experiences have been great – just the normal stress, you know, to look the best you can for the film shoots, and doing your best with the scenes.

What made Taurus such a great costar for you?

He raped me for hours!

Do you have some big plans for your XXX career?

I have so much on my mind. With sex I don't like to do the same all the time, so I am always open for new experiences. There is no limit.

What things do you usually do to prepare for a film shoot?

When I have a shoot coming, I get on a diet, work out double what I usually do, and think about how hot and fun it is going to be.

So what is your typical workout routine?

I run three times a week, go to the gym four to five times a week for two hours working two muscle groups each day. And diet. For me more than 70% of it is what I eat.

And how do you usually spend the evening after a day of shooting?

After I just go directly to bed, alone or with some hottie – if one is available.

If some young guy came to you for advice about getting into this business, what would you tell him?

Go for it. Everything you want in life is there if you want it. You have to take what you want and do what it takes to achieve the things you want to achieve.

If you were making a movie called Jessie's Orgy who would you want as your four costars?

Wow! Alex Collak, Carlos Morales, Francois Sagat ... Yeah!

And I take it you would be the fourth.

Of course.

Is it funny, arousing, educational, or painful to watch yourself on screen?

I don't like to watch myself in a scene. It's too funny and uncomfortable for me.

When people meet you who know you only from your films how do they say you are different from what they expect?

It's always a surprise for them because I am just a normal and very real guy, Jessie Balboa is a fantasy.

What about making XXX films has been the biggest surprise to you?

The reaction of people around me – my friends and family. It is amazing. I didn't expect such a good thing.

Speaking sexually, very few guys are as skilled as me when it comes to ...

Fisting.

What is the secret to fisting effectively?

Relax and take it (laughing). That's how it is for me.

Describe your ideal romantic evening.

A nice dinner with wine, chatting with a good connection between us, For me it's all about the connection. I have to have that, without the connection there is nothing.

Where is the wildest/most unusual place you've ever had sex?

At a cinema in Peru where me and my ex-boyfriend were playing at the back. I can't even remember what the movie was!

Describe your dream vacation.

On the moon all by myself watching the planet earth spinning and rolling.

Where do you hope this career takes you?

I want this career to keep paying my bills and I want it to keep bringing fun into my life.

STATS

BIRTH DATE: May 8, 1969

SIGN: Taurus

HOMETOWN: Boca Raton, Florida

HEIGHT: 5' 7"

WEIGHT: 180 lbs

FAVORITE MUSIC: Any song performed by Tina Turner, The Best!

FAVORITE XXX MOVIES: *Communion, At Doctors Orders, Arabian Fist, Country Man*

FAVORITE MOVIES I'VE BEEN IN: *Tough Stuff, Man Country* (Colt Studios), *FistPack 6.*

XXX COSTAR I'D DO AGAIN IN A MINUTE: Taurus

IF I COULD MAKE ONE REQUEST ON A PORN SET IT WOULD BE: Topping Carlos Morales.

AS A TEEN I ALWAYS FANTASIZED ABOUT SEX WITH: Big Toys!

CURRENT FANTASY MAN: Nick Piston

SEXIEST PART OF A MAN: Butt and legs.

THREE INGREDIENTS OF MY HOTTEST SEX FANTASY: Connection, no fear, going with the flow.

FAVORITE ITEM IN MY SEXUAL TOY BOX: My metal cock ring.

MOST PRIZED POSSESSION: My family and friends

HOBBIES: Sports and sex

Jessie Balboa [PHOTO COURTESY HOT HOUSE ENTERTAINMENT]

ANTONIO **BIAGGI**

How did you get into the business?

By a friend in the industry, he recommended me to Raging Stallion Studios

What were you looking for when you got into it?

To do a movie, maybe two. My goals were pretty modest. Raging Stallion has helped me to exceed my expectations from the industry

What were you biggest concerns starting out?

How I was going to project in front camera.

Were the people who knew you shocked or surprised?

No, my family and friends knew that I did magazines before so they were OK with it.

What about making XXX movies surprised you?

Nothing really. I had been thinking of doing movies for several years and finally I did it.

So Antonio, when did you realize you had such an exceptionally large cock?

People always ask the same question, I don't know. I always thought that I was just normal until I started

STATS

BIRTH DATE: June 10, 1978

SIGN: Gemini

HOMETOWN: San Juan

HEIGHT: 5' 10"

WEIGHT: 150 lbs

TWO BEST CHARACTER TRAITS: Honest and Responsible

TWO WORST CHARACTER TRAITS: Honest and suffer from ADD

FAVORITE MUSIC: Opera, salsa, and meringue

FAVORITE MOVIES: Comedy, horror, and epics. My favorite is *Under the Tuscan Sun*.

FAVORITE MOVIES I'VE BEEN IN: *Trouser Trout* and *Grunts*

XXX COSTAR I'D DO AGAIN IN A MINUTE: Dominic Sol

IF I COULD MAKE ONE DEMAND ON A PORN SET IT WOULD BE: Food and more food, and don't forget the chocolate.

AS A TEEN I ALWAYS FANTASIZED ABOUT SEX WITH: George Clooney and Harrison Ford.

CURRENT FANTASY MAN: I have three – my boyfriend, George Clooney, and Tom Ford the designer.

SEXIEST PART OF A MAN: Gray hair on the temples and his ass.

THREE INGREDIENTS OF MY HOTTEST SEXUAL FANTASY: A hot day and being outdoors with two nasty pigs.

FAVORITE ITEM IN MY SEXUAL TOY BOX: A cock ring.

MOST PRIZED POSSESSION: My family.

HOBBIES: The beach, gym, movies, bowling, traveling the world, and food.

PETS: I travel too much to have any pets.

Antonio Biaggi [PHOTO BY KENT TAYLOR, COURTESY RAGING STALLION STUDIOS]

to fuck with other men. That's when I first realized it was bigger than most.

If someone were to come to you for advice about getting into the business what would you tell him?

It is not that easy of work, there are long days. Also, don't expect to make a living from it. It should be fun and for extra cash. Then you will have the right attitude.

What is the most aroused you have ever been on screen?

I am a total exhibitionist. When there are "visitors" on the set that is when I am most aroused.

Antonio, I'm curious. If you are an exhibitionist and get turned on having sex in front of people, what is the largest audience you have ever had sex in front of?

Maybe ten or more. To be honest I am too busy to take a head count.

Do you find it educational, hilarious, arousing, uncomfortable, or unbearable to watch yourself on screen?

It is funny.

If you were to make a movie called Antonio's Orgy who would you want as your four costars?

Billy Berlin, Trey Castille, Dominic Sol, and any other hot Raging Stallion Latino guys!

What things do you usually do to prepare for a film shoot?

No sex the night before .... if I can.

And how do you usually spend the evening after a day of filming?

Sleeping mostly, watching TV – overall it is just a chill day.

Do you think the adult film industry has an obligation to promote safe sex in movies?

Yes, but they also have an obligation to provide fantasies. I am fine with condoms, of course, but I do not need them to be a big deal in my movies. As long as they are there, discreet is fine.

"I always thought that [my cock] just normal until I started to fuck with other men. That's when I first realized it was bigger than most."

XXX movies are sometimes notorious for having guys get into some rough positions for the sake of the shot. What has been the most difficult sex position you have had to assume on screen?

On an old wood burning stove, in the kitchen of a rustic log cabin, it was in *Trouser Trout*.

Looking back to when you were a child or adolescent is there some memory where you just shake your head and think, "That kid was destined to grow up to be a porn star"?

Not as a child but as a adult, yes, I always like to show-off.

Where is the wildest place you have ever had sex off screen?

In a police patrol car.

Antonio, I need to hear more about that.

A policeman stopped me. I did not know why because I was driving slowly and was wearing my seat belt. When I asked him why he was pulling me over, he told me that he wanted my number. The next thing I knew I was fucking him in his patrol car.

When you pass a hot looking guy on the street what about him gets you to turn around and do a double take every time?

A masculine face and I always turn to see his ass.

What sort of man would you be looking for personality-wise?

I look for some one intelligent and fun that makes me smile and that I can trust.

If you had to choose between love and sex which would it be and what are your thoughts on fidelity?

I choose love because even hot sex is empty after a while if you are not connected with the person you are with more deeply than on a physical level.

Describe your ideal romantic evening.

A great dinner, then a theatre, opera, ballet or a musical, then dessert and a great fuck.

Describe your dream vacation.

Going to multiple cities one after the other like Tuscany then Mykonos then Barcelona , or Marrakech, Cairo, Istanbul and I am also planning a trip to Puerto Rico with my boyfriend.

Antionio Biaggi [PHOTO BY KENT TAYLOR, COURTESY RAGING STALLION STUDIOS]

JACK **BOND**

How did you get started in the business?

I had a few friends who had done it and was talking about it with them. I was intrigued by the industry. So, I spoke to a couple of companies who were interested and became an exclusive with one.

What do you think you were looking for when you got into it?

I was not looking for something. I do however think that life is short, that you should experience and pursue what you want to experience in that journey with courage. And, without fear of what others may or may not think.

Were the people who knew you surprised?

Totally! I don't party, do drugs, go clubbing, nor am I a hooker. It seems that people assume that all these are the only ingredients that makes a porn star. It is kind of a limited view to be honest. And there is nothing wrong about doing any of these things. I teach and design during the day. Also, when you are British, Americans tend to think we just drink tea (Laughing). So porn is a stretch for the people who knew me. I don't think the Brits are perceived as hot, unlike the Latin guys here who are hot almost just because they are Latin. So yeah, it surprised them.

Jack Bond [PHOTO COURTESY LUCASENTERTAINMENT.COM]

What was the most surprising to you about making XXX films?

That it was a fun, liberating experience because for me I had to let go of my ego in order to feel free to perform and that is a great feeling. Life is more interesting when huge egos don't get in the way of it.

Speaking of that liberation, how is your porn persona Jack Bond different from your everyday self?

One influences the other. You can ex-

STATS

BIRTH DATE: April 6, 1967

SIGN: Aries

HOMETOWN: London

HEIGHT: 5'11"

WEIGHT: 201 lbs

TWO BEST CHARACTER TRAITS: Honest with myself and others, a sense of justice, humility, not judgmental/prejudiced, a sense of humor about myself and life in general, and optimistic.

TWO WORST CHARACTER TRAITS: Impatience (working on it that! Laughing), Shy about love stuff (working on that, too).

FAVORITE MUSIC: Pop. Pretty much all from the '50s through to the present day.

FAVORITE MOVIES: *Being Julia, My Fair Lady, Elizabeth* (Cate Blanchett), etc., but I love all film so it's hard to name them all here.

FAVORITE MOVIES I'VE BEEN IN: I have not done enough to compare yet, but *La Dolce Vita* was a good scene, my second. And, I've been told that my upcoming scene with Spencer Quest in the Lucas Entertainments *Encounters* series is very good.

XXX COSTAR I'D DO AGAIN IN A MINUTE: I loved kissing Jason Ridge on set, but we did not do a scene together, but he's a great kisser. Erik Rhodes is hot, nice/sweet guy as well in person.

IF I COULD MAKE ONE REQUEST ON A PORN SET IT WOULD BE: I don't know, but to always have a smile on my face. I generally laugh a lot on set. It should be a fun experience.

AS A TEEN I ALWAYS FANTASIZED ABOUT SEX WITH: Rex Chandler, Harrison Ford (he's still hot)

CURRENT FANTASY MAN: I don't really have one now, I like strong men with strong characters, who know who they are and are at ease with themselves ... that is really sexy to me!

SEXIEST PART OF A MAN: Legs! I like big thighs/butts and calves.

THREE INGREDIENTS OF MY HOTTEST SEX FANTASY: Passionate, dirty, piggy, and romantic all at once.

FAVORITE ITEM IN MY SEXUAL TOY BOX: I don't have one.

MOST PRIZED POSSESSION: My silver cross and chain around my neck

HOBBIES: Movies, gym, painting and drawing, designing, hikes in the country (I love both land/sea), horse riding (I love horses).

PET PEEVES: Being around snobbish, petty, narcissists – very irritating types to deal with. Oh and people with an overbearing sense of entitlement. They are never thankful for anything as a result, which is unattractive to witness.

plore one side of your self, but integrate those experiences into the whole person.

How do you think the experience of appearing in XXX features has changed you?

It has not changed me per se. It was liberating, but it did not bring about a fundamental change within me.

If some young guy came up to you and asked for advice about getting into this business what would you tell him?

Only do it if you are clear about who you are and have weighed the pros and cons of what the consequences for that individual might be on their lives. That is unique for us all, so I would never say, "Yeah, it's great, do it," if I was asked.

Have you personally experienced any repercussions thus far as a result of this career?

Personally I have not, but let's be realistic about the conservative culture we live in.

Have you watched yourself on screen yet, and if so what were your impressions?

Yeah I watched myself, but actually to me it is just another creative process of making images. Whenever I finished a painting it was over and I moved on. That has been true for all design projects I've worked on and film is no different. It just so happens that I am part of the image this time. So, I'm not that interested to view myself for too long.

If you were to make a movie called Jack Bond's Orgy who would you want as your four costars?

Luke Savage, Eric Rhodes, Jason Ridge ... hmmm, and that is it for right now.

"I don't think the Brits are perceived as hot, unlike the Latin guys here who are hot almost just because they are Latin."

Where is the wildest place you've ever had sex?

Wildest place? In public – on a set – that is probably considered pretty wild to a lot of people not in porn.

So what was unique or wild about having sex on a film set? Can you describe what the experience was like for you?

There was nothing wild about it. I think there is an element of auto-eroticism involved, and the idea of being watched is hot.

So then is it difficult to become aroused and remain so given the circumstances of filming?

Hello! Viagra! No, it's easy (Laughing).

What is the best way for you to unwind when you return from a day of shooting on the set?

Make a hot cup of Italian coffee, love all things Italian, and sit down and watch a great movie or The National Geographic Channel, a current viewing pleasure.

When you pass a hot looking guy on the street what causes you to turn around and do a double take every time?

Big butt and legs ... leg man here.

Speaking sexually, very few people are as skilled as me when it comes to ...

There are too many people who can do so many things in every generation in a spectacular way, that I could not compare or compete.

So Jack, what is your definition of La Dolce Vita (The Sweet Life)?

Drinking a great cup of coffee in the morning, going out into my day, experiencing exactly what I am meant to experience in it and being thankful for it always. I don't want "things," I want to live fully and be who I am honestly.

Describe your ideal romantic evening.

I have no scenario, but to be with a guy who can be affectionate, who can hold my hand and hug. That is cute and few guys do that to me. So, wherever the date was, so long as that happens I'd be happy.

Describe your dream vacation.

My dream vacation. Hmmm. To be near the ocean, and mountains (a vast landscape), silence, a blue pool beneath trees to swim in and a cool breeze, caressing my skin on a late afternoon beneath a golden sun. A loving boyfriend (I'm single) handing me a Sea breeze cocktail and the rest is private.

Jack Bond [PHOTO COURTESY LUCASENTERTAINMENT.COM]

TOBER **BRANDT**

How did you get started in the business?

When I was 18 in college, I read an ad for some extra cash. It was asking for males who did not mind being photographed naked. I've always loved being naked in front of other people and it actually paid pretty well – the fact that the photographer was also a good lay helped, so I kept going back. It wasn't long until I was working with other photographers and eventually I met the right people who pretty much told me I should give sex on video a try. I was comfortable with my body and being with other men, so they thought I would do well. The rest, as they say ...

What were you looking for when you got into it?

Truly at the time I was just looking to save money – porn doesn't pay often, but when it pays, it's good money.

Do you recall the first movie you did and the first bit of direction you were given?

The first movie I did was a First Time Tryers Series for All Worlds Video. It was a very friendly, non threatening set. First direction? To show up sober. You wouldn't believe how many goofballs show up with some sort of substance in their system.

What was the best advice you were given starting out?

Never let anyone sell you short. Director Dirk Yates for All Worlds gave me the best advice and I've never forgotten it. On my third or fourth movie for AWV, I was making $1,000.00 a movie – which at the time was kick ass for a newbie 22-year-old that was not signed as an exclusive. I was about to work for another company and he looked at me and told me I was worth the money, to never take less than $1,000.00 from then on, and to actually start asking for more. You should see my rate now ... actually, let's not go there. I don't want my boss to see this and start thinking about how much he's paying me (hee hee).

And if some young buck came to you for advice about getting into XXX work what would you tell him?

If you are doing this for approval, self validation, or to boost your self esteem, turn around and run. If you are here to have fun, make fast money, and enjoy the ride no matter how short or long it lasts, then jump in.

So how did the name Tober Brandt come about?

Tober was my piercer's name in college. I liked it so much, well ...

What about making XXX movies has come as the biggest surprise to you?

What really surprises me is how much competition seems to spring up between the studios. There are a billion sexually deprived humans living in the United States. This means that there is plenty of money to be made. I understand the need to have a competitive edge within each studio, but there is no need to be catty and bloodthirsty. The other thing that surprises me are the amount of divas in this industry. We're being filmed having sex – good God almighty get a grip on yourself and quit acting like your saving the rainforest. Buying donuts for Oprah's backstage green room has more merit.

What are the perks of being a Raging Stallion exclusive and how did that come about?

The entire package is a perk. The men at RS are quality men of integrity and I love being in their presence. It's also nice to be able to be myself around them. I can go out drinking with my boss or co-stars. I'm not put in lockdown two days before a shoot and forced to abstain from sex, other men, or the outdoors ... I really enjoy being around these gentlemen. They pretty much picked me up when my third contract with Titan was up. Titan and I parted on great terms and I was able to pretty much step right into the new deal with RS. Simple as that. JD Slater was such a sweetheart and over

STATS

BIRTH DATE: October 31

SIGN: Scorpio

HOMETOWN: Dayton, Texas

HEIGHT: 6'1"

WEIGHT: 225 lbs

TWO BEST CHARACTER TRAITS: I'm very personable and like being around people – I'm always smiling and having a good time (oh yeah, my cock and my ass).

TWO WORST CHARACTER TRAITS: I'm too nice to people that would take advantage of me – I'm very demanding of myself ... too much so.

FAVORITE MUSIC: I was a music major – I truly love it all.

FAVORITE MOVIES: The *Saw* series, *Romancing the Stone, The Long Kiss Goodnight*

FAVORITE MOVIES I'VE BEEN IN: *Missing Link* (Chi Chi LaRue directed), *Side Effects, Lifeguard, Road to Redneck Hollow* and *SpyQuest 3*

XXX COSTAR I'D DO AGAIN IN A MINUTE: Jake Deckard (oh wait ... we have slept together again), and Bo Knight – he and I never had sex. We did some photo work together, but put me in a bed naked with him again ...

IF I COULD MAKE ONE REQUEST ON A PORN SET IT WOULD BE: Let sex happen naturally and don't fucking micro-direct something that is supposed to be fun, hot and turn people on.

AS A TEEN I ALWAYS FANTASIZED ABOUT SEX WITH: The entire high school football team and the local Baptist Church pastor's oldest son

CURRENT FANTASY MAN: John Cena!

SEXIEST PART OF A MAN: Whatever part is closest to me (I am fond of a guy's mouth and waist line though, and the curve above his ass, and the head of a man's cock, and his hands ... you get the idea).

THREE INGREDIENTS OF MY HOTTEST SEX FANTASY: Restraints (for him, not me), a belt, and a set of very sharp medical tools ... and any good Korn CD to set the mood

FAVORITE ITEM IN MY SEXUAL TOY BOX: Either my bit and bridle or a very large plug

MOST PRIZED POSSESSION: My privacy and my knives

HOBBIES: Ice skating, sky diving, scuba diving, roller blading, sex, traveling and going to parties

PETS: Hell no.

PET PEEVES: Gossip, fake people (aka – small time socialite bar divas), cheap LA promoters, liars, being called a liar

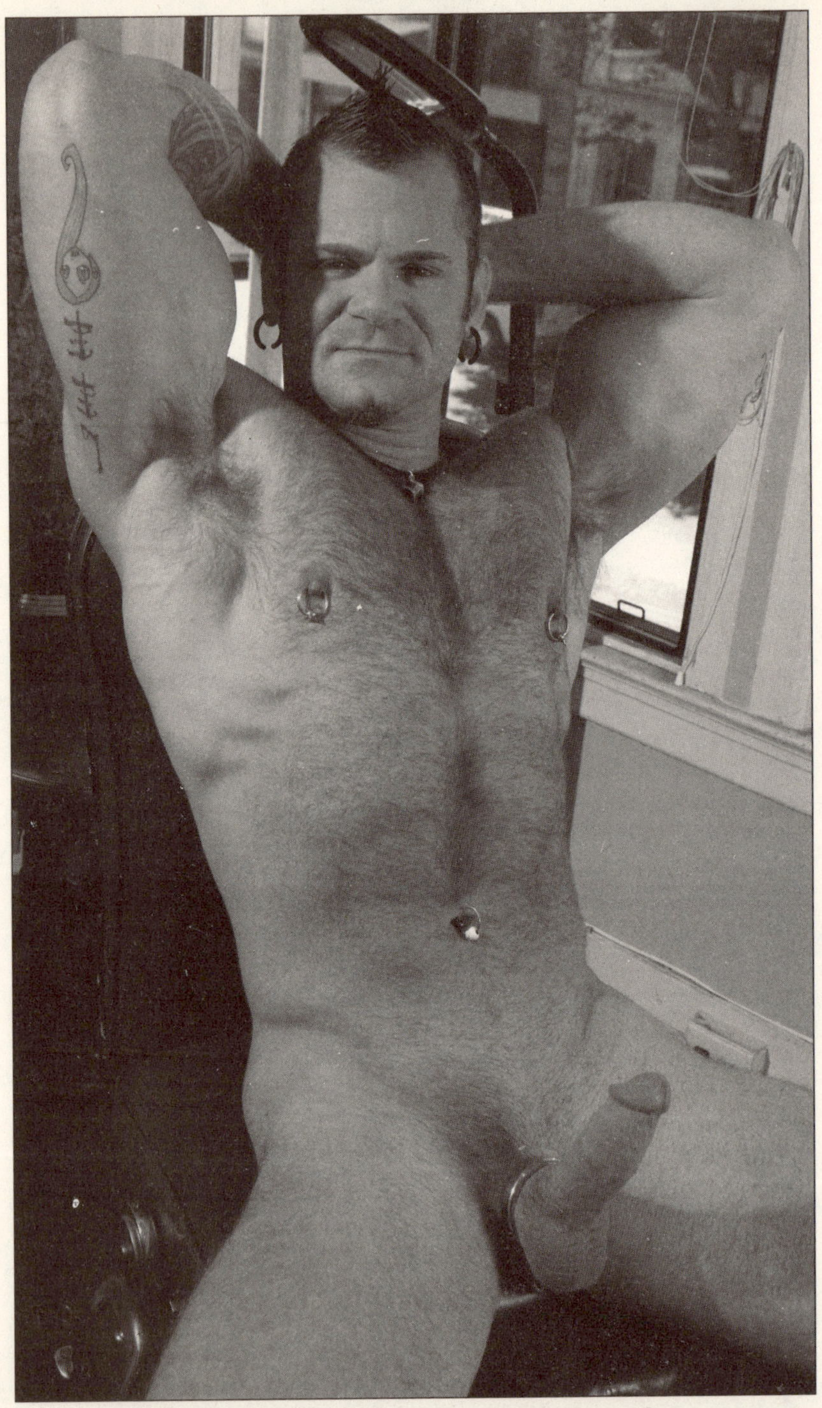

Tober Brandt [PHOTO BY KENT TAYLOR, COURTESY RAGING STALLION STUDIOS]

the years while I was at Titan, he and I had become friends. He was pretty much the guiding instrument in my coming onto RS. I owe him, Michael Brandon, Chris Ward and Jake Deckard a great deal of thanks.

What is the most aroused you have ever been on screen?

It's happened several times and usually in one of two ways. If, when I'm bottoming, the other guy hits my prostate (which is apparently somewhere in my chest since it practically takes a baseball bat to reach) I'll shoot across a football field. I had one co-star hit it so directly that I grabbed his hips, looked him right in the eye, smiled and told him not to even breathe it felt so good. The other way (and this is going to sound so vain) is if there is a mirror around and I can see myself fucking the other man, it goes right to my brain and I cum so hard. I like to watch.

So was this on a set when the guy hit your prostate and caused the explosion? If so, care to name the guy?

Yes – this was on the set. I hate naming names. But check out *Folsom Leather* ...

So *Folsom Leather* was the movie huh ... does that mean the magic cock belonged to Tyler Saint or Rick van Sant?

Ahhhh ... Tyler. What a nice name ...

Have you ever gotten a crush on any of your costars? Care to name names?

A crush? No. My biggest problem is my inability to focus on just one naked man. Developing a crush would require me to actually think about sex with a particular man for more than five minutes.

If we were making a movie called Tober's Orgy who would you want as your four costars?

Daniel Craig. John Cena. The bass guitarist from Velvet Revolver. Dale from Top Chef Miami (2007)

What things do you always do to prepare yourself for a shoot?

I try to get some good sleep, eat, and drink a lot of water. I love champagne – I drink it all the time. Pretty much that and water are my staples. I do try to cut that out the day of shooting though. I pretty much do the things that I do all the time to take care of myself.

And how do you unwind after a long day of shooting?

I usually do one of two things, depending on how I feel and where I'm at. I'll either crawl into bed with a glass of Dom, turn on the TV and hopefully have a good man there with me to do the same, or I'll go the other way entirely. I'll go out, take in the night life, and get laid until the sun comes up.

Is it tough, educational, or hot to watch yourself on screen?

Actually, I can't watch myself on film without laughing.

Where is the wildest place you've ever had sex?

This is very hard for me to answer. I'm pretty bold and have sex when and where I want. I've had so many (not bragging, it's just me) wild experiences – I really feel like I've led a very full sexual life. I will say this – my favorite was on a Southwest red eye flight to NY for the Black Party. Both of the flight attendants were attractive males. After bringing me all the free liquor I wanted, one of them told me the other was interested, and that if I wanted, I could come into the back, pull the curtain and fool around. Long story short, I sucked both of them and got blown in the back. The one fucked me in the back area and then the other and I went into the john and I fucked him. It was the best flight I've ever had and the probably the quietest sex I've ever attempted. The entire cabin was pretty much asleep, so it was easy to get away with, but still ... pretty damn risky.

Have you ever done anything sexually on screen that you would do in your personal life?

Everything I do on screen, I would do in real life. I have no hang ups except rude or stuck up people.

I am always curious about things like this – is there a difference between you and Tober Brandt? Is he just a pseudonym for convenience sake or has he become a kind of other?

Tober is a kind of other. He offers me a kind of duality that is like a warm blanket of anonymity. Everything that he does sexually, I would also do ... probably more so. But with Tober, I can do and say without having to give up who I really am to the entire world. Whereas, myself – Joshua – I can reserve for those that I really want to become close to in life. But, we are one and the same as far as our sexual appetites and fashion sense (hee hee).

"In fetish films, I've actually gone farther than the director planned. I've made camera men leave the set and throw up."

Lots of people consider XXX stars to be these ideal physical specimens, but if you could change one thing about yourself through cosmetic surgery what would it be?

As far as cosmetic surgery, I'm still pretty well preserved and young. I would have a few lines removed though. Other than that, I've always been comfortable in my own body.

Speaking sexually, very few people are as skilled as me when it comes to ...

Very few people that I've met are able to be as sexually comfortable with their own bodies as I am. I figure, it's cool to want more, but at least afford yourself the joy of loving the skin you are in and maximizing your pleasure instead of scrutinizing perfection.

So when fans meet Tober Brandt, how do you differ from what they're expecting?

Usually when people meet me, they say one of two things: first, that I'm much taller in person than they would have thought. The other thing they always say is that I'm both nice and genuine as a person. There are a lot of porn characters out there who would think that they are God's gift to mankind just because their naked ass is on film getting plowed. I've said it before – "Who gives a shit?" Being in porn does not make someone a better or more important person. It's no reason to act high and mighty, like a diva, or treat people with disrespect regardless of whether you are attracted to them or not. I hate the "all muscular guys are assholes" stereotype, and I do all I can to try and show that not all of us are jerks with egos writing checks their personality can't cash. I genuinely like people and meeting new faces – people really are surprised by this and I think it's refreshing to them. It's good to see people smile back when I get through talking to them.

You mention a couple times not being able to tolerate diva or that behavior. What has been the biggest example of diva behavior you have ever encountered on a XXX film set?

Two words for you – "West Hollywood."

No example you would like to share?

Not unless I wanted to start a war, but I will say that anyone who uses the terms "my fans," "career," or "celebrity" regarding porn should be drug out of their imaginary trailers and shot.

Porn sets are often the place of some surreal and hilarious incidents. Do you have any personal tale you would care to share?

I'll just say this : If you are going to do a fisting scene and stop at the grocery store on the way to the set to get Crisco, check to be sure you don't pick up the tub that has been made to look, taste, and smell like real butter.

If you could change one thing about the way the industry is currently run what would it be?

Directors need to quit hiring straight men to work in gay porn scenes. 'Nuff said.

I first realized I was a bona fide porn star when ....

I don't think of myself as a porn "star." I actually hate that phrase. It sounds self absorbed to me.

If you were offered a role in a fetish film, how far would you go?

In fetish films, I've actually gone farther than the director planned. I've made camera men leave the set and throw up, and one shoot I even had a costar come to tears when he saw seven hooks pierce my flesh. It was such a sweet gesture that he would feel pain for me to the point of weeping for my own safety. Ahhh ... I love men. Truly, we are strange and wonderful creatures.

Do you have any childhood or adolescent memory that you can look back upon and say, "Oh yeah, that kid was destined to grow up to be a porn star"?

Actually, I was five years old standing naked in my neighbor's basement, and I think he said something similar just before turning on the camera ...

How would you describe yourself in a personals ad and how would you describe the man you were looking for?

Wow ... a personals ad? Really? I actually hate those things. Pretty much, the only profiles I've ever had show lots of pictures of me and say very little about me except that I want to fuck and how I want to do it. Profiles are for getting laid – let's not lie to ourselves here. The other person or group can decide if they like me as a person while my cock is in their ass or down their throat. I don't like personals ads because I like meeting people face to face – first impression and all. Word descriptions misrepresent a person, which is probably why I'm evading this right now. If someone reads this, likes my picture and wants to get to know me, I'm pretty easy to find. Just ask the bartenders in most major cities (ha ha). What I'm looking for in a man? Someone who will love me above all others, who trusts me completely and always listens, who will never try and change one damn thing about me (even if I change every day – as I tend to do), is sexy, fun to look at and touch, great in bed, and treats me like family. Let's leave it that or I'll throw up.

If you had to choose between sex and love which would you choose and what are your thoughts about fidelity?

That question makes no sense. Love is something that would never require its recipient to choose between it and something else. Personally, I like letting love and sex run hand in hand as a choice avenue of self expression to a partner. And as far as fidelity goes (I assume you mean monogamy), I have no problems with it, but here is where most people that ask for it (especially straight women of their husbands) make it near impossible to achieve – when you ask a person to be sexually monogamous, you aren't just promising to not sleep with other people. You are also asking that person to trust you and you alone with their sexual needs – all of them. That means if they are needing sexual attention, you have made it your responsibility to see that they get it when they need it. You are basically playing doctor to their patient – when a patient needs their meds, the doctor doesn't get to decide if they feel like providing them. It's a commitment with a hefty demand.

That's an interesting comparison. What is the biggest misconception people have about you when you meet them?

That I'm the Big Bad Wolf. I have the reputation of being an extreme player and a sadistic brute in many of my films, so people often forget that off camera I turn back into a real person. Don't get me wrong – when given permission I'll wrap a belt around a man's throat, bind his wrists, cut him open a few dozen times, let him bleed all over me and my sheets (or floor), and suck the open wounds while I fuck the feeling out of his asshole. I'm also the same guy who will spend hours in foreplay, make love gently, and then cuddle up in bed.

Do you think the industry has a responsibility regarding the use of condoms and/or promoting safe sex?

No more responsibility than our beaches have to promote the use of sunscreen. I believe most of them actually say swim at your own risk.

Describe your ideal romantic evening.

I don't really have an ideal romantic evening. Most of the people who have been out with me say there is something almost magical about the way things move around me, and I agree. I've lead a very blessed and charmed life. Most of my evenings are very romantic – almost movie-like, full of more than one perfect moment. As long as the evening contains myself and someone I love, the rest seems to take care of itself – and it's always different – and it's always a surprise.

Any idea as to the secret for living a charmed life?

Well, when people meet me, they always tell me what great energy I have. I guess I would have to say, just be as joyful, positive and welcoming as possible. Have an idea for your day, month, life, etc., but allow for change, adjustment and complete redirection. Find a reason to celebrate something in every situation – even if it sounds sarcastic. Look for ways to help others instead of being solely self-serving. Smile and be nice.

That's a very cool philosophy to have. I can see why you are charmed. Seriously, I think that attitude would bring the magic on. If you had to compare yourself to an animal what species do you think best captures your essence and why?

A Virus – it doesn't stop until it has taken all that it wants in its entirety.

If your life had a theme song what would it be?

"Open your Heart" – Madonna.

Does your cock have a nickname and if so how did it come about?

No. But I have nicknames for some of the dicks that I've dated ... does that count?

That's a good one, can I use that? Better yet, let's compare nicknames sometime. Describe your dream vacation.

My dream vacation is Alaska. Ice diving. Swimming to the bottom of an iceberg. Listening to whales underwater. The ice, the cold, the beautiful blue endless depths underneath me – yeah.

Where do you want/think/plan for this career to take you?

Tober Brandt [PHOTO BY KENT TAYLOR, COURTESY RAGING STALLION STUDIOS]

I'm loving the ride. If it takes me anywhere, I will be more than thrilled and grateful. Right now, it affords me the opportunity to help charities raise funds; a chance to play around the world and throw parties. It's a wonderful moment in my life, and I'm blessed for every second that passes with success. I'm in school pursuing a second degree though, so it's not as though I have all my eggs in one basket.

So what other basket are you putting your eggs into, or what is the degree/ field you are studying?

Ha ha – too personal.

After all we've shared that's not too personal.

Well, right now I like keeping that info secret. I don't want to jinx the whole thing.

COREY **CADE**

So tell me how you got started in the business?

I was approached at the gym – someone had asked me if I ever thought about doing porn. I was really strapped for cash at the time, but also knew that I had a killer ass, so I agreed to come in for a meeting, and the rest is history.

What were you looking for when you got into it?

My first paycheck. haha. Really, I had no expectations about anything. I'm an avid porn fan and I was just happy to be a part of something that I had watched so much of in the past.

Were the financial rewards of a XXX career what you expected?

Yes and no. Starting off, I feel that I signed a very low contract and did so just because I wasn't familiar with the pay scale. Now, I'm sure to negotiate a suitable contract to meet my expectations.

As an avid porn fan what are some of your favorite films?

You know, I am a huge fan of Sean Cody's work. The boys are great, the

STATS

BIRTH DATE: December 17, 1980

SIGN: Sagittarius

HOMETOWN: Kalamazoo, MI

HEIGHT: 5'8"

WEIGHT: 155 lbs.

TWO BEST CHARACTER TRAITS: Humble and honest

TWO WORST CHARACTER TRAITS: Blunt and overly optimistic

FAVORITE MUSIC: Classic rock

FAVORITE MOVIES: *Stand By Me*, the best movie of all time.

FAVORITE MOVIES I'VE BEEN IN: *Encounters 2*, Lucas Entertainment

XXX COSTAR I'D DO AGAIN IN A MINUTE: Jimmy, we've only done an oral scene together, and I would love to get a bit more intimate!

IF I COULD MAKE ONE REQUEST ON A PORN SET IT WOULD BE: To provide slippers, my feet get really cold walking around barefoot everywhere. Haha, I'm such a pussy.

AS A TEEN I ALWAYS FANTASIZED ABOUT SEX WITH: Marky Mark

CURRENT FANTASY MAN: Bruce Willis, always and forever!

SEXIEST PART OF A MAN: A five o'clock shadow

THREE INGREDIENTS OF MY HOTTEST SEX FANTASY: Muscles, sweat and a big dick

FAVORITE ITEM IN MY SEXUAL TOY BOX: My Falcon replicas of Jeremy Penn and Matthew Rush

MOST PRIZED POSSESSION: My Calvin and Hobbes Complete Box Set

HOBBIES: Writing and cooking

PETS: None anymore, used to own a Rhodesian ridgeback

PET PEEVES: People who chew their nails

Corey Cade [PHOTO COURTESY LUCASENTERTAINMENT.COM]

filming is great, and you can't ask for anything better then the idea of hot straight guys getting it on.

Going along with that if you could make a film called Corey Cade's Orgy who would you want as your four costars?

Honestly, give me four of Wilson Vasquez and we'll call it a day. But, to answer the question fairly, I'd have to throw in Brad Star, Joey Foster, and Chet from Sean Cody.

How did you come up with your nom de' porn or is Corey Cade your real name?

Obviously I'm one of the smaller guys in porn, and a name like Rex Titan just wouldn't fit. So, I remember I had a big crush on a guy named Corey ages ago. He was masculine but sweet at the same time, so that kind of stuck with me.

What was your initial interview with Lucas Entertainment like?

It was fairly short. I came in, took a couple of photographs and then was escorted into Michael's office where he asked me to strip down. He made note of a couple of areas I could focus on in my workout and then took a look at my butt hole (for what reason, I have no idea) and we started scheduling my first scene. It all happened pretty fast actually.

Do you recall the first movie you made and the first bit of direction you were given?

One of my first scenes was with Chad Hunt, directed by Chad Hunt. I really took a liking to him, he's kind of a big brother to me in a way, only the kind that fucks. Since he was directing and starring in the scene, I basically followed his lead. We never paused to discuss angles or anything, just went at it, and the scene turned out great!

What about making XXX films didn't you expect?

The royal treatment! People have been very kind to me. I thought I might be looked down upon in some circles, but I believe if you spread good energy, good energy will come your way.

If a guy came to you and asked for advice about getting into the business what would you tell him?

I would tell him to make sure it's definitely something he wants to do before taking the plunge. The only regret I have is not being able to run for president. After these past seven years with Bush in office, it seems they'll let anybody do the job, and I could have been a shoe in!

How do we get you in bed and what do we do with you once we get you there?

Take control. I love men who take control, tell me what they want, and dominate the playing field. I love men, not pussies. Big arms help, too. And as far as what to do when we get there, all I have to say is just get it hard, I'll do the rest. haha.

Speaking sexually very few guys are as skilled as me when it comes to …

Being able to take a big dick. I can't deep throat that well at all, but when it comes to taking a 9-10 incher in the ass, please, no sweat!

When it comes to driving a man crazy I've found nothing works better than ...

Pretending to be interested in what they're saying. haha. Sometimes the best turn on is knowing that someone is just listening to you. I know everyone expects me to say whisper in his ear, or touch his thigh (which works on me!) but I found that when you listen, or even just pretend to listen, they get turned on that much more.

So is there anything in your background or past that would suggest that "one day that kid is going to grow up to be in porn movies"?

Besides my dad's stacks of Penthouse that I used to jack off to when I was younger, I don't believe so. I've always craved attention, so that could have been a clue ... maybe.

What do you usually do the day before to prepare for a XXX shoot?

I try to talk to the co-star, ask if there is anything they like, don't like. Basically introduce myself to the person who's going to be licking my asshole the next day.

And what is your typical evening like when you get home from filming?

Eat and Sleep. In that order.

What is the easiest way to get your dick hard?

Fuck me in the ass.

Do you have some XXX fantasy you are just waiting for some director to ask you to film?

I want to do a group scene. Doesn't have to be the caliber of *Heaven to Hell*, but I'd like to be surrounded by men fucking. I think that would be hot.

Porn is notorious for putting guys into some very awkward positions for the sake of the shot ... what is the most unusual or uncomfortable position you have ever had to assume?

God, I feel so vanilla. I can't say that I've been put into a position that is too compromising.

Maybe you're just extremely flexible? What is the biggest misconception people have about you when you meet them?

I think people see my smile and think that I'm naive and impressionable. In all honesty, it couldn't be further from the truth. I'm very intelligent and am not easily taken advantage of.

If you could change one thing about the way the industry is currently run what would it be?

The stigma that all porn actors are unintelligent.

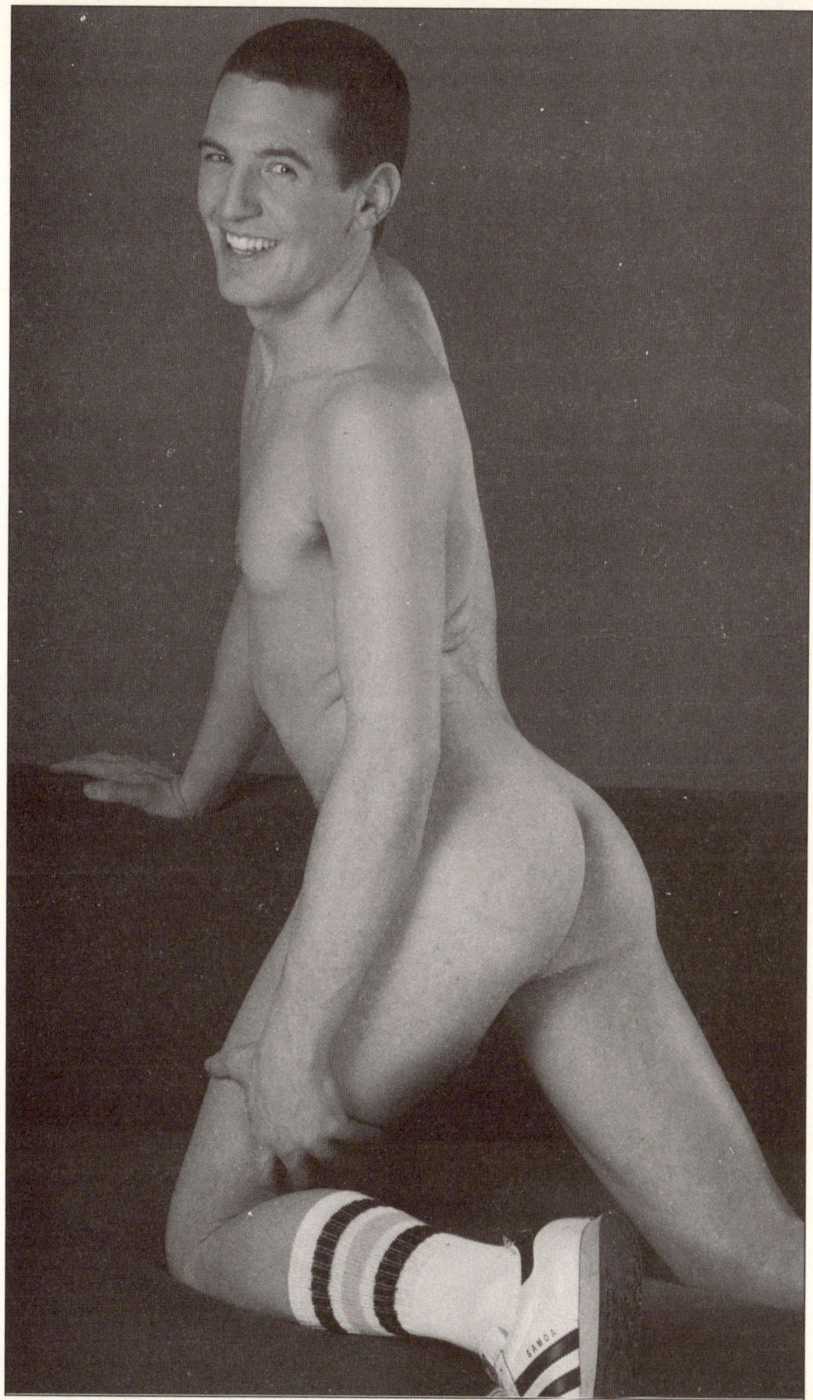

Corey Cade [PHOTO COURTESY LUCASENTERTAINMENT.COM]

Do you think the industry has a responsibility regarding the use of condoms and/or promoting safe sex?

I used to, but now I think the responsibility lies on the performer rather then the industry. The industry could care less about your health. It's sad to say, but very true. You are responsible for you, and you have to stand up for what you believe is right as a performer.

Do you have some best example of bad behavior on a XXX set you would care to share?

I can't say I've ever had a bad experience. If I have, I would have addressed it at the time so it wouldn't turn into a big deal. I don't like stressful situations.

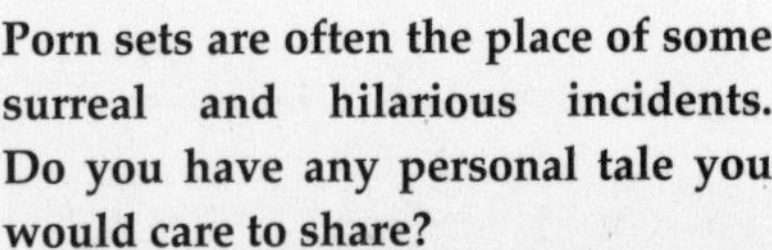

Porn sets are often the place of some surreal and hilarious incidents. Do you have any personal tale you would care to share?

Well, my experience with porn sets have been pretty vanilla. But, in my personal life I have found myself in weird locations. One summer I was vacationing on the Jersey shore. I met this really cool guy and we hit it off right away. Neither of us was able to bring the other home, so we found a small playground with a great jungle gym. It wasn't until he was pounding my ass that I looked up and saw we were in the playground of a private Catholic School! Haha. It was really hot and dirty all at the same time!

How would you describe yourself in a personals ad?

Sweet, outgoing, blunt, honest, optimistic, and well read.

When you pass a hot looking guy on the street what about him gets you to turn around and do a double take every time?

Basically, if we make an eye connection, I'm doing a double take. Muscles really get my interest. I love a big chest and big arms.

If you had to choose between sex and love which would you choose and what are your thoughts about fidelity?

I would choose sex. Love is great, but a lot harder to find. I think that fidelity depends on the relationship and the people involved. For some, an open relationship works, for others it's death. I'm not one to judge. If it works for you and makes you happy, that's all that should ever matter.

If your life had a theme song what would it be?

It does have a theme song – "Glory Days" by Just Jack on his newest album, Overtones.

Describe your ideal romantic evening.

God, I'm so easy. Dinner and a movie, as long as I'm not paying. hahaha. But, I like to try different restaurants. NYC has so much to offer, you have to be original when picking a place to dine. That's romantic to me.

Do you think this twist in your life path has been surprising?

I wouldn't say I was destined to be a porn star, but I don't think it's surprising either. I was always very easy going and loved to experiment in all aspects of my life. I think it kind of found me, and I just happened to be good at it!

ADAM **CHAMP**

How did you get started in the business?

Actually, Colt talent coordinator and personal friend Manfred Speer contacted me two years ago inviting me to become a Colt model. I took some time thinking about it, but I must admit I've always wanted to be in this business.

What were you looking for when you got into it?

I knew sooner or later I was going to become a Colt model. I've got some proposals from other companies but I declined them because my goal was Colt Studio always. I was looking for and I am looking for being remembered as an iconic Colt model. I love all these men. They are the epitome of masculinity and sensuality.

What about making XXX movies didn't you expect?

Actually I knew many things about the industry, but I was not expecting to have so many liberties in choosing my

STATS

BIRTH DATE: October 10, 1976

SIGN: Libra

HOMETOWN: Buenos Aires, Argentina

HEIGHT: 5'10"

WEIGHT: 215 lbs

TWO BEST CHARACTER TRAITS: I think my body and my generosity

TWO WORST CHARACTER TRAITS: My behavior – sometimes I'm a bad boy and I am very lazy

FAVORITE MUSIC: I'm charmed by Tchaikovsky music. Surely The Nutcracker is his most enchanting piece.

FAVORITE MOVIES: I love all the old movies. I love divas who play bitchy, mean characters

FAVORITE MOVIES I'VE BEEN IN: I've enjoined filming all my movies, but I can never forget the one who made me and Carlo Masi fall in love. Unfortunately the title is unknown yet as the movie is not released.

XXX COSTAR I'D DO AGAIN IN A MINUTE: I chose him as a life partner and I would choose him again and again for all my movies. He is my beloved partner and lover, Carlo Masi

IF I COULD MAKE ONE REQUEST ON A PORN SET IT WOULD BE: It would be nice if they would remember that my favorite champagne is Dom Perignon, but I seriously doubt it is ever going to happen.

AS A TEEN I ALWAYS FANTASIZED ABOUT SEX WITH: Superman

CURRENT FANTASY MAN: I know I start to sound boring but I am living a very special moment of my life with him so I will answer again: Carlo Masi.

SEXIEST PART OF A MAN: Eyes and butt

THREE INGREDIENTS OF MY HOTTEST SEX FANTASY: Mirrors, cams and domination

FAVORITE ITEM IN MY SEXUAL TOY BOX: My 12-inch dildo

MOST PRIZED POSSESSION: My dog, an Italian mastee

HOBBIES: Modern art and musicals

PETS: Dogs

partners in movies. That's something great! And also I was not expecting my fellows at Colt to be such sweet, nice and friendly people.

So what are the perks to being a Colt exclusive?

They are so many. Especially the love and recognition from the fans. They are all very warm.

And what are some things about Carlo Masi that makes him your dream man?

Wow, there are so many things. Carlo is great! The best. We are alike physically and mentally, same points of view about life, same height, same weight, same size cock. Haha! He makes me laugh and smile all the time. Also we don't need to explain or hide from each other anything about our jobs. I feel so happy and lucky to have met him.

Is it easier to have a partner who also works in the industry? How does that work and do either of you get jealous about your shooting partners?

Mmm ... Sometimes it is not very easy. If you mix an Argentinean and an Italian boy it might be very dangerous. We talk about everything about our jobs. We have a deep respect about our decisions from work, but we talk seriously first. Of course we are always jealous of each other when we shoot scenes with some other guys, but we understand it. It is our job.

So when you made the leap into porn was filming difficult at first?

No, not actually. It was pretty natural to me, as if I'd being doing it for years. I believe I was born for this job.

Do you recall your first film and the first bit of direction you were given?

Sure, I do remember it. It was just last June after all. Moreover, shooting that scene with gorgeous, sexy Luke Garrett made it unforgettable. On that very same movie I remember John (Rutherford) telling me to grab Luke's leg with my other hand (I was covering Luke's face with my hand from the camera). I also remember John asking me not to look at the cameras and to try to catch as much sun light as possible on my body.

What things do you usually do to prepare for a shoot?

Before shooting a scene I don't have sex for three or four days to insure a big load. That's so important to me. Also I reduce carbs. I'm always on a diet, but in the last week I adjust it more. And sleep!

And what is the average evening like when you get home from a day of filming?

After a day of filming I try to relax on Carlo's chest. Hugging and kissing each other. Also I eat some ice cream and watch TV or some movies. I really got very tired after filming, especially in the summer.

OK, I must hear more about the three ingredients to your sexual fantasy. Fill in the blanks regarding mirrors, cam, and domination.

OK, I like to have sex in front of mirrors and watch everything, especially when my cock is pounding. I love all the positions and have sex for a long long time and at the same time take tons of pics or I'm filming all the action. About domination I must say I love leather! I also love to dominate and role play, controlling at all times the situation. But mirrors are my favorites.

Adam Champ [PHOTO COURTESY COLTSTUDIOGROUP.COM]

"There are a few secrets to making me horny. One of them is looking at myself in a mirror. Another one is showing me a beautiful, bubbled, spread ass."

So you like watching yourself in mirrors ... then is it educational, interesting, painful, embarrassing, or impossible to watch yourself on screen?

Well, that depends on my mood. It can be all those things at the same time. Educational because watching at myself I can see and hence I can correct my weak points. It is interesting because not many people know what they look like when they have sex. It is painful because I have a boyfriend and we are very jealous of one another. It is embarrassing because I think of my friends might watch this movie somewhere sooner or later and that is pretty awkward. And it is impossible when I am in a bad mood so I can't see anything but my defects.

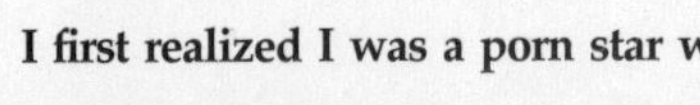

I first realized I was a porn star when ...

I first realized I was truly a porn star when in December last year (2006). I went to Rome, right on the other side of the globe and people recognized me. I didn't expect that people living so far from me knew not only my name but also them to be able to recognize my face among hundreds in a club. About the same time I was in Italy a friend of mine sent me a message telling me I was very well known in London, too. And I also was voted "The Most Gorgeous Man in South America" by a very popular web site. I was aware I was popular in the U.S.A, but I was not expecting to be known all around the world.

You must receive many fan requests. Has there been a most unusual one you would care to share?

Sure I remember. I was asked for some of my pubic hairs.

Speaking sexually very few guys are as skilled as me when it comes to ...

Pounding very hard and for a long time

If you were making a film called The Champ's Orgy who would you want as your four costars?

Of course all the Colt men. They are the real champions: Carlo Masi, Gage Weston, Luke Garret and Skye Woods.

XXX is notorious for putting guys into some pretty uncomfortable positions for the sake of the shot. What is the hardest position you've ever had to assume while having sex for a movie?

The hardest position I ever had to assume was during the shooting of the scene with Carlo Masi on a Harley Davidson motorbike. The movie has not been released yet.

What has been a sexual experience you think would have made a fantastic film if cameras would have been around?

I was in Rome with my boyfriend Carlo Masi. We were both in leather and playing with a dildo.

Where is the wildest place you have ever had sex off-screen?

I had sex inside a closet once, underneath the bed. But I must confess the wildest place it was under a Roman aqueduct. That day was fucking freezing outside, but me and my boyfriend (Carlo Masi) got horny and we decided to make it right away. Those wild places are always with a boyfriend for me.

When it comes to seducing a man I've found nothing works better than ...

A big, big smile.

If someone came to you for advice about getting into the business what would you tell him?

Actually I've never been asked for some advice, but if I were I would say never dye your hair.

Do you plan on eventually moving behind the camera in some capacity?

I'm not moving in that direction at this moment. I'd prefer to explore all the possibilities as a porn actor.

How do you think you are a typical Libra?

I am 100% typical Libra. We are supposed to be balanced, but it is not true. I'm an extreme boy. I mean there are no points in between at all. Also I love the arts, especially music and painting. But I define myself a typical Libra because I've got a fanatical obsession for beauty – physical beauty. I have a deep feeling for aesthetics.

How would you describe yourself in a personals ad?

This is a very challenging question. I guess I would say I am not only gorgeous but I am also very intelligent and full of surprises. This is totally flattering myself, but I deserve the compliments.

What is the biggest misconception people have about you when you meet them?

I am a very quiet boy, but I am not shy. Actually people's conception about me is exactly the way I am. Sometimes people think porn stars are totally perverted boys and in my case it is absolutely true.

What is the secret to turning you on sexually?

Well, there are a few secrets to making me horny. One of them is looking at myself in a mirror. Another one is showing me a beautiful, bubbled, spread ass. If you don't know what I mean check out my boyfriend's ass. One last secret I will mention is to lick my nipples. I love my nipples to be licked and sucked.

What is the best pick-up line you have ever used or fallen for?

I don't need a lot of words with a smile like mine, but I totally melt when my boyfriend calls me Amore Mio. It might be not original coming from an Italian, but I like it so much.

If you had to choose between sex and love which would you choose and what are your thoughts about fidelity?

I choose love, but I don't refuse sex either. Sex with love is the best thing you can ever do. It is very difficult to me to separate love from sex or sex from love. Fidelity is my first value. Belonging to someone gives life a real meaning. I always prefer to talk about fidelity and loyalty in the relationship. If you are not able to be loyal to me I prefer to let you go.

If you were offered a role in a fetish film how far do you think you would go?

100 km? Haha. I am kidding. But I really can go further than many people can imagine.

Porn sets are often the place of some surreal and hilarious incidents. Do you have any personal tale you would care to share?

One time, before shooting I was not saying a single word to my sex partner because I thought he was a boy who was speaking ill about me, so I decided not to talk with him. After two hours I heard his name and I realized he was not the guy I thought. Therefore, I started talking to him. I felt so stupid and I began to laugh and laugh.

Do you think the industry has a responsibility regarding the use of condoms and/or promoting safe sex?

The industry has a huge responsibility promoting safe sex and the use of condoms. I will never shoot a bareback movie, unless the other model would be my real life partner. Porn models and movies are a reminder to people and can show them they can have fun and play safe at the same time.

Adam, adult film stars are often considered these ideal specimens, yet if you could change one thing about yourself through cosmetic surgery what would it be?

Actually I am extremely satisfied and proud of my look. In my personal opinion cosmetic or plastic surgeries are too often used in excess, but it is also true that in some cases it is necessary, especially when one needs the help of surgeries to repair some obvious defect. For many people surgery can help to make them feel happier and self-confident, which is a very important thing.

What things do you think have been the greatest contribution to your success as a XXX star?

Surely I was very lucky to be in the right place at the right moment, but most of the merit of my success is due to the support of Colt Studio owner John Rutherford and the rest of the crew, who trusted and believed in me from the first moment. I also have to mention the entire Colt Studio stable, without them it would have been impossible to become an iconic Colt model.

Is there some episode in your childhood which looking back you just think, "Boy that kid was destined to grow up to be a porn star"?

Haha! There are many episodes. The most prominent one was when I was seven or eight years old. One day I almost got expelled from the swimming club because I was touching my fellows and forcing them to show me their ass. That same day I spent a good amount of time staring at the older guys in the shower and scoring them.

Wow. That is telling! Any others?

I remember I loved to play with Superman and Batman dolls, take their uniforms off and make them have sex. I had a huge imagination at that time.

Well, now that you are in it where do you hope this career takes you?

Who knows? I'd like to get a big big house with my boyfriend and many cats and dogs.

If you had to compare yourself to an animal what species do you think best captures your essence and why?

I would say a wild black horse, especially a wild one; those ones you cannot ride. I have loved horses since I was a kid. Horses are strong but at the same time they are weak and also full of pride.

Describe your dream vacation.

My dream vacation is with my man, Carlo, of course. Naked on a lonely beach and making love on the sand. Only the ocean, the sky, my man and me. That's all I can ask.

MATT **COLE**

How did you get started in the business?

It has been quite an amazing year for me. If you told me two years ago that all this was going to happen I would have just laughed. The whole experience has been nothing but positive and quite frankly I'm having a blast. This all came about exactly one year ago when a friend of mine sent some pics of me to an agent. Within two days I had an agent and three of the biggest porn studios expressed that they wanted to work with me. Three weeks later I was out in San Francisco filming my first movie. The rest as they say is history. I have been fortunate enough to work for the best in the industry.

What were you looking for when you got into it?

I really had no expectations. I knew that my life was going to be changed forever and that things would never be the same again, but I prepared myself for that. Quite honestly the experience thus far has been nothing but positive. I've met amazing people from all over the world and have had the opportunity to travel more than I ever could have imagined.

Were the people who knew you surprised?

At first yes, but I think deep down it wasn't that shocking. I have always

STATS

BIRTH DATE: December 4, 1977

SIGN: Sagittarius

HOMETOWN: Michigan

HEIGHT: 5'10"

WEIGHT: 190 lbs

TWO BEST CHARACTER TRAITS: Humorous, intelligent

TWO WORST CHARACTER TRAITS: Shy, self critical

FAVORITE MUSIC: Coldplay

FAVORITE MOVIES: *Citizen Kane*

FAVORITE MOVIES I'VE BEEN IN: *Trunks 2, Boot Boy, Trapped Pt 2, At Your Service*

XXX COSTAR I'D DO AGAIN IN A MINUTE: Jason Kingsley

IF I COULD MAKE ONE REQUEST ON A PORN SET IT WOULD BE: No junk food!

AS A TEEN I ALWAYS FANTASIZED ABOUT SEX WITH: Men!

CURRENT FANTASY MAN: Any tall, dark, Italian will do.

SEXIEST PART OF A MAN: His eyes

THREE INGREDIENTS OF MY HOTTEST SEX FANTASY: Sweat, lots of kissing and lots of noise.

FAVORITE ITEM IN MY SEXUAL TOY BOX: All of them

MOST PRIZED POSSESSION: My health

HOBBIES: Working out, biking, rollerblading, movies, dancing, cooking.

PET PEEVES: Bad kissers

Matt Cole [PHOTO COURTESY HOT HOUSE ENTERTAINMENT]

been a very sexual person and my friends know that. I think the biggest shock came to them when people started recognizing me on the street. It was different for them to see people reacting to me in that way.

What is the first thing you do when you come home from a XXX set?

Haha. Eat! Days on the set are long and rigorous. Imagine it to be like working out for over six hours. When I get back to my hotel I want to unwind, eat, and relax. Usually later that night I'll be horny again at which point I'll usually just jack off and go to bed.

"My boyfriend at the time couldn't wait until we got in the bed, so he just pulled my pants down and fucked me over the mailbox."

So you were a bit coy with your sexual toy box answer in the opening questionnaire, do you have anything specific that you enjoy using?

I'm really not big on toys. I much prefer the real thing. Nothing plastic is a substitute for the real deal. I will say that uniforms and props can sometimes be sexy and create the mood. But after I rip that uniform off, I want to be playing with the real thing.

Speaking sexually very few people are as gifted as I am when it comes to …

Kissing. I have been told on many occasions that I'm a great kisser. It's such a big part of my sex life, too. I think it makes the experience that much more intense. The secret to amazing kissing is all in the lips.

So if a guy is a bad kisser is that definitely a deal breaker for you?

Absolutely! Kissing is the most important thing to me. In order for sex to be amazing there has to be intense kissing. Quite frankly if you can't get me excited by kissing me, chances are I'm not going to be excited when I'm having sex with you.

What is the most turned on you have ever been on screen?

I just filmed a scene with Francesco D'Macho. This man could not have been more my type. This man is one hot fucking Italian with the body of a Greek God. We fucked like crazy on the set. I have never been so turned on by a costar. At one point he leaned down and whispered, "You're a very good actor," and I replied "I'm not acting, baby." Very rarely do you find that sort of chemistry on a set, but when you do it's amazing. There were several times I had to stop because I thought I was going to cum accidentally, and that almost never happens.

Where is the wildest place you've ever had sex?

On my front porch in the early morning after coming home from the bars. My boyfriend at the time couldn't wait until we got in the bed, so he just pulled my pants down and fucked me over the mailbox.

Describe your ideal romantic evening.

A night of cuddling and kissing. Those are two of my favorite things. It's especially good if it's cold and/or rainy outside. You just snuggle up in bed and enjoy one another all day long.

Matt Cole [PHOTO COURTESY LUCASENTERTAINMENT.COM]

JAKE **CRUISE**

How did the Jake Cruise Company come to be?

I was a web designer during the dot bust and needed money. My shrink suggested I start a porn site. That's right – my shrink!

Why do you think you said that made your therapist suggest a XXX site?

I was in a financial bind because of the dot bust. I had quite a high paying job to strike out on my own and I was about to lose the house. My therapist told me he had a longtime client who was in his 30s and living in his parents' garage. The guy had no social life and no job. One day he asked the therapist if he knew of a good accountant. The therapist, surprised, asked him why he needed one. The patient told him he had made so much money off of porn sites that he didn't know what to do with it all. So, basically, my therapist thought it might be a good way for me to get out of my financial hardship. He was right, but it took a year for me to figure out what to do and another year after launching JakeCruise.com before the site began to turn a profit.

STATS

BIRTH DATE: March 21, 1958

SIGN: Pisces

HOMETOWN: Miami

HEIGHT: 5'11"

WEIGHT: 200

TWO BEST CHARACTER TRAITS: I'm easy to work with and I love having fun.

TWO WORST CHARACTER TRAITS: Workaholic and workaholic.

FAVORITE MUSIC: Anything from David Bowie

FAVORITE MOVIES: *2001: A Space Odyssey and The Bad Seed*

FAVORITE MOVIES I'VE BEEN IN: *The Bad Seed* (Just Kidding), *Cruise Collection 15: Who's My Daddy,* and *Cruise Collection 56: Brendan Sharpe.*

XXX COSTAR I'D DO AGAIN IN A MINUTE: Carlo Cox

IF I COULD MAKE ONE DEMAND ON A PORN SET IT WOULD BE: Make the cameraman exit and leave me alone with this hunk!

AS A TEEN I ALWAYS FANTASIZED ABOUT SEX WITH: Good Catholic boys don't have sexual teen fantasies!

CURRENT FANTASY MAN: Pierre Fitch

SEXIEST PART OF A MAN: The back of the neck.

THREE INGREDIENTS OF MY HOTTEST SEX FANTASY: Me, Identical Twin Stud Number 1 and Identical Twin Stud Number 2.

FAVORITE ITEM IN MY SEXUAL TOY BOX: My Malibu Ken Doll.

MOST PRIZED POSSESSION: My sanity

HOBBIES: Sex, work, movies, sex, work, collection old Mac computers, sex, work.

PETS: 2 dogs and 1 cat.

PET PEEVES: They better not! I just cleaned the carpets!

Was it and has it been therapeutic?

Some say laughter is the best medicine. Well, I like to have fun and laugh while having sex, so in my case laughter and sex are the best medicine. Dr. Cruise highly recommends fun sex for anyone who is down and out.

What was the toughest part about getting the company off the ground?

Starting with no capital. I leased a video camera and used my Staples credit card to buy a digital still camera. I almost had to close up shop at the first anniversary due to lack of funds.

Did you have any idea starting out that it would get this big or this popular?

Not in the least. When I started out I was hoping to make a few hundred dollars a week. Now I have nine full time employees.

So with this company, when was the first time it really clicked with you that it was going to be a success?

At my first anniversary, I was about to shut the site down. I was working full time as a mainstream web designer and also working full time on JakeCruise.com. But I was only making enough money to pay the models. I was not making a profit. My house cleaner was my cameraman and CCBill processed my credit card payments. But I did everything else: web design, updates, photo editing, video editing, customer service, marketing, casting, etc. I was about to go crazy. Then the idea of putting up a one minute preview of my then most popular scene occurred to me. I had been warned by others not to because my bandwidth would go through the roof. But I did and overnight my sales quadrupled! It was amazing. I hired a video editor first and began to produce my line of DVDs. It's been growing strong ever since. I still have free previews for all of my movies.

I am an idiot about these things, but you mentioned that people warned you about a one minute scene because your bandwidth would do through the roof? What is the danger of increasing your bandwidth?

Web site owners have to pay a hosting company for the movies and pictures that transfer from the web site to the user's computer. This is called bandwidth. So if you download a movie to your computer from a web site, the owner of that site has paid a hosting company for you to get that file. The larger the file size of the movie or picture, the more bandwidth it takes to movie it from point A to point B. Think of it like a moving truck. If you're moving a couch from one house to another you just need a small truck, maybe even a pick up truck. But if you're moving an entire house full of furniture (files) you need a much larger truck (bandwidth), which is more expensive.

Thanks for the explanation. So how do you usually find your models?

Most apply through my two sites. Some are referred by scouts as well as former models.

Can you give me the typical scenario you follow from initial meeting to filming?

Actually, there's no initial meeting. It's all over the phone and email. Usually when we shoot the scene will be the first time we've met.

So if a lot of contact is over the phone

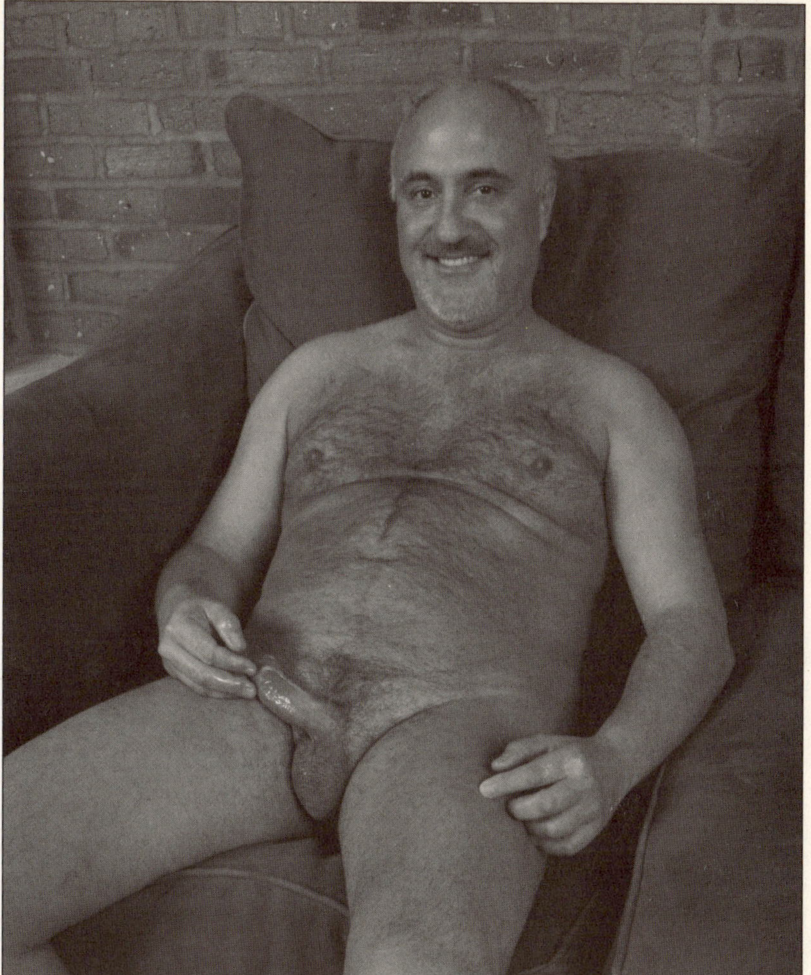

Jake Cruise [PHOTO COURTESY JAKECRUISE.COM]

and via email do models sometimes show up looking not at all like their photos/description or like that you expected? If so how do you deal with that sort of situation?

Oh, that has happened. Let me tell you. I'm a bit of a nice guy so, when a guy shows up 40 pounds heavier then the picture he submitted, I shoot him anyway. But these are usually guys from outside of Los Angeles. What I've learned is that you never know what the reaction of my customers is going to be. This particular guy had cellulite on his butt. He had buck teeth (he never smiled in his pics) and I thought it was going to be a disaster. He sold like hotcakes and is still popular today. Why? I don't know. People saw something other than his fat and buck teeth and they liked him. It's a crazy world.

Have you ever recruited anyone? Just gone up to them and said, I'd love to have you in a movie of mine?

I would die. I have never been able

to do it. I take it back. I did do it once. I went into a local adult video store to buy some lube. The cute guy behind the counter recognized me and we started talking. I invited him on and he accepted. His name was Ian.

Buying lube is always such an ice breaker. Who are your favorites of all the models you have discovered?

I wouldn't say I discovered him since he applied, but Michael Von Steel has been great to work with and has been very popular. I can only think of a couple of guys that I didn't like working with. I've been lucky in that most models have been fun. I think it's also that I provide a fun environment to work and play in.

What is the most aroused you have ever been on screen?

There have been three times that come to mind. The first was when Tommy D and I had sex and he threw me on the bed and literally ripped my shirt off – buttons went flying everywhere. The second was in Michael's Bonus when Michael Von Steel topped me. He is a fantastic lover. And most recently I did a scene with Trevor (Jude Collins from Randy Blue) where he topped me with his big cock. It's not on the site yet. But what was great was all the horsing around we did. We wrestled and he pinned me. When he fucked me, he would thrust real hard and make me scream with joy. But the best was when he began to kiss me. That was unexpected as he had never kissed a guy before.

What is the biggest drama or example of bad behavior that has ever occurred in a Jake Cruise production?

I have been *soooooo* lucky. I've never had a big issue with a performer. Well, some things have been very big, but that's another story. No, I had one real asshole very early on. I hired a straight porn star who was a real ass. He was doing a solo but didn't want me to shoot his butt. I insisted. Then he didn't want to cum on himself. I insisted. At the end of the shoot, when he was jacking off while watching straight porn, I mentioned something to him and he just screamed at me to shut up. Mind you, I have it on tape and it shows that I didn't speak a word for the previous 11 minutes. I almost kicked him out, but at the time I couldn't afford to. I needed the scene for the weekly update. On my way driving him to the bus stop (yep, this loser didn't have a car in LA) he told me he didn't understand why producers usually won't work with him a second time. I just shrugged and told him I didn't know why. And that's it. No one else has been a hassle to work with.

Can we expect any derivation from the Jake Cruise format, meaning any plot based films sometime in the future?

It is my intention one day to do a more professional, scripted movie. After five and a half years of amateur reality based porn I sure am ready. It's actually in the works right now. I'm talking with a famous gay porn director of years back and hopefully we will be able to work together. I'm also toying with the idea of doing a bisexual scene on Jake Cruise. But I don't know what my member's reaction would be to see me fucking a girl, even if I'm sucking cock at the same time. What do you think? Should I give it a try?

First off let me ask – when you men-

tion possible getting into plotted films ... what are the sort of plots or themes that would most interest you?

I like everyday situations that turn into sex. I don't mean when the doorbell rings and the pizza boy is at the door with a smile and a slice of ... you know. But let's say Adam is looking for a new puppy and goes to the dog shelter. He's shown some dogs by Steve who works there. They play with a couple of puppies and become playful themselves. But they don't have sex right then and there. Steve tells Adam that he's also a dog trainer. Adam hires him to help him train his new pup. At home Steve begins to train Adam's pup, but then he begins to train Adam's rooster, too. Or did I mean cock? I like plots that have a bit of meat to them. I don't want to see the sex right away. It's actually the opposite of what I do on JakeCruise.com.

OK, in answer to your earlier question – yes – I think you should add a woman to a sex scene with you and sort of test the waters, yours as well as the viewers'.

I'm thinking about it! It's a bit scary, but I'm ready to take the plunge. Hey, after five and a half years a little change is good.

I notice you are starting to do some strictly hetero movies as well but with the focus on the woman servicing the guy. How is that different from doing the strictly gay stuff and how is it being received?

My Straight Guys for Gay Eyes line is doing well. We're in our third year and membership and recognition is growing. The girls don't service the guys only, they also get fucked. It's full blown, 100% straight porn made for gay men. When it first launched I got a few letters from people complaining that I was demeaning gay men and that gay men shouldn't like straight porn. I found it ironic, and sad, that some members of our community decided that they knew what gay men should, or should not be, be attracted to. After fighting the religious right for our rights to have gay sex, now some of our own were trying to restrict us as well.

So now that the business is such a success does your partner ever say something like, you don't need to do it all or is level of involvement and all just part of your persona?

Well, we have nine full time employees so I definitely don't do it all any longer. But I try to stay involved as much as possible in the editorial aspect. By that I mean that I want to make sure that the scenes are fun for the performers, so that the fun comes across on camera. I had several movies shot in Philadelphia and Prague when I wasn't present and I regretted how some turned out. I think if I could have been there cheerleading it would have been more of my type of movie.

Has finding success yourself as a porn star surprised you as much as the success of the business?

Like you wouldn't believe. About three years ago a friend sent me a press release from a VOD (video on demand) site that had started running my movies. The press release went on to say something like, "... great porn stars from the past like Joey Stefano and Ryan Idol, as well as new stars like Michael Brandon and Jake Cruise." I almost fell out of my chair. Porn star? Me? It was strange because I don't know of any other middle aged, husky (overweight), normal cock sized gay man who became a porn star in his 40s. I could understand it if I were a muscle hunk with a nine inch rod. But I'm just a normal middle aged Joe who likes to eat.

Are you the company's most popular star?

There are two types of members. Those who join my site for the hot men and tolerate my being with the guys. The other type are the members who, for some odd reason, find me attractive. I have a straight woman in Seattle who is just bonkers about me. Go figure.

What things do you personally do to prepare for a film shoot?

Well, after trimming my beard and nose hairs, I shave my balls. Then I have someone take an electric trimmer to my back. No, not a lawn trimmer! Then if I'm going to bottom I clean myself out and play with a dildo for a bit to loosen the old girl up. And that's about it. Oh, and I brush my teeth, too.

How do you usually spend the evening after an hour of filming?

Passed out drunk in front of the TV with my life partner. OK, well, maybe not passed out drunk. But I live a very typical middle class life. I work during the day and come home to a house in the San Fernando Valley with two dogs, a cat, and a husband. He's the company's Chief Financial Officer, which means he keeps me from wasting all of our money!

One of my favorite scenes in a movie is where you suck off the cameraman. Does that sort of "audience participation" thing happen often on a JC set?

Well, he wasn't exactly in the audience. And no, it hasn't happened often on the set. In that case my cameraman, and model, Giovanni, had been off working at a camp for two weeks and hadn't been able to jack off in all of that time. He's straight, but even seeing me service the other model, Fernando, got him hard. So I asked to suck him off and he was more than willing. What followed is the best cum shot I've ever shot, and probably ever will. He let loose stream after stream of thick spunk all over my face. I didn't even know how much there was until I saw the footage. It was *deeeelicious*! I just posted a new scene last Friday in which Tristan, a male stripper, is brought in by my employees during our five year celebration. Tristan plays with me, strips off his clothes, and then he goes a lot further. He ended up fucking me right there in full view of my crew. What you see is a re-enactment of what actually happened a few days earlier. I got Tristan to do it over on camera. He also went on to do a few more scenes with me, and a scene for *Straight Guys for Gay Eyes*. And today we just finished shooting a scene where I have sex with Tommy D in my office while my employees worked around us. It's kinda fun. You know, a typical day at work. (Laughing).

Has featuring barebacking movies been any sort of problem for you and how do you respond to critics who claim the porn has a responsibility to portray safe sex?

I wouldn't say that I feature bareback movies. Some of my movies are bareback, but most aren't. Currently there are 23 out of 261 movies. That's less than 10%. My view on this is that I am an entertainer and not an educator. Over the past 24 years we have all been educated enough to at least understand that unprotected sex is unsafe. Some believe that adult gay men should be treated like children who might copy exactly what they see in porn. But think that through and you'll see that it doesn't stand up to logic. If gay men imitated in real life what they saw in porn, there would never have been an AIDS epidemic. There would have been AIDS, but the reason it would not have been an epidemic is that everyone would have been cumming on their lover's backs or bellies, not internally. The virus would not have spread as quickly. I believe the premise that adult gay men imitate what they see in their porn fantasies is false. A fantasy is a fantasy and an adult man will understand that.

There is a vocal minority in the gay community, many with a lot of power in the adult industry, who strongly hold the opposing view. I have never been personally attacked by them, at least not to my face. Some people have written in saying that I am like Hitler for showing two men having sex naturally. I wonder if these people know how closely they resemble the religious right in their words and attitudes. I walked in my first gay pride parade in San Diego in 1976 at the age of 18. From a very young age I was told that having sex with men is sinful and wrong. Now gay men are telling me that having gay sex without a condom is sinful and wrong.

The fact is that I shoot bareback scenes the same way I shoot straight scenes. Everyone, including me, is tested at the Adult Industry Medical Clinic (AIM) using the PCR/DNA test for HIV. The same safety precautions that are used for straight performers I use for gay performers. I don't discriminate. The only exception I make is when the performers are a couple in real life. If they normally have sex without condoms, then I'm not going to require them to take the AIM test.

"I live a very typical middle class life. I work during the day and come home to a house in the San Fernando Valley with two dogs, a cat, and a husband."

Do you have a favorite (non-Jake Cruise) porn production or two?

I never watch porn! (Laughing). Actually, I really like some of the old school porn. I loved *The Big Switch* which was a big production bisexual movie from the late '80s. And anything with Rex Chandler will make me cream my pants. *Woof.* I love the John Summers movies, too, especially *Two Handfuls* with Brian Maxon – another god!

What five men walking the planet would you love to get on your massage table for fifteen minutes?

Ryan Reynolds, Matthew McConaughey, Jake Gyllenhaal, Christian Bale, Bea Arthur

You are kinky! Speaking sexually, very few guys are as skilled as me when it comes to ...

Making a guy feel like he's having fun while having sex.

What is the biggest misconception people have about Jake Cruise before meeting you?

That I'm a sex fiend. Seriously, people think all I ever do is have sex with hot studs all the time. There is more to me than just that. I also have sex with guys who aren't so hot.

When you pass a hot looking guy on the street what gets you to turn around and do a double take every time?

The face and upper body. My eyes never go to the crotch. Just not much interested in that. It's always the face and the chest. Show me a man with strong pecs and beautiful eyes and I'll follow him anywhere. But show me the same guy with a cigarette in his mouth and I won't even glance.

Where is the wildest place you've ever had sex?

In the back room of a bar in Madrid when I was in Spain during my college years. I was kissing a hot guy named Pierre while another guy sucked me, a third guy rimmed my hole, and other guys were touching my body. The same thing was happening with Pierre. We did nothing but kiss, and other guys serviced both of us. It was fucking amazing and wild.

Describe your ideal romantic evening.

Sitting on the lawn in front of the Eiffel Tower at sunset with my lover, eating fresh bread and cheese and sharing a really good bottle of wine. Watching the lights come on the Tower. Then slowly walking back home along the Seine just a little drunk. Getting into a soft, cozy bed and making love slowly, quietly, and not in front of any fucking cameras!

If you had to choose between sex and love which would it be and what are your feelings about fidelity?

I can't really answer that question because it's not possible for me. I can't fall in love with someone who is jealous and insecure. The question, in my mind, is similar to asking, "If you had to choose between dining out and love, which ...." In my life sex is a natural part of life just like eating and sleeping. Love is an emotional component to one's personality that sometimes includes sex and sometimes doesn't. I've been in a relationship with the same man for almost 18 years. We have lived together since two weeks after we started the relationship. Two months after that we had joined all of our finances and still do so today. He manages all of the financial dealings of the business (he pays those bandwidth bills!). For us sex with each other is part of our loving relationship. And sex with others is a natural, fun part of life. It's also my job.

Describe your dream vacation.

I'm on a Mediterranean isle with my lover and a few close friends. We hang around at the beach, go boating, snorkeling, etc., during the day. At night we have a good, fresh cooked dinner al fresco, then relax drinking wine while having good conversation. The young local boys (all of legal age) come by and massage my feet and shoulders. My lover and I take one back to our cabana to share. In the morning we get up slowly, drink strong coffee, along with bread and olive oil. But the most important thing is that my iPhone is no where to be found. No one else has a phone either. I have no computer with me. In fact, there is no Internet connection on the entire island. Scary, huh? My gut actually clenched as I wrote this. But yes, I think that would be my ideal vacation – disconnected and content.

HANK **CRUZ**

How do you consider yourself a typical Capricorn?

I'm confident and strong willed.

What was the best advice you were given starting out?

To work for an established company (director) first.

If someone came to you for advice about getting into the business what would you tell them?

That it is not at all the business as it has been portrayed in bad TV versions of an adult film star's life.

What things do you always do to prepare for a shoot?

Gym, steroids, haircut, body grooming, rest. Lots of rest. Avoid sex for at least three days, longer if possible.

And how do you usually spend the night after a day of filming?

Sleeping.

What is the most aroused you have ever been on screen?

Licking a dude's wet moist quivering hole, sweet.

Speaking sexually very few guys are as skilled as me when it comes to ...

STATS

BIRTH DATE: January 15

SIGN: Capricorn of course

HOMETOWN: Earth

HEIGHT: 5'10"

WEIGHT: 180 lbs

TWO BEST CHARACTER TRAITS: Intelligence and confidence

TWO WORST CHARACTER TRAITS: Intelligence and confidence

FAVORITE MUSIC: Yes

FAVORITE MOVIES: *Valley of the Dolls, What Ever Happened to Baby Jane, Being There, Harold and Maude*

FAVORITE MOVIES I'VE BEEN IN: *Truck Stop on I-95*

XXX COSTAR I'D DO AGAIN IN A MINUTE: Any of them; I'm a professional.

IF I COULD MAKE ONE REQUEST ON A PORN SET IT WOULD BE: Adequate showering facilities.

AS A TEEN I ALWAYS FANTASIZED ABOUT SEX WITH: My friends

CURRENT FANTASY MAN: Anonymous dude in tight jeans I saw today.

SEXIEST PART OF A MAN: His ass

THREE INGREDIENTS OF MY HOTTEST SEX FANTASY: Mirrors, lots of touching, candlelight

FAVORITE ITEM IN MY SEXUAL TOY BOX: Tit suction tips

MOST PRIZED POSSESSION: Memories

HOBBIES: Dining out, travel, experiencing art

PETS: Miniature Dachshund named Klaus

PET PEEVES: Rules.

Hank Cruz [PHOTO COURTESY HANK CRUZ]

Having a useful tongue and thick lips. Latinos are advantaged there.

How would you describe yourself in a personals ad?

Gym body stable guy with no agenda seeks absolutely no agenda.

What would you bring to a relationship? —

Hot House, their models are closest to my type of guy. Perhaps Titan. Any four professionals would do.

What are the best and the worst parts of being a porn star?

That people think you are sexy and unattainable. That people think you are sexy and unattainable.

"I was a nerdy kid. I didn't hit the gym until after I was told I would die from HIV/AIDS. Then suddenly I became desirable. Ironic as heck."

Describe your ideal romantic evening.

Dinner by candlelight, hugging and kissing by a fireplace, then more hugging and kissing with every intention of fucking all night, but opting for just cuddling and sleeping instead. That's intimacy. Fucking is not intimacy. It's a means to an end, but it's not intimate.

So if you had to choose between sex and love, which would it be and what are your thoughts about fidelity?

Love, and fidelity is bonded in the heart, not in your pants. Fucking is not intimacy. Kissing and discussing philosophy and cuddling are intimacy.

Starting out, what was your biggest fear about making the XXX plunge?

That somehow my sexual notoriety could be used against me, which is false. Vanessa Williams and Anna Nicole Smith didn't have any problem becoming successful after participating in the adult entertainment industry.

If you were making a movie called Hank Cruz' Orgy who would you want as your four costars?

It's just work. I'd pick four from

Is it hilarious, educational, painful, or arousing to watch yourself on screen?

I don't watch myself on screen, in the mirror maybe, but that's a private showing.

Do you think the industry has a responsibility regarding the use of condoms and/or promoting safe sex?

There is only safer sex. Condomless sex with the money shot hitting the lens is very safe on that scale. We have a responsibility as individuals to promote safer sex. It isn't the industry's responsibility, it is our responsibility as individuals.

Looking back on your childhood and adolescence is there any memory that you think of and say, "That kid was destined to grow up to be a porn star"?

Absolutely not. I was a nerdy kid. I didn't hit the gym until after I was told I would die from HIV/AIDS. Then suddenly I became desirable. Ironic as heck. Also, there are no porn stars. They are adult film performers.

If you could change one thing about the way the adult film industry is currently run what would it be?

That, like in more commercial films, the actors could be better paid, and possibly participate in the sales in an equity share, especially if the film is successful.

What is the craziest bit of drama you have ever encountered on a XXX set?

There is no place for drama on the set. The worst stuff that happens is that someone doesn't show up, or can't get it up, or can't cum on time.

When you pass a hot looking guy on the street what gets you to turn around and do a double take every time?

A nice butt.

Many people consider porn stars to be these ideal physical specimens, but if you could change one thing about yourself through cosmetic surgery what would it be?

A lot of people love hairy guys, but I wish I weren't quite so hairy. It comes with being a mammal.

Describe your dream vacation.

Paid for.

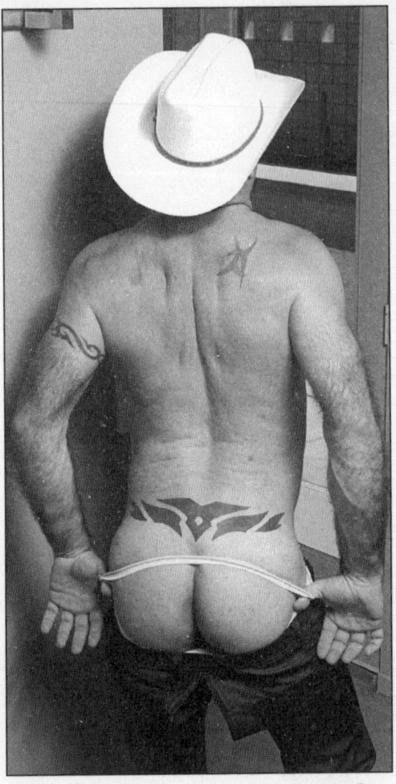

Hank Cruz [PHOTO COURTESY HANK CRUZ]

Where do you hope this business takes you?

My business will take me places, and my hobby of having done adult films can only make me more interesting at dinner and in bed if you get that far.

STEVE **CRUZ**

So is Steve Cruz your real name or is there some story of how that *nom du porn* came about?

Steve is my real name. The last name is a common Portuguese last name, like my real last name. It's as genuine as a fake name can get.

How did you get started in the business?

I was approached by a few studios and weighed the decision before signing on. I knew a few people in the industry going in.

So Steve, when you say the studios approached you about getting into movies how do you mean that? What was the scenario?

I hired Kent Taylor, photographer at Raging Stallion, to do some contract work for one of the gay men's public health campaigns I designed and art directed. While in the studio I met the director and it kind of evolved from there. Chris Ward approached me

STATS

BIRTH DATE: November 4

SIGN: Scorpio

HOMETOWN: San Francisco Bay Area

HEIGHT: 5'5"

WEIGHT: 140 lbs

TWO BEST CHARACTER TRAITS: I'm honest and considerate.

TWO WORST CHARACTER TRAITS: I over analyze and give small things too much meaning. I'm stubborn.

FAVORITE MUSIC: Classic Rock. Alternative Rock. New Wave. No Wave. Synth. Electronic.

FAVORITE MOVIES: *Boogie Nights, Chinatown, Streetcar Named Desire, Hairspray, Rebel Without a Cause, LA Confidential, Donnie Darko, Blade Runner*

FAVORITE MOVIES I'VE BEEN IN: (Most of my work is not out yet, so these answers are based on the experience pre-edit, packaging and release) *Lords of the Jungle, Mirage.*

XXX COSTAR I'D DO AGAIN IN A MINUTE: François Sagat.

IF I COULD MAKE ONE REQUEST ON A PORN SET IT WOULD BE: I always need water.

AS A TEEN I ALWAYS FANTASIZED ABOUT SEX WITH: Colt Man Rick Wolfmier

CURRENT FANTASY MAN: Dean Phoenix.

SEXIEST PART OF A MAN: The groin, the baseline of the obliques, lower abs leading down to his shaft.

THREE INGREDIENTS OF MY HOTTEST SEX FANTASY: Muscles, sweat and foreskin

FAVORITE ITEM IN MY SEXUAL TOY BOX: Nipple clamps

MOST PRIZED POSSESSIONS: My Power Mac G5, my MacBook Pro.

HOBBIES: Playing my bass guitar. Graphic design.

PETS: A cat named Kitty

PET PEEVES: Self-deprecation. It's the biggest turn off when a guy puts himself down constantly. Oh! and that smoked stale cigarette smell and taste. Both make me go limp ...

seriously with an offer that involved travel to Hawaii and Palm Springs, and significant roles. I'm glad I said yes. Shooting both *Mirage* and *Lords of the Jungle* was a blast!

Did you surprise yourself by taking the plunge?

Yes. Although I was more surprised by the offers. I never saw myself doing this until I saw my film. Then it all made sense to me.

What were you looking for when you got into it?

I wasn't looking for anything really. I found myself recently single after a six-year relationship. I was in the process of re-examining my life and my identity and what I wanted. The offer came at a perfect time to make that change.

Did going into porn provide the life change you were hoping it would following that relationship?

It was a catalyst for change yes. The therapy helped also! (Laughs) In the end I am glad to be single. I wouldn't be doing this if I was partnered. I don't think much about the life that ended because the life I am living is so much more fun!

Do you have any plans or idea of where you want this career to take you?

You can't make any real money in porn unless you are a producer or partner. So as a performer I hope to work with the best while I'm here, make some great movies, turn out hot performances guys will get off on. If in the process I get to travel and enjoy life, hey why not? I'm an ambitious and creative person, post production fascinates me. Editing, Product Packaging, maybe even directing ... Or maybe I'll start a rock band! (Laughs) ... anything is possible.

Do you recall the first bit of direction you were given in a XXX movie?

Sure. You can watch the behind the scenes DVD of *Lords of the Jungle* and see it for yourself. Chris Ward was great. He was encouraging and always checked in to make sure I was in a good head space. He says, "the bottom is always in charge."

What are some things you always do to prepare for a XXX film shoot?

I usually stop all sexual activity a week or two before production. I save myself. I hit the gym hard and I get plenty of rest. Diet is a little more restricted than usual.

And what is a typical scenario when you get home after a day of filming?

Pure exhaustion. Sometimes there's a residual buzz from the energy of filming, but mostly I'm spent. I'm ravenous after sex. Who eats before a shoot – right?! So I reward myself with a huge meal and sleep. Maybe something fatty like French Fries and Chocolate Gelato.

Can you give me a typical casting scenario or what the experience of casting has been?

Each studio handles me differently. Some treat me like gold. I choose who I want to work with. That has been great! In most cases the director or casting director had someone in mind for me going in ... Brian Mills at Titan chose François Sagat. It's like Brian

Steve Cruz [PHOTO BY KENT TAYLOR, COURTESY RAGING STALLION STUDIOS]

picked my brain or something. A dream come true! Chris Ward at Raging Stallion chose Jake Deckard, again straight from my fantasies. Chi Chi LaRue paired me with Arpad Miklos, another one of my favorites. It's kind of been a charmed ride so far.

If you were to add to your resume a specific sexual prowess what would it be and what do you think makes you so good/skilled/gifted at it?

I like to serve? (Laughs) I love sucking cock! Seriously, I don't know why I am good at this except for practice makes perfect. You do well what you enjoy and it's just in my nature. Sexually I've always been a natural performer ... and I've always been very open and in touch with my sexuality. I've little to no shame or inhibition at 34. I hope to stay that way as I get older in spite of our attitudes about aging and sex.

When it comes to seducing a man what works best for you?

I'm direct. No nonsense. Whether that's the best approach for every man, I can't say. I put it out there and if he's interested and not put off by honesty ... it's a go! I know sometimes I'm too forward for some guys, but my guess is it would have been a bad match any way.

What is the key to turning you on sexually?

I like masculine uncomplicated men. Someone in great shape who's strong and down to earth. Sexually intense. Self possessed, maybe even a little quiet. Dominant but not opposed to letting me take over when I want to. Physically he's worked out and muscular, even beefy. He's a little older than me. Maybe he's graying. He's probably hairy. Facial hair. Has an edge, maybe a few tats. Hung. Uncut.

And François Sagat, what made him a costar you would like to do again?

I mentioned before I've watched his films. He's a physical ideal: The face, the body, just perfect. I also like the tattoo, it's very distinct. And a he's sweet, sweet man. Very tasty.

If a guy came up to you and asked advice about getting into the business what would you tell him?

Depends on the guy. Some guys are more marketable than others, it's a business. So know your worth and what you bring to the business, ask questions. Make more allies than enemies. Treat people well even if they are freaks. Learn fast. Work hard (yes, making porn is hard work). And most of all have fun with this. Relax, it's only porn! Don't take it or yourself too seriously.

Do you have some deep dark fantasy you are just waiting for some porn director to ask you to film?

I have a character I want to play that has a dark side. I am developing his story and the trouble he always finds himself in. Like me he survives on his instincts – but I am basically a good person at heart, so to play someone who's first impulse is totally selfish and unscrupulous sounds liberating.

How is your porn persona Steve Cruz is different from the non-XXX you?

Not much. We're the same person. You take a stage name because you need to, but other than that I just want to be me.

If you were offered a part in a fetish film how far do you think you would go?

I go back and forth on the topic. I am cast in a fetish film next month. I will do some light kink, water sports maybe. Bondage is hot. Aggressive sex is cool. No whipping or blood sports. No piercing. My thought is to set limits early in the career and keep evolving and pushing limits in time. The worst thing would be to do something extreme on film only then to be type cast.

Where is the wildest place you've ever had sex?

I have been having a lot of sex in bars lately. Not penetration, just blow jobs. Last week I got one in front of the back bar with the bartender and half the bar watching. The bartender was hot. And he had a big dick which he kept flashing me on my request. And then I got my dick sucked twice at a bar a few nights ago. I came once and went back for seconds. It's kind of a new thing for me to get serviced. I like it though.

I am curious is this exhibitionist streak something that was always part of your persona, is it a reaction to being single, or do you think making porn has heightened it? Any armchair psychologist insights?

As I get older and more comfortable in my skin, the exhibitionist comes out more and more. Either porn has made me more confident or more ballsy. It has certainly sparked a fire! I was in a relationship that had a lot of sexual freedom, so it's not like I am making up for lost time or anything.For now I am enjoying being unattached and enjoying the attention I am getting on and off camera.

Have guys started to recognize you through your movies and if so how have they treated you differently?

They are just starting to since *Lords of the Jungle* was released. Someone in a video store recognized me. Overall people are being very nice.

Speaking of that have you had any interesting fan requests?

Nothing too extreme yet! Just emails for autographs. Or during a public appearance they want to play with the hair on my chest. I get a lot of that anyway.

As someone newly single how would describe yourself in a personals ad.

That's tough because if I were to place an ad, I would be advertising or seeking companionship. That's not how I go about things. I don't even use the Internet for hook-ups. But if had to I'd say: Hot hairy versatile/bottom with tats and no attitude. Down to earth guy up for anything though not seeking. Make me the offer too hot to refuse.

Porn sets are known to be the magnets for some very funny/dramatic/surreal experiences. What's the most unusual experience you have had on a set thus far?

Funny: The funniest is a line Dirk Jager delivers in Mirage as he pulls me in tow: "Your boyfriend is too loose. You fuck him!" (which is actually not true, check my references) Surreal: The beauty of the Pacific Ocean, the blue Hawaiian sky and Jake Deckard on his knees in front of me slobbering on my cock – Jesus! It was all too much to deal with for my second scene, and first project. You can see that in *Lords of the Jungle*.

"I have been having a lot of sex in bars lately. Not penetration, just blow jobs. Last week I got one in front of the back bar with the bartender and half the bar watching."

What is the best pickup line you have ever used or fell for?

I don't usually use words to pick guys up. Lines are corny, right? Usually it's with eye contact. I'd rather stare a guy down. If he likes it, he's usually intense enough to match my energy, an indicator that we'll have a good time.

How do we get you in the sack and what do we do once we get you there?

Be direct. If I want it, I don't play hard to get nor do I waste time. Once you get me there bring on the energy and intensity. I like passionate sex, connected sex, uninhibited – safer sex.

Do you have an all time favorite sex scene from a XXX video? Or if it's easier just your favorite porn flick?

I'm a sucker for classic Colt movies: Killer and Butch, Bruno, Mike Betts and Rick Wolfmier. Or anything with Al Parker ... Falcon's classic *The Other Side of Aspen*.

If you were making a movie called Steve Cruz' Orgy who would you demand as your four costars?

I only get four? Dean Phoenix, François Sagat, Francesco D'Macho and Carlo Masi (or bring Colton Ford out of retirement – Woof!)

OK, I am going to let you have four more people at your orgy ...

Hot! The more the merrier right! Chris Wide, Adriano Marquez, Jake Deckard and Damien Cross. Of course most of these guys are exclusives for different companies so it could never happen. But a guy can dream!

Steve, congratulations of being named a Raging Stallion exclusive. How did

that come about and what sort of perks does being an exclusive entail?

Stallion has wanted me from day one. I'm the perfect Stallion fit. But I needed to sow my oats before settling down. I wanted to work with best talent that the industry had to offer, and I had the privilege of being directed by Brian Mills of Titan (twice), legendary Chi Chi LaRue (twice) and Steven Scarborough. I learned a lot about how to deliver a great performance from each. I think Chris Ward understood my need to get my feet wet. He said I'd be back, and he was right! So when the opportunity was still on the table I jumped at the chance. It feels great to have a studio home. It was a lot of work to represent myself. Now I have a great studio to handle publicity and co-navigate my career. It's a relief and it's an amazing feeling of support. I couldn't be happier.

People tend to think of XXX stars as these ideal specimens, but if you could have one bit of cosmetic surgery performed on yourself what would it be?

I am very comfortable in my skin. I wouldn't change a thing.

So can you give me a bit more info about your cat named Kitty?

She's all white with green eyes and she's beautiful. I have had since she was about four months. Food and sleep is her life, more food than sleep. I had to put her on a diet because she weighed in at a whopping 27 lbs during her last visit to the vet. "Kitty Kitty Fat Ass!"

In what ways do you think you are a typical Scorpio?

I'm passionate. I'm ballsy. I'm driven and very creative. I work hard and I want the best from life. I love to fuck. I can be stubborn. I can also get a little obsessive especially around work. I can probably learn to relax more and slow it down a bit.

Have you ever been stalked?

Sort of. I had a date with a guy once, it was just good sex basically. No connection. I thought I heard him say "I love you" when he left my room that night ... He never showed up places or followed me around but called me at home every day for about a month. It got a little crazy when he wanted me to move in with him, two hours away in some backward town! I told him that he was obnoxious and not to call me anymore. That's when he threatened to knock me unconscious and take me "home" in a bag in the trunk of his car. Freak show! I wish this was exaggeration.

Describe your ideal romantic evening.

ZZZZZZ. I'm kind of through with romance. I don't trust romance. I'd want to him for what he is not for what I'd like him to be or what he'd like me to see. Sex and intimacy is instinctive for me. We click or we don't. We fit or we don't. A good date includes how well we connect, if we have anything in common, if we have fun, if it feels natural and if the sex is hot. Everything else is fog on a windshield. You're dazzled by the colored lights on your way to a head-on collision.

Describe your dream vacation.

Peace and quiet on a remote beach in the Pacific. Tahiti. Bora Bora. I'm doing nothing. No plans. No obligation.

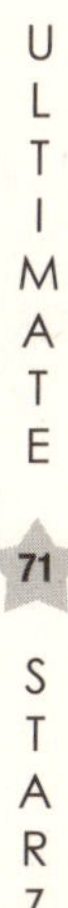

Steve Cruz [PHOTO BY KENT TAYLOR, COURTESY RAGING STALLION STUDIOS]

Where do you see yourself or where would you like to see yourself five years down the line?

Maybe I'll be playing bass in a band, writing my own stuff. Maybe I'll go back to painting. In five years I'll be about 40 and hopefully in the best shape of my life, the ideal age, so maybe I'll still be in movies but knowing me I'll have to be doing something creative. Maybe editing or directing? Anything is possible!

What are you the most grateful for in your life?

That's tough to narrow down. I don't want to sound like a new age zealot or a born again Christian, but I'm really grateful for everything in my life. I feel like one of the most blessed people I know, its sometimes unbelievable the opportunities that come to me and the wonderful people in my life. I'm grateful for my luck and for the experience of life itself!

VINNIE **D'ANGELO**

How did you get started in the business?

They had been talking to me for years. I was just more prepared for it now after taking a long four years think about it.

So it took you four years to make up your mind about getting into the business. What were your concerns or hesitations?

I just wasn't ready for it at that time, a lot of personal issues.

What were you looking for when you got into it?

Notoriety, also just a chance to travel and see lots of different places.

Has the XXX career brought you the notoriety you wanted?

It's starting to.

Were the people who knew you surprised?

No, I toured the country stripping. It was more a natural evolution.

What was the first movie you did and the first bit of direction you were given?

Trunks 3; and the first bit of direction was "Relax and take your time." I was very nervous.

What about making XXX sort of came as a surprise to you?

How easy it really was for me. They say I'm a natural at it. Go figure.

STATS

BIRTH DATE: December 10, 1977

SIGN: Sagittarius

HOMETOWN: Chicago

HEIGHT: 5'11"

WEIGHT: 205 lbs

TWO BEST CHARACTER TRAITS: I'm outgoing, and easy going

TWO WORST CHARACTER TRAITS: I can be blunt and aggressive

FAVORITE MUSIC: From club music to regular pop to classic ... it varies on my mood.

FAVORITE MOVIES: *The Matrix* films

IF I COULD MAKE ONE REQUEST ON A PORN SET IT WOULD BE: Hmm ... I pretty much get it all ... (Laughing) ... hot guys

AS A TEEN I ALWAYS FANTASIZED ABOUT SEX WITH: Max Grand and Jeff Stryker

CURENT FANTASY MAN: Arpad Miklos

SEXIEST PART OF A MAN: Masculinity of the hair, that pubic hair area.

THREE INGREDIENTS OF MY HOTTEST SEX FANTASY: Masculine, facial hair, big cock

FAVORITE ITEM IN MY SEXUAL TOY BOX: None

MOST PRIZED POSSESSION: My big heart

HOBBIES: Movies, friends, socializing, beach, swimming, roller blading

PETS: 2 cats

PET PEEVES: Negativism

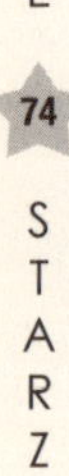

Vinnie D'Angelo [PHOTO COURTESY HOT HOUSE ENTERTAINMENT]

If a young buck were to come up to you on the street and ask for advice about getting into the business what would you tell him?

I would tell him a little of my experiences and point him in the right direction.

Do you have any expectations of where you want this career to take you?

Yes. I would like to be a star.

Going along with that, how exactly will you know when you get there? How do you define being a star?

I define being a star by going places and people recognizing you and wanting an autograph and having a lot of publicity such as in magazines, etc.

When it comes to seducing a man I've found that nothing works better than …

Charm.

Where is the wildest place you've ever had sex?

On the beach in Miami.

Describe your ideal romantic evening.

Candlelight dinner and a movie. Then a nice snuggle and kiss session before sex and after.

Where do you see yourself five years down the line?

Living life to the fullest.

What is the most aroused/sexually excited you have ever been on screen?

My scene with Steve Cruz – *1 on 1* for a web broadcast for Hothouse.

Have you ever developed a crush on any of your co-stars – would you care to name names?

None so far.

How would you describe yourself in a personals ad?

Hot n' horny Italian.

What is the best way to get you into bed and what is the best thing to do with you once we get you there?

Charm and give that ass up. Oops. Did I let the dog out? (Laughing).

Describe your dream vacation.

My dream vacation would be going somewhere that is warm with lots of sun. I can sunbathe on the deck of a boat and jump into the blue ocean and swim and play with other hot buds of mine. Then swim ashore and have sex on the beach. That would be ideal.

Vinnie D'Angelo [PHOTO COURTESY HOT HOUSE ENTERTAINMENT]

FRANCESCO **D'MACHO**

How did you get started in the business?

Well, I had been a fashion and fitness model for a number of years. But I'm addicted to working out and body building, so I realized that if I was going to bulk up I would have to find another career. Then one of my best friends, also in the porn industry, sent a few pictures of me around to well-known companies like Hot House and I got a very good response. So I thought to myself "What the fuck, let's give it a try." The thing that scared me a little was that it all happened really fast, without having the chance to think it through. About ten days later I was on a plane ready for my first scene. I didn't know what to expect, but I ended up having one of the most rewarding experiences of my life. I went to do my first movie being booked for one scene only. Since I'd never been in front of a camera before, the guys at Hot House wanted to see how I'd react to everything first. Well, I ended up getting in two scenes and on the cover, too! When Director Steven offered me an exclusive deal to perform for them I was overwhelmed.

Since you didn't know what to expect for your first film what was the biggest surprise?

STATS

BIRTH DATE: January 28, 1979

SIGN: Aquarius

HOMETOWN: Rome

HEIGHT: 6'

WEIGHT: 210 lbs.

TWO BEST CHARACTER TRAITS: I'm outgoing and smart.

TWO WORST CHARACTER TRAITS: I'm lazy and I suffer from ADD (Attention Deficit Disorder).

FAVORITE MUSIC: Tribal House

FAVORITE MOVIES: *His Secret Life, Serial Mom*

FAVORITE MOVIE I'VE BEEN IN: *Trunks 3*

XXX COSTAR I'D DO AGAIN IN A MINUTE: Robert Van Damme

IF I COULD MAKE ONE REQUEST ON A PORN SET IT WOULD BE: Only one request?

AS A TEEN I ALWAYS FANTASIZED ABOUT SET WITH: Superman

CURRENT FANTASY MAN: The Dieux Du Stade Men

SEXIEST PART OF A MAN: Footballer's legs.

THREE INGREDIENTS OF MY HOTTEST SEX FANTASY: Muscles, sweat, and sand.

FAVORITE ITEM IN MY SEXUAL TOY BOX: François Sagat

MOST PRIZED POSSESSION: My brain.

HOBBIES: Traveling, working out.

PETS: None, but I want a dog soon.

PET PEEVES: When your best friend turns out to be a back stabber, when all the movies that are playing suck, when people think only about themselves.

Francesco D'Macho [PHOTO COURTESY HOT HOUSE ENTERTAINMENT]

How professional the whole environment you work into really is. I feel like being on set of a real movie. But I think that is a Hot House thing.

What were you looking for when you got into it?

Another interviewer once asked me, "What is your biggest fear?" At the time I told him "death and subsequently being forgotten. I don't want to live on this earth and leave no footprint or memory of my time here." Obviously, just getting into the business at all means that we are exhibitionists. Knowing that someone is turned on when they watch me have sex is both enormously flattering and a huge aphrodisiac. But I think on a deeper level getting into the gay adult business was about leaving my mark, my footprint, my memory. Hopefully many of these images that we are filming will live on in people's minds for many years to come. I also enjoy provoking people and taboos. I would like to think I'm also part of a process whereby we can make porn more mainstream and accepted by the public. And I hope it's working. Tommy Hansen, one of the beautiful Bel Ami boys, has appeared on the Czech Big Brother television show with almost no fuss. Because you know, at the end of the day, everybody watches porn, from politicians to priests in the Vatican. I hope it doesn't sound conceited, but I really do think that we can be an engine of change.

Do you recall the first film you made and the first bit of direction you were given?

My very first scene was with the incredible Robert Van Damme. It was part of the award winning all-sex leather movie *Black-n-Blue*. I was extremely nervous but trying desperately not to show it. Playing it so cool. But I didn't need to worry. Everyone on the Hot House crew is so friendly and professional that my life in front of the camera is easy. I guess the movie Black has become famous for the part where Robert slaps me across the face. Really hot! What was lost on the edit was that I had initiated it and slapped him first. He was really surprised but went with the action. Either way, it's hot. Of course, I can't talk about direction without mentioning Steven Scarborough. And that name says it all. Twenty years in the industry, directing some of the best gay porn movies of all time. I feel flattered that he has always told me, since our first movie, that I'm a natural and don't need much direction. I guess what he meant is that I like to show it off to the camera, and that is what being successful in this business is all about.

If someone came to you for advice about getting into the business what would you tell them?

Be ready for a very competitive world. At present porn is incredibly popular worldwide, but it also means that there are a lot of production companies and a lot of guys who want to be stars. But having said that, you have to also make sure you keep a level head and have fun doing it. You just have to approach it all with a good attitude. I love where porn has taken me in the last twelve months, and I'm looking forward to a great future. Right now my life is so exciting. And for that I'm very grateful.

What was the best piece of advice you were given starting out?

Don't believe anything people tell you.

What is the most aroused you have ever been on screen?

The day I was in a silver Corvette sitting next to Christoph Scharff on the set of *White Heat (Trunks 4)*. The chemistry between Christoph and me was intense. I know the sex was the most real I've had to date while filming. I also have to tell you that the Corvette was a pretty big turn on as well. But, just like Christoph, Steven Scarborough would only let me play with it for one day. But I also want to say that I have filmed scenes with some amazing stars, including Robert Van Damme (*Black-n-Blue*), Arpad Miklos (*Private Lowlife*) and Jason Ridge (*Communion*). It is so hard to pick one time in particular. They have all been unbelievably hot. My latest movie is *Jockstrap* in which I was partnered with the new Hot House Exclusive Ty LeBeouf. He's a sexual dynamo (he claims LeBeouf means Little Bull). Things went so well and he was so aroused by the scene that he actually came twice. I love that I can have that effect on someone.

"Everybody watches porn, from politicians to priests in the Vatican. I hope it doesn't sound conceited, but I really do think that we can be an engine of change.

What things do you always do to prepare yourself for a day of filming?

Plenty of sleep, a good workout and as much mental relaxation as possible. Days on set can be long. The only way I can get through it is to be as physically and mentally ready as possible.

And how do you usually spend the evening after being on the film set all day?

We usually find time to have dinner together, which allows us all to relax in a humorous environment. Try having dinner with Alex Collack. He has one great story after another, all done with some amazing voices and outrageous actions.

After that I like to have some time to myself. I'm usually in a hotel when we film, so I lie on the bed and will spend time talking with friends on the phone or updating my blog. I think it is important that we all remember that we're nothing without the fans. My website, www.francscodmacho.com, is set up to allow as much interaction with my fans and friends as possible. So when I'm in my hotel room I like to take time to answer questions or reply to comments that fans have left on my blog. Then it's time for bed because most days I will be up by 6:00 am the next morning to start my work-out.

What is the biggest misconception people have about you when they meet you for the first time?

That I'm not a divo (That is the Italian masculine version of diva, there you go I gave you a little Italian lesson). Most people seem to think I'm

Francesco D'Macho [PHOTO COURTESY HOT HOUSE ENTERTAINMENT]

very approachable and friendly. But really I am a huge divo. OK I'm being silly. I think because of my size and look, at first glance people can be very intimidated by me. But if they get past that intimidation and talk to me they generally find that I am pretty attitude free and friendly. I'm very down to earth. And everyone should know that one of the best things about being in this business is the interaction with fans. Whether I'm at the Folsom Street Fair in San Francisco, IML in Chicago or Hustlaball in Berlin, it is always such a thrill and privilege to meet the fans who are buying my movies.

You mention the importance of your fans and they certainly love you. What is the most interesting or unusual request you've had from a fan?

Before I answer you with this, let me just say that I'd do almost anything for my fans! They are the reason why I'm standing out and proud right now. OK, enough with the sugar. I've way too many strange requests at times. I still get shocked by people's fetishes or turn ons. I feel like such a saint. OK, this guy once asked for my chewing gum during a signing at IML Chicago, I looked at him and didn't know if he was serious or not. Well, he was.

What is the biggest example of divo behavior you have ever encountered on a XXX set?

Being on set can be very challenging at times, you are working together with a crew of people, everyone is focused on doing his own job. The actors are the center of everything in that situation, if they fuck it up, everyone is affected. Divo behavior is part of this game, the better I'm treated the better I deliver for everyone. But let's not talk about me any further. You'd have to ask someone else for my being-a-divo on set. (Like to my publicist David, he would give you the real dirt!) I can tell you that Alex Collack requests a full tray of Krispy Cream donuts when he is on set, and no one is allowed to touch them.

Have you ever developed a crush on any of your costars? Care to name names?

All of them! (How political).

And if you were making a movie called Francesco's Orgy who would you want as your four costars?

Matthew Rush, François Sagat, Julian Vincenzo and Jenna Jameson.

XXX is known for putting guys in some very awkward positions for the sake of the camera shot. What is the toughest position you have ever assumed when filming?

For the sake of the shot you gotta show it good in positions you wouldn't assume normally. That is a given for people who work in the industry. At first I used to think, "How in hell is this position is going to look natural the way it is staged?" Then you take a look at the final cut on video and I think, "Dammit! This looks so good!" I can tell you that I hate when they ask me to cum standing up. The money shot (or the cum shot) is already the toughest part of the shoot for me. I'm tired, it is always happening at the end of the day, everyone wants to go rest, and I feel the pressure is on me big time! So when they ask me to cum while standing up I'm like "No! This is going to take forever now!"

Have you ever done anything sexually on screen that you would never do in your personal life?

Leather is not my thing, but I've done two leather based movies to date (*Black* and *Communion*, both for Hot House).

How would you describe yourself in a personals ad?

You mean one of those dating ads!? "Big dork, dumb as a puppy dog, big heart and huge romantic, impulsive, aggressive and outgoing, looking for another fallen angel in hell to take care of one another." Pretty lame, right?

Speaking sexually, very few guys are as skilled as me when it comes to ...

Definitely kissing.

Where is the wildest place you've ever had sex?

On my sister's bed with her boyfriend. I'm so bad!

Describe you ideal romantic evening.

Couldn't you ask me what my ideal sexual situation would be? That's easy, sex on a beach with two muscle guys, with me as the filling in a muscle sandwich. Romantic. Hmm. Talking, enjoying a glass of wine, some Belgian chocolate, a fireplace, snowing outside, looking deep into the eyes of someone you find not just visually stimulating but mentally stimulating. Lots of gentle touching. The animalistic passion can come later. True romance is so much about connecting on a mental level.

Describe your dream vacation.

A trip around the world with a loved one.

ROLAND **DANE**

So Roland, which end of that whip do you like to be on?

I like to hold the whip and dominate.

How did you get started in the business?

In '98 a Hungarian model agent looked for an English-French translator. I was a poor college student, so it was a great offer. Then in '99 I worked for Falcon International as a translator in Budapest, and John Rutherford who was the supervisor of that project offered me a Falcon exclusive contract

What were you looking for when you got into it?

Much less than I reached. I feel very lucky. I was counting on a little extra money on the side for the university. Now, directing and acting for Colt Studio Group is my life and I cannot imagine any other job for myself. Being the producer-director of Colt's Olympus line is the biggest honor, more than I ever could imagine in the past.

And now you have become a producer/director/star. Which of those three jobs gives you the most pleasure and which is the most trying for you?

I love challenges and when I can do all the three at the same time, that's what I like most.

And if you could name 10 guys to form your dream cast who would they be?

Julian Vincenzo, Fernando Nielsen, Lucio Maverick, Jose Ganetti, Giovan-

STATS

BIRTH DATE: October 19, 1976

SIGN: Libra

HOMETOWN: Budapest

HEIGHT: 5'10"

WEIGHT: 175 lbs

FAVORITE MUSIC: Trance

FAVORITE MOVIES: Tarantino movies

FAVORITE MOVIES I'VE BEEN IN: *Hostile, Casting Couch* (Colt)

XXX COSTAR I'D DO AGAIN IN A MINUTE: I've had sex with so many of them in private I'd rather choose from civies.

IF I COULD MAKE ONE REQUEST ON A PORN SET IT WOULD BE: I'm the producer-director so usually things are up to me.

AS A TEEN I ALWAYS FANTASIZED ABOUT SEX WITH: Young Alain Delon (he was amazing in the '60s).

SEXIEST PART OF A MAN: Chest, abs, smile.

THREE INGREDIENTS OF MY HOTTEST SEX FANTASY: Group, domination, tools.

FAVORITE ITEM IN MY SEXUAL TOY BOX: Whip.

MOST PRIZED POSSESSION: Exotic travel, expensive cars.

HOBBIES: Fitness, boxing, travel, history.

PETS: I spend too much time abroad, so I cannot have one.

ni Floretto, Tom Chase, Brad Patton, Brian Hansen, Carlo Masi, Kane O' Farrell. I chose these men not only because they look amazing, but they are very professional, perfect models.

How do you go about casting the models/actors for your films?

I know all of the Hungarians and Czechs. If I want a foreign guy I ask for photos and talk to him on phone before the shooting.

Why do you think Eastern Europe has become such a rich market for making and producing gay XXX movies?

There are so many beautiful guys here fortunately, on the one hand. On the other hand, honestly, they don't have too much money and this is a very good income compared to the alternatives. When it started in the mid '90s, it was so cheap to shoot a movie here, but thanks to the good American economy it's not true anymore, but Budapest is still the European porn capital because of the well-built system. During that 10-15 years we learned this business very well.

What is the best sex you have ever had on camera?

A very hot scene between Brian Hansen and me in *Casting Couch* (Colt Studio Group).

What is the biggest difficulty/challenge you usually have when filming a movie?

After directing 30 movies the only difficulties are if the models don't show up on shooting day for different reasons, and they forget to call me about this.

What things do you usually do to prepare yourself for a day of filming?

I need at least six hours sleeping. Lots of Xanax—just joking. But I don't really need any special preparation.

And how do you usually spend the evening after a long day on the movie set?

With sleeping, especially when I'm directing and acting at the same time. It can be exhausting.

When you mention that you got into this as a student ... what was your intended career before porn?

High school P.E. teacher

Where is the wildest place you have ever had sex?

The most disgusting place was a sex club in San Francisco where my shoes almost became glued onto the floor. I guess they gave up cleaning the club. But the biggest turn on was beside a 200-foot tall waterfall in Thailand.

Describe you ideal romantic evening?

Although I'm not a very romantic guy: by the ocean, white sand, palm trees, a fancy restaurant with soft chill-out music and a good bottle of Cabernet Sauvignon or a Long Island Iced

"Budapest is still the European porn capital because of the well-built system. During [the past] 10-15 years we learned this business very well."

Roland Dane [PHOTO COURTESY COLTSTUDIOGROUP.COM]

Tea (if the guy is not cute enough) can be effective.

Describe your dream vacation.

Again, I can tell I'm very lucky. I always spend two months on a beautiful island in Thailand each year with tanning, training, riding my big chopper motorbike, excursions to the jungle, diving, jet skiing, partying on the beach, meeting tanned, cute guys in shorts on the beach.

How do you think this experience in XXX has changed you?

I became much smarter, I traveled around the world, so I became very open-minded for the different cultures. I already lived much more than a regular 30-year-old guy, and I have life-experiences like a 50-year-old man, which is good and bad at the same time.

DEREK DASILVA

How did you get started in the business of porn?

Well, I was kinda curious about doing it for a while and was even asked a few times in my 20s to do roles – but these never panned out. I loved the idea of being like those old AMG guys in the Bob Mizer photos – they are hot forever, and I thought it was cool to that I still found these men hot, 30 or 40 years later. And there is a weird *Videodome* effect – doing it on video somehow makes it seem bigger and more real, even as it is actually more artificial.

When I hit my mid 30s, I kinda figured it was now or never – plus I had been getting in better shape due to my martial arts and yoga regimes – so I actually looked better in my 30s than I did when I was younger. I was watching a Shotgun video at a Fort Troff party thrown by Joe G and I mentioned to a friend that I had always wanted to do what I saw in Roger's vids. My friend knew Roger, had played with him, and encouraged me to look him up. So I did. He seemed dubious of my claims of being into really heavy CBT, but after a few conversations he was interested into seeing if I was for real. Of course he delivered a scene the likes of which I might never experience again – it became the video *Breaking Point*. He pretty much sent me right off a cliff with almost no warm up. The whole scene, which lasted many hours, was done entirely without bondage – I had to force myself to be still for his attacks on my balls. By the end I was in tears – my will to take more was waning, and I was getting angry – I was certain I couldn't take more but he kept pushing me.

Of course after breaking down I did take more, but only after he let me recompose myself. While it seemed fast when it happened, on tape it's totally different – I slowly start to self destruct, piece by piece, until I finally fall completely apart. It was intense, and in my strange way, I really enjoyed the experience. It's hard to break me, but Roger was more than able. My balls were huge and swollen for days afterwards, which made sparring in my Jiu Jitsu class a rather challenging task. After this I did more work at the different small houses that did the videos I liked – and in general the experience was great. In a way, doing porn is a very heady experience. It's really an altered state of mind where for a few days your whole purpose in life is to be intensely sexual – and to do it without the shame or secrecy that usually comes with sex.

What do you think you were looking for when you got into it?

That's a complex question and one I doubt many guys are entirely honest with themselves about. On the most basic level, it was about having a new experience, and getting to play with a CBT player whose work I had long admired in video. But at a deeper level it's more complex, I think. Most porn performers are looking for validation, someone saying "yeah, you're hot," and knowing there are hundred of guys wanking off to your image. Of course everyone wants validation on some level, but not everyone is willing to transgress social norms to do it. But I've always been the sort to question these boundaries and I certainly have a mixed view of myself and like the ego boost that being behind the camera gives me. And while I'm not the

STATS

BIRTH DATE: January 26, 1968

SIGN: Aquarius

HOMETOWN: Ex-Detroit area, now Chicago

HEIGHT: 5'6"

WEIGHT: 168 lbs (but this varies wildly depending upon shoot schedules and jiu jitsu tournaments.)

TWO BEST CHARACTER TRAITS: Smart and thoughtful

TWO WORST CHARACTER TRAITS: I don't suffer fools gladly, and socially go from shy silence that looks like anger to rambling on to the point of being a brainy bore.

FAVORITE MUSIC: I'm a music freak – I love old punk rock, funk, dub reggae, free jazz, Detroit techno, electro, hip hop, garage rock, rootsy country – and anything else. I like nearly all genres, but only the most interesting music in each. I play in two bands, own a recording studio, worked as a successful music promoter and have run small Indy record labels.

FAVORITE MOVIES: *Fight Club, Sin City, Videodrome, 8 ½, 8 ½ Women, Blue Velvet.*

FAVORITE MOVIES I'VE BEEN IN: *Painful Pleasures* and *Ball Bash 1*, both came out so amazingly well.

XXX COSTAR I'D DO AGAIN IN A MINUTE: Roger from Shotgun, and Johnny Bondi are both amazing BDSM tops.

IF I COULD MAKE ONE REQUEST ON A PORN SET IT WOULD BE: Make it real! Unless I'm right there in the moment of intensity I don't enjoy it and that means the scene isn't going to be hot. Often I'm with tops that I've not met before, so convincing them that I really like a heavy BDSM scene is sometimes a challenge.

AS A TEEN I ALWAYS FANTASIZED ABOUT SEX WITH: Probably the only one I can mention that anyone would have heard of was that dude leaning up against the white rock in the early Calvin Klein underwear ads. At the time it was a pretty radical thing to sexualize a man that way. Now I'm more into brains than beef (though that rare combo of both together is perfection itself).

CURRENT FANTASY MAN: My boyfriend? I know that's lame. I'm also fond of a certain West Coast top who shall remain nameless since he's not a public figure or anything – but I'm hoping to see a lot more of him.

SEXIEST PART OF A MAN: Area at the bottom of the abs – though when having sex I really love feeling the sheer bulk of a guy's lats.

THREE INGREDIENTS OF MY HOTTEST SEX FANTASY: Pleasure and pain and someone that is smart enough to make me unsure which one is which!

FAVORITE ITEM IN MY SEXUAL TOY BOX: I have a rubber flogger that I rather like for when I'm topping a scene. I'm vegetarian and strict enough that I don't wear leather or use leather toys. Finding non-leather BDSM toys that are mean enough without being crazy is tougher than you'd think. But this one manages to be pretty versatile.

MOST PRIZED POSSESSION: My record collection

HOBBIES: Music, Jiu Jitsu, modern and contemporary literature, contemporary art, cutting edge fashion.

PETS: I used to keep lizards. When the last one died (it was 14 years old) I decided that I couldn't keep animals as pets anymore with a good conscience.

PET PEEVES: People who can't think beyond their own wants. While we're all like this to varying degrees some people make it into a sociopathic art.

sort that gets off on the idea of being a porn star (and there are guys that revel in the star aspect of it), I do like the notoriety to a certain degree. It's sort of a "fuck you" to that part of the world that would confine you to what is considered proper behavior. And while it sounds pompous, I also like the educational aspects of porn – it can show you how to be safer while still have mind blowing fun. And it acts as an escape valve for those that the fantasy of the kind of edge play we do in vids, but who cannot or would not do these things themselves in real life.

OK if one of the things you like about making porn is the educational aspect then would you ever be involved in a barebacking video?

Never. Barebacking is just plain fucked up. I mean we know that new diseases and new strains of existing diseases come around all the time. So why are so many guys insistent on spreading them everywhere as quickly as they can? Having come out at a time when droves of the guys just a few years older than me died so insanely young, I cannot comprehend the short sightedness of throwing out all caution and concern for the general well being of our whole community.

So what are some of the things you typically do to prepare yourself for a film shoot?

Nothing too unusual. I run more while continuing to lift, and I cut my calories down so I get more cut. And I hit the tanning bed of course. A few days before the shoot I abstain from sex, but mentally get myself as sexually revved up as possible by reading a lot of porn so that when the day to film arrives I can hardly wait to get down to business. I also try to work with the director to understand what he wants and to try to add to his vision with ideas and fantasies that I have, or even with things I can bring along as props. And I try to fantasize a lot about the kinds of things I expect to do in the video. Lately I've been doing so many videos that it's been tough to balance the bulking and cutting phases of my diet/weight training regime – as soon as I think I'm going to have a few months to just eat, another video shoot comes along and I'm trying to quickly lose the bit of extra fat that I gain while bulking up. This can get frustrating, especially when a shoot falls through last minute after weeks of feeling starved. I'm vegetarian and I'm also a natural body builder. Because of this I've already got the deck stacked against me when it comes to building mass, so not getting in a solid bulking period always makes me feel even further behind.

And what is your usual mode of unwinding afterwards?

Well first I usually like to eat a lot of the foods I'd stopped eating! Which isn't much different from what I do after a wrestling tournament, really. Then, once I'm home, I tend to get very domestic: it's all about dinner and a movie with my boyfriend, and wallowing in creature comforts of being home again. And I'm usually still pretty damn horny after a shoot, so getting back to having sex with my boyfriend is always really nice.

What about making XXX flicks didn't you expect?

While doing the videos for the smaller companies was very much what I expected, doing more elaborate productions was pretty surprising. There is a level of artifice to it and, just like in the real movies, editing does a lot of the work. Things that seem weird and unnatural when you shoot them end up looking great somehow through porn editing magic. And video is such a poorly resolving medium that lots of things just don't show – though after watching the Detroit Tigers in the World Series in High Def and getting to memorize every pore on the pitchers' faces, I think that porn is about to change in ways that might not bode well. Too much resolution won't be flattering to a good many stars. I just hope it doesn't end up pushing things even more in the young twink direction that is so popular right now.

Tell me a bit more about how you see high definition changing the face of XXX?

Let's just say that too much detail can work against even the hottest guy – there is a reason why bar lighting is generally dim! I expect a swing to absurd amounts of close detail at first until the novelty wears off and we decide we'd rather not see the little pimple on some guy's ass. On the other hand, I've done video BDSM scenes where having a clearer picture would have been better. In *Painful Pleasures*, Bondi left some nice single tail welts on my chest that you really can't see very well in the video. But realistically this technology is unlikely to hit BDSM porn for a while – it's just too expensive.

I am also curious if you find it arousing, uncomfortable, or educational to watch yourself on screen.

At first I really had a hard time seeing myself on the screen and could only see my faults – which really is hard because you want to make something hot and you just can't see it at all. But over time I've learned to watch my videos to improve my performances, and occasionally I've even got off on watching my own videos. I even managed to get into *Knots and Ball Bash* 1 enough on the first viewing to jerk off right away. The weird thing about all this is that, when I watch porn I generally imagine myself as one of the guys in the video and the desire is to be that guy. When I watch my own stuff, I am that guy – and I'm reliving a hot scene.

So how did you start getting into the BDSM scene? Was it where your fantasies always lingered/wandered? Was it something a partner introduced you to that made you think, "Where has this been all my life?" Was it a gradual evolution?

I pretty much started having BDSM fantasies when I was 4. I had an imaginary playmate who would tie me up – oddly enough this playmate was a female. In grade school I was pretty obvious if you look at my school work: I would do my reports and dioramas on things like the Native American Sun Dance, Puritan punishments, and Classic Maya blood rites. No matter the topic, I'd find a kinky spin on it, even at that age.

Trust and a sort of surrender always seem such integral parts of BDSM. I'm curious if that makes it tough for you to do on film because you're oftentimes working with a guy you don't know?

Not really. Mostly the really intense and complex scenes I've done with players that know what they are doing and who I know by either their video work or by their reputation. When I'm doing stuff with a novice top, it's more a matter of helping to understand how to read me and how to build me up to higher and higher levels – this is an art and it takes time. But I'm tough enough that really for most BDSM scenes the worst that happens if the top isn't getting it right is that I'm not turned on and lose my hard-on. Topping new guys can be a challenge. They are still learning about the whole thing and a video set is a rough place to learn about this stuff. So it makes it tricky to do a real intense scene since you can't just interrupt the scene to talk them through and help them process like you normally would in a scene with a newer player.

"Barebacking is just plain fucked up."

So what for you is makes the blurring of pleasure and pain a peak sexual experience?

Supposedly pleasure and pain both trigger the neurotransmitter dopamine, just as many popular recreational drugs do. So when you are flooding your neural connections with both kinds of stimuli you end up increasing the overall intensity – or at least you do if you're wired the way I am. I do think most people find that at least a little bit of pain increases sexual pleasure: a love bite or a pinch to the nipples seems to find its way onto the sexual menu of even the most vanilla of couples. My pain threshold is very different, and so I can take a lot of pain before it's too much, but along the way something happens to intensify and deepen the whole experience – whether it be endorphins or dopamine or adrenaline or whatever I don't know. The medical literature on the topic is interesting, but doesn't really tell a consistent story. Taking it away from the clinical level, the psychological effect is intense. You are both loving and hating what you feel and, as a result, your physical and emotional response becomes really intense. After a good heavy SM scene I feel content and relaxed – the stupid shit doesn't bother me the way it otherwise might.

So how far do you think you would go in a fetish film?

Well, I try to stick with stuff I actually enjoy. I have limits on what I will do especially around safety, and I have limits on what I enjoy. I will sometimes do something I'm not really into because it makes sense in the film. For example while I don't really like rimming and had never done it before it made sense in *Folsom Filth* and I did it, not because the director asked, but because it seemed the right activity for my character in that film. And because it was done on camera, it became a turn on even though it would have normally grossed me out. That said, there are some things I will never do. I don't think you'll ever see me on either end of a fisting scene!

I'm curious too about the difference between Mark and Derek. Is Derek da Silva a sort of separate segment of your personality?

While I'm tempted to pass off some

Derek Da Silva [PHOTO COURTESY TITANMEN.COM]

bullshit answer about it being like the heteronyms of Pessoa, really it's just a name I use to keep a bit of privacy. I wanted to keep a Portuguese surname, I thought Derek was a sexy sounding name, and I liked the fact that you could loosely translate the whole name as King of the Jungle. But I generally answer to Mark ... or Ears when I'm in LA. Blame Vaginal Crème Davis for that nickname!

For you where do music and porn overlap?

Well, there is a performance aspect to both, but they don't meet as much as I'd like. I play porn star and rock star against each other as each as a certain aura that people get into – but that's all marketing. I use the fact that I play mostly naked on stage in my punk band to lure in those who think it's going to be a hot strip show, but once they hear us they run for the doors. We aren't a cute and funny band – we are a real punk band and we're into old school audience confrontation, absurdity and shock.

On the porn side, when I get into directing – hopefully soon – I hope to help change the role music and sound plays in porn. Some good ambient industrial stuff would work so much better than most of what you hear today, as would actually scoring the music to match the full action of the scene. Sequencer loops need to be banned – they make me feel like I'm on hold on the telephone. A lot more could be done to really make it so music adds to the video, but doing it right is a lot of work and unlikely to add to the bottom line – so no one is likely to bother. As it stands, the only vids I listen to with the sound on are the ones that have no music at all.

I'm interested in hearing more about your directing aspirations. What sort of things do you think we can expect to see from Derek Da Silva behind the camera?

Well, I wouldn't be literally behind the camera for starters – that's not an area I have talent in. My own approach to creating anything comes from the D.I.Y. ethics and aesthetics of the punk, industrial and techno music scenes. Technology in the digital video world has gotten to the point where you can do some fairly ambitious things rather cheaply – if you spend the time to do them. Porn is a business and we know time is money, but if you put aside the purely commercial aspects you could make something that has broad appeal, but that is more singular and groundbreaking.

I don't want to give away my specific ideas and approach since then I've boxed myself in before I even start, but I have been storyboarding scenarios, figuring out pacing, and just thinking about how to do something that is bigger than a bunch of guys fucking on a cool set with good lighting. In this I'm taking my cues from the guerilla video movement. I'm hoping to create BDSM videos that break out of the old conventions and that feature some really creative play. One thing that I'm still exploring is how to get a storyline that adds to the erotic energy of the video rather than takes you out of it. As a big fan of written porn, I want to figure out how to tell an erotic story economically and with the same impact as my favorite stories from old issues of Drummer and MR. There is a cerebral element to good BDSM that is rarely tapped in video – I want to figure out how to bring that in.

How do you think the XXX experience has changed you or influenced your life?

Well, it certainly has made me learn to take care of my body better. I exercise more, eat better and make a point of simple things like sleeping enough, using moisturizer, etc. All of which is really positive. It also gives me a certain feeling of accomplishment – I've done something that most people don't really respect, but it's something I like and that I find worthwhile. It's also opened me to people and experiences I might otherwise have been oblivious to – some of these are negative, but understanding the darker sides of humanity is important, too. On the negative side, appearance really is superficial and as you grow older you inevitably age. So it's tough investing a lot of psychic energy in a self image that is 100% guaranteed to fade in time. In this respect, doing video could almost be looked on as a way to fight one's own mortality. While I'm sure fame has its impacts on many porn stars, I'm not one of them. Because I work in such a specific niche, I'm rarely recognized by strangers – and when I do it's because I'm in a band, not because I'm a porn actor.

Are you a natural exhibitionist?

I'm not sure. I would have to assume yes, but it's actually one of those things that I have a hard time being introspective about. I'm probably a certain kind of exhibitionist, but I'm not sure how to differentiate the various species of exhibitionists. I mean, can anyone with a decent amount of body ink claim to be anything but an exhibitionist?

Speaking sexually, few guys are as skilled as me when it comes to ...

Getting turned on by heavy pain and delivering a great cum shot in the middle of it all, without using any drugs at all.

Where is the wildest place you've ever had sex?

On the top of a pyramid on the central plaza of Tikal – it was dusk and the guards were clearing the park.

It also seems that some form of ritual is a huge part of your sexuality. How do you think that aspect comes into play?

I'm not sure that it really does, but maybe you're seeing something that I'm so close to that I can't see it. For me BDSM scenes are really about sharing an experience that is meaningful yet very enjoyable. What are you seeing that makes you think I'm into ritual play?

Because of A) Your interest as a kid leaned heavily in that direction; B) The wildest place answer was sort of in that vein, and C) BDSM strikes me as similar because of the use of tools/implements, the border between pleasure and pain, and the act of losing oneself with a formal ecstatic experience. Does that make sense?

Ah, now I see why you'd think that. But it is a misread of what I'm into – but you're a very good company on that one. Before he passed away I used to play with Tony DeBlase a lot at an annual BDSM run. The first few times we played he tried to bring Maya ritual elements into the scenes much to my confusion. I had to explain that I didn't tick that way. I wanted to be right there with him in the moment, seeing his eyes, taking in his energy, surrendering to his control, and giving all the energy back until the whole scene became an intense arc of white light. I'm what they call an "energy player" and I get my focus and drive from the guy I am doing the scene with not from some external fantasy. This is true whether I top or bottom.

Derek Da Silva [PHOTO COURTESY TITANMEN.COM]

While it's true BDSM uses tools, I've always gravitated to those tools that allowed the closest, most intimate contact (I love strikes with hands and fists), while longer range things like having your back whipped don't do much for me since I cannot connect so well. Oddly, while it would seem the opposite with the gloves and sterile precautions, play piercing is perhaps the most connected and intimate scene of all in my mind. Topping or bottoming, when I do play piecing with someone who is of the right mind set, I pretty much merge with them. Topping a needle scene gives me the same endorphin high that I get bottoming a needle scene. And while all the sterile preparations are arguably formal and precise, that formalism is just a set of crucial safety precautions I take and not part of some medical fantasy as it would be for certain guys.

Describe your dream vacation.

I really love escaping to the jungles of the Peten in Guatemala, getting completely away from people and letting everything slow down to the point where I can sense every animal and all the intense life swarming in the trees and in the brush. The first time I was in the jungle I was so overwhelmed by it that I cried – it was really the most at home I had felt in my entire life.

BRENDAN **DAVIES**

How did you come up with your porn name?

I use Brendan on my ads for escorting. The last name is taken from Davie Street, the main gay street in Vancouver ... thus Brendan Davies.

What is the key to being a great escort?

I don't consider myself a great escort, but being able to carry on a relatively educated conversation, being a good listener, and making your client think being with him is the greatest thing happening to you. I'm pretty relaxed when I escort ... and I know I'm rocking their world for that moment. And be the one in control, always!

How did you get started in the movie business?

I put a profile on BigMuscle.com and a day later I had at least three companies ask me if I would be interested in doing porn. I always had thought about it and I knew it was something I wanted to do, so I decided to go ahead and say yes.

What do you think you were looking for when you got into it?

I wasn't really looking for anything. I was just filling out a fantasy!

Do you recall your first XXX and the

STATS

BIRTH DATE: March 24, 1958

SIGN: Aries

HOMETOWN: Mission B.C.

HEIGHT: 5'10"

WEIGHT: 200 lbs

TWO BEST CHARACTER TRAITS: Generally I'm a very happy, calm, and grounded person.

TWO WORST CHARACTER TRAITS: It has to be my way!

FAVORITE MUSIC: Baroque

FAVORITE MOVIES: *The Lord of the Rings*

FAVORITE MOVIES I'VE BEEN IN: *Folsom Filth*

XXX COSTAR I'D DO AGAIN IN A MINUTE: Blake Nolan

IF I COULD MAKE ONE REQUEST ON A PORN SET IT WOULD BE: A massage therapist on site for between shoots.

AS A TEEN I ALWAYS FANTASIZED ABOUT SEX WITH: A group of cops.

CURRENT FANTASY MAN: I have this thing for Blake Nolan.

SEXIEST PART OF A MAN: Ass ... I am a total ass pig.

THREE INGREDIENTS OF MY HOTTEST SEX FANTASY: Cops, force, restraints, and double fucking.

FAVORITE ITEM IN MY SEXUAL TOY BOX: Vibrating sounds.

MOST PRIZED POSSESSION: My truck (Nissan Titan).

HOBBIES: Gardening.

PETS: Gus, my Yorkie who thinks he's a Rottweiler.

PET PEEVES: Bad drivers.

first bit of direction you were given.

The first movie was *Folsom Filth* and the first bit of direction I was given was: "Don't look at the camera."

What about XXX movies surprised you?

What surprised me is how professional most of the studios are to work with. I have been treated very well by everyone I have worked for and the other stars have been awesome. There are some very cool dudes in the industry, and I have a lot of respect for a lot of these guys.

"I like to see myself perform and it is educational because you can see how you can improve your performance the next time."

What is the most turned on you have ever been on screen?

Punch fucking this very sweet boy from Amsterdam. I don't know his name at the moment but it was last week when I was shooting for Titan. It was for their IML movie which will be released this year at IML

What is punch fucking?

Really! You've never heard of punch fucking? It's fisting and you work up to punching – you actually are punching your fist right in and out of the guy's hole. In this scene, I would punch one hand, remove it fast, and punch in the other.

Did you have some hesitation getting into the XXX industry as a somewhat older guy?

None. I wasn't really entering it with any expectations. I think for an older guy I look pretty good!

That's definitely true! What things do you always do to prepare for a film shoot?

Sleep, eat well, exercise, and keep hydrated. I'm pretty relaxed. I don't get nervous before a shoot.

And what do you usually do whenever you get home after a day of filming?

Call a friend back home and discuss my day, and eat. I like to eat. I usually clean-up and go to bed or relax watching a movie or listening to music. I very seldom will go out after a shoot.

Give me the run of a "filming day" scenario in your experience?

Well, show up at set at given time, say 7: 45 am, wait around for the set an camera crew to do their stuff, do stills from say 9:00-11:00, wait around for a couple hours while others are having stills. Lunch break. Rimming from 1:00 pm-2:30 pm., wait for set changes, fuck scene 3:00 pm-5:00 pm, wait around and then usually continue the next day with cum shots, watersports, etc. Sometimes we do cum shots at the beginning of the day. It changes all the time.

Would you like to someday direct or produce your own work?

Yes. Definitely it is something I would like to do. I would love to direct and produce my own work. I think I would be very good at it. I'm good at anything I do!

So with wanting to direct and produce, what are the main things you have learned in front of the camera that will come in handy behind it?

Patience. You have to give the performer his time, be patient because too much pressure just kills it! Then I would have to say, being able to play to the camera and the lights, opening up to the camera, the camera has to be able to see the dick. Most importantly, I think if the chemistry is good between two stars, I would encourage them to do what they feel best doing – just go with it and have fun. If they are in a hot moment, I wouldn't stop them – keep the passion going so it's not so fake. I would also try to set scenes up with guys who are attracted to each other; sometimes I am really shocked at the selection of guys or pairings.

So for future reference for directors who are a few of the guys you would like to work with in XXX?

Definitely love to work with Blake Nolan, Matt Cole and Jason Branch.

Is it arousing, educational, or uncomfortable to watch yourself on screen?

I find it somewhat arousing, but I don't watch myself much. I like to see myself perform and it is educational because you can see how you can improve your performance the next time.

What is the most uncomfortable position you have ever been on screen?

The most uncomfortable position would have been me getting fucked in the tire sling in *Hard Mechanics 3* by Blake Nolan. It was very hot and I loved it but the ropes were cutting into me and burning my thighs and neck and I kept sinking into the middle of the tire. I had rope burns for two weeks afterwards, but believe me I would place myself there any time to go through that fuck again with Blake. Woof!

What is the key to getting you in the sack and what do we do with you once we have you there?

I'm very attracted to Big Muscle Guys with nice asses. Once you have me there it is free for all – anything can happen. I can top or bottom, go from vanilla to very wild!

How wild is wild? What are your limits?

I haven't come across a limit yet! Blood and Scat, that's all I can think of. But I do like the smell and taste of a hot muscle ass – raunchy and sweaty!

When it comes to seducing a man I've found nothing better than ...

Being very direct about what I want.

How would you describe yourself in a personals ad?

VGL Muscular Dude, into other VGL Muscular Dudes for uninhibited sweaty man to man.

What is your favorite all time scene from a XXX film ... or if it's easier, your favorite couple XXX DVDs?

I think my all time favorite scene is with Massive Studios for *Hard Mechanics 3* where I rimmed Blake Nolan and then ended up getting fucked by him in a sling made from a tire hung

Brendan Davies [PHOTO BY KENT TAYLOR, COURTESY RAGING STALLION STUDIOS]

from a hoist. I like that pairing!

Speaking sexually, very few guys are as skilled as me when it comes to ...

Rimming. I love rimming a hot guy.

Where is the wildest place you've ever had sex?

In a Pentecostal Church Baptismal tank. Does this mean I am going to hell?

Of course it does, but give me the details please .

It was just prior to my leaving the church ... a visiting choir from the southern USA ... I saw this very cute boy, caught him checking me out. After the service he stayed behind with me because there was going to be a baptismal service that evening and he volunteered to help with the preparations. It's a huge immersion tank. It was empty and we were cleaning it. It was obvious that we were both attracted to each other, so I moved things along. We didn't fuck in it, just jerked each other off. But the setting was very hot. Guess I will burn for that one!

Do you have some great fantasy that you are just waiting for some director to ask you to film?

I am very much into the outdoors and 4x4ing. I would love to be asked to do a raunchy fuck scene, outdoors with another hot muscle dude that I am 100% into. I could write the scene if the director wanted me to!

Describe your ideal vacation.

My ideal vacation is with a very hot guy or boyfriend, in the mountains camped next to a river with no one around. I spend as much time as I can 4x4ing and camping in the summer and I like the solitude of the wilderness. I am even comfortable being out there on my own ... which I do often. I have an awesome truck and I know thousands of kilometers of back roads in Southern British Columbia's Mountains. And yes on a few occasions I have actually had encounters with other off roaders.

Describe your ideal romantic evening.

I like a nice restaurant, wine, good conversation, a stroll along the Sea Wall and then passionate making out on the beach or behind some bush. Is that considered romantic? Or return to my house to a cozy fire in the fireplace, my big bed or the playroom.

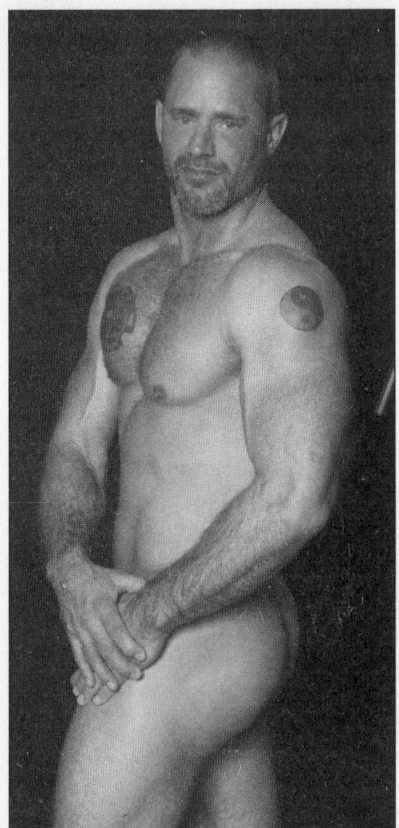

Brendan Davies [PHOTO BY KENT TAYLOR, COURTESY RAGING STALLION STUDIOS]

Where do you want this career to take you?

I am happy where it is leading right now. I don't expect to be in it too long. My priority is my own business so for now we will just have to wait and see. I am surprised at how in demand I seem to be at the moment and am liking it very much. I guess I really want to be a superstar.

ERYK **ELLIOTT**

How did you get started in the business?

I had gone through a break-up with a guy, and felt really unattractive. I was horribly depressed. I felt because this one guy didn't like me, that I must've been some three-headed freak. A friend told me, "I'll bet if you sent your photos to Chi Chi LaRue, he'd call you back." And he did.

So has the guy who dumped you and then prompted this career come crawling back begging for a second chance?

No he didn't. Seriously, it's OK though. I took something from the destructive situation. It made me more humble and thoughtful of other people's feelings. So I grew from it.

What were you looking for when you got into it?

More confidence, a self-esteem boost.

Do you recall the first movie you made and the first bit of direction you were given?

Yes, in *Never Been Touched*, I was giving a blow job to Bobby Williams and I was told to keep my hand out of the shot ... stop blocking the shot.

So what made Bobby Williams such an amazing costar?

Probably the physical attributes. He is a total Californian beach hottie. And he kind of reminded me of Ken – *a lá* Barbie and Ken.

What about making XXX movies surprised you?

To see clothed people like make up people and camera men on the set. People with jobs to do who may or may not be personally turned on by what was going on.

Who offered the best advice to you starting out?

My long time best friend Breezy Cross. She told me anyone who would say anything negative about doing a film for Falcon or Chi Chi LaRue was only jealous.

If some young guy came to you for advice about getting into the business what would you tell him?

Have a real job and life goals. Don't get caught up in any of the reviews or publicity you may receive. Porn is a short term, life is long-term. And to have fun with porn. There are so many people in the world that fantasize, about being in it ... and only a small percentage are actually cast in films. When I look back at my youth and time in porn. I will wear it as a badge of honor vs. the scarlet letter.

Were the people who knew you surprised when you started making porn?

Definitely. Although. I danced at a club in Lansing, Michigan, as a go go dancer and made a lot of money at it. So I am sure there were some not as surprised. I never saw this path in life for myself. I never set out to become involved in porn. I have friends and old co-workers and even an ex fiancé that still have a hard time with it. But that's their problem.

Given your pet peeve list it doesn't sound like you would tolerate much bad behavior on a XXX set? What is the worst example of on set antics that you have witnessed?

No, I wouldn't. A sex shoot is no place for drama, just lotsa man lovin'. I wouldn't work with someone like that again. Someone bitching about being promised $50 dollars more. For real. Oh ,and his check was like three times what mine was. No kidding.

How did the directing styles of Joe Gage and Chi Chi LaRue differ?

Chi Chi is very vocal. Oh "that's fucking hot ... don't stop fucking him. That looks hot." Joe is very to the point.

Have you ever developed a crush on any of your costars? Care to name names?

STATS

BIRTH DATE: May 15, 1979

SIGN: Taurus

HOMETOWN: Mt. Morris, Michigan

HEIGHT: 5'9"

WEIGHT: 140 lbs

TWO BEST CHARACTER TRAITS: Compassionate bleeding heart and real. If something sucks, I'd tell you.

TWO WORST CHARACTER TRAITS: Shyness ... really it's true; and indecisiveness.

FAVORITE MUSIC: 90s pop, hip hop, dance, R&B, current popular music

FAVORITE MOVIES: *Save the Last Dance, Scary Movie 3, Brokeback Mountain*

FAVORITE MOVIES I'VE BEEN IN: *Never Been Touched* – Chi Chi Larue is so amazing. *Getting It in the End* – The atmosphere off the set was so fun. We colored at the crew dinner. How bad is that, a day shooting, literally. (Laughing) And we colored at dinner! *Deep Water Beach Patrol*, for the opportunity to work with Joe Gage, Mason Wyler, and Dylan West ... need I say more?

XXX COSTAR I'D DO AGAIN IN A MINUTE: Bobby Williams, hands down that boy is hot.

IF I COULD MAKE ONE REQUEST ON A PORN SET IT WOULD BE: To have a twink personal assistant.

AS A TEEN I ALWAYS FANTASIZED ABOUT SEX WITH: Tony *&^%$'s dad. For real, dude was big-time into free balling before I even knew what it was.

CURRENT FANTASY MAN: Chad Hunt

SEXIEST PART OF A MAN: Face.

THREE INGREDIENTS OF MY HOTTEST SEX FANTASY: Big cock, dirty talk, cheating bi-married men.

FAVORITE ITEM IN MY SEXUAL TOY BOX: I've got a Feshlight that is the fucking bomb. Can I say that? ... if so ... it fucking rocks.

MOST PRIZED POSSESSION: My Chevy Camaro.

HOBBIES: Radio broadcasting, production, imaging (geeky stuff).

PETS: Diva the amazing Dobergirl. She's my freaking home girl. She is the most important thing to me, like a child. She is my version of Sugar Pie from the Anna Nicole Show. Bud Pointer Dog, he is inexhaustible and is so protective and smart. He is a rescue dog from L.A. Animal services. He has been with me for two and a half years now. He is a total man's man. He loves beer, popcorn, and cleavage.

PET PEEVES: Difficult people, dishonesty, complainers, hysterics, unsolicited drama, narrow minded and judgmental people.

Eryk Elliott [PHOTO COURTESY TITANMEN.COM]

Well obviously the very dreamy Bobby Williams. Justin Wells, what a sexy southern guy. Between his accent and eyes, I was spellbound. For real!

If you were to make a movie called Eryk's Orgy who would you want as your four costars?

Jan Fischer, Nick Capra, Bobby Williams and Rod Barry.

What things do you usually do to prepare for a film shoot?

Tanning. Manicure: Do you want to see my chewed and jagged fingernails in someone's ***? Pedicure: You never know when someone might want to suck on your foot on cam. It's porn, stranger things have been filmed. Hair cut and trim.

And how do you usually spend the evening after a day before the cameras?

Eating high protein foods and sleeping.

Is it educational, unbearable, arousing, or amusing to watch yourself in a movie?

A little of all of the above. The bonus footage of me jacking off on *Manplay 20*. Hot! I love it. I've jacked off to it about 20 times. I'd do me! (Laughing).

So describe the typical casting scenario for your getting a role in a film?

It has been everything from an email from a director to a phone call from a producer. It is always good to send photos and thank you notes, even if they go unreturned *ahem you know who you are* It has paid off for me a few times.

If you were offered a role in a fetish film how far would you go?

Chances are almost 99.9 percent that you would never see me in a fetish video. I am *sooooo* vanilla. I need to work on that.

So do you have any plans of how you intend to be less vanilla or any idea what direction you would move in?

I am not sure at this point. I am only 28. I am still becoming comfortable in my own skin. I am still learning a lot about myself and what makes me hot.

Do you have some amazing fantasy you are just waiting for some director to ask you to film?

Not that I can think of.

Have you ever done anything sexually on film that you would never do in your personal life?

Water sports.

XXX is notorious for putting guys in some very uncomfortable positions for the sake of the camera, what is the most uncomfortable position you've ever had to assume on film?

Never Been Touched – I was doing a five way fuck scene on a sofa as part of a fraternity hazing scene. While I was on top of this guy fucking him my knee was in the back side of the couch being poked by a very hard piece of metal sticking out. Chi Chi was yelling, "Fuck him, fuck him, that looks great on camera." I didn't want to let my scene partner or Chi Chi down so I kept going. I didn't bleed, but damn close. It left a mark.

I first realized I was a porn star when …

I received fan mail from all over the globe telling me they had seen my movies and wanted to see more. I think the term star is perhaps a little trite. Is everyone who goes on film a star?

What has been the most interesting fan request you've had thus far?

I have been asked to come visit. We all know what that means right. Show me the money!

What are the best and the worst parts of being in this business?

Best: Getting all glamorous and taking photos. Knowing people masturbate looking at me. Fan Mail – is a big pick me up sometimes. Interaction with people who have seen my films. Woo hoo I'm a frickin porno star! Worst: Short shelf life of porn careers. Preconceived notions about porn stars. Uncertainty if people really like you.

So what are some of the preconceived notions that people have about porn stars?

Promiscuous. Dirty and diseased. Uneducated. No moral values. Drug use. Broken homes. Emotional psychological mess. Been molested … I have.

Do you think the industry has a responsibility regarding the use of condoms and/or promoting safe sex?

I do think that an industry which promotes sex also morally should be responsible for the promotion of safe sex. It's just the right thing to do. Which is why I loved my experiences with Channel 1 releasing. Chi Chi Larue (Larry) and I see eye on the condom issue.

What is the most turned on you have

ever been on screen?

Fucking Jeremy Jordan in *Getting It in the End.*

Porn sets are often the place of some surreal and hilarious incidents. Do you have any personal tale you would care to share?

I find lunch chats during a porn set interesting. Some of the most mundane life details are sometimes exchanged, then right back to fucking after lunch. You gotta love it!

Do you have a favorite all time XXX movie (that you haven't been in) or a favorite scene that made you think, "Now that's what I want to do"?

Yes: *The Original Little Big League* from Rascal Video. I've always been a fan of Chi Chi. So even appearing in one of his films was a huge rush for me.

Was there any episode in your randy youth that you look back upon and think "Oh yeah, that kid was destined to grow up to be a porn star"?

Certainly, I was always a bit of a showboat and loved to be watched. Dancing in a strip club as a moonlighting job, should have been an indication. At the time I was holding down a fulltime job as an on air personality at a local radio station.

What is the secret to being a good go-go boy and making mega tips?

Actually to be a good performer. If you are a good performer the money will come easily. Flirting and connecting with the audience. I am actually very shy, but I can take my clothes off in front of a room full of people (and they pay me). How weird a paradox is that?

Speaking sexually, very few guys are as skilled as me when it comes to ...

Kissing.

How would you describe yourself in a personals ad and how would you describe the man you were looking for?

First off. I tend to like guys in their early to mid 30s. I like built guys with huge cocks and pretty faces. I know that sounds like a tall order, but I've snagged some. I would describe myself as a Young/Smooth/Hung/Sexy guy looking for the aforementioned male (see above).

"I am *sooooo* vanilla. I need to work on that."

Does being in this business make dating hard or easy?

That depends! Sometimes easier, sometimes harder. I am a pretty shrewd judge of character. I dated a guy once who loved to tell people about my XXX film career. It bothered me a lot. It felt like a lot of my worth was based on my adult film career. Needless to say, it didn't work out. He is great guy and we still talk.

How are you different from your porn persona Eryk Elliot or is there no difference?

Eryk Elliott isn't real (Laughing). That's the difference ... *scratches head* although if I could get a different social security number hehehe ... I don't do stripes well.

What is the biggest misconception people have about you when you meet them?

That I am naked all the time or feel sexual 24 hours a day!

If you could change one thing about the way the industry is currently run what would it be?

To have directors be respectful enough to return an email or phone call.

People tend to think of porn stars as these ideal physical specimens, but if you could change one thing about yourself what would it be?

I'd want an even larger penis. Chad Hunt (drools) get out of my way.

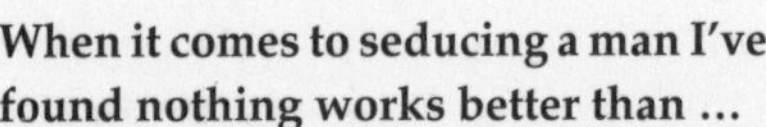

When it comes to seducing a man I've found nothing works better than ...

Being coy and playing a little hard to get. Flirting. I love nothing more than to work them up. The pay off is always passionate and hot.

How do we get you in the sack and what do we do with you once we get you there?

If we met it might be online, or through friends, I would probably smash you in the pants with my member. I am a top who loves a lot of oral attention. I am huge into kissing and passionate body contact.

Where is the wildest place you've ever had sex?

I met this closeted guy back in 1999 on Gay.com. We ended up sucking each other's cock in a church parking lot, and in an adjacent cornfield. I continued to hook up with him until I relocated to Los Angeles in 2004.

Describe your ideal romantic evening.

This is an interesting question. There are so many possible answers and including them all here would fill this entire book. An ideal is intelligent witty conversation over din-

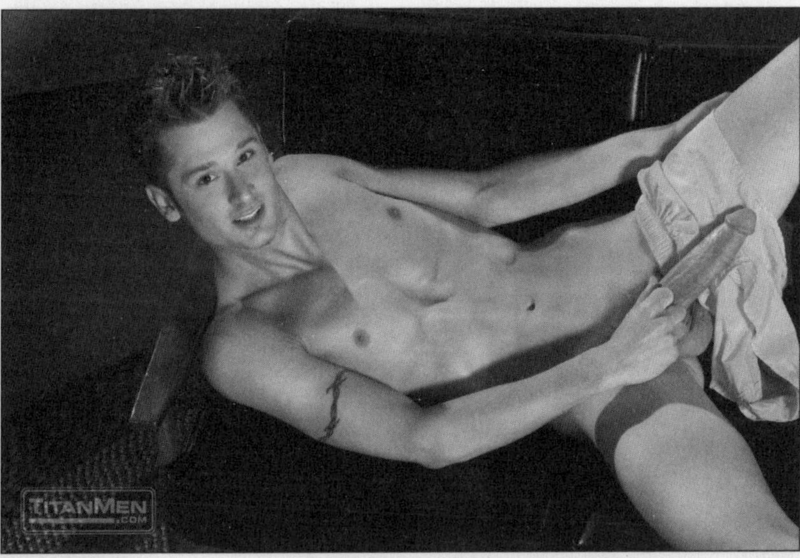

Eryk Elliott [PHOTO COURTESY TITANMEN.COM]

ner/drinks ... flirting ... lots of flirting. I love to flirt, what else can I say? Doesn't it feel good to flirt or be flirted with? That's what life is all about ... feeling good.

If you had to choose between sex and love which would you choose and what are your thoughts about fidelity?

I love myself. So I do not need someone else's love to feel whole, or complete – you know. I definitely need sex to feel complete. So I would choose sex. I do not believe wholly in fidelity. I know this is going to piss off a few handfuls of people, but I don't care. The stinging truth of reality is we are men. Men love sex. So if we are not getting it from our partner, like little dogs we stray. If fidelity is something you believe in, you are operating in fantasyland.

If you had to compare yourself to an animal what species do you think best captures your essence and why?

A fox ... I am sly like a fox.

If your life had a theme song what would it be?

"Everyday Is a Winding Road" by Sheryl Crow

Does your cock have a nickname and if so how did it come about?

Nah! I haven't named my penis. If I did. I would've changed its name twenty times by now. Besides, dick is a strong name.

Describe your dream vacation.

Something tropical like Negril Jamaica sounds great right about now.

Where do you hope this career takes you?

Porn is never a career. I hope that it takes me into the will of some rich ninety-year-old ailing man with more money than J Howard Marshall. I would definitely be up for giving some sugar for a few million, wouldn't you? Thanks Anna Nicole, I'll be getting everything in writing.

FRED **FAURTIN**

So how did you get started in the business?

Before I begin I want to thank my boyfriend (Gil Nemo). I'm here today because he contacted Cazzo Film three years ago, and after a quick casting interview in Berlin, I started in this business. You can see this first scene on *Berlin Private 3* on Prick DVD (Cazzo Film Division).

What were you looking for when you got into it?

I wanted to take part in a porn movie just to see. It was a fantasy for me to be part of a porn movie, but to make lots of films is a dream come true! Especially with Cazzo. It's exactly my type of movie (and my type of porn actor. Thom Barron was a big fantasy of mine for a long time and finally I've done a film with him now!). And with U.S. porn movies – I'm very proud to be a part of these as well.

Were the people who knew you surprised?

I'm a very sexual guy; it's not a very big surprise for my friends who knew me. It's just a little bit strange to see me on screen in a different bar and sex-club. My friends don't like to see me on screen, but they love to see me in print like on a magazine cover!

STATS

BIRTH DATE: 07/28

SIGN: Leo

HOMETOWN: Paris

HEIGHT: 5'9"

WEIGHT: 152 lb

TWO BEST CHARACTER TRAITS: I'm passionate and a perfectionist.

TWO WORST CHARACTER TRAITS: I'm egocentric and impatient.

FAVORITE MUSIC: Pop, rock, dance

FAVORITE MOVIES: *American History X* (Edward Norton was so sexy in this movie!), *Volver* (Almodovar)

FAVORITE MOVIES I'VE BEEN IN: *Kolbenfrsser-Oil Change 2* (CAZZO FILM), *Fuck Fiction* (CAZZO FILM)

XXX COSTAR I'D DO AGAIN IN A MINUTE: Darren Robbins

IF I COULD MAKE ONE REQUEST ON A PORN SET IT WOULD BE: To have my choice of positions.

AS A TEEN I ALWAYS FANTASIZED ABOUT SEX WITH: Marky Mark

CURRENT FANTASY MAN: A muscular Latino guy with tattoos and piercings

SEXIEST PART OF A MAN: Shoulders

INGREDIENTS OF MY HOTTEST SEX FANTASY: SEVERAL GUYS, Uniforms, industrial places (like a factory)

FAVORITE ITEM IN MY SEXUAL TOY BOX: Handcuffs

MOST PRIZED POSSESSION: My partner (Gil Nemo) in my life since 1994

HOBBIES: Travel and sports.

Fred Faurtin [PHOTO BY KENT TAYLOR, COURTESY RAGING STALLION STUDIOS]

Do you recall your first XXX film and the first bit of direction you were given?

My first sex scene was with my boyfriend, of course it was probably easier for the first time in front of camera (not upsetting). We did not get too much information from the director, just to have fun!

Speaking of directions – I noticed that what you would like to ask for on a movie set would be to choose your own positions for sex while making a film. What is the most uncomfortable position you've been "arranged" in by a director?

The most uncomfortable position was on *Fuck Fiction* (Cazzo). After a long week of sunny weather and indoor shooting, the last sex scene was set for outside. Unfortunately it was the worst day of the week, raining, freezing, and lot of mosquitoes! Finally we changed the location just before the beginning of the shoot because the grass was damp. It's a good memory, but not a very comfortable sex scene (but it definitely wasn't the director's fault).

Speaking sexually, very few people are as skilled as me when it comes to …

Pissing during sex action. Also I'm also very flexible. It's very easy for me to be given new directions during a scene.

So tell me a bit about your fantasy in a factory with several guys in uniforms – and throw those handcuffs into the mix as well.

I'm very excited by uniforms (firemen are my favorites), but in this case I prefer the military look. It will be in a factory (depot, cells) something very homoerotic. It will be possible to fasten me with handcuffs, several very muscular and virile guys will have fun with me (versatile positions will be great).

Describe your ideal romantic evening?

My ideal romantic evening are with my boyfriend of course, at home with a dinner prepared by me (I'm a great cook), a bottle of red wine, flowers and candles on table, and an excellent movie on DVD player. I prefer the winter for this kind of evening (especially when I have the Christmas tree at home).

Fred Faurtin [PHOTO BY KENT TAYLOR, COURTESY RAGING STALLION STUDIOS]

LUKE **GARRETT**

How did you get started in the business?

In my head, or in real life? In my head, let's be honest, I always wanted to "Party like a rock star and fuck like a porn star." But the actual chance to live out this fantasy came to me and my former partner (fellow Colt Man, Gage Weston) when Colt talent director, Manfred Speer, contacted us asking if we'd be interested in doing a scene together as a couple. We had to wait until Gage was out of the military (he's a Marine) but as soon as we could, we jumped at the opportunity.

I had been approached by Colt before – and kick myself to this day for missing the opportunity to work with legendary photographer, Jim French "Rip Colt" himself – but the timing hadn't been right for me personally or professionally until I met Gage. When he and I talked about it, both of us really wanted to try it out and we figured, "Hey, if it's not for us, we can always say we just did it the one time and as a couple." The thing is, though, we loved it. We signed exclusive contracts with Colt the day after we shot our scene together. To this day, that scene ranks at the top on our list of favorite movies.

What were you looking for when you got into it?

I'm an exhibitionist who doesn't do moderation well, so I was looking for the ultimate avenue to charge ahead full-throttle with being totally out there sexually. And I have that now and it's very fulfilling – amazing actually. Because what came along with it was so much more than I ever anticipated: travel to places I probably never would have gotten to myself, meeting people I would never have had the chance to meet, and doing things like this interview which is one of the multitude of ways I've been afforded to interact with others out there. Ultimately, that's what puts a shine on my soul – connecting with other people, sharing our stories, maybe even finding some similarities between each other and making the planet we share a bit cozier, friendlier, more intimate.

What was your biggest fear in getting into this business?

I have a career outside of Colt as a manager with one of the top telecom companies in the U.S. I've been with them for twelve years now and hope I have a solid reputation as a hard working, intelligent professional. I'm sane enough to realize that, at least with certain people, being in the porn industry (not to mention gay porn) carries a certain stigma – to put it lightly. What kept me from signing on with Colt earlier in my life was the fear that I would damage my career.

STATS

BIRTH DATE: August 10, 1970

SIGN: Slippery When Wet

HOMETOWN: Visalia, CA

HEIGHT: 5'8"

WEIGHT: 210 lbs.

TWO BEST CHARACTER TRAITS: I'm like a puppy – I'll love you to death, and look happy even when I'm wetting myself.

TWO WORST CHARACTER TRAITS: The wetting myself thing isn't very popular, and I can be dumb as a box of rocks, but I can lift heavy things!

FAVORITE MUSIC: Both kinds – Country and Western

FAVORITE MOVIES: Anything by directors John Rutherford and Kristofer Weston. Hubba hubba. There's a reason I chose to be with Colt and those guys epitomize the best from end to end, head to toe.

FAVORITE MOVIES I'VE BEEN IN: Anything with a partner, or two – with *Wide Strokes* and *Man Country* topping the list.

XXX COSTAR I'D DO AGAIN IN A MINUTE: Carlo Masi – but believe me, he can last longer than a minute. Five hours is our record, and I think we can break it.

IF I COULD MAKE ONE REQUEST ON A PORN SET IT WOULD BE: More special effects. We're talking demons flying out of hell, swooping into locker rooms and carrying off football jocks for pagan orgies. But live web cams are cool, too.

AS A TEEN I ALWAYS FANTASIZED ABOUT SEX WITH: Um, let's see ... oh yeah, men.

CURRENT FANTASY MAN: John Cena ... tell him, please.

SEXIEST PART OF A MAN: His face; that moment when your eyes first lock and you catch yourselves with a look of "Woof! This man is Hot," spreading like a surge of testosterone across your faces, followed by a sly smile and the first exploratory steps closer, on your way to knowing each other much, much better.

THREE INGREDIENTS OF MY HOTTEST SEX FANTASY: An unlocked door, an empty six pack, and the possibility that it could really happen.

FAVORITE ITEM IN MY SEXUAL TOY BOX: Uh oh, am I supposed to have a toy box?! Donations gratefully accepted at [address somewhere in California] c/o Luke Garrett. Hell, I may even use it on my webcam show. It only hurts the first time, right?!

MOST PRIZED POSSESSION: This moment, right now, every minute of every day.

HOBBIES: Working out, collecting erotic art, writing, reading, and breaking out the killer dance moves ... in my head when I'm doing cardio and looking like a total geek.

PETS: Haven't been able to bring myself to getting a new one since I lost my Bovus, a 190 pound Old English Mastiff. My cuddle buddy. And, just for the record, he drooled a lot more than me.

PET PEEVES: Size queens. But I love their boyfriends.

Come to find out, however, my pursuits outside my "normal" job have been met with a great deal of acceptance – and even some downright excitement by some. I've received tremendous support and if anyone is unhappy with my decision, they've kept that sentiment to themselves. If I'd known it would have been such a non-issue, I would have signed with Colt years ago.

Do you recall your first movie and the first bit of direction you were given?

The first movie, my scene with Gage Weston in *Wide Strokes* is unforgettable. Being able to do something like that with the love of your life, fully immersing yourselves in this very public display of carnal intimacy for the whole world to see, made it the perfect introduction for us. We like to say we entered the business by entering each other on film. *Grrrrr*, baby! And the direction was so easy. John Rutherford (an amazing sweetheart of a man with an acumen and vision for the business rivaled by none) basically just let us do our thing. We arrived on the set with a pre-existing attraction to one another, intimately in tune with the pleasure we get from being together, and immensely turned on by doing it in front of the camera.

We shot the scene inside a cozy little cabin in Malibu Canyon – fire in the fireplace, Navy recruiting poster on the wall, big inviting bed. There were these really solid posts running across the ceiling from wall-to-wall and we made really good use of those. Hubba hubba. In fact, we totally let ourselves go. There were times we were going at it so hard that I forgot there was anyone else around. I'd glance over, see a camera and think, "Oh hell, they're catching this on film ... hot damn!" But the ultimate, the thing that left John speechless and what still turns us on to this day, was the "climactic conclusion" when Gage literally plastered me in the most incredible volume, blast after blast, of man-DNA that any of us had ever seen. OK, I have to go take a cold shower now.

What is the most aroused you have ever been on screen?

In *Man Country* doing a three-way with Gage Weston and Carlo Masi. Carlo is this Italian super hunk, sexy as sin from head to toe. We went out into a field at a ranch in California and defiled a tractor in ways I fantasized about as a country boy myself. You know those big tires tractors have? Carlo had me bent over one, gripping the lug nuts like my life depended on it, his big Roman self planted inside me while Gage simultaneously plowed into him. Every time Gage thrust into Carlo, Carlo surged deeper into me. I was so turned on that I started cumming just from the sensation of being topped this way. I had to reach down and grip my fist around myself to stop from unloading completely right then and there. We went on to shoot that scene for a total of five hours ... .enjoying every minute.

How do you typically prepare yourself for an upcoming film shoot?

Aside from increasing my workouts from two hours per day to four hours per day (45 minutes of cardio in the morning, then weight training and another 45 minutes of cardio at night), dieting and then dehydrating a few days before the shoot, I say my serenity prayer: "God, grant me a piece that stays hard like that time even after I came; Strength to accept guys hung like a beer can; And stamina to go the distance." My Catholic school priests told me that God listens to all prayers.

And how do you usually spend the evening after a day of filming?

Eating! I'm all about the seven deadly sins, and after a day of filming I dive into gluttony like a demon possessed, savoring every mouthful, every swallow, every delicious drop on my lips, across my tongue, down my throat. Don't you just love eating?

So is it hilarious, educational, hot, or painful to watch yourself in a movie?

This is going to sound vain as all hell, but I get turned on big time watching my scenes on film. It's actually watching the other guy, as I've found I'm as big a voyeur as an exhibitionist, and reliving the experience of filming the scene. Of course, I always think I could have done something differently to make it better or turned my body in a different way to give more of a visual for the camera. But to give you an example of what a charge I get watching, Gage and I only made it through viewing half of our scene in *Wide Strokes* before we were totally on each other and going at it like we were right back there in Malibu.

You seem to enjoy a lot of positions sexually, but porn is notorious for putting guys in some very uncomfortable positions for the sake of the camera. Which is the most uncomfortable you've had to assume?

For movies, I haven't had to endure anything too arduous. At 210 pounds, I'm not the most flexible guy on the planet and we're often looking back at the camera to catch the expressions on our faces during certain vigorous moments. Since I diet down and dehydrate for these shoots (to show more definition in my body) I'm prone to cramping. But I think every bodybuilder learns to keep that look of, "Dammit this hurts!" off our faces when a cramp seizes our bodies. That being said, I've put a guy in a painful position for the sake of the shoot: Carlo Masi in *Man Country*. Gage Weston and I had the poor guy buck naked and sitting between the two of us, leaning back against a tractor tire and alternately going down on each of us. The lug nuts of the tire were digging into his back and the blazing California sun was beating down on his naked flesh. Fortunately for Carlo, he's great at what he does ... oh so very great ... and had Gage and I both giving him his reward soon enough. The real contortions for me happen when working with the photographers. And, buddy, I love working with the photographers. We have some great ones at Colt. To work with them is to know you're going to capture some amazing images, poured over in the years to come by multitudes of men. So if any of them want me to engage in a solo game of Twister Extreme for a stretch of five hours, I'll do it and ask for more, Sir.

Have you ever done anything sexually on screen that you would never do in your personal life?

No. John Rutherford is great about filming real-life passion and genuine sexual chemistry. I can't imagine he'd ever even ask us to do something we wouldn't be totally into. If anything, we ask him how far we can push it to do the things that turn us on the most. The end result is a movie bursting with these big muscular men living out fantasies in the flesh and, at least for me, fueling personal – and very powerful – sex drives in private as well.

If someone were to come to you for advice about getting into the business what would you tell him?

Know deep in your bones that it's going to be out there forever. If a guy has any discomfort with that, it may not be a good step to make because there is no going back. And know equally well that everyone – from your family to your friends and colleagues to the check-out person at the grocery store – is going to know about it. Some of us thrive on that or, at the very least, accept it. If you welcome that kind of thing, then the next step is to look for a company that fits you – a studio maybe that you've always thought made great movies, with men you'd love to appear beside, and people running the company you trust. Trust is something implicit in my relationship with Colt. Having that kind of working relationship in the pursuit of something so erotic can be absolutely life-changing.

How do you think the XXX experience has changed you?

Are you talking about that movie, xXx with Vin Diesel?! I love that movie. I came out of the theater determined to get a hold of that jacket he wore, all lined with fur and sexy in a very tough way – seriously, that jacket rocks like Gibraltar. And, dayum, getting' a hold of Vin would warm me up just fine, too. I'm cold without you, Vin; you big hunky bastard.

(Laughing). You crack me up. If you were offered a role in a fetish film how far would you go for the sake of the camera?

That depends a lot on who I'd be with. I can open up to a lot of things with the right guy. And, sometimes, I'll see a man who conjures up fantasies that I may never live out in the flesh, but give me a surge of pleasure merely to think, "What if ..." At the same time, I can be maddeningly sane. I have this annoying knee-jerk propensity for saying, "No". I don't think that's all a bad thing, either. All things in moderation, right? And the "all" part leaves the door open for so, so much.

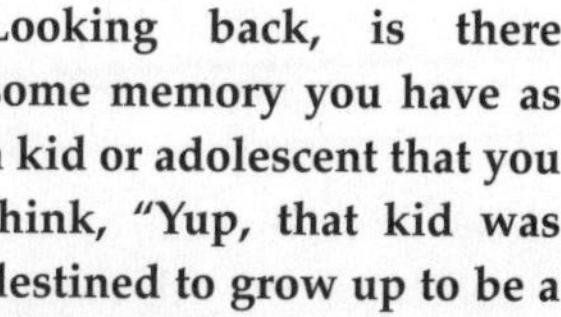

Luke Garrett
[PHOTO COURTESY COLTSTUDIOGROUP.COM]

Looking back, is there some memory you have as a kid or adolescent that you think, "Yup, that kid was destined to grow up to be a porn star"?

Dude, I grew up in a tiny little farm town. Not once

did I think any of the bubbas in my little burg were headed for a life in porn. I may have wanted to do a porn with them, but always thought that was other people ... you know, like Los Angeles people. Ha!

Speaking sexually, very few guys are as skilled as me when it comes to ...

Spankin' it 'till the howler monkey screams. I get a perverse pleasure in edging it until the floodgates are nearly bursting open, then keeping it all held back, building up again and again and again until all that exists is an animal desire – an overwhelming need – to release. And I can grill a steak that'll roll your eyes back into your head, too.

So can you give me an idea of the sort of erotic art that you collect?

My personal intrigue with erotic art started with Tom of Finland. I love that kind of uber-masculinity and raw sexuality ... the dominance of men with men. Recently I've become even more greedy to collect the works of Tom Jones and Ira Smith. Tom Jones does these really hunky, incredibly hot nudes of men and has a wrestling series which I display with proud prominence in my bedroom. And Ira Smith nails the obsession I have with men's' butts – these perfect globes inviting the viewer in for a deeper inspection. And the more artists I discover, the more I want to collect. I have an affinity for well-built men, though strength in any form gets my attention every time. The art I'm most drawn to is bold in character, totally unapologetic for the sexuality it depicts, and damn if it doesn't depict exactly what I'd like to be doing or looking like myself.

Where is the wildest place you've ever had sex?

The back of a moving Hummer, stripped naked and tied down while a guy in a cop uniform drove and his buck-naked buddy planted himself on top of me, using every dip in the road to become much more deeply connected with me than I ever thought possible. The cop became my bro in heart and soul years ago. He and I share a very rich fantasy life and he relishes every opportunity to make the best of those fantasies come true. This particular day was delivered to me as a gift for my birthday and the whole Hummer experience was just the beginning. Gotta love friends like that.

Is maintaining a relationship with both partners in the business difficult?

Being in the business definitely adds another dimension to a relationship, but I think it actually helped Gage and I being in the business together, and especially that we entered the business together as a couple. Of course, I'm saying that and I'm no longer together with Gage, so what do I really know, right? Then again, I know I love people, I know I'll always love Gage, and I know he loves me, too. So maybe the real difficulty doesn't derive from the business – maybe we simply have too much love to confine to just the two of us! There are a lot of great things – opportunities and experiences – that came our way early on with Colt that actually cemented Gage and me closer together. We enjoy a bond that holds us together today in part due to those experiences and the shared journeys we've taken to arrive where we are today. We can look back, smile, and appreciate what got us here, fully knowing a huge portion of that joy and gratitude rests with each other.

When you go out in a city are you completely besieged by Colt fans and have you ever made any of their Colt fantasies come true?

"I get a perverse pleasure in edging it until the floodgates are nearly bursting open, then keeping it all held back, building up again and again and again until all that exists is an animal desire – an overwhelming need – to release."

I think I enjoy seeing them every bit as much as they may enjoy seeing me. I get massive amounts of energy from the friends and fans of Colt – it's like being filled to overflowing with feelings so powerful, appreciation so abundant, that I can't contain it all and want to share it with everyone. There's a rush I get from a really good work out and I get the same heart-thumping elation from meeting and talking with and connecting with these guys.

And yeah, Gage Weston, Carlo Masi, Adam Champ and I recently did a tour from Mykonos to Paris. When we got to Paris, Gage and I went to one of the local, gay-oriented gyms to work out. Yeah, I know, some people go to the Louvre, we went to the Gym de Louvre! Upstairs is the main floor of the gym and we met some really cool guys – sexy, too, especially with those French accents ... .oooh la la! Downstairs is, shall we say, the shower complex. After the workout, when Gage and I were rinsing off, we saw one of the sexiest men we've ever run across. Wow. Along with a body that will be fueling fantasies in my head for years to come, he had a smile and a look in his eyes that said, "Come here you big Americans. Let me show you the other side of Paris." And he did show us – the front side, the back side, top and bottom. Later that night, we ran into a couple of guys at our appearance (at La Scene Nightclub). They were smiling from ear to ear and said, "I heard you met our friend at the gym today. He's a huge fan of yours and you made his day." Well, the feeling was mutual, as the best feelings often are.

What's the most unusual request you've ever had from a fan?

This guy contacted me letting me know his birthday was coming up and, for his present, he wanted to hire me to come out and spend the weekend with him. Now, I'm not an escort, but it's somewhat flattering when someone wants to give up some greenbacks in exchange for your time. So I politely told him I was honored to receive the request from him, but that escorting just isn't my thing. He wrote me right back saying, "No, I don't want sex from you. I want you to come out and help me build a new barn on my property!" And, you know, I actually considered it! It's hard to say "no" to working with power tools.

Describe your ideal romantic evening.

John Cena, a bottle of tequila, and an Ambien. Romance isn't dead; it's big, buff, and unconscious. Trust me John, it only hurts the first time.

How would you describe yourself in a personals ad?

A few miles, some of them over rough road, but solid body and fresh interior. Great for road trips, mountain getaways, or staying at home. Heart of gold or best offer. No serious inquiries declined.

When you pass a hot looking guy on the street what gets you to turn around and do a double take every time?

Making eye contact with a handsome man. I just can't keep turned away. I keep looking back, wondering if he's looking back at me, too. And if he is, maybe we share a sly smile in seeing the mutual attraction. That kind of thing stirs me to the core. Have you ever experienced someone looking at you and feeling like they're really seeing you? I mean, not just looking at you and noticing you, but taking in all he sees, absorbing what he sees with barely concealed eagerness, with an appetite for more? That's so erotic to me – to see him savoring you with his eyes in equal measure to the hunger growing inside you for him, and, most importantly, not hiding it from each other – putting it fully out there because you want each other to see, to know. I think I'll go for a walk now.

How do we get you in the sack and what do we do with you once we get you there?

The John Cena equation would work for me, too – a bottle of tequila and an Ambien. I really wouldn't have much say in what happens after that, would I?

Describe your dream vacation.

Sailing the Hawaiian islands, hopping from one secluded spot to the next, with a group of close friends; ship stocked with food, just enough workout equipment to keep us from feeling too guilty about our time away from the gym; sun shining bright, water warm and inviting, good conversation, laughter, and new memories populating every moment of every day, the kind that get even better with the telling year after year.

How far do you hope this career takes you? Do you have any interest in moving behind the camera as well?

My ambition is to write, though I'll definitely keep my eyes open for any opportunities, any interesting and potentially fulfilling avenues that may open up in front of me. I'm completely devoted to Colt. Jim French, way back when I was a teenager, offered up images of a masculine, vividly erotic ideal of male sexuality which has become, in an astonishing real way, a wholly integral part of who I am today. Any future that includes Colt is a good future to me.

ERIK **GRANT**

How did you get started in the business?

I guess it was pretty easy. I applied online at LucasEntertainment.com and about three days later I received an email from Michael. He wanted to meet me in person. I took the train to New York and met him in his office. He seemed really cool. We talked for a few minutes and he asked me to undress and get hard. So I did. And I guess we all know that I got the job.

What were you looking for when you got into it?

I don't think I was looking for anything in particular. I nice paycheck isn't bad. But really, I am a camera whore; well that's what I am told. I love being naked and I love being watched. So what's better? I get to be in front of the camera, naked, and being watched! Love it!

So being a camera whore does that mean you like to watch yourself on screen as well or does it make you uncomfortable?

Oh hell no! I won't watch myself. I think I would critique myself too much. And I would think that's a little conceited. I just like to be watched and entertain others.

What makes/made Wilfried Knight such a great costar?

Besides the fact he is crazy hot? He's a really cool and down to earth guy. He loves hot, sweaty, rough sex. Who would make a better costar?

If you were making a movie called Erik Grant's Orgy who would you want cast as your four costars?

Good question ... As I said before Wilfried Knight, I think that's a given, Edu Boxer, Kent Larson, and Fredrick Ford because I know he can take an ass pounding.

If a guy were to come to you for advice about getting into the business what would you tell him?

It's not as easy as you think. It's a lot of hard work on and off camera. You have to have dedication to the company and maintaining your body.

What was the best piece of advice you were giving starting out?

Honestly, I can't remember. If I heard any, I still would do what I am going to do anyway.

What about making XXX movies didn't you expect?

How quickly you become noticed in your own town as "Erik."

You mention how quickly Erik became known in your hometown. Did you have any negative repercussions because of that?

Yeah, most people think that a porn star is a whore. I am not going to lie, I have had my experiences, but that's really not me. Erik is a persona that I created. In real life, I am very edgy with my looks, piercing (most people don't see them because I have to take them out), and tattoos. I love sex, but I am not a whore, I just play one in the movies.

It also brings up an interesting point. How different are you from your porn persona Erik Grant?

Aside from the things I have already mentioned ... I have a very confident side, but at the same time I have a very sensitive and insecure side of me. I really don't show that in the movies too much because I am too caught up in myself and whoring around.

So how did you come up with your porn name?

Michael and I came up with my name during the making of *Manhattan Heat*. I remember it was during an interview, and we stopped halfway when we came to my name. I had mentioned one name, he said it was too "pornish" from what I remember. Now what is too pornish? Is that even a word? Anyway, so he made a few phone calls and waited and we finally got a call back on the name Erik Grant.

BIRTH DATE: October 29, 1979

SIGN: Scorpio

HOMETOWN: Binghamton, NY

HEIGHT: 5'10"

WEIGHT: 145 lbs

TWO BEST/WORST CHARACTER TRAITS: I am going to answer these two questions with one answer. I can be fun loving and easy going one minute, cross me the wrong way and well, you'll see my worst character traits.

FAVORITE MUSIC: I like almost everything. If you look through my CDs you could find anything from Fleetwood Mac, Janet Jackson or Janis Joplin or Lil' Kim. I do have to say, my favorite to listen to is Hip Hop. Good beat, makes ya wanna dance.

FAVORITE MOVIES: I'll just assume it isn't XXX ... I love horror movies, (like) *Saw*. I think those are my favorite. I love anything with Angelina Jolie in it, too; she got me hooked in *Gia*.

FAVORITE MOVIES I'VE BEEN IN: *Manhattan Heat* because it was my first starring role, and *La Dolce Vita* because it was just hot and fun!

XXX COSTAR I'D DO AGAIN IN A MINUTE: Wilfried Knight in a New York minute.

AS A TEEN I ALWAYS FANTASIZED ABOUT SEX WITH: I know this is weird, but I always had a thing for MacGyver.

CURRENT FANTASY MAN: That would definitely be David Beckham. He is hot no matter what – short hair, long hair, shaved, shit I don't care.

SEXIEST PART OF A MAN: Arms! Love some big strong arms bulging out of a tank top, or through a perfectly fitted Tee around his sculptured body. Is it getting hot in here or is it just me?

THREE INGREDIENTS OF MY HOTTEST SEX FANTASY: This is an easy one. The first ingredient would be David Beckam. The second, an endless supply of lube. And I guess it wouldn't be my hottest sexual fantasy if I wasn't included. So yeah, I am definitely that third ingredient. That would be something to remember.

FAVORITE ITEM IN MY SEXUAL TOY BOX: That would be my dick!

MOST PRIZED POSSESSION: Most people would say their dogs or even their boyfriend. Fuck them, it's my Mercedes Benz SLK 230!

HOBBIES: Riding my bike when it's warm, going to the gym, my friends, music, anything to relax.

PETS: I have three dogs. Two are Pomeranian and Poodle Mixes, and I have a teacup Chihuahua. Yeah I know, I'm really gay. You haven't heard their names yet ... Gucci is the mother, Gabbana is the daughter. If you're wondering where is Dolce, we had to give him up to a friend, he's the father. The little guy is Louis.

Erik Grant [PHOTO COURTESY LUCASENTERTAINMENT.COM]

Do you recall the first movie you made and the first bit of direction you were given?

Yes, like it was yesterday. The first movie I did was *Manhattan Heat* and I had a hard time with the lines at the beginning of the movie. If you've seen the movie, you've seen the outtakes. I am talking to Wilfried on the phone and I could not get the words out right, or I wasn't speaking loud enough. I just remember hearing "Talk Louder! Talk Louder!" I think it took about forty takes.

When it comes to driving a man wild in bed I've found nothing works better than ...

Being a complete and total whore. (Laughing). Nah, it helps though. But I've found that being passive/aggressive drives men fucking wild.

It worked for me, worked for him, so there you go.

What things do you do to prepare for a shoot?

Nothing really I guess, the usual. Make sure my hair color is at its natural. Remember, the carpet has to match the drapes! Shower, trim up, and smoke about a pack of cigarettes. Then I'm ready!

And how do you usually spend an evening after a long day of filming?

Depends on where I am at. Fire Island, evenings were spent out or lying by the pool. While I was in New York, I usually went out. We all have a curfew while shooting; feel like I am back at home with Mom.

Where is the wildest place you've ever had sex?

That would have to be going down the New Jersey Turnpike at about 3:00 a.m. coming from New York. Here's a tip: A moon roof really comes in handy in these situations for those more creative positions.

How would you describe yourself in a personals ad?

GWM 5'10", 145 lbs, brown hair and blue eyes, nice abs and toned. Shy, but can be crazy. Confident, sexy and loves sex. Just give me one night.

What is the best pick up line you have ever used or fallen for?

I don't get picked. I pick you! No lines and no other bullshit. If you

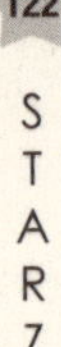

Erik Grant [PHOTO COURTESY LUCASENTERTAINMENT.COM]

want it, come and get it!

When you pass a hot looking guy on the street what makes you turn around and do a double take every time?

Now that depends, it's always the arms. If they have big arms wearing a tank or a fitted tee then I do a double take and check out that ass, too. Dark hair and light eyes will do it to, but the body has to fit.

Speaking sexually very few guys are as skilled as me when it comes to …

Being a top. I think I really know where to hit the spot on a guy. I know when to do it long and hard and soft and slow.

When it comes to seducing a man I've found that nothing works better than …

Being passive/submissive top or bottom. That can work both ways.

What is the secret to getting you hard faster than anything?

Many many ways. I love having a guy tell me exactly what he wants me to do to him or the guy to take complete control and be a complete slutty bottom, the louder the better. Damn, got a hard-on now thinking about it.

If you were offered a role in a fetish film how far do you think you would go?

I don't do scat, water sports or crazy shit like that. I can be a freak. I have a line of people that would probably agree. Just once, unscripted sex, and just let me do what I do best. If toe sucking is a part of that, then hey, let's roll.

"I have a very sensitive and insecure side of me. I really don't show that in the movies too much because I am too caught up in myself and whoring around."

You mention dedication to your company and maintaining your body. What has been the biggest sacrifice you have made to date in either regard?

I have many things that I am dedicated to. My company, my job, my body and my boyfriend. I can't really say that I have made any major sacrifices besides taking time off from work, not seeing my boyfriend for a week or so. As for my body, I just do as I always have, the gym.

I first realized I was a porn star when …

I realized I loved being watched.

Where do you see this career taking you? Do you have plans someday to move into another aspect of the industry?

Wherever Michael wants to take me, I'll just leave it at that.

JEREMY **HALL**

How did you get started in the business?

In 2004, I met Falcon porn star Roman Heart at a night club in Vancouver. He told me about his work for Falcon, and I was immediately drawn in by the idea. He connected me with Chris Steele who at the time was Director of Production for Falcon Studios. Within two months I was starring in *Spokes 3*. That was my first porn experience.

So what exactly did Roman Heart say that made you think their porn world was meant for you?

Roman told me about his traveling, dance work, video work. The money sounded good. It all sounded really fun.

What were you looking for when you got into it?

I ask myself the same question almost every day. I could give you an assortment of reasons, I was bored, horny, feeling adventurous, wanted the money ... The more interesting question is why after three years am I still here?

So what has kept you in the business after three years?

Well, it's not the money. Believe me, there are easier ways to make money. I think I'm still here because it is such a challenging and stimulating career.

STATS

BIRTH DATE: October 6, 1981

SIGN: Libra

HOMETOWN: Vancouver, BC

HEIGHT: 5'11"

WEIGHT: 170 lbs

TWO BEST CHARACTER TRAITS: Hardworking, honest

TWO WORST CHARACTER TRAITS: Compulsive, impatient

FAVORITE MUSIC: House, electro

FAVORITE MOVIES: Classics from the '80s

FAVORITE MOVIES I'VE BEEN IN: *ClubJeremyHall.com*, *WildLands* (Studio 2000), *Bottom of the 9th* (Channel 1).

XXX COSTAR I'D DO AGAIN IN A MINUTE: Dean Monroe

IF I COULD MAKE ONE REQUEST ON A PORN SET IT WOULD BE: Get rid of the cameras, "I'm trying to fuck here!"

AS A TEEN I ALWAYS FANTASIZED ABOUT SEX WITH: Guys on my hockey team.

CURRENT FANTASY MAN: Always changing.

SEXIEST PART OF A MAN: Armpits.

THREE INGREDIENTS OF MY HOTTEST SEX FANTASY: Good personality, big dick, nice body.

MOST PRIZED POSSESSION: I will give you a hint: its nine inches, and I'm playing with it right now.

HOBBIES: Wish I had time. I still travel, and enjoy the little bit of time I have off.

PETS: None, travel too much.

PET PEEVES: When people judge.

The travel, the boys, the general interest that people around you have. It's rewarding when someone is interested in what you do for work. And I know it sounds silly but I think I'm trying to prove to some people that I can't be pushed out of the business. There are no hard feelings towards anyone, but this is how the business works. Most people get used up. I want to be in control of my career. That's why I started up ClubJeremyHall.com.

Were the people who knew you surprised?

Well at the time I was sort of closeted. Living a double life. So the straight ones were, but not so much the gay ones.

What is the most aroused you have ever been on camera?

Lust Resorts, my scene partner was smoking hot!

What is the best advice you were given starting out?

Chris Steele told me if you want to make it big, be very picky about whom you work for and don't do more then five or six movies a year. It was good advice.

If someone were to come to you for advice about getting into the business what would you tell him?

Stay away from drugs, especially crystal meth! Know what you want out of the business, money, acknowledgement, etc. Have a plan. If all else fails, find the exit before the exit finds you!

What are the best and worst parts of being a porn star?

The best part is definitely the trav-

Jeremy Hall [PHOTO COURTESY CLUBJEREMYHALL.COM]

el. And the worst part is that some people can't see beyond what I do for work.

What things do you usually do to prepare for a movie?

Psych myself up and take Viagra.

And how do you usually spend your evening after a day of filming?

Just as though it were any other evening.

If you were offered a role in a fetish film how far do you think you would go?

Not very far ... I am pretty vanilla. I think a sling can be hot though.

Do you have some best example of bad behavior on a XXX set?

Not on a set, but one time Chris Steele took all the models out to a movie. Some girls thought we were hot and offered up $20 to show off our dicks ... I took them up on the offer.

Looking back on your childhood or adolescence is there some scene or episode where you think, "That kid was destined to grow up to be a porn star"?

Yes! The signs were all there.

Can you give some specifics?

Well I read an article on this topic. It said that most people who do porn have distant relationships with their parents. I very much fit into that category. It's not a bad thing. I love my parents, they just were not there a lot ... I hope I'm not sounding melodramatic, that's not my intention!

Do you think the adult film industry has an obligation to promote safe sex?

That's a hard question to answer because a lot of good people in this industry have chosen to produce bareback content. They have made a legal business decision. It's not my place to attack them for it. The emphasis should be on discouraging models from entering that side of the business, and identifying and weeding out bareback producers that pressure models into performing without condoms. But I think this question is misdirected. You could put that responsibility on the industry, but it won't change anything. There will always be bareback porn produced. Does Hollywood have a responsibility in not depicting certain violence in movies? This is a huge question that society still has not answered ... My personal opinion is: I would like to see all porn videos with condoms used.

Let's talk a bit about your site. So how did Club Jeremy Hall come about?

I've always had a thing for jocks, and thought there was not enough porn on the Internet for my niche. I've got a thing for jock straps, too, especially on soccer players. There is something about soccer players that just does it for me!

What was the toughest part of getting it all in order and off the ground?

It took me almost a year to put the site together. I did everything myself and learned a lot! The toughest part was and still is balancing everything, handling production, editing, marketing, web development. Giving all of these areas the appropriate amount of attention and still go to the gym.

"Believe me, there are easier ways to make money."

What can guys expect to see who check out your site?

Well, the theme is "Real Jocks Fuck," so if you're into jocks, you'll like my site. But Club Jeremy Hall is not just a site, it's a brand. I'm launching an affiliate site called JockBucks.com, which will have additional sites branch off. I'm also starting to put out Club Jeremy Hall DVDs. People can expect a consistent brand, masculine, athletic, and hardcore.

Jesus, you're a conglomerate. Good luck with all that. When you pass a hot looking guy on the street what about him gets you to turn around

Jeremy Hall [PHOTO COURTESY STUDIO 2000]

and do a double take every time?

Confidence.

Speaking sexually very few guys are as skilled as me when it comes to ...

Topping.

So what do you think it is you do that makes you so skilled at topping?

I just focus on the sex and controlling the other person.

How would you describe yourself in a personals ad and what sort of guy would you be looking for?

Honest, consistent, open minded, non judgmental.

Describe your ideal romantic evening.

I've always thought a hot air balloon was really romantic!

Describe your dream vacation.

I have *sooo* many ... the beach in Rio, Brazil.

DERRICK **HANSON**

How did you get started in the business?

It's actually a funny story. In the same week, Michael Brandon from Raging Stallion Studios saw my profile on BigMuscle.com and just emailed me out of the blue asking if I wanted to do videos. Later the same the week, Chi Chi LaRue emailed me after seeing my profile on Friendster.com. I figured if these two huge porn moguls thought I should be in adult video, maybe I should.

What were you looking for when you got into it?

I really had no expectations. I hadn't pursued it on my own, so I didn't know what to expect. I just wanted to have some fun and hopefully some really hot sex!

Were the people who knew you surprised?

Not at all. I'm naturally a really sexual person. I've also been involved in modeling almost my entire life, so the transition to porn was not too big of a stretch.

What was your biggest fear at taking the plunge into the porn world?

I didn't really have many concerns. A lot of guys might worry that it could

Derrick Hanson [PHOTO BY KENT TAYLOR, COUTESY RAGING STALLION STUDIOS]

maybe interfere with their professional careers at some point, but I'm studying sex education and HIV/STI public health, so I knew it would not be too much of a problem.

What was your first movie and do you recall the first bit of direction you were given?

My first big movie was back in spring 2005, *Team Players* from Raging Stallion Studios. I don't remember my first bit of direction, but I do remember having to bend over and show my hole in between every take because that was what turned my co-star on, which I thought was really funny.

What surprised you about making XXX films?

I was surprised about how much like other professional careers it was. There are plenty of office and industry politics. It definitely is a job. While it sure beats sitting in any cubicle, anyone who says that making porn is easy, obviously hasn't made a porno.

What is the most sexually aroused you have ever been on screen?

It's hard to pick just one. My scene in *Night Callers* from Unzipped was really hot because I had asked Chi Chi if I could work with Jon Galt (who I had jerked off to for years) and she put with me with not only him but also sexpot Jake Deckard! I also loved filming my scene in *Boners* from Raging Stallion Studios with Joey Russo. Joey and I hit it off from the moment we met, we actually ended up dating for several months after the shoot and are still good friends today!

If we were making Derrick Hanson's Orgy who are some of the folks who would need to get an invitation?

Eric Hanson, Bret Wolfe, Chad Hunt, Jason Branch, Erik Grant, Joe Foster, Parker Williams, Nick Piston, Johnny Hazzard, Dean Phoenix, and Ricky Sinz.

What things do you usually do to prepare for a film shoot?

I make sure to work extra hard at the gym the week before. I get a haircut and trim my facial/body hair. I tan a few days before. I try and look at the script or at least find out about the story line and my character and get familiar with the feel of the movie.

And how do you usually spend the evening after a day before the cameras?

As soon as the cameras stop rolling, I just want to go home or to my hotel room and take a nice long hot shower. Then I treat myself to a big meal and a few drinks!

If someone were to come to you for advice about getting into the business what would you tell him?

I would make sure they understood that this is a business. If they just want to have some quick fun or have a quick laugh by doing something a little wild, I would tell them to just do amateur. If their head is in the right place, and I believed they might do well in this industry, I would make some calls for them and recommend them to my friends at the different studios. If I did not know them well enough to make personal recommendations, I would tell them to hit the gym, clean up their look, and contact which ever studio they feel they would work the best with.

What are the best and worst aspects of being a porn star?

The best part of being a porn star is being well known and popular. The worst thing about being a porn star is being well known and popular .

Speaking sexually, very few guys are

STATS

BIRTH DATE: April 12, 1980

SIGN: Aries. I am the very definition of an Aries male with just two exceptions. I am not a jealous person (nor am I particularly fond of jealous people), and I am not as selfish as most Aries men.

HOMETOWN: Austin, Texas

HEIGHT: 6'2"

WEIGHT: 170-175 lbs

TWO BEST CHARACTER TRAITS: Even though most people say we finish last, I really pride myself on being a truly good person! People also tell me that I'm a really down to earth fun guy.

TWO WORST CHARACTER TRAITS: I am extremely independent (which is sometimes wrongly perceived as selfishness). I strongly believe that everyone should live their life the way they want and however they choose and do whatever they want to (or not do). I'm going to do my thing, you go do your thing, and hopefully we'll end up doing a lot of stuff together in the end! I also have a tendency to talk too much at times.

FAVORITE MUSIC: Jazzy Soulful House! Chillout Lounge, 2-Step, Hip Hop, DrumNBass, Soul/Funk, Jazz, Miguel Migs, Blue 6, David Harness, Mark Farina, Roy Davis, Jr., King Brit, Dee-Lite, Moloko, Missy Elliot, Eryka Badu, EBTG, Portishead, Bjork, Tori Amos, Billie Holiday, Kristine W, SugaBabes.

FAVORITE MOVIES: *Party Girl, Amelie, Labrynth, Steel Magnolias, Beautiful Thing, Half Baked, Run Lola Run, The Joy Luck Club, House of Yes, Silence of the Lambs, Happiness, Requiem for a Dream, Say Anything, Secretary, Hedwig & The Angry Inch, The Salton Sea, Heathers.*

FAVORITE MOVIES I'VE BEEN IN: *La Dolce Vita* (Lucas Entertainment), *Night Callers* (Unzipped), *Lifeguard: the Men of Deep Water Beach* (Titan), *Lock Down* (Falcon/Mustang), and *Bedroom Eyes* (Raging Stallion).

XXX COSTAR I'D DO AGAIN IN A MINUTE: Chad Hunt, Tober Brandt, Dean Monroe, Doug Jeffries, and Rik Jammer!

IF I COULD MAKE ONE REQUEST ON A PORN SET IT WOULD BE: To play back what has been filmed during the breaks! I would like to see how the scene is looking on camera so that I know what is looking hot that day and what's not. Usually you never know how the scene looks until you get your copy of the final product!

AS A TEEN I ALWAYS FANTASIZED ABOUT SEX WITH: Hot, hairy, older, masculine men.

CURRENT FANTASY MAN: Eric Hanson

SEXIEST PART OF A MAN: There are soooo many. I love the space between a man's balls and his hole (perineum, taint, etc.) I also love a hot happy trail, hairy muscular forearms & thighs, and a nice ripe armpit!

THREE INGREDIENTS OF MY HOTTEST SEX FANTASY: Hot, hairy, fun guys ... Lots of sex toys ... Everyone cumming on me in the end!

FAVORITE ITEM IN MY SEXUAL TOY BOX: I really love sex toys! I have a really big collection – but I'd have to say I love my leather gear – chaps, harnesses, boots, cuffs, etc.

MOST PRIZED POSSESSION: I don't really put much value on the material things I own ... my most prized possessions are my memories! I have lived such an interesting and crazy life and that's something no one can ever take away from me!

HOBBIES: Music, movies, sex, dancing, parties, computers, swimming, friends, photography, wrestling, house music, men, raves, traveling, psychology, Indie films, video production, acting, politics, astrology, gay/lesbian issues, sex education.

PETS: I love animals, but I haven't owned any pets for the last few years.

PET PEEVES: The quickest way to get on my nerves is by trying to tell me what to do! Or by talking to me about or trying to impress me with how much money you make or how much your designer outfit cost! I also can't stomach people who are constantly moody, unnecessarily negative, pessimistic, materialistic, shallow, users, pretentious, fake, plastic, prejudice, homophobic, or who think declaring oneself a Bitch is something to be proud of or makes one cool!

as skilled as me when it comes to ...

Eating ass!

Where is the wildest place you've ever had sex?

SEXY Vers STUDS w/ ATHLETIC BUILDS! Body hair, Tats, Piercings, Big Balls, BIG Shooters = BIG +! U MUST BE: REAL, LAIDBACK, OPEN-MINDED, & HAVE A FACE PIC!

"I do remember having to bend over and show my hole in between every take because that was what turned my co-star on, which I thought was really funny."

I'm a full time student, and in between classes I sometimes cruise the bathrooms on campus.

How would you describe yourself in a personals ad ... and what sort of man would you be looking for?

Hot Young Piglet Lookin' 4 FUN! I'm 27, 6'2", 170#, dk brwn/blue, naturally smooth & tan, with a nice 7.5" cut cock. I work out 5 times a week, I'm clean-cut but with a lil bit of an edge ... I have a few body piercing, a couple tattoos, etc. ... I'm extremely open minded and I can get into a wide variety of different things ... from j/o, showin off, porn, or oral/fucking, to leather, toys, kink, role play, wrestling, w/s, groups, 1-on-1, etc. ... HIV- but cool w/ poz guys. I'm lookin for FUN

People often consider XXX stars these ideal creatures, but if you could alter or change on thing about yourself through cosmetic surgery what would it be?

I wish my ass was bigger.

Where do you hope this career in XXX takes you?

I'm a psychology major specializing in human sexuality and gay/lesbian studies. I also am very public health oriented. Lately my porn career has provided me with a platform to help reach my community in a variety of ways. I just hope that porn continues too be a fun and exciting career that provides me with further opportunities to help people and try and make some kind of difference.

Derrick Hanson [PHOTO COUTESY HOT HOUSE ENTERTAINMENT]

ANTTON **HARRI**

How did you get started in the business?

I always liked porn as I always enjoyed watching other men playing among themselves. I was curious about taking part in a porn movie and back in February 2002 I happened to meet in Barcelona an actor-turned-producer called Lucas Foz who was looking for a lead figure to perform in his first project. He had previously taken part in porn movies as an actor and he re-assured me that everything would go alright and that I would enjoy working in his movie. I accepted the role and that was my debut in the business.

What were you looking for when you got into it?

After reading so much about it, I guess I wanted to learn what the business was like from the inside. I am a curious person in the positive sense of the word and I enjoy trying out new things. At that time, I had recently resigned from a position in a French fashion house because I was getting bored. There is nothing worse than boredom in life and most regular jobs are unchallenging and usually lack stimulus. I wanted to be stimulated and I also wanted to have some fun. As a newcomer, porn was a challenge for me, a challenge that offered good prospects of stimulating fun.

STATS

BIRTH DATE: February 17, 1974

SIGN: Aquarius

HOMETOWN: London, UK

HEIGHT: 5'8"

WEIGHT: 192 lbs

TWO BEST CHARACTER TRAITS: Friendliness, patience.

TWO WORST CHARACTER TRAITS: Opinionated, stubborn

FAVORITE MUSIC: Eclectic: techno-dance, house, pop, rock & roll, symphonic melodies and folk music.

FAVORITE MOVIES: *The Lord of the Rings*

FAVORITE MOVIES I'VE BEEN IN: *Manly Heat*, *Scorched* and *Quenched* by Kristopher Weston/Colt.

XXX COSTAR I'D DO AGAIN IN A MINUTE: Josh Weston

IF I COULD MAKE ONE DEMAND ON A PORN SET IT WOULD BE: Not to have any stops during a sex scene.

AS A TEEN I ALWAYS FANTASIZED ABOUT SEX WITH: Muscle men

CURRENT FANTASY MAN: Luke Garrett

SEXIEST PART OF A MAN: His face

THREE INGREDIENTS IN MY HOTTEST SEX FANTASY: A pretty face, a muscular body and a big dick.

FAVORITE ITEM IN MY SEXUAL TOY BOX: The lube

MOST PRIZED POSSESSION: My library

HOBBIES: Traveling, body-building, cycling, reading.

Antton Harri [PHOTO COURTESY HOT HOUSE ENTERTAINMENT]

Were the people who knew you surprised?

More than surprised, they were excited and thrilled. My flat mate and my closest friends knew that after I quit my previous regular job I was toying with the idea of getting into porn, therefore they saw it as a natural step to start taking part in porn movies. It was new and exciting to them, too, as they didn't know anybody else in their circle of friends who had done any porn. They were very supportive of my new career, and I am thankful to them for their encouragement.

What about making XXX movies didn't you expect?

The constant interruptions of the scenes: Freeze! Stop! Don't move! A porn movie is the graphic depiction of amazing sex but that is the final product. The actual sex in a movie set is a little bit frustrating because one cannot follow his own natural instincts but the orders of the film director who needs to interrupt the play in order to be able to take good pictures from different angles. The best directors and studios are aware of this and try to ease the whole process by making the actors feel as comfortable as possible during the sex scene.

Do you recall your first movie and the first bit of direction you were given?

The first movie was called *Working Day* (produced by Lucas Foz and produced by Private Studios) and the first instruction I received was: Don't look at the camera! My first scene was filmed in a bedroom where I pretended to sleep and to wake up in the morning. I wasn't used to the presence of cameras and my eyes kept on looking at the camera lens which annoyed the director ... until I learned to ignore the cameraman who was standing up and down on my bed.

Describe your ideal romantic evening.

There are many ways of enjoying a romantic encounter, but I would probably like to go to the theater to either watch an entertaining musical or an epic movie before having dinner in a restaurant serving Mediterranean or Japanese food. That would appease my stomach and would get me into a chatty mood. Strolling along the seaboard after dinner, drinking a cup of strong coffee while being caressed by the ocean breeze and then going back home with my handsome date for some sexy fun before going to sleep would complete my ideal romantic evening.

Speaking sexually, very few people are as skilled as me when it comes to ...

Kissing. There is no enjoyable sex if kissing is not involved. Foreplay is very important for arousing the senses and kissing is the essential part of it. When kissing, people get face to face and smell each other, feel the texture of each other's skin, play with their tongues ... so many senses are activated by kissing that I cannot imagine kiss-less sex!

What is the best pick up line you have either used or had used on you?

I am more visual than verbal when it comes to this, a mischievous smile and a lustful look get me hooked.

What is your typical regiment when you start to prepare for a film shoot?

I am usually a very regular person in my habits which means that I follow a regular pattern of diet and training, therefore there isn't much change before or after a film shooting except the fact that I get more strict with myself regarding my diet and my training a few days before the film shoot in order to achieve a more muscular and leaner look. I basically follow a high protein low fat diet and when approaching a film shoot I reduce my carbs intake to achieve a ripped look which is difficult to get.

And what are the first things you do when you get home from shooting?

I remove my shoes and lay down on the sofa ... Just kidding! I always check that everything is alright at home and then I relax a little bit before going through all the house chores that have been neglected during my absence. I also check my mail and I respond to my email messages.

You mention that there is nothing worse in life than being bored. Do you foresee that happening at some time with XXX films and if so what methods are you using to try and prevent the boredom from settling in?

I really don't think that I will ever get tired of taking part in XXX films, probably the production companies will discard me long before I get bored with porn movies. There aren't many jobs more interesting than that of a porn star where you get paid for having sex because, unfortunately, most jobs in this planet are damn boring, especially if you aren't your own boss. That is why people take holidays, to get away from the boredom that daily routine creates.

prospective porn star should consider carefully what his main source of income will be because doing porn only doesn't pay the bills. If the model feels comfortable with being naked in front of others and there are no other issues that might affect his current or future life in a negative way, then he should go ahead and do porn but always keeping in perspective both the negative and positive aspects of the business.

"So many senses are activated by kissing that I cannot imagine kiss-less sex!"

When you pass a hot looking guy on the street what causes you to turn around and do a double take every time?

The look on his face. If he looks at me, then I will probably look back and if he is a handsome man, I will turn around again after he is out of my sight. If the man is in good shape and he shows it by wearing tight clothes, then I will definitely turn around to have a second and, probably, a third look!

If someone were to come to you for advice about getting into the business what would you tell him?

I would first ask them to consider if they are sure they want to do porn or not. Why do they want to enter this industry? How is this going to affect their life? The consequences of getting into the business need to be considered because if they have a job and their job is going to be compromised by doing porn and they intend to keep it, then they shouldn't do porn. Also, how family and friends are going to react needs to be considered. Take into account that once a model is filmed naked, those images will remain regardless if the model has done one movie or dozens of movies. The

Do you have some nasty sexual fantasy you are just waiting for some director to ask you to film and if so can you give a brief description?

I really don't have any nasty fantasies worth talking about, but I do have this fantasy that involves an old cable car in Donostia, my hometown (in Basqueland). This is an antique red-colored wooden cable car with lots of charm that is very popular with Donostians due to the fact that it is kept in its original early twentieth century look. The cable car travels up a steep hill where amazing views of the city and the ocean can be enjoyed. I fantasize about shooting a scene on that red cable car and having sex on the wooden benches while looking into the beautiful scenery down below.

Where is the wildest/kinkiest place you have ever had sex?

On the floor between two garbage containers in a back street in Old Town Philadelphia. I was visiting a good friend of mine for a couple

Antton Harri [PHOTO COURTESY HOT HOUSE ENTERTAINMENT]

of weeks in Bethesda, a Maryland suburb north of DC, and I took the train to Philadelphia for a day trip. I wanted to see the renown Liberty Bell and other historical Revolutionary sites. It was early afternoon, lunch time, and I was heading for a market near City Hall for something to eat. I was planning to feed my stomach, but when I came across this hunky man, I decided I would also feed my lust. He wasn't local, so we had to accommodate ourselves to whatever discretion that Old Town Philly offered, which wasn't much by the way! I returned to Bethesda fully satisfied.

Describe your dream vacation.

My dream vacation would involve visiting a place with either charm or amazing scenery or unusual architecture or everything combined. It could be a trip to a tropical island, to a glacier in the mountains or to some ancient ruins, but it would have to be fulfilling in the sense that at the end of my vacation I would need to feel like I learned something new and that the trip was worth the effort.

LUKE **HASS**

How did you get started in the business?

I used to meet a lot of guys online with my web cam and finally I figured, why not make money doing this! I created an account on a live streaming site and one day this guy – that today I happily call a friend – asked me if I ever thought about doing porn. He used to be an editor for a number of adult publications and he had some connections. He told a few studios about me – and I was surprised to be honest, but I got many nice offers. I also had this desire to meet and work with Brent Corrigan and do some scenes for his site ... probably before I ever considered doing studio porn myself actually. So, that was my first porn experience. We spent 12 days together and we shot 3 amazing scenes. After that, I met with a few of the studios ... and Raging Stallion made me a terrific offer! They cast me in the 3-part video *Grunts* and for a first-timer I knew that was an opportunity I couldn't pass up.

Luke Hass [PHOTO BY KENT TAYLOR, COURTESY RAGING STALLION STUDIOS]

What were you looking for when you got into it?

Experience. Exposure – no pun intended. My own site (lukehass.com) does well, but there is nothing like doing porn that would open up even more doors and introduce me to even more fans. I love producing my own scenes. I know someday, if I'm lucky, they'll let me produce or direct for a studio. While doing my first scene with Raging Stallion, I pretty much thought ... this is amazing. I hope they like me as much as I like doing this! They offered me an exclusive contract and they were gracious enough to let me keep working on my site. There was no way I could say no. The money is very good and it allows me to keep my business running. So it's a win-win situation for me.

Were the people who knew you surprised when you took the XXX plunge?

To be honest, I had mixed reviews from friends and family. Also it's not something I usually talk about a lot. I value my privacy (I do!) and even though this line of work contradicts that statement (I know!) once you do a video, it's not exactly like people aren't going to know about it. My closest friends either love what I do or don't seem to care (I mean, they're just so many stories to tell every time I come back from a shoot). Others find it funny, and others simply don't speak about it. I haven't had any really negative response to my decision. I'm sure that will come with time, after all no one can please everyone. And I'm not going to lose sleep worrying about it one way or the other. And, if I had friends who had a problem with it they wouldn't really be good friends now, would they?

Since you just made Grunts was the experience tough for you? Was adapting to having sex in front of the crew and all a challenge or did it come easily?

It was a lot easier than I thought it would be! When I did the scenes with Brent Corrigan, there were only

STATS

BIRTH DATE: February 22

SIGN: Pisces

HOMETOWN: Born Rio de Janeiro, Brazil but now live in Providence RI.

HEIGHT: 5'10"

WEIGHT: 140 lbs

TWO BEST CHARACTER TRAITS: Sense of humor and personality; I'm always happy.

TWO WORST CHARACTER TRAITS: I'm impatient, which is kind of ironic since I'm personally always fashionably late!

FAVORITE MUSIC: Coldplay and U2

FAVORITE MOVIES: *Hedwig and the Angry Inch* (Which is funny since I have so many inches!)

FAVORITE MOVIES I'VE BEEN IN: Hopefully by the time this book is released I've made more than one professional video, so for now – *Grunts*.

XXX COSTAR I'D DO AGAIN IN A MINUTE: Brent Corrigan

IF I COULD MAKE ONE REQUEST ON A PORN SET IT WOULD BE: When you work for Raging Stallion Studios you don't have any desires. They treat you like a king, they feed you constantly, they run your errands, they give you choices on your co-stars, and they're the best. What else can I ask for?

AS A TEEN I ALWAYS FANTASIZED ABOUT SEX WITH: Leonardo DiCaprio

CURRENT FANTASY MAN: Matt Damon for a movie star you know. There was also this hot guy, Neil Haskell, on *So You Think You Can Dance*.

SEXIEST PART OF A MAN: Eyes and lips.

THREE INGREDIENTS OF MY HOTTEST SEX FANTASY: A cabin in the woods with the snow coming down with a fireplace going. And a bottle of wine with a hot guy under a blanket. Oh wait, that was five.

FAVORITE ITEM IN MY SEXUAL TOY BOX: Why use plastic when you can use the real thing? But if you really wanna know, my anal beads.

MOST PRIZED POSSESSION: Besides my cock, my iPhone.

HOBBIES: Photography, traveling, meeting new people. I also love watching movies, dancing and last but not least, my blog.

PETS: I have the cutest Jade Plant called Cidney. And don't tell me she ain't a pet.

PET PEEVES: Slow drivers. Loud and rude people. And people who don't put the toilet paper correctly (it should be outwards, not inwards!)

Luke Hass [PHOTO BY KENT TAYLOR, COURTESY RAGING STALLION STUDIOS]

a couple people present in each scene which in theory should have made me more comfortable, but no! Filming *Grunts* was such a turn on for me. The huge crew, the amount of models there, having that many people watching me was actually a complete fucking thrill! Especially the days following my scenes when I was having so much good feedback, everyone genuinely complimenting me for something I did or how a scene went. I couldn't ask for more.

"I don't think I will cosmetically change any other part of my body but if I have to pick one, I'd say my potato-shaped nose. ...But if I'm naked, no one is looking at my nose."

Do you have some amazing XXX fantasy you are just waiting for some director to ask you to film?

I've never been this big fantasy type of guy. I like reality! I mean, I do have some minor things I'd live to do in my private life that I wouldn't mind doing on camera, but for the most part, I'm a very passionate guy when it comes to sex. I like lots of foreplay and I could honestly last for hours fucking someone I'm really into. And although it could sound boring for some just changing positions after some time it does the trick for me. I'll save the whole fuck-me-in-a-sling-with-a-leather-harness-on or I'm in a sailor suit, for my videos. I'm sure the directors are going to have a lot more imagination than I will when it comes to fantasies, and it's not like I mind living them anyway. OK, on second thought I wanna have a four-way with the Kershner triplets, but hey! Who doesn't?

People often consider porn stars these ideal physical specimens, but if you could change one thing about yourself through cosmetic surgery what would it be?

Nice question! Maybe I will charge you for my therapy bills now! All jokes aside, I used to think I was a really ugly kid. I was also, in my opinion, an ugly teenager. I had helmet hair, very smooth legs which my brothers would always make fun of me about (I have four older brothers by the way – none of them gay, sorry) I had this huge outtie belly button that really bothered me and kinda ruined my confidence especially when I had to go to the beach. Some of the things I just mentioned are easily corrected. I got a new haircut, as I grew up the hair on my legs finally decided to show up and a few years back I got rid of the huge belly button. I don't think I will cosmetically change any other part of my body but if I have to pick one, I'd say my potato-shaped nose. But honestly I learned how to live with it. And I'm going to take a wild guess here but, if I'm naked, no one is looking at my nose.

Where is the wildest place you've ever had sex?

That's a hard one. I'm going to have to dig in my memory and get back to this one in a couple minutes ... (OK, 15 minutes later) it wasn't really a wild place, per se, but a wild situation. It was early evening in the back of this guy's SUV parked in the middle of a fairly busy street in a residential area. I'm going to omit most of the details here to preserve some privacy (his privacy of course) but it was for me an unexpected situation where things just really happened on the spur of the moment. People walking by the car, other cars driving by us unknowingly aware. It's just something I will never forget, probably because one minute we were driving and the next minute we were fucking. The car stopped of course! And I only have him to thank, since it was primarily his idea.

Sexually speaking, very few guys are as skilled as me when it comes to ...

Fucking someone for the first time and actually having the other guy enjoy it. Even with a dick as big as mine. Most first experiences usually come with pain, and I blame the top. You can't just worry about your own enjoyment and shove your cock into the bottom like they're a pro. Just to shorten this answer I'm going to say I'm a pro on breaking the seal and I'm very proud of that!

How would you describe yourself in a personals ad?

Oh my, this is a hard one. There's a famous Brazilian song that sings "Moreno alto, bonito e sensual, talvez eu seja a solucao do seu problema, carinhoso, bom nivel social. Inteligente e a disposicao de um relacionamento intimo e discreto, realize seu sonho sexual ..." It's a very corny song, and when I translate it, you'll think it's describing me. Tall, handsome, tanned and sensual guy, maybe I'm the solution for your problems, very sweet with good social skills. Intelligent and available for an intimate and discrete relationship, in sum, your sexual dream come true ..." If you know me well enough, you'll know I ain't lying!

Where do you hope this career takes you?

Hopefully where a desk job wouldn't. No, really. Success with my site, recognition. The opportunity to look back in many years to come and not regret anything I did. My goal in life is to be happy and to make people happy. Going to work and being miserable the whole day isn't for me. I want in the future to be able to be recognized as someone that brought light into someone's darkness. Sex is one of the most, if not the most, important part of someone's life. If you don't have a good sex life you don't have a good life at all, you develop issues, you create drama, you get bitter, which will eventually create even bigger problems. So, if I can be someone's fantasy – if I can from the other side of that camera make someone's day because they love looking at me fucking someone else so much that they reach their climax – then this is it, this is what I want from this business. And if you ever cum watching one of my scenes, I absolutely want to hear that from the fans because that'll be the same as a huge compliment coming from a renowned director. Foremost, I want to be able to live comfortably and keep working until I take my last breath. And, hopefully, that will be many years in the future!

NICK **HORN**

How did you get started in the business?

I'd been thinking about it for a long time. I kept telling myself that when I was happy with my body I'd do it. One day I was chatting with a bear friend of mine who's been in a couple films, I realized there were all types of guys doing films, and I was actually comfortable how I looked in front of a camera.

What were you looking for when you got into it?

Fame, money, power, the chance to rule the world! Seriously, I just did it for fun and thought it'd be nice to have a couple extra bucks for fun. I realized after I started that maybe I did it to feed my exhibitionist side a bit, too.

Do you recall the first film you did and the first bit of direction you were given?

I was so nervous when I started! I just remember standing there with the cameras rolling trying to keep a hard-on and thinking "Don't fuck this up!" then not being able to keep an erection because I was so nervous – I kept thinking, "I'm totally fucking up, I'm blowing it, no one's ever going to work with me again!" My heart was racing. The director could tell I was

Nick Horn
[PHOTO COURTESY HOT HOUSE ENTERTAINMENT]

STATS

SIGN: Yes, I'm a Leo!

HOMETOWN: Eugene Oregon

HEIGHT: 6'

WEIGHT: Usually around 180 lbs

TWO BEST CHARACTER TRAITS: I'm easy ... going. I'm nice and don't have an attitude, try to be friendly to everyone I meet.

TWO WORST CHARACTER TRAITS: Hmmm ... probably still that I'm easy ... going, nice and don't have an attitude and try to be friendly to everyone I meet.

FAVORITE MUSIC: I like dance music, it gives me energy. I also like an eclectic mix of alternative, pop, and jazz.

FAVORITE MOVIES: My favorite movie of all time is *Muriel's Wedding*. It was the first movie I saw when I moved to Los Angeles when I turned 18, and I really identified with everything the movie is about. I even went to Australia and checked out the places where they filmed the movie!

FAVORITE MOVIES I'VE BEEN IN: I've really enjoyed all of them, everyone on the set has been fantastic- all the directors, crew, and actors were so fun to work with! Some of my specific favorites were *Justice* from Hot House, *CopShack on 101* from Titan and *Blue* from Hot House. I also really enjoyed working with Steven Scarbourough and Chi Chi LaRue.

XXX COSTAR I'D DO AGAIN IN A MINUTE: Kent North, Dean Monroe, and Collin O'Neal.

IF I COULD MAKE ONE REQUEST ON A PORN SET IT WOULD BE: To direct, of course!

AS A TEEN I ALWAYS FANTASIZED ABOUT SEX WITH: Bruce Willis, he is super hot and just keeps getting hotter! Bruce, call me sometime.

CURRENT FANTASY MAN: I don't need a fantasy man, I'm out doing my fantasy men whenever I want, but if I had to pick one I've been lusting after Zachary Pierce, he's really hot!

SEXIEST PART OF A MAN: I think it depends on the man. I'm usually drawn to the face, stomach and cock. Love snuggling up next to all of those parts though.

THREE INGREDIENTS OF MY HOTTEST SEX FANTASY: Me, various other individuals, mixed with the juices from one or more men.

FAVORITE ITEM IN MY SEXUAL TOY BOX: My bottle of Gun Oil

MOST PRIZED POSSESSION: My mattress, of course!

HOBBIES: Traveling, poker with my buddies, movies and the gym.

PETS: None. I wish I had a cat though.

PET PEEVES: When people are flaky or late, unless it's me being flaky or late.

nervous, so he pulled me aside and calmed me down. He explained that everyone has times when they are nervous. After that (and some help from a blue pill) I went back and finished the scene. It was the difference between night and day – everything went fantastic after that!

What things do you always make sure to do in the days leading up to filming?

I would up my cardio the two weeks before and cut out carbs. I'd up my training and just try to get as lean as possible.

What and what is your typical evening after you've been shooting all day?

I really enjoy going out to dinner with the cast and crew after filming and then getting a good night's sleep. On the last day of the shoot it's fun to go out and have some drinks on the town to unwind!

You mention wanting to direct and you've worked with some great directors – Steven Scarbourough, Joe Gage, Chi Chi LaRue ... what things did working with those guys teach you about the top porn directors?

They are consummate professionals – they have the ability to direct the action and guide the models to a great

Nick Horn [PHOTO COURTESY TITANMEN.COM]

performance by noticing and keeping on top of small details as well as looking at the big picture all the while making you feel comfortable and like you are the star.

Where is the wildest place you've ever had sex?

Up the butt ... oh, I mean, probably on the dance floor during New Years in San Francisco once. I was dancing with this guy and I got behind him, he reached around and we started fucking right there on the dance floor – nobody could tell, it just looked like we were dancing closely!

"I'm a sucker for mean looking guys who are really nice."

And what things do you think you would be especially aware of as a director coming from the other side of the camera as a model?

I think I would be conscious of people's stamina – different people can work for different lengths of time before they wear out. It's important to allow people time to relax and rest their bodies so they can keep the action coming!

If in your directing efforts you were to film yourself in Nick's Orgy who would you want as your four co-stars?

Hmmm ... that's a tough question! If I had to just pick four, I would love to do an orgy scene with Zak Spears, Kirk Ziegler, Steven Scarborough and Jake Deckard.

When you pass a hot looking guy on the street what gets you to turn around and do a double take every time?

Sexy eyes and beefy body.

Speaking sexually, very few people are as skilled as me when it comes to ...

Kissing, it's definitely one of my strong suits.

How do we get you in the sack and what do we do with you once we get you there?

Buy me a drink and I'm yours for the night! Well, maybe it's a couple. Really what it comes down to is that I'm a sucker for mean looking guys who are really nice. I think what we'd do in the sack depends on the chemistry. I'm open to everything! Versatility is a good thing though.

Describe your ideal romantic evening.

If I had a checklist that I needed to complete, it would make for a really boring evening. I like spontaneity and having someone just take me and show me a good time – something that they enjoy doing, too, so we both have a romantic evening. If we do something that is special to them, that they want me to share, it means a lot. A nice dinner is always a good starting point though!

TY HUDSON

Hey Ty, Can you set the scene for us about where you're answering the questions?

I am sitting here writing on Memorial Day Weekend. I live in the West Hills in Portland, Oregon, on the side of a mountain. There are the sounds of drumming circles from some directions, jazz and classical live bands coming from other directions. Still more, the sounds of laughter coming from a neighboring house. I hear the yipping of coyote in the forest and fields nearby. This place is magical and unsurpassed in originality. I feel blessed to live here. Tomorrow my wolf dog and I head for the rain forests to shoot some photographs. This seems like life beyond living! I love it here!

How did you get started in the business?

Destiny? Seems that issues of intimacy vs. male sexuality have been present in my life from an early age on and that I was somehow meant to embellish on the matters and make it my career. My photo opportunities have been ongoing since I was 18, using myself as a model for my Caravaggio/Sargent-esque style paintings. I was my cheapest and most available model. Since then I have been undergoing various self-portraiture projects all fitting under the main title of Mythos-Pathos: Legend of the Mind. Other sub-topic endeavors fall underneath that and are part of a growing collection of self-portraiture photo projects I hope to get published in the near future. My first XXX movie opportunity was offered by Colt/Buckshot productions. It was really a wonderful experience and I really offer great thanks to John Rutherford and Jerry Douglas for their support and amazing talent. They have provided themselves as great examples for me. Side note: While they are my original mentors and I follow them closely, I am not involved with them at the present time. I would be self-unforgiving not to mention that my present dedication, unfailing, goes to Jett Blakk who has had faith and an open presence to me. He is my ultimate hero and I hope to grow further with him. Thank you, Jett!

What were you looking for when you got into it?

I was looking to grow and expand on my concepts of intimacy. The Colt/Buckshot production had a great potential for that given the tremendous support and family-like atmosphere there during the shoot. I was also looking for more behind the camera experience since my ultimate goal is/has been to write some screenplays ... not necessarily in the standard XXX format but what I call Graphic Cinema format

STATS

BIRTH DATE: June 24, 1960

SIGN: Cancer

HOMETOWN: Portland, OR.

HEIGHT: 5'11"

WEIGHT: 187 lbs

TWO BEST CHARACTER TRAITS: I have a deep sense of intimacy that I value in my life. Intimacy operates on every level of my life, not just physically but emotionally, psychologically, spiritually and even the mundane aspects of basic living. It's the foundation of who I am and I cannot imagine life without it! All of my passion, motivation and drive for life and living generates from that point of departure. My second best character trait would be my depth of feeling. I'm not talking about drama, but genuine feeling, multifaceted. It's connecting the two that makes one complement the other and it involves sharing that with all the other things around you whether that means friends, a partner, work, whatever. We are not on this Earth to be alone in it. We are here together. I find my strength by infusing feeling into the Art of Intimacy. It is not restricted to just the people around me but my general surroundings as well and the journey of life holistically.

I definitely have heart and compassion, the ability to love and be loved. I like to connect with people on terms that they are comfortable with and at the level they are capable of and then share in not only that part of each of us but pushing our boundaries together. I've shaken hands with death on a few occasions and it has had an effect on how I view what is important.

I nearly drowned when I was seven years old and then I was born with congenital hypertension, (high blood pressure), and had a stroke when I was 24 years old. Word was that I would be a statistic by the time I was 35. I've surpassed that and even reversed the damaging process of hypertension through nutrition and my pursuit/knowledge in the medical sciences. My educational background, (multiple undergrad and masters levels course work), was in part self serving, but I did use all of that to help others by getting involved in cancer research, physical and nutritional programs for guys who are HIV poz, running a provision program for homeless folks and working in various health care centers and in the hospital setting. It's important to give back what you have learned if it can help other people too. I'm trying to do that through my photography and graphic cinema projects now. They are not simply porn or erotica but concentrate on topics of our intricate human being but uncensored.

It might seem that the two traits, (intimacy & heart/ Compassion) are the same, but it's a matter of focus and application. You can feel things, but intimacy involves an aspect of sharing with someone or something other than yourself. That is my strongest grace. I feel blessed in that sense.

TWO WORST CHARACTER TRAITS: I'm personally impatient with myself. I have high personal expectations and am personally demanding. I don't like to fail others or myself. I can be my own worst enemy occasionally think myself to sleep at night thinking about what kind of worth and contribution I've made to the day. In one sense it is a good thing in that I really love to learn and have pursued my education with a variety of bachelor's degrees and master's work. On the down side, my brain never seems to stop and I can get into this very detail oriented mode of thought.My second worst character trait ... Hmm. I think that would be my creativity. Sounds funny maybe but it's very demanding on a partner. They have to put up with my never-ending, seemingly random inspirations. I live in that mode though. Doesn't matter if it is at an event or a party. The more there is around me the more creative I get with possibilities. Get me alone and in bed though, then you have my full attention ... and creatively so.

"Worst" and "Best" qualities are sort of a point of perspective. Sometimes my best qualities bite me in the ass and sometimes the worst ones are my saving grace. Life's funny that way.

FAVORITE MUSIC: Depends on what I'm looking for. On top of being in front of the camera, I am behind it as well. I write screenplays, so I look at a lot of different kinds of music and my extensive travel schedule exposes me to a number of different trends and styles. On a personal level I really love Elliot Smith who wrote some of the score for Good Will Hunting. I also like the Shins, (Garden State score). There is a station in Seattle I connect to on line even while I am traveling and I draw from there frequently for original sound. It's KEXP, really great for fresh music. For a while I was blasting out Tom Jones Greatest hits. Especially before filming. I loved "What's New Pussy Cat?" and "Thunder Ball." I move around from Alternative to old country to European club mixes to opera to classical and symphony easily. Why limit yourself? Recently I've been listening to some bands called Wild Royale, Bittersweet, Boozoo Bajou and some of the Xbox video game soundtracks.

FAVORITE MOVIES: *Farewell My Concubine, Memoirs of a Geisha, The Pillow Book, Saved, Batman Begins.* I really have come to love the series, *Buffy the Vampire Slayer.* Joss Wedon's writing and character development is pretty amazing!

FAVORITE MOVIES I'VE BEEN IN: I've really enjoyed filming with all of the productions I've been in by Jett Blakk, (*Dirty Little Sins, Bonesaw,Mars Needs Men, World Class Slash Sex Orgy, Masque*). *Masque* was incredibly fun and the cast and crew were all wonderful! He is *soooooo* supportive and organized it just makes the filming fun and natural as possible. Of course, the hot, sexy men he casts helps as well. Jett is an amazing inspiration and I respect him wholeheartedly. I am in awe of his professionalism as well as his capacity for just being a friend. He amazes me! His personal and business integrity is unsurpassed and impresses me to no end! Thanks Jett! You honor me with your presence! As written by so many others before me, you are Brilliant! I've had some very good experiences with Doug Jeffries as well. It is more then his beautiful blue eyes and heart warming charisma. On one movie, (*Color Blind*), He partnered me with Tiger, this beautiful black man ... Amazing! Hot natural real time sex caught on film. I loved the connection. *Grrrr!* Again, great cast and crew. I've loved working around Chi Chi, (*World Class Splash Sex Orgy* and the opening film for the Grabbys in Chicago 2006). I guess the magic combination is the films that have content and context with dialogue as well as hot man sex along with high production values. I am currently writing screenplays that I categorize as Graphic Cinema. They are basically Hollywood movies without the censorship of human sexuality imposed.

XXX COSTAR I'D DO AGAIN IN A MINUTE: Tober Brandt, Trevor Knight, Shane Rollins, Manni Torrez, Zachary Pierce, Troy Punk, Jason Ridge, Shawn Steele. My wish list is pretty extensive. I'll just name two: Mathew Rush and Carlo Massi.

IF I COULD MAKE ONE REQUEST ON A PORN SET IT WOULD BE: More content and character context along with residual payments to cast members on post production market items, (post cards, calendars etc. ...). I've often pondered the pros and cons of having some sort of program to assist the welfare of the models. It's an unpopular concept at best, (and complicated), but the

Ty Hudson [PHOTO COURTESY HOT HOUSE ENTERTAINMENT]

industry is growing and changing and there is at least potential for growth in this area as well. I'm not talking about a union or anything like that but the Industry has grown considerably over the past thirty years and for some people modeling in front of the camera is a profession. More immediate though, I'd like to see Kimono large sized rubbers or Beyond Seven's offered as an option to the ever-present Magnum's because they are more comfortable and accommodating size wise. They former are "almost like wearing nothing at all," except you are, (and I fully support safer sex practices both in and outside of the industry).

AS A TEEN I ALWAYS FANTASIZED ABOUT SEX WITH: One of my math teachers. He was sort of a stocky, walking testosterone type of guy, kind of muscle bound. You could tell he was packing a big ol' piece of Man Tenders in those tight polies he wore. I flunked math class that term because I could not keep from staring at his crotch. Sigh.

CURRENT FANTASY MAN: I'm single right now but if I was looking. Mr. Fantasy Man would have an open heart and a sense of beauty that he would apply that to our lovemaking and daily life. He'd be a guy who is intelligent and conscientious of the world around him, someone I would listen to speak and be blown away by his dynamic

"The part of a man I find most erotic in bed is his voice. Some guys can make me cum really, really fast just by being very close to me and talking gently in my ear."

presence. I would want him to compliment and challenge me with both our similarities and our differences. That allows us the opportunity to share life and grow as well. It would help if he had long muscular legs, thick black hair, brown eyes, darker skin, long eyelashes, nice big balls and was highly sensual. I really like that darker Mediterranean look. "Sense of humor and enjoys laughing" is a must on the criteria list! I'm an adventurer and very hardy in the outdoors and so he'd also have to be similar in that respect. He would have a strong sense of "self" and the able to assert it. Being driven, intense and a creative problem solver myself, it would be a good thing if he were my equal in that respect. If he had children and a family I would want to be part of that fully: an in-law and not an outlaw. I have always been in long-term relationships prior to my present career in the industry. I still hope for that at some point. The beauty of youth, finances, health, etc. changes over time and I want someone who will hang in with me regardless. We all eventually lose our independence and reach some ending point in our lives. It's good to have a partner who is also your best friend so you can be there for each other when hard times come. Obviously, I have a unique past that includes escorting and pornography. Both have been important and valued experiences in my life. It's really been a great opportunity for me to learn about my own sexuality as well as others and how we incorporate that into the various facets of our lives. Mr. Bohunk, (as in hunky bohemian), has to be fine with all of this. I don't care much about physical monogamy but overall emotional monogamy is a must.

SEXIEST PART OF A MAN: His back, (shows his strength). A man's eyes because they tell me the story of his past and his present heart. Lips are erotic because they can write novels of passion all over my body. His heart and mind, too because they can illustrate/elaborate on his lust, love and the intensity and intricacies of his masculine personhood. Let it also be known that the part of a man I find most erotic in bed is his voice. Some guys can make me cum really, really fast just by being very close to me and talking gently in my ear. Legs turn me on because I just like great looking legs. Feet ... hands ... nipples, body hair, balls, cock ... Well, hell ... What's left? I like men, what more can I say?

THREE INGREDIENTS OF MY HOTTEST SEX FANTASY: Hot, sexy men, being outside while we are having sex, partners who have heart and are into a mutually intense and passionate sexual experience.

FAVORITE ITEM IN MY SEXUAL TOY BOX: Lube & lotion! It makes everything better!

MOST PRIZED POSSESSION: I'm either very fortunate or very selfish. I have seven – none of which I actually possess. I embrace them all though and rely on them frequently. These are my lucky seven: intimacy, my heritage, my creativity, today/tomorrow, my dog Nanook, Stuart and Lisa, (my partners in life). Without them my life would seem incomplete.

HOBBIES: Photography, screenplay writing, creating graphic novels, mountain climbing, scuba diving, surfing, sailing, landscaping with tropical plants here in Oregon, exploring wilderness areas, camping, crabbing on the coast, writing music, playing drums, guitar, piano, drawing, painting, building furniture, stone masonry, rafting, kayaking, snowboarding, skiing, riding horses, traveling, searching the world over for good chocolate and bakery, learning languages and study philosophy, science, medicine, nutrition, breed fish, birds, cats and dogs. With the exception of traveling, school things, hunting for chocolate and breeding critters. I do the rest naked whenever possible.

PETS: My illustrious dog Nanook! He has an unyielding gentle heart and brave sensibility about him. He is an independent thinker and intelligent. I'm incredibly proud of him! If he were a man instead of a dog, he would be my fantasy man! Don't worry. There's nothing funny going on there. Get your mind out of the gutter!

PET PEEVES: Dirty bathrooms, violence, pointless raging, thoughtlessness, sand fleas, abusive use of cologne and perfume, apathy, sugar, grass and inappropriate fear.

and cable/Gay TV ready format. I really want to expand on the boundaries of both porn and Hollywood cinema, using real life intimacy issues and redefining the modern/future gay male definition. Those issues need to be updated. We seem to be in the middle of the post '70s, '80s, early '90s versions of them but sexuality on a broader scale seems to be expanding. I talk to a lot of people, straight, bi, gay, trans ... younger populations don't seem to differentiate or feel the strong need to dedicate oneself as straight or gay but concentrate on the value of a person and the relationship they have with other people in the world. I follow in that suit.

Our value as human beings should not be defined by a particular sexual preference but by our character and connection or inter-intra-action with ourselves and between the world/events/people around us. Seems like when we identify ourselves firstly by the foundations we build on but then neglect the reality of who we are as human beings we lose perspective. For example, there are plenty of people who prescribe to a particular religion or political faction. There are people who would never consider being gay or straight. They are in some sense products of the society and culture around them. They make the ideals "who" they are although they may feel differently inside or not have any true understanding of those foundations. They view their understanding as complete and not partial and may never consider optional ways to view the world or themselves. They just accept the standard dogma of the day.

I wonder if that stifles growth and understanding. My involvement in my current professions offered opportunities to bring up questions on a broader scale, challenge old beliefs and encourage people to reconsider things. Media can be a strong tool for raising awareness.

If someone came to you for advice about getting into the business what would you tell him?

Think about why you want to do this – for money? Prestige? Recognition? What do you want to gain and what do you want to contribute? If you were watching porn or any indulging in any other type of media what would you be looking to gain from it? Life and living does not simply embrace what you gain from it but how you contribute on both a conscious level and how people interpret what you do/say. Think about what your words and actions and consider how it may influence others. You are not without value or impression to those around you. We are the hope for those behind us and the example for those ahead of us. Your impressions of everything in front of you are in some form or shape of understanding, a reflection of your own beliefs and comprehension. So determine how this business, (or any other), is a reflection of you and consider how you want to move within it. Your actions won't just affect other people but also yourself. That would be my Native American foundations talking to you/me. Just like anything else: determine your goal, find a plan of action and go for it. If you don't succeed try again. If you don't like it, change and do something else. Do what you are most passionate about.

Speaking sexually, Very few people are as talented as me when it comes to ...

Intimacy. Sexuality is an arena. I don't place an emphasis on sex, but value individuals and self-exemplification of who we are as persons on an intimate level. So, sexually speaking, whatever I do with another person is unique and has our own personal intimacy signature on it ... special and not like any other experience. We play in the sexual arena mutually and find the places that are most meaningful to us and move from that point of departure. In strict sexual terms I am a talented kisser, ass eater and equally skilled and able to receive as a Top, (more often), and Bottom as far as intercourse goes. Getting really down to basics, ass turns me on. Let me go there and we can create history with the rest of our bodies.

What is the most aroused you have ever been on screen and why?

I was in a production called *Color Blind* by Unzipped video. I was to do a scene with this guy in a barn stall setting. I wanted to introduce myself on an intimate level with him, so while in between filming, I gave him a back rub and started kissing. He was reciprocal and very sincere and passionate about giving of himself. By the time we started filming, there was a very strong connection for me towards him and I think it showed up on film. It felt very intense on my end while having sex with him in front of the camera. I was happy to give my ass up for intercourse with him. I just wanted to be with him on all levels regardless of the filming but not completely unconscious of wanting it to be powerful on camera for others to enjoy or strive for. There was also a scene where I topped a guy on Jett Blakk's production of *Masque* for Oh Man Studios. His name is Sean. Although the whole energy and intensity level and type of sharing was different, it was equally impressive to me on its own merit. In *Color Blind*, the man I worked with topped m. In *Masque*, I topped Sean. Both powerful experiences but, very different and personally complete. I am really more of a top sexually but in either one of those productions it was not about topping or bottoming but rather meeting on deeper levels while we played sexually. I wanted to give and receive fully since my partner(s) were both really receptive to connecting on levels that were not strictly sexual.

What are some of the things you do to prepare for a XXX shoot?

Actually, I do a lot! First I get my script memorized. Then I visualize the potential scene as best I can. The night before I put my script, clothing, props, lube, condoms and toiletries together. I eat high protein up until two days before the shoot and then load up on carbs, lecithin, zinc and fluids to keep myself hydrated and produce a nice thick creamy load for the camera and my viewers. The night before the shot, I eat light meals. I don't have sex for five days before my call date. I prefer to stay in my own place and generally have one. That way I can get good sleep and have a quiet space where I can be very private. In that privacy, I assume the role of my character and keep it there until we shoot. The day before shooting motivates me to get a haircut, manicure and pedicure.

On the morning of production, I do some basic hygiene rituals – floss, bleach my teeth, douche, re-check my fingernails and toe nails. Trim my

Ty Hudson [PHOTO COURTESY HOT HOUSE ENTERTAINMENT]

beard, sit outside and clear my mind of everything. Being quiet is really important for me – private, quiet and by myself – that is a three-hour process minimal. I nurture my film presence there. Finally, I get in the car and start to head to the site or studio. I generally put on some music that gets me in the mood. One time it was the SHINS. Another time it was the best hits of Tom Jones. Still again, it can be opera or classical, alternative or '60s classics and all dependent on what puts me in filming mode.

Once at the site, I have very little time to get to know who I am working with both in respect to cast and crew. What I am doing sexually may be an unknown but because being on some personal level is important to my work process, I become very social if not charismatic. Some people might view this as promiscuous or whorish. It's really an attempt at getting to know my team members so that we can make the best movie possible. I'll talk, hug and kiss on cast members and flirt with the make-up and/or camera crew. Creating a situation that has intensely good energy and camaraderie adds to my performance and seems to be a constructive force for other cast and crew. My hope is that all of that energy shows up on film. If time permits, I will isolate myself for a few minutes and just be thoughtful and quiet before filming.

When call time comes, I put everything aside and focus only on my scene. Lights. Camera. Action! My concentration is there and generally directors allow me the artistic freedom to express myself with my partner. Although fully in character, I have this side of me that maintains a technical fetish of a sort and I am fairly conscious of the camera's eye. I want to be sure that neither my cast mates nor myself are blocking anything that is essential to what viewers are looking to see on film. Breaks are distracting for me and I generally find another cast member to be intimate/

sexual with or go off by myself and keep my hard on going, maintaining my camera/character high. Once we are done, my hard on subsides and I let go of the moment. I shower and part with the experience. Afterwards, I thank everyone and give hugs.

And what are the first things you do when you get home from a XXX shoot?

After shooting and bidding farewell, I will get in my car, drive a few blocks out of range and get out to smoke a cigarette. Nasty habit but I get a sense of release from it. I'll smoke an American Spirit Organic light or two and listen to some music that brings me to a plateau of serenity. At that point, I call Stuart, (mentioned previously), and ask him about his day. Hearing about his day levels me out and makes me feel good. I tell him how the shoot went and then traditionally go to Jerry's Famous Deli in Los Angeles and eat a bowl of Matzah Ball soup, turkey sandwich and have an Éclair for desert. I come home and sit outside or about twenty minutes, smoke another American Spirit, come in and check my email, work on photos or screenplays and then snuggle up into bed. Nice full day. I feel satisfied. I lay in bed planning and thinking about what the up and coming week holds for me. Sleep finally comes when I picture my wolf dog Nanook jumping into bed with me and snuggling up close. I imagine coming home to him and then start to dream. Zzzzzzzzz. That's my boy!

Is it hot or tough to watch yourself on screen?

I'm very critical of myself ... "Hmmm ... should have cheated to the camera more this way or that way" ... "Need to develop my chest or seratus muscles more." "I should have read that line differently and need to relax my eyes." That inevitably leads me into thoughts about how I would direct and film a production of my own – you know, being on the other side of the camera. On the other hand, it's really interesting as well as erotic to see myself having sex with some hot guy. It doesn't necessarily turn me on, but I am endlessly fascinated by the whole thing! It's not just me there but me as this particular character plus having sex with someone and putting the two together is both inspiring as well as amazing. It's generally a very "learning" experience for me. Again, I indulge in technicalities and look at editing and dialogue, acting and lighting, film angles. My mind races with ideas.

How far would you go in a fetish film and would you be more likely to push the envelope in a movie or in your private life?

How far do you want to go?! I will always push the boundaries and limits for a film! If you don't have ideas I will give you some and we can start a new film project. My goal is to provide the most amazing experience to the viewer that I can. I'm creative and energetic on film. I'll hang from bars, find entertaining uses of medical equipment, construction sites, tractors, rivers, fire, water, sand, rope, anything to bring the concept of entertainment and thought provocation to some new interesting level. I may be limited by the construct of the production context but always willing and able to go beyond and above the expectation: safe and sane always. I have a tendency to be rather dominant on film as either a top or bottom, athletic and as extreme as possible. There is something about being in front of the camera that transcends me into some "other" place. I'll pick a man up and thrust him onto my hard throbbing dick, supporting him with one arm and just driving into him. I'll push a top down and mount his engorged penis and milk his cock with my ass, looking him straight in the eye and penetrating his soul as he penetrates my ass. Tools, devices, role-playing, toys, love. I want an impression to be presented on film. If you have faith in me and give me the opportunity I won't disappoint you and will give my all! I want the viewer to be satisfied. I want ultimately to do a great job.

There is no field or endeavor I have undertaken in my life where the motto was not, "Excellence in Execution." If you are going to do something, do it right, do it well, and to the best of your ability. Things that you fall short on are opportunities to learn how you can do it better the second time. Don't waste your time on things you have no passion for. Discover and present your assets, potentiate them to the fullest extent possible. In my private life I will give myself fully to my partner. Explore together the things that will bring us to a closer sense of understanding and be there with him to reach our fullest potential. Life is for living and experiencing! Let's do it! You want to make Love and cry because it's so beautiful; I'm there and will cry in the beauty with you. You want to talk nasty and just be dirty boys, let's be dirty. Overall, it's about partnership, trust, living and loving with my mate. With a life partner, life itself may set the boundaries for us, but we will push the limits and create an empire of our own, forthright and driven! While I will give 150% in front of the camera, with a partner I will give 1000% to make a difference and set the pace for those watching. I would be more than fine with putting that on film for others to see.

"To let someone objectify you as simply a penis or to view a client as simply an income seems limited and unfulfilling at best."

If you were to make a film called My Orgy whom would you want as your four costars and why?

I have no descript answer to this question. Although, I am researching this since I am casting for my *Dante* production. There is no orgy scene there but my hope is to cast guys who are very open and uninhibited about expressing not only their sexual presence on film but also an emotional, spiritual, psychological presence a well. I would like them to be able to connect with their partner or partners and give freely on all levels. Sometimes guys will meet for the first time on set and then go right into filming. The connection is lost and the viewer picks up on this from the get go. I talk to a lot of guys who watch all sorts of genre of porn. They dislike the lack of connection. It's noticeable, very obvious and then seems mechanical or contrived. In my own productions, I want to bring the cast and crew together, let them intermingle, see how they interact and how they express or withhold themselves with regard to the people around them and then place them accordingly or give them the opportunity to develop a deeper bond so that when they get in front of the camera there is the foundation of a natural relationship. The price of a pool and good food is a small price to pay for the presence of honest emotion and bonding in front of the camera. The audience of any film production will prey upon insincerity instantly and unforgivably. I would try to do everything in my power to lessen the potential for this injustice to the viewer. I want the productions I am in or produce to have some value, meaning, real life application and/or reference. As with my clients, I don't want anyone to go home thinking, "Wow, I had another orgasm". I want people to go home and think, "Wow ... my life has been enriched."

If I weren't making porn or involved in the sex industry I would be ...

Well, considering I've been a teacher, construction worker, landscaper, painter, photographer, film write/producer, philosopher, partner, corporate manager, athlete, counselor, trainer, student, father, parent, lover, philanthropist, archeologist, musician, linguist, lone ranger and more ... All of these things have led me to the place of my choosing. I chose to do this. I am where I want to be and have purpose behind being here and want to progress further, contribute to life and the growth and understanding of others exponentially through the reflection of my own experiences. I fully respect and congratulate the efforts and achievements of my forerunners and hope to make advancements in the understanding and definition of what it means to be not only a sensual, sexual man but what it means to be a human being. I can't imagine being any other place. I feel blessed and privileged. The potential and regard of this industry is underrated and underestimated. I believe in it and give myself fully to bring a better understanding of intimacy between individuals whether homosexual, heterosexual, transsexual, transgender, multicultural, interracial, interpersonal. I firmly believe that as a species we can be significantly above the superficial human constructs of politics, religion, culture and personal self-image. Those things are facets of our social development and while I have no intention of discrediting them or underrating their influence or importance, I feel that there is something about our existence that is even stronger, more powerful – a fuel that feeds the development of these conditions but is not fully perceived and directed appropriately. My life goal through the format of film, photography and writing is to explore and present an opportunity to focus on this potential. I was born with a voice, a body, and an intellect. It would be disrespectful not to use it.

If you were a woman would you still be involved in this industry?

Absolutely but I would want to augment how I display myself sexually. I would make my sexuality part of my strength; take pride in being a woman with firm tits and nice tight love dish.

It wouldn't be about overpowering anyone but just being strong within myself and taking that femininity and making full use of it, illustrating who I am through my gender. Male, female, neither both, young or old, take what you are and be amazing.

You mention having an escort past ... what qualities do you think are the most important in being a top-notch escort?

First, study the profession. I actually did this prior to entering the field. I eventually concentrated on the original Geisha around the Edo period in Japan. They were male, educated, skilled in music and literature, socially graceful and often times acted as counselors and confidants to officials and Emperors.

I've dedicated myself to strive and provide those similar, though embellished upon, contributions and really believe in making the time I spend with my clients meaningful and valuable to them on a wide variety of levels. Decide whether you want to work as a prostitute or an escort. I conduct my profession differently then a lot of guys out there. I do not take on multiple clients per day because that diminishes the quality of the time a client and I will spend together. I am strictly paid for my time and so do not add on additional charges for extra interests. I think some guys call that the cafeteria plan. I think there are a lot of guys out there who will meet a client, maybe ask for money upfront, show off a little, have sex and then zip up and leave to meet the next client. That seems more like prostitution to me. They don't take the time to get to know their client or vise-versa.

Escorting on a professional level is more involved. You have a better chance of improving the service to your client if you have some understanding about each other. Additionally, you improve your own personal safety by getting to know your client. You are dealing with another human being and I believe that implies a need for mutual respect, compassion and understanding at least. People are three-dimensional and their sexuality is not some separate entity but an integrated part of who they are on the whole, (no pun intended). Simply providing sexual relief does not require much. A person could stay at home and masturbate and feel good for a bit but then still have that odd sense of void, unfulfilled. Spending time with a client involves understanding the void or needs of this person to the best of your ability and meet with them on mutual ground, be in a space with them where they are free to be the person they are without judgment, sometimes venturing into ideas of how they would like to manifest themselves as they move ahead in life.

To let someone objectify you as simply a penis or to view a client as simply an income seems limited and unfulfilling at best. My goal is always to at least meet and hopefully exceed my client's expectations. You always want to be clear thinking, have an open heart and mind, and be safe and sane. Move in tandem on as many levels as the client feels comfortable with. Try to know yourself as well as possible. Understanding who you are gives you an understanding of what you have to offer and how you can improve your service to this other human being. For me, a true escort should make the goal to have the escort and client look back on their experiences saying, "Wow, my life has been enriched", rather then, "I had a bunch of orgasms", or "I made a lot of money".

What is the key to getting you in the sack and what do we do with you once we get you there?

Good question, since I rarely play outside of professional interests. I rarely masturbate as well. It takes away from my work in front of the camera or my clients. Better to mention things that really turn me off. I'm a rather creative individual. I draw from all sorts of experiences. Prevent me from moving around in my life and indulging in my seemingly random adventures and you can pretty much count on me being an unwilling bed partner. Turn me on by telling me about your day and asking about mine. Love me and let me love you back. Of course then there is that thing where playing with my nipples is a sure bet. I find the combination of a gentle, compassionate heart, cultured, open mind and feral penis and ass extremely attractive. Good eye contact and hugging get me going. From there it can go from sweet, passionate sex to crazy wild sex.

Let's start with a midnight swim. Come in wet and refreshed, then start kissing, feeling our breath mingle at the corners of our mouths with lips barely touching, moving back and forth into each other in an undulating embrace, drawing in the warm scent of our bodies as they rise and mix forming an intoxicating cologne of love ether, feeling our fingers travel and explore the landscape of our bodies – lips and mouths suckling on nipples, hungry, thirsty, biting gently, feeling our bodies give into each other in contrast to the hard swelling of our prowess pressing against our stomachs, moving into the salty sweetness under your arms, licking my way down your sides until I reach your penis. I concentrate on the heat being thrown off onto my lips as it pulsates. I explore every fold, vein, curve, writing novels with my tongue and moving back further to your heavier musk where the sweat is silkier, smooth, opening you slowly with kisses and fingers. Coming up to share your scent with you, now staining my mouth and hands, penetrating you just a little and letting you open up to me, drawing me in deeper and deeper, a firm and steady push when I have reached an apparent end.

You open up further and we embrace tightly. Looking into your eyes and talking. We kiss, moving in a tidal force, creating an ocean of our own, our scents suddenly blossom, our pupils dilate, we fill our ocean with surges of semen, our hearts still pounding we are overcome by exhaustion and the serenity of the night passing. Soft snoring creates tiny breezes, drying up the rivulets of sweat along our bodies and caressing our dreams. The bed cools, the sun rises ... mmm.

How would you describe yourself in a personals ad?

Roses in your bathwater, tongues seal secrets between the parted lips and firm presence of two gentlemen's glances. My presence is graceful, masculine, sensuous, intelligent, well mannered yet naughty. I am responsive to your touch and masterful with my own. Sophisticated without attitude. Capable and willing to be lusted after as well as lustful for you, Loved as well as love you. The beauty of two men sharing deeply & intimately in life makes me hard and wet. Salt passes between our lips making our souls sweeter. Experiences shared make our lives richer. Life should be about this always! Why waste you heart with unrealized Dreams when we can still fall asleep in the afterglow of our awakened life, playful adventures, and the creamy pearls of our virile imaginations! Uninhibited, adventurous, openminded, love to explore and discover the private moments of the deepest intimacy on the landscape of our minds, bodies and in the world we can create together! Top to Bottom: I give myself 110%. Mutual satisfaction, sweet kisses, open me, open you, holding tender or holding tight. A Man as well as a gentleman. A Tyger of character. wrestle a little, play a little, and groom each other's musky pride. Purrrrrrr!

What is the kinkiest thing you have ever done?

I've had sex on a large canvas in paint, in front of large groups of people, behind a clothing rack, on rooftops, suspended in air, role-playing, (as a doctor of sorts, student, construction worker, lost boy on his way to his straight date), played with rose petals, candy, ice cream, toys and medical equipment but really the kinkiest thing I ever did was date this one guy. After about seven months into it, I was invited to the family Christmas party. Shortly after arriving it became apparent that I had sex with his brother about one month before starting to date this guy. I had no idea they were brothers. What can I say? They both have a similar look that I like. The brother felt compelled to disclose this to my boyfriend. That didn't go over well.

Additionally, this guy's mother had at some point decided she had fallen in love with me and lost sixty pounds for this party so she would look more attractive to me. She cornered me in the kitchen and planted an unexpected French kiss on me just as the boyfriend was coming into the kitchen. That was pretty much the end of our relationship. Very unsettling.

Do you have some particular sexual fantasy you are just hoping some director asks you to film?

Something surrounded by powerful dialogue and a compelling story line that eventually finds me and another character in some intense act of making love on film. Not just two guys having hot sex but something where there is a reason for us having it, some type of forbidden love situation or over coming impossible odds. Maybe we make love in the desperation of our last moments together? A role that I can invest my entire being into completely and give fully on a sexual level in front of the camera, uncensored and unedited even if we laugh or cry. I don't really care how we express ourselves sexually but want the content and context of our characters to make whatever it is that we do on a sexual level meaningful and moving. Top, bottom, toys, whatever – put one of us in drag and have it be about our sexual identity differences and how we can never be together given our different preferences so, we put all that aside and make true love for the last time. The bottom line being that we are making love. Hmm, suddenly I have another idea for a film. I think I'll call it, "Straight to Earth".

You mention wishing Kimono or Beyond 7 condoms be used on XXX sets ... can models use their own condoms or do they have to be chosen by the director/studio/production people?

Well, I can't really speak for the studios. I generally bring my own condoms and lube though. I prefer the Kimono extra large and Beyond 7's because they are micro thin but very accommodating and strong as well. The other larger brands are so industrial as far as thickness goes. I want to feel my partner and not abrade him with rubber friction. Reciprocally, I don't want rubber burns up inside my ass. Ouch! Condom safe lotion works best for me with regard to intercourse as well as or jerking off. Silicone lubes dissolve my contacts if I get any in my eyes and water based lubes get sticky.Yuck!

I have a few preferred lotions I like that are condom safe and just soak in making your skin vibrant and refreshed, giving you baby soft skin and an unparalleled youthful glow. On the set there seems to be the two usual types of lube, silicone and water based. Sometimes there are a variety of different condoms there but never these two that I like. Trojan seems to have this big corner on the market in California. Not much variety there as far as condom choice. So, I stock up here I Portland. On my own productions I will most likely provide the standards plus my own personal faves.

Do you view sexual preference as a product of genetics, nurturing or choice?

It's a little naive and rigid to think that it is simply one or the other. Reality probably falls somewhere in a variety of combinations of all of them and maybe include other considerations

Ty Hudson [PHOTO BY TYGER'S EYE IMAGING]

we don't know about yet as well. On a genetic level I think there are probably a number of different scenarios. Some people may be born with a genetic predisposition to heterosexuality or homosexuality or even celibacy. XY, XX, XXX, XXY, those genetic combinations exist not to mention varying hormone levels during fetal development, adolescence or the aging process. There may be hormones that do not contribute directly but rather influence perhaps our emotional responses and they may contribute indirectly.

Some people are doing active research and redefining homosexuality as a potentially treatable disease but what if being gay is also a matter of choice? I like the way a man feels in my arms, the way he plays back with me physically and expresses his body. I like it and choose to continue enjoying the experience of men on all levels. Sexuality is a physical expression but not solely. It also operates on emotional, psychological and spiritual levels. Sexual expression functions as a form of communicating those aspects.

Why shouldn't choosing to be gay or bi be valid? Does making the choice to love the same sex or both somehow negate the fact that a person may be a great and loving parent, good teacher, a hard and diligent worker, an honest and contributing citizen worthy of the same legal rights and freedoms collectively as those who follow different faiths and political venues? The word democracy comes to mind, especially the part about principles of social equality and the respect for the individual within a community. I think it follows the part about the majority rules to which I site Yahoo encyclopedia: Such a philosophy places a high value on the equality of individuals and would free people as far as possible from restraints not self-imposed. It insists that necessary restraints be imposed only by the consent of the majority and that they conform to the principle of equality. Seems a-OK…so I use the internet.

But it's the words, "principal of equality" that seem relevant to me. It amazes me that you can follow any faith and a variety of political parties and be entitled to the securities and privileges of having a home, holding a job, (reflecting back on measures 9 and 13 in Oregon), receiving inheritance, tax benefits and sharing insurance coverage in a heterosexual or even nonsexual partnership. If you form a homosexual partnership however, life, liberty, health and property have all been compromised with regard to the principle of equality. Homosexuality has been around a long time and is not confined to our own species. It's been documented to exist in cultures even when they were isolated from each other and before the gene pool was as hybridized as it is today.

Coming back around to gay, "The Disease," treating the "disease" without considering and addressing the cause/source does not eliminate it. Do we not, each of us, come from an ovum and sperm? Is there something about conception, about sexual reproduction, that causes/allows for homosexuality? Is it perhaps innate or even instinctual in all of us? (I am simply posing questions, challenging even some of my own personal beliefs and trying to expand my own understanding). Conditions of nurturing including joy or stress may leave impressions on a person and open the potential for expressing themselves sexually or in a physically intimate way with one or both genders. I think there used to be some theory that you were gay because you had a bad relationship with your Father or Mother. I know plenty of gay individuals who had great relationships with their parents and lots of heterosexual people who had awful relationships with their parents. So, I don't place too much weight on that. If anything, I tend to think that there is a lot of pressure from both heterosexuals and homosexuals to "pick a preference", forging a division among people. Adolescents seem to bare the greatest burden of this. Overall, I personally choose to believe that people and maybe mammals in general, are "sexual" beings. It's a part of our make up; natural, intentional and of value. There are other more important things that define us as human beings than our sexual preference. Whether genetic, cultured, chosen or a combination of all of them. I am always a human being and all that goes with that. And, by the way, yes, I enjoy the company of other gentlemen.

If you had to choose between sex and love which one would you choose and what are your thoughts on fidelity?

Can't I have both sex and love? I like it when sex is the physical language of love spoken between my partner and I. Eventually, sex will subside and so I would have to choose love here. I really am not concerned with sexual fidelity. Emotional fidelity is a strong concern for me though.

If you were an animal what animal would you be and why?

I'd be a cross between a wolf and an eagle. Some creature that is integrated with the beings and things around him, majestic, social, self assured without being pretentious. Elegant, graceful, understanding of his need without being abusive or extravagant, intuitive, aware, contributing, sincere, instinctual but not without thoughtfulness and consideration, calculating, confident, free, challenging, dedicated, nurturing, flying, howling at the moon, legendary, controversial, impressive by action but stealthy in movement, nomadic, aware of life and death, appreciative of both, visually comprehensive, omnipresent but not obvious, loving but not without regard to independence or merit of growth through free will.

Ty, I am also an admirer of your screenplays. I thought you did an excellent job with the ambitious film *Dante*.

Well, thanks Owen! It was a collective effort and I had a really great cast and crew. It was an amazing experience to work with Jett on the production side. He is practical as well as creative. I always feel honored to be part of his productions and doubly blessed to have him working with me on this one.

What most interests you when it comes to bringing "plots to porn"?

Well, Owen, I really hope to add context and content to the characters with the idea of making the intimate and sexual details less generic and more personable. I would like to set up a situation where the viewer cares about the characters, looks at them as villains or heroes, buddies even, someone that they can relate to: attainable/ approachable role models. I would like the characters to mean something more then simply hot guys having sex. It gives you more to personally connect with. I pursue the idea of giving people enough Fantasy to remove themselves from the mundane or difficulties of daily living but enough three dimensional reality, (through character development), to constructively influence their real life.

When looking at your screenplays what themes seem to emerge?

Mainly things that investigate or bring to question who we are as human beings or "Men." Stories that intrigue me the most are those that challenge my thinking, expand my understanding of myself or the world around me. We are born into a world of definition and meaning so if a story doesn't address that somehow, I just don't see the point in it.

Describe your ideal romantic evening.

Ahhhh ... Start the day off scuba diving off of some Tahitian Island and diving for pearls in Bora Bora. Feed sharks and rays in the afternoon. Swim naked with dolphins in the early evening. Catch a tuna and stir him in salt and lime, crack open a coconut and pour on a little milk, shave some and throw that in there too. Go sailing, ride horses on the beach or ride bikes around on one of the Islands. New Zealand Lamb for dinner and a nice bottle of wine. Retire to our over water bungalow with the glass floor. Light a few candles, kiss and snuggle in bed while the trade winds blow the curtains. Lick the heat of the sun and salt of the ocean off each other's bodies, lay naked in bed surrounded by fragrant tropical flowers and don't come out for two days. My second scenario – canoeing or kayaking by day, rubbing oil all over each other and sun bathing naked in the woods somewhere, building a fort together and have wild sex under the stars, fall asleep in our fort and cooking breakfast over a fire! Eggs and pancakes and a naked man out in the wilderness! Yum!

MARC LaSALLE

How did you get started in the business?

I originally got started in Seattle with a smaller company where I recognized the owner of the company at a friend's birthday party. I walked up and introduced myself to him then as we casually got to that point of the conversation I told him my intentions.

Are you a natural exhibitionist?

I'm actually somewhat shy.

So how does a "somewhat shy guy" overcome his inhibitions and make XXX movies?

That's been years in the making and gym training. Secretly it's always been a fantasy of mine to do XXX movies.

Is that what were you looking for when you got into it?

I must admit, as a child I was always looking for attention and I guess that carried through to adulthood.

So has being a XXX star brought you

STATS

BIRTH DATE: October 1

SIGN: Libra

HOMETOWN: Born-Santa Barbara, CA

HEIGHT: 5'9"

WEIGHT: 170 lbs

TWO BEST CHARACTER TRAITS: Charming, polite

TWO WORST CHARACTER TRAITS: Too hard on myself, controlling

FAVORITE MUSIC: Deep House, Funky Disco House

FAVORITE MOVIES: Scary movies

FAVORITE MOVIES I'VE BEEN IN: *Notorious C.H.O., Lords of the Jungle*

XXX COSTAR I'D DO AGAIN IN A MINUTE: Anthony Martinez

IF I COULD MAKE ONE REQUEST ON A PORN SET IT WOULD BE: To be more efficient

AS A TEEN I ALWAYS FANTASIZED ABOUT SEX WITH: Tom Hanks, Rick Donovan

CURRENT FANTASY MAN: I sleep with him every night.

SEXIEST PART OF A MAN: I like a man with a nice strong back and biceps.

THREE INGREDIENTS OF MY HOTTEST SEX FANTASY: Crisco, toy chest and a great imagination.

FAVORITE ITEM IN MY SEXUAL TOY BOX: My 12x7 black dong. It helps me prepare for deep scenes.

MOST PRIZED POSSESSION: I don't really have anything that is prized, I could lose everything in a second; it's all just stuff and replaceable.

HOBBIES: Netflix, playing with the dogs, gardening, shopping with my man, dining out and hanging with friends, reading.

PETS: My partners' two dogs – black Lab/border collie and yellow Lab/golden retriever/chow mix, both girls

PET PEEVES: When people don't follow through with what they promise

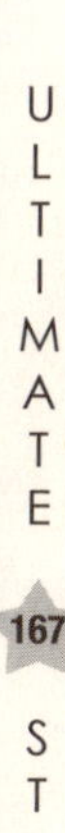

Mark LaSalle [PHOTO BY KENT TAYLOR, COURTESY RAGING STALLION STUDIOS]

the level of attention you were hoping for?

I really don't consider myself a star, just a porn personality and it hasn't brought me the attention that I was hoping for yet. I don't know if that will ever happen, but it's nice to know that I am forever immortalized in print and video.

And has there been a downside to that notoriety?

No.

What about making XXX films surprised you?

The thing that surprised me is how closely it resembles the making of a real mainstream movie. I've been in a couple and on TV soundstages so it all felt sort of at home with me.

Speaking of that your movie credits list *Notorious C.H.O.* as one of the favorites you've been in – I gotta hear about that. What was it like? Details.

It was filmed in Seattle at the Paramount Theater. Margaret was shooting her movie in Seattle and I happened to be at the right place at the right time. It was fun with the cameras there and all the hoopla. Anyhow, we signed a release and that was that. I get calls every now and then with friends saying they saw me on TV. I'm in the beginning and the end of the movie and I'm in the movie trailer. It's fun.

That's very cool. Marc, you mentioned that you wanted adult film sets to be more efficient. Would you please explain or elaborate a bit on that?

Well, the thing that doesn't change between mainstream and X-stream is the fact that there is always waiting around for the grips, directors, sound, stills to get the show started. I am pretty much ready to go when it's my call time, but unfortunately the actors are always waiting around for set-up to begin and get started so we can just get it on. I could say that I'll just start being late because I know we won't start on time, but then that's not very professional and I look at this as a profession and treat it accordingly.

If a guy came up to you and asked advice about getting into the business what would you tell him?

That has recently happened, a friend of mine is interested in the business and I told him to get in shape. He had some questions for me. We talked about it and I told him how I got in.

What is the most aroused you have ever been on screen?

The most to date hasn't been released yet. I did a scene with Anthony Martinez; we had good chemistry both on and off screen. That scene is still in the pipeline to date.

What is the most drama you have ever experienced on a XXX set?

I'd have to say on the set of *Lords of the Jungle*. I didn't have any specific drama towards me but there was plenty with one of the cast members. It got to the point where we were ready to leave that person on the island.

So what is the difference between you and Marc LaSalle the porn star?

Not a whole lot, except when I'm out as Marc I play up the role a little bit more. In this type of field you have to be somewhat of a showman and I'm used to it.

If you were to make a movie called Marc LaSalle's Orgy whom would you want as your 4 costars?

That's a tough one since I don't really know a lot of the other actors. I'd have to say after being at the awards and seeing the few that I do recognize in person, Erik Rhodes would be at the top of that list. I might have to take a look at my Myspace page to pull a few names, too.

Have you ever developed a crush on any of your costars, care to name names?

I have hooked up with co-stars off screen, but as far as crushes, no. I know the life of the adult film star and I know it wouldn't work out as I'd imagine I like it to.

What things do you typically do to prepare for a XXX shoot?

It depends on what type of shoot I'm doing. Overall I go to the gym more frequently towards a film/photo shoot. Prior to the day I trim down on my eating and I prepare myself internally if you get my drift.

"As a child I was always looking for attention and I guess that carried through to adulthood."

Is it tough, educational, arousing, or impossible to watch yourself having sex on screen?

I've talked to many performers and a lot of them have said that they have never or won't ever watch themselves on video. On the other hand with me, I like to watch for purely perfecting my craft and learning from myself. I like to know what to do, what not to do, so next time I can be better for my viewers.

So where do you stand on the whole agent vs. no agent question and why?

It's nice to have the security of a studio backing me especially starting off, but I have seen other co-stars who have done three times the amount work I have done and been on at least a dozen magazines and movies. With an agent you do get the chance to work around with different studios. For right now I like building my core as an exclusive model and then perhaps later I'll see where I want to go with it.

And what do you usually do when you are finished filming?

I eat and have time to myself. It takes a lot out of me. Most people who only watch the movies don't realize what it takes to make a movie. It really is a lot of hard work, no pun intended. It's physically and mentally draining from time to time. It's almost as if I need time to come out of character.

Do you have some special XXX fantasy you are just waiting for some director to ask you film?

There is a scene from the movie *Last Exit to Brooklyn* that is a secret fantasy. However, it's probably far too graphic for portrayal on XXX video.

Adult films are somewhat notorious for putting actors in really difficult poses and positions for the sake of

the camera. What is the most trying position you have ever had to assume for the good of a scene?

Being under a hot sun, twice on a big rock, leaning against a tree, having my leg up for over an hour, and mosquitoes.

If you could change one thing about the way the industry is currently run what would it be?

Add some more color in the mix with the bigger studios.

Do you have some best example of bad behavior on a XXX set you would care to share?

What happens on the set stays on the set. There's no need in fucking with anybody's fantasy.

Do you think the industry has a responsibility regarding the use of condoms and/or promoting safe sex?

I think individuals are responsible for their own use of condoms in the industry. That is why there are those studios that cater to specifically condom-less play. We are not responsible, but we are in fact setting an example of a healthier way to play and exist.

People often think of XXX stars as being these perfect specimens, but if you could have one bit of cosmetic surgery done what would it be?

I'd probably get a little lypo and some anti-aging work, you know, a little nip/tuck here or there, but overall I'm pretty satisfied with myself. Nothing a good trainer couldn't help out with.

Do you have any childhood or adolescent memory that you can look back upon and say, "Oh yeah, that kid was destined to grow up to be a porn star"?

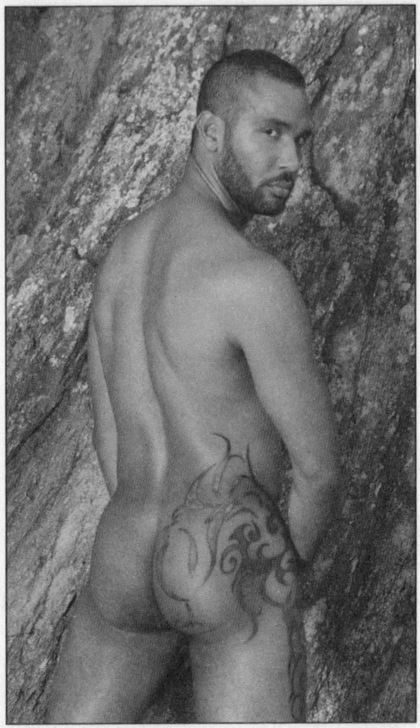

Mark LaSalle [PHOTO BY KENT TAYLOR, COURTESY RAGING STALLION STUDIOS]

I didn't even know what gay porn was then. I knew it got me off looking at men's parts in magazines or what have you.

When it comes to driving a man wild I've found nothing works better than …

Being myself.

How do we get you in the sack and what do we do with you once we get you there?

Who would we be? And if you have to ask what to do with me then you have no business being in the sack with me.

When you pass a hot looking guy

on the street what causes you to turn around and do a double take every time?

Crotch, face, arms.

How would you describe yourself in a personals ad?

5'9", 31"waist, 170, brn/dk brn, good physical shape, good-looking, down to earth, funny, fun to hang out with and good in the sack. Also I have been told I'm a great kisser. More than mild to extremely wild. See attached picture.

Where is the wildest place you have ever had sex off camera?

In my younger days I was all over the place. I remember having sex in the middle of the ring of trees one night around midnight and then running across the park naked to the bathroom. I've done it on the ground next to a guy's truck when traffic is going by on the other side, sex on a boat and on a beach. I've done it in a parking garage, in a pool and hot tub. I guess no place really unusual.

Describe your ideal romantic evening.

Sometimes I like to shake things up and do a simple routine backwards. Perhaps I might decide to work up a good appetite by having a roll in the hay first, then go out to eat or eat in, then cuddle up on the sofa and watch a movie and have dessert and then go to bed and sleep nude and cuddle until we both fell asleep. I'm pretty simple and easy when it comes to this.

If you had to choose between sex and love which would you choose and what are your thoughts about fidelity?

With all of the sex I've had in my life it's about time for some love. As for fidelity, I am loyal to my mate, but don't get me wrong I'm not dead. It's only healthy to look at all the other hot guys around and compare to see what each of our tastes is. I don't have any desire to sleep around, besides I get to do that whenever I do a scene. It's almost having the best of both worlds and getting paid for it too.

Describe your dream vacation.

Since I love to travel that is a hard one. I recently went to Paris with my boyfriend. It was my first time to Europe and we went for Christmas and New Years for ten days. We dined, shopped, did a lot of site seeing, shopped and walked, then shopped some more. I'd have to say that so far that would be number one until my next big vacation. The only setback if any was that is was very cold.

How do you consider yourself a typical Libra?

I have all the character traits of the Libra, I can be indecisive, but it's usually bad when I'm hungry or tired. I am artistic and refined. I've been told that I am charming. I do like to mediate and balance and I always look calm. Those are just some of what makes me, me.

What is the biggest misconception people have about you when you meet them?

That's a good question. Maybe people think that I'm a hooker for hire, or perhaps that I'm a bit stand offish at first? I'm a bit quiet until I get to know you. For the most part when I'm in the public eye, I try to be as straightforward as I can be.

If you had to compare yourself to an animal what species do you think best captures your essence and why?

A black jaguar because I'm very independent and don't require the pack mentality. I'm very capable of going out by myself and having a good time.

If your life had a theme song what would it be?

As cheese ball as it sounds I'd have to say "Fame" by Irene Cara

Does your cock have a nickname and if so how did it come about?

Not really, but years ago before the movies friends and I would laugh as I would twirl my cock about and sing the "Tootsie Roll" by 69 Boyz.

That's better than a nickname. Do you have any plans or hopes about where you want this career to take you?

I did attend my first GAVYN Awards in 2007. That would be very cool to win an award.

What factors do you think have been the most instrumental in your success as an adult film star?

I think the fact that I have remained true to myself about what industry I'm in and not let it go to my head is one of the main factors. I also do my best in remaining professional and treating this like any other job. I also keep a clean body, health and mind. I like the idea of people wanting to work with me again.

LEEROY **LELLEK**

How did you get started in the business?

After having a very spiritual nearly non-sexual phase in life I didn't know what to do next and found an ad in a Berlin gay newspaper (Siegessäule) that a new porn company was looking for actors. I did a public casting in a Berlin club and landed on the cover of the movie.

What were you looking for when you got into it?

For new experiences and a way to show my sexuality since I believed that I do not need to hide it and that it's natural. Also I wanted to express with my look (shaved head, piercing, tattoos which were not mainstream in Berlin at that time; people called me a Nazi in the street because of that shaved head!) something special. And the look succeeded!

Did you surprise yourself? Was it

STATS

BIRTH DATE: January 22, 1969

SIGN: Aquarius, ascendant Gemini

HOMETOWN: Berlin, Germany. Born in Bacharach very close to Loreley, Rhine River, Germany

HEIGHT: 1.86 meters

WEIGHT: 82 kilo/164 lbs

TWO BEST CHARACTER TRAITS: Honesty, sensitivity

TWO WORST CHARACTER TRAITS: I do expect a lot of myself and others; that can be too pushy or pitiless. I live my fantasies.

FAVORITE MUSIC: Soul, Celtic harp, heavy metal. Aretha Franklin, Annie Lennox, Michael Jackson, loads of stuff.

FAVORITE MOVIES: *The Piano, The Thief of Baghdad*, everything without cars and explosions.

FAVORITE MOVIES I'VE BEEN IN: *Bulging Bavarians* by Cazzo, Berlin, *French Kiss* by Reddevil, Los Angeles/Paris, *A Night at Bruno's* by Chi Chi Larue/Rascal, Berlin/Los Angeles

XXX COSTARS I'D DO AGAIN IN A MINUTE: Johnny Hazzard, Thom Barron

IF I COULD MAKE ONE REQUEST ON A PORN SET IT WOULD BE: Everybody on the team should be naked, including director, cameramen, and photographers.

AS A TEEN I ALWAYS FANTASIZED ABOUT SEX WITH: An anonymous half naked hunk walking down the railroad, and the butch employee of my father, and a cute sexy punk living in my village, and ...

CURRENT FANTASY MAN: None. I concentrate on the moment.

SEXIEST PART OF A MAN: The ear (when I lick it ...)

THREE INGREDIENTS OF MY HOTTEST SEX FANTASY: White briefs, a lot of huge black dicks and oil. I like contrasts.

FAVORITE ITEM IN MY SEXUAL TOY BOX: Ayurvedic mud powder

MOST PRIZED POSSESSION: Freedom.

HOBBIES: Sports (fitness, bike) gardening, traveling

PETS: A white rabbit with blue eyes and a bunch of goldfish.

PET PEEVES: Disrespect, self destruction.

Leeroy Lellek [PHOTO BY JEORG WENDT-GAUDREAULT, COURTESY LELLEK]

something you didn't really foresee yourself doing until you just jumped in?

I always liked to show off, but never naked, always with clothes. I even learned fashion design and made really eccentric clothes for myself and others. But I never expected my exhibitionism to lead me into XXX movies. When I was 21 I had a two-year relationship with a black dancer, and I must say I was shocked when he danced one day nude on stage. I was also raised very conservative.

Were the people who knew you surprised when you started making adult films?

Yes, some. But I must say most of the time in my life I was a lone rider, not caring too much what other people thought about me. When I presented my first porn cover to my parents on the coffee table their faces looked pretty surprised.

Do you recall the first movie you made and the first bit of instruction the director gave you?

After the *Order*: he (Thom Barron) is peeping out of a bush on you and you are chipping the wood with an axe. The director just said who would be active and who would be passive. We enjoyed it so much that we lengthened it and switched.

If someone were to come to you for advice about getting into the business what would you tell him?

First I would say: don't do it! Look for another job! If he insists I'd say do only what you'd also do it without a cam, don't let someone urge you in any direction. Be creative, spontaneous, authentic. Dare to change orders if they appear stupid to you. Stop immediately if anything seems strange or feels bad! Don't do it for the money if you don't have fun while doing it! And don't take drugs. If your partner does not give you a kick ask for the next one!

What is the most sexually aroused you have ever been on screen?

The scene that was very real for me was in *Army Dreams* – the sleeping room scene, a typical teenager fantasy. You are in a room, everything dark, all beds are full of naked guys with big dicks. You realize the guy in the other bed stares at you and starts wanking off. I came without touching myself as the atmosphere was really tense and hot. Guess it gave me such a thrill that I never had that in my youth.

If we were making a movie called Leeroy's Orgy who would you want as your four costars?

Bobby Blake, Ray Dragon, Marco da Silva and Tim Hamilton.

As your porn set demand you listed the crew must be naked, too. Do you have some fantasy that goes along with that?

A naked person is more sensitive when he's aroused. The sexual atmosphere would increase a lot if the cameraman's dick would get a short blowjob in between. Also I wouldn't mind the director wanking it on the set. He'll do it later anyway. The fantasy of it would be to have some magic moments where the whole crew is having sex but still functioning and filming the movie. If the actors can concentrate while having sex (where's the light, the hand, the camera) the others should be able to do their jobs erect, too, I guess.

So you have worked in movies in both Berlin and in the States. How would you say the two differ in terms of the industry?

German producers do not ask for pumped meat. You can be natural, meaning 72 kilos having 186 cm. Also they would not book you to perform a fetish you don't have. The U.S. market asks for more pounds and bigger dicks. They have no problem putting some leather on a smiling beach boy. There's much more weight on the pictures / stills (for advertising) in the U.S. market. The sexual action needs to look hot in the U.S. – and to be hot in the German productions.

What things do you usually do to prepare yourself for a film shoot?

Besides exercising and a sun tan – creaming my face and body often and I definitely have 2-3 days of no sex before a movie. I check fingernails, feet, ass, shave my hole and balls, burn the hair from my ears, cut the eyebrows – just a lot of taking care of myself.

And how do you usually spend the evening after a day of filming?

Well, to be really honest that ranges from crying in the night up to having fun with friends or simply sex with strangers. Depending on how the movie went. And how much energy it took or gave.

XXX movies are notorious for putting guys in some very awkward sexual positions for the sake of the camera. What is the most awkward position you've ever had to assume on film?

There were several. They really like to do that. The most horrible was a tiny little wooden bench used in *Army Dreams*. First my partner had to lay on that getting fucked by me and then I had to lay on that and it was breaking my back. What a fucking fuck-fuck!

What about making XXX movies has surprised you the most?

The fees that are paid in Germany. The ease with which you are replaced by the next fresh face / body / dick. The fact that if you sell your sexuality you'll loose something. And win something.

So what have you gained and what have you lost?

I lost unfortunately a little of my sensitivity and some of my playfulness. I gained a lot of power and personality. The biz often turned me towards: "Look bad / angry / hard," I regret that there are at the moment no sensitive, romantic sensual types of role models in porn for gays. And I doubt if super-macho is the right way.

What's the biggest example of bad behavior you have ever witnessed on a film set?

One thing I couldn't believe was a director that exploded when any person smoked a cigarette close to (15 meters away from) the set, shouting that that stuff kills people (well that's true ...) but had no problems feeding half of the crew with cocaine from his bag. But I guess this question aims more in the direction of a new actor who was running around and shouting: I am the most beautiful one.

Is it tough, educational, hilarious, or arousing to watch yourself in a movie?

Arousing meaning sexy/horny? No! At least not for me. It's like watching two dogs fucking. I must say I do not watch the movies I do anymore. In the beginning I was shocked. Most people are never confronted with the face they make when cumming. I was. But if you ask in general if it's educational to see yourself acting in a movie I must say yes, it helps to develop a higher consciousness, you see the whole situation from above and from another view. That's exactly what a guru tells you to exercise in life. To change the view.

"A director exploded when any person smoked a cigarette close to the set, shouting that that stuff kills people... but had no problems feeding half of the crew with cocaine from his bag."

Do you have some great sexual fantasy you are just waiting for some director to ask you to film?

I'd love to be the bottom in an interracial gangbang scene, but I guess that is more a kind of usual fantasy. Another one would be a very romantic scene happening by a waterfall with butterflies around.

Is sex for you a spiritual experience?

Good sex is. An orgasm is the closest experience to religious ecstasy. It's the natural state of being of the soul – pure ecstasy. In life we forget that. There were spiritual leaders who said: You have to experience (and live!) sex to discover what comes after. Well, nobody is born holy; you can become holy after you are a sinner; that's my opinion.

Looking back on your youth is there some episode that you recall that makes you think, "That child is destined to grow up to be a porn star"?

Definitely. I had a teddy bear for whom my mother knitted a cap with strips to tie it around the neck. I took that knitted cap, placed the hood on my tiny penis (guess I was five or six or something like that) tied the strips like a tanga around the waist and appeared dancing in front of my parents and the visiting neighbors. Well, they should have been prepared!

Is a tanga like a thong or g-string?

Yes, a tanga is like a G-string, so I invented that at the tender age of five.

When people recognize you from your films, do you notice if they treat you any differently than they would otherwise?

Yes. definitely. Some freeze like "Uh, he's famous / a star / not from this planet!" others think I probably like to fuck 24/7. In Germany most people try to show me that they know what I do but that for them it's nothing special, that it's normal. They don't have that fan-attitude like Americans "Can I take a picture / have an autograph?"

What is the oddest/strangest/most unique request a fan has ever made of you?

There never was anything strange. When fans have addressed to me they have always been very polite and never asked for strange stuff. They've been very respectful. I'm thankful for that!

Have you ever been stalked?

Yes. It was a person that adored me, built an altar with my pictures and tried to make me kill him. A kind of demon that tried to swallow my existence. It was very hard to get rid of him. It sucked and spoiled two years of my life. That's the price.

That's creepy. When you pass a hot looking man on the street what causes you to turn around and do a double take every time?

Talking about cars the only car that makes me turn around my head is a jaguar E-type from the sixties. And you can imagine as often as I see that car it's about that often that I see a man who causes me to turn my head. Maybe once a month or less. He needs a strong personality, something special in the eyes and a kind of dancer's walk. It's not any special type, it's more an attitude or state of being.

How do we get you into bed and what do we do with you once we get you there?

Either you make me tired and I fall in your bed! Or you are able to flirt without pushing. A good talk helps to raise my interest. If the kissing is good the job is done. What to do with me in bed? If I'm still there in the morning you did the right thing! I'm versatile and very open-minded and like to play. Any creative idea will catch my interest! Offer me a bed of roses! And then be sensual!

Where is the wildest place you've ever had sex?

In a an open cable car moving slowly above the Rhine River, the vineyard, and passing a lot of tourists ...

I want to hear more about that ...

This cable car was in Rüdesheim/Rhine Valley. You drive one way uphill toward the Germania, one way downhill towards the village, the downhill cars pass by your car. The cars are open, but you see only till the waist. I was young, twenty and unpacked my dick in the sunshine, my at that time boyfriend sucked it and wanked it till I came, that was it. For a movie I would make the scene a bit more extravagant.

Speaking sexually, very few men are as skilled as me when it comes to ...

Riding on a big dick professionally. At least I've heard that.

So you like to ride a nice big dick, huh? In that case who has given you "the ride of your life" on screen?

I must say this did not happen till now on screen. My biggest talent is still not caught on celluloid. But I must admit I became more joyfully passive over the last year and had my best scenes privately without a cam in sight. So there's still a job to do!

How would you describe yourself in a personals ad?

Is that the stuff when you try to get married in a newspaper?

Yes.

38/186cm/84kg, male, attractive, used, with a little damage and decoration available now! (Or for rent?)

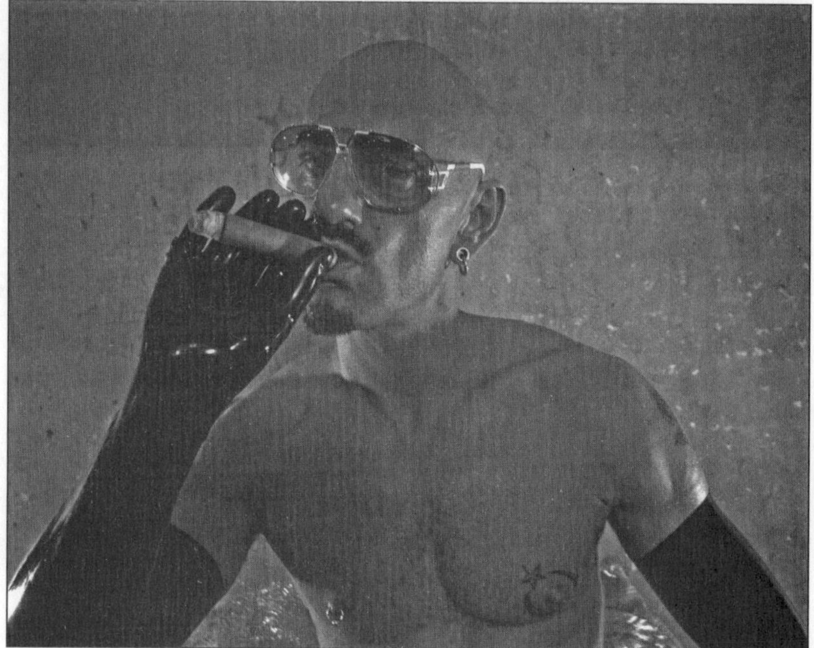

Leeroy Lellek [PHOTO BY JEORG WENDT-GAUDREAULT, COURTESY LELLEK]

How do you think you are a typical Aquarian?

Aquarians are said to be creative, full of fantasy, like to idealize, talk/discuss, be philosophical and rational, live in fantasy worlds, want to make the world better than it is. All that is typical me. But also I learned a lot from partners/lovers/friends, so I gained new character aspects like exploring the unconsciousness (what most Aquarians hate, as it's not logical), to be eager like a Capricorn or balanced like a Libra. What a lot of Aquarians do not have is the inner fire, like an emotional outburst, but after twenty years in Berlin I can do that very well.

Describe your dream vacation.

It should be in Asia, Thailand or India, a very colorful strange country with an ocean, warmth, palm trees, nature, things to discover, strange temples, plants, animals. Somewhere I can walk around only wrapped with a scarf around my hips without people staring. I should be accompanied by a very nice guy, trying to fulfill all my wishes – a kind of muscular black sultan with a huge dick. An alternative would be Mexico, but that holiday would be a more spiritual experience.

How do you use Ayurvedic mud powder?

It's a very fine powder consisting of minerals and herbs. You wet the body (shower) then you massage the powder on the whole body, including face/hair. It gives a sensation to the skin. If you look right away with that stuff in the mirror you won't recognize yourself, you look like a native and feel like an animal. If you are alone I'm sure you will wank off, if you are not alone, have fun! It goes with condoms (they should be the stronger ones)

Describe your ideal romantic evening.

A warm country, sea view, having a dinner in an open restaurant with candles, live music and wine. Afterwards a walk on the beach, then sex in a natural place (a waterfall, the ocean, sand dunes) with a lot of touching, talking and kissing. Quite normal, isn't it?

Where do you hope this career in XXX takes you?

When I started 1997 I never thought it would lead anywhere or that people would remember my name, recognize me or that I would still be doing it successfully after ten years. Now I hope that I can be something like a guiding star for youngsters and also people who are not brave enough to follow their impulses. Personally for me I expect experiences (yes, there are still a few sexual experiences I have not done) and in the upcoming two years a house with a garden in a beautiful warm country with palm trees, a loving husband and lots of children. I want a life full of happiness where at the very end, when I fall down dead I will not think: "Ah, well I forgot to do that and now life is over ..." In one word: Satisfaction on several levels. And then I'm on to the next planet.

CJ **MADISON**

What kind of dog do you have?

A Lab/pitbull mix named Chelsea.

How did you get started in the business?

Chad Donovan met me go-go dancing at KRAVE, Las Vegas, and asked if I ever wanted to do porn, I said maybe, and the rest is history.

So what is the secret to being a successful go-go dancer?

Give them what they want – but not too much, never wear underwear or G-strings. I only wear outfits that are homoerotic – black boots, camouflage shorts and dog tags for example.

What were you looking for when you got into making XXX movies?

An outlet for my exhibitionism.

Have you always been an exhibitionist?

Yes, I remember being 14 and having our roof being fixed on a Saturday morning and they had a ladder out my window, so when I heard the guys working I got naked and pretended I was asleep hoping they'd stop and stare as they went by my window.

So is the exhibitionism of being a porn star and knowing all those people are going to be at home with their DVD players watching you better than being a go-go dancer and having a smaller audience there live?

STATS

BIRTH DATE: October 15, 1971

SIGN: Scorpio

HOMETOWN: Philadelphia

HEIGHT: 6'3"

WEIGHT: 210 lbs

TWO BEST CHARACTER TRAITS: I'm honest and trustworthy.

TWO WORST CHARACTER TRAITS: I'm sometimes lazy and bored easily.

FAVORITE MUSIC: Alternative

FAVORITE MOVIES: Action movies

FAVORITE MOVIES I'VE BEEN IN: *Miami, Drifters*

XXX COSTAR I'D DO AGAIN IN A MINUTE: Roman Raggazi

IF I COULD MAKE ONE REQUEST ON A PORN SET IT WOULD BE: Red Bull!

AS A TEEN I ALWAYS FANTASIZED ABOUT SEX WITH: Antonio Sabato, Jr.

SEXIEST PART OF A MAN: His smile.

THREE INGREDIENTS OF MY HOTTEST SEX FANTASY: The outdoors, a beautiful man, it's raining

FAVORITE ITEM IN MY SEXUAL TOY BOX: Vibrating anal beads

MOST PRIZED POSSESSION: My boyfriend

HOBBIES: Music and friends

PETS: My dog

PET PEEVES: Being late

The exhibitionism in porn for me is the top of the line. One reason I started doing it is because I didn't get off anymore on all the other stuff; I think it's the pinnacle of being an exhibitionist.

When you pass a hot looking guy on the street what gets you to turn around and do a double take every time?

The thought of me wanting to taste his ass.

"I remember being 14 and having our roof being fixed on a Saturday morning and they had a ladder out my window. I got naked and pretended I was asleep hoping they'd stop and stare as they went by my window."

Do you recall your first film and the first bit of direction you were given?

Yes, *Play On* from Studio 2000 and Chad Donovan the director telling me to, "Eat that ass CJ!"

What things do you usually do to prepare for filming?

No sex for two days before filming, no partying, drinking, etc., for about a week before, the gym every day for a week, and I only use Cialis.

And how do you typically spend the evening after a long day of shooting?

In my hotel room bed resting!

If someone were to come to you for advice about getting into the business what would you tell him?

Don't be an exclusive right off. Look around see what companies you like before you commit to working for one for a year straight.

Where is the wildest place you've ever had sex?

Personally, off a second story fire escape on 15th and 9th Avenues in NYC with people walking by watching us.

People oftentimes consider XXX stars to be ideal specimens, but if you could change one thing about yourself through cosmetic surgery what would it be?

I wish I could say – but I really like me, of course I feel fat all the time, but I know that's just mind games and funny mirrors.

Describe your ideal romantic evening.

My boyfriend and I had one not too long ago, a great candlelight dinner, movie, and a snuggle at home followed by dirty hot sex.

Speaking sexually, very few guys are as skilled as me when it comes to ...

Eating ass.

Do you have some great fantasy you are just waiting for some director to ask you to film?

I think it would be hot to fuck with non-porn people watching and taking them by surprise.

How do you think the XXX experience has changed you?

It's freed me sexually.

CJ Madison [PHOTO COURTESY HOT HOUSE ENTERTAINMENT]

Is it impossible, uncomfortable, educational, or arousing to watch yourself in a movie?

Educational. My roommate gives me notes on how I do and how I've gotten better or worse from film to film. Really it's an excuse for us to pull out the vodka and laugh for an hour!

When it comes to seducing a man I've found that nothing works better than ...

Being honest and genuine. (Laughing). Please, I tell it like it is if I want to play with them, I tell them, and if they aren't in my car ten minutes later then I know I wouldn't have had any fun with them to begin with.

How would you describe yourself in a personals ad?

Tall Italian with a fat cock waiting to have fun! (Laughing). Honestly, I would never have an ad. I never needed one. Is that cocky?

If you were making a movie called CJ's Orgy who would you want as your four costars?

OK, get ready! Jesse Santana, Dean Flynn, Francois Sagat, Roman Ragazzi, Collin O'Neal, Trevor Knight, Erik Rhodes, Steve Cruz, Jake Deckard, and Cort Donovan.

That's a few more than four but what the hell. Describe your dream vacation.

One week in Hawaii with my boyfriend on a white sand beach with no clothes.

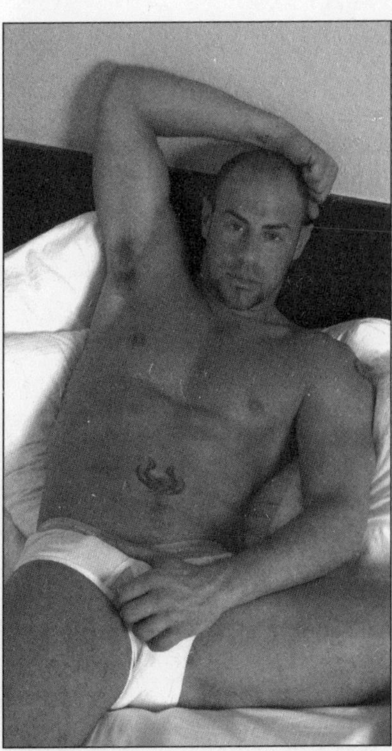

CJ Madison [PHOTO BY KENT TAYLOR, COURTESY RAGING STALLION STUDIOS]

DANNY **MANN**

How did you get started in the business?

I had some pictures posted on Big Muscle and Big Muscle Bears. Teddy Marks from Butchbear contacted me asking if I'd be interested in posing for them, I said yes immediately. They really helped me get my start and I thank them for that.

What were you looking for when you got into it?

I had always wanted to just do one movie, even just one scene, just because I like porn and wanted to do one. I have now done a few, and they have all been great, and the hot sex hasn't been too bad either.

Do you recall the first movie and the first bit of direction you were given?

Oh yeah. I actually did my first scene with a straight guy, we wanted to do porn and his girlfriend said OK but only with guys, so he tried it, and my luck I got to suck him off for a

STATS

BIRTH DATE: December 21, 1970

SIGN: Capricorn

HOMETOWN: Born in Southampton, PA, but I live in Atlanta, GA

HEIGHT: 5'11"

WEIGHT: 210-220 lbs

TWO BEST CHARACTER TRAITS: I'm willing and loyal

TWO WORST CHARACTER TRAITS: I bite my nails – really bad!

FAVORITE MUSIC: Bluegrass, folk,circuit morning music,deep tribal.

FAVORITE MOVIES: *The Big Chill*, the *Bourne* series

FAVORITE MOVIES I'VE BEEN IN: *Centurion Muscle II*

XXX COSTAR I'D DO AGAIN IN A MINUTE: Brendan Davies (*Nailed*); that is one fucking hot sexy man!

IF I COULD MAKE ONE REQUEST ON PORN SET IT WOULD BE: Less talking and more grunts and groans.

AS A TEEN I ALWAYS FANTASIZED ABOUT SEX WITH: Firemen, Lee Majors (The Six Million Dollar Man).

CURRENT FANTASY MAN: John Cena, Randy Orton, Gage Weston, Christian Volt

SEXIEST PART OF A MAN: Bunny patch, the little divot that's hairy right at the top of the butt crack and cheeks.

THREE INGREDIENTS OF MY HOTTEST SEX FANTASY: Big furry muscles, a cigar, and my Fire Department ball cap.

FAVORITE ITEM IN MY SEXUAL TOY BOX: My mind

MOST PRIZED POSSESSION: My Grandfather's department issued sleeping blankets from when he joined the Boston Fire Department in 1928. Very thin wool in red and black flannel checks.

HOBBIES: Gym, travel, camping, cooking, dancing and trivia

PETS: Mr. Hobbs, my cat of 16 years. I've had him since he was three weeks old

PET PEEVES: Bad drivers, ignorant people, bad drunks and rude people.

Danny Mann [PHOTO BY KENT TAYLOR, COURTESY RAGING STALLION STUDIOS]

few hours. It was kind of hot. I think straight guys are hot like so many gay men do.

Do you think you are a natural exhibitionist?

In most cases, not so much with big crowds. I like being watched, but the thought of doing it somewhere crazy or out of the norm, and possibly getting caught excites me more.

When it comes to driving a man wild in bed I've found nothing works better than ...

My blowjobs. I love to suck cock.

What is the most turned on you have ever been in a movie?

Playing with Colin West's ass in *The Red and The Black*. I got to punch his ass and taste his sweet hole.

XXX is notorious for putting the guys in tough positions for the sake of the shot. What is the toughest position you've had to assume for the camera?

Nailed (Mustang) the end scene when we tried to stay balanced on a pile of old tires. The scene was hot, but the tires just wouldn't stay stacked.

Where is the wildest place you've ever had sex – off camera?

Hmm. I gotta to think a few minutes. Boiler room of Roseland Ballroom in NYC for the Black Party. Snuck down there with this huge muscle farm boy and sucked his cock as he leaned against the old grease boiler; it was fucking hot.

If some guy came up to you and asked for advice about getting into the business what would you tell him?

Pick a good name, one that fits you, and take it slow.

Describe your ideal romantic evening.

Curled up in a huge bed with tons of pillows, and a hot furry muscle fireplug on one side and a big furry muscle daddy on the other.

I'm curious, were you always attracted to bears even as a young guy or did you develop the attraction only as you became more of a bear yourself?

I was always attracted to big daddy types and always looked at older mature men. I'd have to say they were always probably bears.

I first realized I was a porn star when ...

I saw the cover of *Muscle Bear Hotel* and realized it was my ass I was looking at.

So what is the main difference between you in everyday life and Danny Mann the porn star?

Not that much, maybe I am more reserved on screen. (Laughing) What you see on screen is really a big part of me, and I wanted it that way. I want people to know that what you see on screen is what you'd get from me at home.

What can we do to get your cock hard in a second?

Whimper.

So you initially only wanted to do one scene to say you had done it and now you have done several. Have you also developed any further career aspirations for the XXX business ... any thoughts about working behind the camera?

I would like to write porn stories. I have always wanted to write stories for *Hand Jobs* magazine. I have tons of stories in my head. I wouldn't mind directing a movie or two. I have a few ideas that I think would transfer to film very well.

Going along with that, what things have learned from being in front of the camera that would help make you that much more skilled as a director?

To give the guys some direction and set up but also to just let them do their thing. It would be very important to get the right guys together. Sometimes I watch a porn and I think, "Those guys don't look right together," or, "That doesn't look right."

So can you give me a typical casting scenario (or a couple) for how you get most of your film roles?

There is really only one thing to say: JD Slater. He has always cast me with the right guys. We talked a lot and still do and he just knows the right guy to cast me with.

Is it educational, arousing, uncomfortable, or unbearable to watch yourself on screen?

Funny you ask. For me it's uncomfortable, but if there's someone else watching at the same time it's unbearable. I just can't do it, but I'm also the type of guy that blushes and doesn't take compliments well.

What surprised you the most about making XXX movies?

How much starting and stopping there is. What you see as 20-30 minutes could be up to six hours.

Do you get recognized very often and if so what is the most memorable fan encounter you have had?

Yes, I have had it happen a few times. There are two times that I remember most. Once I picked up this hot little fucker (I have a thing for short fireplug kind of guys). We went home and were playing for a while, I was fucking him for a good hour or so when I got him face to face, started kissing him and he looked at me and said, "I have been waiting three years for you to fuck me like this, and have jerked off to this moment hundreds of times." He sure was lucky he was so cute, and had a hot ass because I almost lost my hard-on and had to stop. Second time, I was at my fuck buddy's house (well he's my ex we just have great sex together) we had two other guys over, he put in *Centurion Muscle II Alpha*. Well, fifteen minutes into my scene the guy I was fucking doggy style looked up at the TV and starting talking about how hot the two guys are, he went on and on for a few minutes when my friend looks him in the eye, points to me on the screen and says ... "Umm that's who's fucking your hole." He whipped his head around, and I just looked at him and smiled big and rammed my cock into him so hard he blew his load.

Have you ever been stalked?

Oh, God yes. Most times it's just stares, but there's this one guy in Atlanta that knew all these weird things about me, things I didn't know. Whenever I would be out he would always follow me around the club, then one night he actually pushed a friend of mine who I was dancing with out of the way to stand behind me. My friend flipped out on him and the guy starting getting all freaked out. It was a bit much, so I went home and an hour later he was sitting in the parking lot of my apartment complex. It freaked me out

If we were to make a movie called Danny's Orgy who would you want as your four costars?

Wow, only four – Jake Decker, Dean Coulter, Pete Kuzack, Randy Orton and John Cena (WWF wrestlers). They would be at the top of my list but there are so many more ...

Have you ever developed a crush on any of your costars, care to name names?

I was once quoted in an article as saying, "Dean Coulter has an amazing ass. I'd eat it for a week," and I had never met him.

What things do you typically do to help you prepare for a porn shoot?

I'm like I am sure a lot of guys and do have my own routine. Lots of time at the gym, lots of protein shakes, eat eat eat (I am 215 lbs) once I am on set, there's a whole other routine I go through. I like to talk with my partner for a bit, just to get to know each other and make sure we're on the same page.

And what do you typically do after a hard day of filming?

Eat! I love a good milk shake and piece of pie once I'm done.

What is the most drama you have ever encountered on a XXX set?

I have a personal motto is not to kiss and tell. I wouldn't want anyone to do that about me. But for myself, well there's one horror story. Sometimes you need a little help staying hard for a long period of time and I used a little too much of something. Well, after eleven hours I was still hard. I had to go to the emergency room. One hour, a small procedure and some good morphine later, my hard-on was gone. It's a great war story for the grandkids.

If someone were to offer you a role in a fetish film how far do you think you would go before the cameras?

Considering that I have a ton a fetishes myself (Firemen) I think I would get into some pretty kinky scenes. That said, when I started out on this journey, I set some guidelines and parameters for myself. I have wavered on them a few times, but what are rules made for if not to be broken. I guess I wouldn't do anything that would harm or tarnish the persona of Danny Mann, and I wouldn't do anything I'd have to fake being into.

"After eleven hours I was still hard. I had to go to the emergency room. One hour, a small procedure and some good morphine later, my hard-on was gone. It's a great war story for the grandkids."

Do you have some special fantasy that you are just waiting for some director to ask you to film?

More like tons of them. If I had to narrow it down, it would be more along the lines of a locker room scene after football practice, and I piss a few guys off and they end up ganging up on me. I get used by the team – say 8-10 guys, and when I say used, I mean I'm treated like a whore – no mercy, maybe even to the point where I cry.

Do you think the industry has a responsibility regarding the use of condoms and/or promoting safe sex?

To some degree. by now if you don't know what is safe and what isn't well you must be living under a rock. I think it is more up to the individual to hold himself responsible.

If you could change one thing about the way the industry is currently run what would it be?

Bigger muscles, less shaving, more facial hair.

Do you have any childhood or adolescent memory that you can look back upon and say, "Oh yeah, that kid was destined to grow up to be a porn star"?

I always was starting the neighborhood gang or club and initiation always involved some sort of sex act.

How would you describe yourself in a personals ad?

Laid back jeans and t-shirt and wrist cuff kinda guy, and a bit of a musclebear.

When it comes to seducing a man I've found that nothing works better than ...

A deep kiss, one of my blowjobs, and a few strokes in my ass.

If you had to choose between sex and love which would you choose and what are your thoughts about fidelity?

Danny Mann [PHOTO BY KENT TAYLOR, COURTESY RAGING STALLION STUDIOS]

Hmm. I'd have to choose both. I'm a guy that can be in love and still just have sex. If fidelity works for you great; it hasn't worked so good for me. Not that I'm out fucking around 24/7, but I do like to play once and awhile.

What is the biggest misconception people have about you when you meet them?

That I am mean or stuck up. Actually I'm very shy.

Describe your dream vacation.

Las Vegas and Seattle put together. Buffets, slots, heat, with great mountains and forest to hike. I know they are opposites in climate but you asked.

If your life had a theme song what would it be?

"Dive" by Debby Holiday

If you had to compare yourself to an animal what species do you think best captures your essence and why?

I've always thought of myself as a wolf – great alone, but better in a pack. Plus they are beautiful animals.

How do you think you are a typical Capricorn?

Very independent, strong willed, great memory, and an insatiable desire for knowledge.

So now that you are in the industry how long or far do you plan on taking this career?

I think a lot of that isn't up to me. I think some of that has to do with what guys are looking for in porn. I also know that I am sort of typecast, I'm a Muscle Bear, it's not like I can shave off all my chest hair and appeal to a new audience, So that has a lot to do with it. But as long as I am offered work and it looks good and feels good I would keep going, I am getting to the age where I can start playing the sexy older daddy type. Oh wait, I already do.

MARKIE

How did you get started in the business?

I sent in pictures to *In Touch for Men* the magazine in 1998. The owner liked me and flew me to LA for the photo shoot. I also did *In Touch for Men: Auditions Volume 5*. That was my first professional photo shoot, and first ever appearance on DVD.

What were you looking for when you got into it?

I always wanted to be famous. I never knew what I could do as far as talent. I just thought it would be so much. Porn was the first door that opened for me to be famous. I never directly set out to do it. I fell into it. I love it still after all these years. Now, I am looking to win an award. That is the goal now!

Has being in XXX movies brought you the fame you wanted?

Yes it has. About two years ago I went on a little East Coast tour (ten cities) I was with Scott the owner of Factory Productions. We went into every XXX store in all these cities, and some of the clubs, too. The people working in each store recognized me right off, so I signed photos and some DVDs. I

BIRTH DATE: July 14, 1980

SIGN: Cancer

HOMETOWN: Los Gatos, CA

HEIGHT: 6'1"

WEIGHT: 160 lbs

TWO BEST CHARACTER TRAITS: My brain and my cock.

TWO WORST CHARACTER TRAITS: My brain and my cock.

FAVORITE MUSIC: Pop

FAVORITE MOVIES: Horror

FAVORITE MOVIES I'VE BEEN IN: *Swim Meat Lovers, In Pretty Deep, Bone Alone 2: Lust in LA*

XXX COSTAR I'D DO AGAIN IN A MINUTE: Michael Brandon, Desmond Montclair, Benjamin Bradley

IF I COULD MAKE ONE REQUEST ON A PORN SET IT WOULD BE: ID Lube Millennium always

AS A TEEN I ALWAYS FANTASIZED ABOUT SEX WITH: Joey Lawrence, Will Smith, Jeremy Jordan. Antonio Sabato, Jr.

CURRENT FANTASY MAN: Will Smith

SEXIEST PART OF A MAN: His full body

THREE INGREDIENTS OF MY HOTTEST SEX FANTASY: Wine, condoms, ID Lube

FAVORITE ITEM IN MY SEXUAL TOY BOX: 10" dildo

MOST PRIZED POSSESSION: Personally autographed 8x10 from Cher

HOBBIES: Singing, dancing, music, movies, clothes design, plants

PETS: none

PET PEEVES: Lying, arguments, immature people, stealing, yelling, loud people, bareback sex.

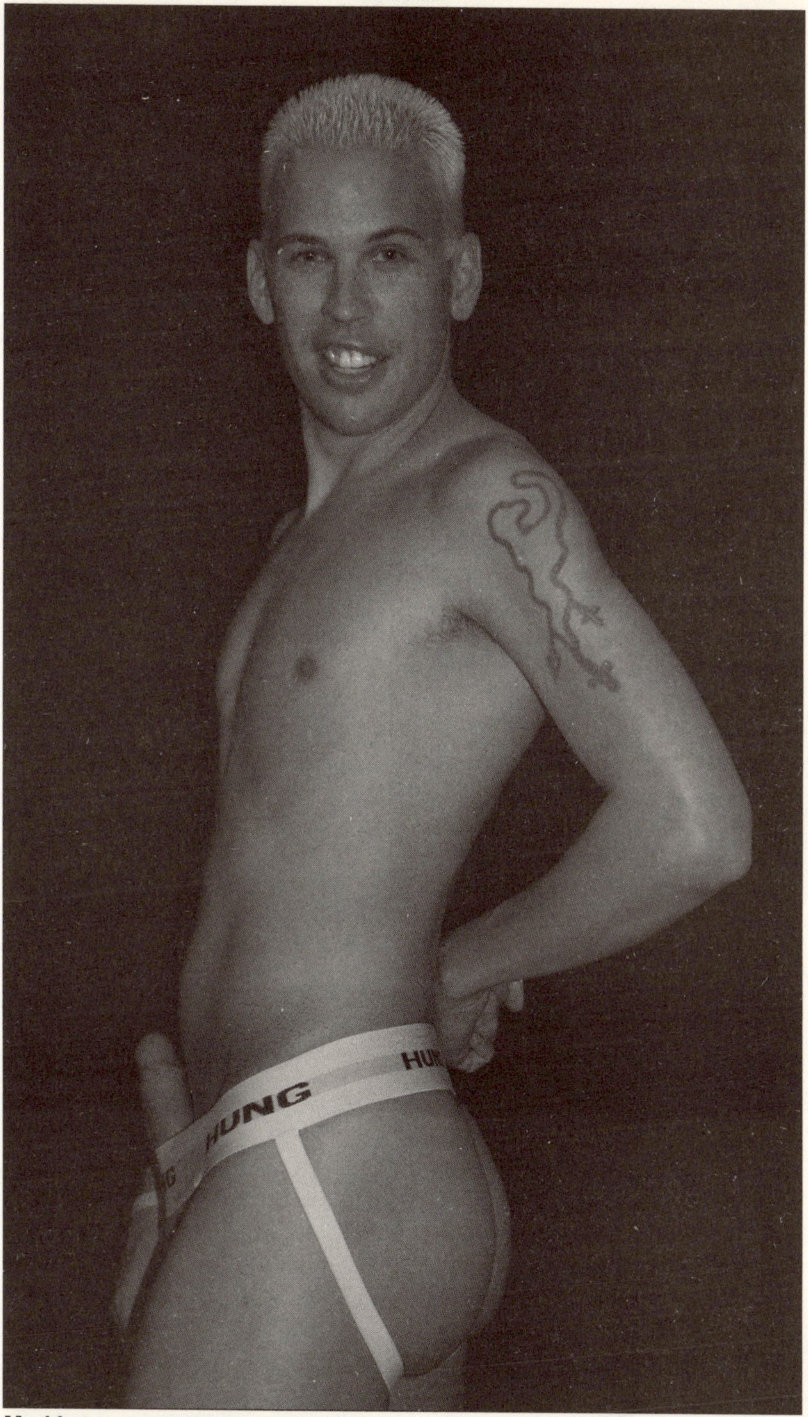

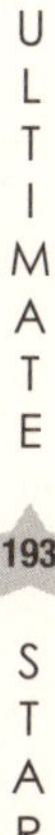

Markie [PHOTO COURTESY MARKIESBDC.COM]

could not walk down the street in the Castro, or in Philly without people coming up to me. In San Francisco I was the biggest. I would still like to be a bigger star! It is a working progress. I also have not changed in my six year career. I think I am good with fame.

Do you recall the first movie you did and the first bit of direction you were given?

The first two-way was for a film series called *New Meat*. I was on the cover and it was *New Meat #25*. I had the option to work with someone or the owner of the company. I chose the owner of the company because he was so hung, and he was experienced. I was pretty good in the film I must say.

What about making XXX movies surprised you?

The fact that no one tests their models or asks if you are HIV negative or positive. I thought that was surprising. The fact that a lot of my peers are not into drugs, and are really sweet guys. That was also really a surprise. When I first started, I never went to the parties or award shows because I thought it was all full of drugs. I was so wrong. I learned a lot, usually the hard way. I am HIV- just for the record. I only have safe sex both personally and professionally.

What do you usually do to prepare yourself for a XXX shoot?

I do a lot. I get a hair cut, bleach the hair, get a manicure and pedicure, tan, keep heavily to my workout schedule, and douche at least an hour before, and eat two hours before. I also do not cum for at least three days which is way hard to do!

And how do you usually spend the night after you get home from a day of filming?

I like to rest, have a nice big meal, glass of wine and rest. Watch a nice movie. I turn off the phones and completely relax. If I do a shoot out of town, I will relax at the hotel, and or call a close friend to talk about the shoot.

What is the most turned on you have ever been in a movie?

Well just recently, for my new site www.markiesbigdickclub.com, I topped this hot black guy named Alyx Lane. I was so turned on that I just had to fuck his wanting ass. He loved it and he shot past his head. I pulled out and shot past his head, too! It was intense and the best cum shot I have ever done so far. That was the hottest!

If a guy were to come to you for advice about getting into the business what would you tell him?

Listen, think, observe, and learn all you can. Find a mentor. Michael Brandon was my mentor on so much I didn't know about marketing yourself and your product. I also learned hell of a lot on my own. I have gotten every video shoot on my own, with the exception of my Catalina video called *It's a Hard Life*. My friend Frank Parker made a call and got me that gig. Stay substance free. Be alert. Never talk about anyone in the industry.

In what ways did Michael Brandon mentor you?

He would tell me things like, never talk about anyone if it is in a negative light. I really just learned from watching him and being around him. I saw how he interacted with his fans and friends. I learned how to network to the hilt. He works it like no one in the biz. He is like Madonna when it comes to marketing. This is something I have learned as well. Also you never know who you are talking to. You should always be nice to everyone. Though, this comes naturally for me. I was raised with manners to respect others.

What advice or pointers did he give?

Just to observe him. He would throw me up on stage with him a few times in San Francisco and Chicago, so I would get stage experience and be able to talk into a microphone with crowds of fans. This was great because I am so terribly shy. After a couple times I loved it. I really just learned a lot from being around him mostly. We're great friends today.

"[Michael Brandon] is like Madonna when it comes to marketing."

What is your secret to driving a man wild in bed?

I am orally talented. I have an ass that drives guys nuts! My ex from three years ago still wants to tap my ass. I am a great top as well. It is true that it takes a great bottom to make a great top. I can make any guy cum with my mouth. I have had straight men tell me they have never had oral from a guy like I give. They have come back, too!

How do we get you in the sack and what do we do with you once we get you there?

Well, if you're real, no bullshit, just yourself, and you have the guts to walk over to me – I am pretty much yours. I've been told that I am intimidating until someone talks to me, then they say, you're nothing like I thought. You're very nice and sweet. I don't know. Once you have me, you can massage me, as I love to be touched and you can do whatever you want. I like all things and I like it safe of course. I treat everyone as if they are positive, no offense, but just being safe here.

Where is the wildest place you've ever had sex?

The wildest place, were there are two actually. Once in my Iroc-Z Camaro with the Tee-Tops off in Chico, CA, in the summer with a hot guy named Josh. To this day he had the biggest cock I have ever been with. He was a true 12x7 cut. I had him in the passenger seat and climbed on top and rode that huge cock till I shot all over him. The other was with my ex (the same one from three years ago) and we met this boy at the pool in Garnerville, CA (just north of San Francisco). He drove his lesbian friend's Suburban. We did a three way in the back on a doggy bed! That was the wildest, cheapest, dirtiest place I have yet to have quick sex! The windows were all fogged up, too. It was funny!

Describe your ideal romantic evening.

I would like to have a nice dinner either at home or out. See a scary movie with my date or boyfriend. Dinner would consist of a nice glass of wine. (Just for the record, I like a nice shiraz, merlot, or Chardonay) love reds better. Just relax and forget about day to day life and wrap all my attention around the guy I am with. This could also consist of an out of town trip for the weekend to a ski resort, or someplace cold and snowy, or someplace warm and tropical. We can get heated up in both settings.

When you said people come up to you and expect you to be very different. Do you ask them what they are expecting?

Yes, they think I am going to be an asshole, like so many in this business. Then they are relieved to know, I have two brain cells to rub together and that I am a real person. They are surprised that I am so down to earth. They sometimes think, if he is all together, what's he doing porn for! I love what I do. It is a great outlet for me to express one part of my personality.

Have you ever done anything sexually on screen that you would never do in your personal life?

I give way better head and have way better sex in private than on screen, unless the guy is fucking hot. (Hello Brad Benton!) It is starting to change however. Owning my own company, the sex on camera is getting really hot for me and much more real.

If you were offered a role in a fetish film how far would you go?

I would not do a fetish film. No interest there.

I first realized I was a porn star when …

When the first fan come up to me and said they loved my films.

You mention being recognized frequently. What is a typical fan encounter like?

It is so cool. A fan comes up to me and usually says I loved you in such and such a film. We chat and I like to find out more about the person. I will ask them personal questions. I spend a lot of time with all my fans. It is a fun experience. I really enjoy it.

And have you had a most peculiar or interesting fan request?

Not really. My fans are really cool. They just want to say hi and are really respectful of me, and my time and whomever I am with.

Is it arousing, informative and educational, tough, or unbearable to watch yourself on screen?

(Laughing). Yes, the first thing I thought when I saw myself was, I didn't know I did that. We are our worst critic. I've seen all kinds of things I don't like or didn't know I did. I just did Jason Sechrest's radio show last Friday (Feb. 16, 2007) and I wanted to see what I looked like or how I came across, or what I forgot to say. You can learn. Cher when she is on tour would have the rehearsal taped, so she could see what to do differently to make the show better. I guess it is the same. You should watch yourself to learn. It's nice to see yourself and get past that part of critiquing.

What things do you think contribute to your success as a XXX star?

Honesty, charisma, down-to-earth, bubbly, sincere, sexy, and sexual. I also always meet every fan, I have spent many hours signing autographs to make sure everyone that came to the event got something from me. I really appreciate the fans because without them I would not be doing the thing that I am famous for. The fans are the biggest contribution.

Have you experienced any negative repercussions from your XXX career?

Not really. Well, OK, it is hard to have a relationship. That sucks out loud. Any other line of work and there is never an issue. The porn biz and it's a big deal.

Do you have some great fantasy you are just waiting for some director to ask you to film?

Hmm. I think I would like to have a gang bang with me and four hung black men. That would be hot!

People often think of adult film stars as perfect specimens, but if you could change one thing about your appearance with cosmetic surgery what would you have done?

Absolutely nothing. I like everything the way it is. My teeth are being straightened as we speak, so I guess that would be the only thing. I like everything the way it is.

What are the pros and cons of agent vs. no agent and where do you stand on the issue?

I sure did it the fucking hard way. It could have been so much easier had I found an agent. Not to say I have never tried. I have looked for years. Never found one that was worth a shit, and or one that would follow up on what he said. I have gotten used to doing everything on my own. Just seems to be the way I am supposed to go in life. I have it a little gritty. Just seems to be the way it is.

Do you think the industry has a responsibility regarding the use of condoms and/or promoting safe sex?

Absolutely! I think this whole bareback thing is way out of control. No wonder the government has stepped in. But with that being said you never hear much about the straight world using condoms. We all know they mostly do not. I guess the HIV is still alive and well and being promoted to the gay community. It's mystifying to me that anyone would risk death for a quick fuck. I always use and have used condoms.

If you could change one thing about the way the industry is currently run what would it be?

I would change that fact that we need more ethnicity. We need more Blacks and Latinos, and other races. I also think we need more body types. It seems that all that is out there is buff.

Do you have a game plan for your career in the business? Where do you want this to take you?

Ummm ... No. I put one foot in front of the other each day. I have no idea what I was doing when I started. There is no handbook on becoming a huge porn star. No one gives you advice. It is not an easy business. I have a real grasp on how it works now. I decided that becoming a company owner would do two things. One is piss the people off that thought I was a flash in the pan and would just

Markie [PHOTO COURTESY MARKIESBDC.COM]

go away. Two it would move me up to a level in this industry that few achieve. Michael Brandon is one that has achieved this status. I would like to do more films. It would be nice to work with one of my famous peers. I'm going into this new business phase of my porn career for the long haul, not to get rich quick. But when I am in my 40s and 50s I will still be earning a check from my web site.

Do you have any childhood or adolescent memory that you can look back upon and say, "Oh yeah, that kid was destined to grow up to be a porn star"?

No! But famous, yes. I was really popular in school. I didn't even know it until I left. (Laughing) People were still talking about me two years afterward. So I have this really cool thing I did when I was about 14. I would tape myself singing to Cher songs. The old video recorders you know VHS (Laughing). I have them and about over an hours worth of me, off key and dancing and such. But I have them now on DVD. I played it for a couple of close friends. They thought I really had star potential then and should really pursue music. So I guess I have always wanted to be famous and making a lasting impression has always come natural for me all my life. Just seems fitting. I love that I make a lasting impression. That is really the coolest thing. I love it!

How would you describe yourself in a personals ad?

Sexy, fun, blonde, talented, interesting, easy-going, sensual, seductive, eccentric, a realist, humorous, smart, clever, romantic, caring, thoughtful, and generous.

When you pass a hot looking guy on the street what gets you to turn around and do a double take every time?

Body usually or awesome eye contact. I am not shy here! Strange dichotomy I know. (Laughing). If I see someone I like, I go right up to them. I am human like everyone else, so I get turned down. I can honestly say that I'm happier to get turned down then to leave and think, shit I wish I would have went over and talked to that guy.

What is the best pick up line you have ever used or fallen for?

Hmm. I usually ask what is your name. Seems to work. (Laughing). Guys never come up to me. I have never fallen for a line. I don't believe in that kind of stuff. I believe if you want it just ask.

What's the easiest way to get you to cum?

Suck my cock and play with my balls. I love that. Or put a cock in my mouth.

If your life had a theme song what would it be?

"Ain't No Body's Business (If I Do)"

If you had to compare yourself to an animal what species do you think best captures your essence and why?

Leopard! Because I can be tame and sexy, and wild and sexy. I also try to look fabulous all the time. I think leopards look nice all the time. I also think they can be cute and nice when they are young, and can also be tough and wild.

Describe your dream vacation.

Gosh that is so far from my reality. I would like to have two weeks in a cabin in the snow with a hot boyfriend on Christmas. No family, just me and my boyfriend in a wooded cabin in the snow on the week before and the week of Christmas. That has always been a dream of mine. See, I'm very simple and easily amused,

ADRIANO **MARQUEZ**

How did you get started in the adult film business?

It is a very long story. I was in Miami. I just arrived from Europe, and I met a man named Robert. We started to talk about doing some movies with Kristen Bjorn ... and we did.

What were you looking for when you got into it?

Nothing in particular, in the beginning it was simply a matter of money and fulfilling one of my fantasies.

So did making XXX movies turn out to be the sort of fantasy you had in mind when got into the movies?

I must say yes, but it is not now. It is just a job for me. I try to give the best of myself every time, but when I finish, I go back to my life, and that's what is wonderful.

What advice did Kristen Bjorn give you when you were starting off in the business?

He has always been very nice to me. We are both in Barcelona now, too. It is very funny, but he never gave me any advice at all. I didn't need it. I was very aware of that world and all the limitations – the good things and the bad things, too.

I'm so curious, how does he get all you guys to cum without touching yourselves?

Adriano Marquez [PHOTO COURTESY TITANMEN.COM]

When we work together, the truth is after three days we where *soooooo* tired you just do it. And remember this was before there was Viagra. It was very hard mind work, especially if you are working with heterosexual guys. But as a real professional, cumming in situations like this was just fine.

What is the most sexually aroused you have ever been on screen in a XXX movie?

It was *Guardian Angel* – the place and the all cast was perfect for the movie and the results are there. The direction was fantastic, Bruce (Cam) for me is one of the best directors in porn because he works like a photographer, too bad things are not the same in that company but life is all about changes.

What things do you always do to prepare for a XXX film shoot?

The regular stuff. Get a clean hair cut, trim the beard, just get myself looking as good as I can for the camera. And it depends too on what the director asks me to look like.

And what do you usually do when you come home at the end of a day of filming?

I just say thanks and goodbye for the day. I take a very long bath, watch a movie, and go to sleep.

If you were offered a role in a fetish film how far sexually would you go for the camera?

Very far if the cast was fantastic, and the film has a big budget.

Have you ever developed a crush or strong feelings for any of your costars?

No never for me. It is just a job and I'm a very good professional. I never mix my life with work. I go to work, get paid, and then go home to my life.

You must have so many fans who ask you all sorts of things. What is the most unusual request any of them has ever made of you?

What always happens to me, and it is because I work all the time in the service industry, is: Wow, but you are so nice. Like I shouldn't be and I don't know if they are sad or happy about it. I have to say I've never had a bad time. But when I have a boyfriend then things change. They get really jealous and they go to him and say the bad things that they don't say to me. It is sad but it is part of this world. I'm very used to it.

STATS

BIRTH DATE: August 25, 1965

SIGN: Virgo

HEIGHT: 6'2"

WEIGHT: 200 lbs.

HOMETOWN: Barcelona

TWO BEST CHARACTER TRAITS: I get really excited about little things and I'm not scared of making changes in my life.

TWO WORST CHARACTER TRAITS: I'm very self-critical and a perfectionist so I expect the same of other people – so I'm frequently disappointed.

FAVORITE MUSIC: I love chill out music, all the Buddha Bar CDs.

FAVORITE MOVIES: *Moulin Rouge*

FAVORITE MOVIES I'VE BEEN IN: *Desert Train*

IF I COULD MAKE ONE DEMAND ON A XXX SET IT WOULD BE: I'd love to work in natural places with lots of beauty around us like in the Caribbean or in the desert.

AS A TEENAGER I FANTASIZED ABOUT SEX WITH: Big older men ... and I still like it.

MY CURRENT FANTASY MAN: If they have a baby face with a very tight body I'm totally lost. I prefer tight bodies to big bodies.

MY FAVORITE PART OF A MAN: Of course the butt. I just love a beautiful bubble butt. They are so powerful and people don't realize that.

FAVORITE TOY IN MY SEXUAL TOY BOX: I will say a big dildo is always good to have and all kinds of leather stuff. A mirror, too – I'm very visual.

MOST PRIZED POSSESSION: I think the less I have the freer I am.

HOBBIES: Cooking is my passion.

PETS: As much as I love dogs, I would like to have a big space for them to run.

Adriano Marquez [PHOTO COURTESY HOT HOUSE ENTERTAINMENT]

And the other thing I get a lot is: "You are much more handsome in real life," which I prefer to take as a compliment.

Where is the wildest place you have ever had sex?

I always get really nervous when I'm in a public place because I don't know the place.

Speaking sexually, very few men are as skilled as me when it comes to ...

Role playing. It is difficult sometimes to change for real. I guess that's what makes a good actor, and a good sex partner.

I enjoyed what you said about role playing. In sex, what is your favorite role to play?

I have many: daddy, slave-master ...

What is your favorite way to drive a man wild in bed?

Well sex for me is just physical and I listen to my partner. I always try to make sure he is happy, but I always make sure he knows what he has to do. I'm very bossy.

You mention you love to cook and I was wondering how you think cooking and sex are alike?

For me cooking is a way of living since I'm becoming a chef in July in Barcelona, so it is more than a passion, and I'm very very good. But to answer your question, I love to cook for people that I care about because into each plate I put lots of time and love. In sex it is similar to wanting to please people when I cook.

What is your dream vacation?

I would love to find a place to live and feel I'm on vacation when I return from my trips. The place closest to that for me is Miami, but if I have to choose a paradise I will choose any of the Caribbean Islands.

"The thing [fans will tell me] is: 'You are much more handsome in real life,' which I prefer to take as a compliment."

Describe your ideal romantic evening.

I'm very simple about that – a fantastic dinner where we can talk, maybe a play followed by a walk.

So Adriano, do you think you are a typical Virgo?

Not at all because my ascendant is Leo, I think I get more things from Leo than Virgo, even if my very close friends think I'm a very typical Virgo but I don't see it.

Where do you see yourself in life five years down the line?

Where I may be is in Miami because I have a great job offer to run a salon there, and as I said before it is paradise to me. If that doesn't work I'm in Barcelona finishing cooking school now and I will be chef in July. Then I may open something in Palm Springs. I have lots of projects.

What are you the most grateful for in your life?

My parents, and the place I come from, and the fantastic life I have. It is a dream. I've always done what I wanted to do and not many people can say that.

TRISTAN **MATHEWS**

What kind of dog is Bruizer?

He's a miniature Chihuahua.

How did you get started in the business?

Well, I had this friend that ran his own Internet porn company and he asked me to do a scene for him, and I really liked it and I asked him if knew any agents in the biz and here I am today.

What were you looking for when you got into it?

I was looking basically to have fun, have hot sex with guys, and make money while doing it.

What was your greatest fear about taking the plunge into XXX?

I didn't really have a big fear when entering the XXX business. I'm very comfortable with my sexuality and with sex in general.

Do you recall your first movie and the first bit of direction you were given?

STATS

BIRTH DATE: December 27, 1986

SIGN: Capricorn

HOMETOWN: East Haven, CT

HEIGHT: 5'8"

WEIGHT: 140 lbs

TWO BEST CHARACTER TRAITS: My outgoing personality and great sense of humor.

TWO WORST CHARACTER TRAITS: I talk a lot and I get mad real easy.

FAVORITE MUSIC: I love all kinds

FAVORITE MOVIES: *Halloween*, and porn of course, *The Rise and Fall of Heidi Fleiss*

FAVORITE MOVIES I'VE BEEN IN: Studio 2000/*In Too Deep*, Falcon Studios/*Hustle and Cruise*, Adonis Pictures/*Butt Heads*

XXX COSTAR I'D DO AGAIN IN A MINUTE: Trevor Knight

IF I COULD MAKE ONE REQUEST ON A PORN SET IT WOULD BE: I would have to say better food but only sometimes.

AS A TEEN I ALWAYS FANTASIZED ABOUT SEX WITH: Porn stars and now my fantasy has come true!

CURRENT FANTASY MAN: Johnny Castle. I was in a movie with him, but we did not get to do a scene together.

SEXIEST PART OF A MAN: Their pecs all the way to their penis.

THREE INGREDIENTS OF MY HOTTEST SEX FANTASY: Pecs, abs, and a huge dick

FAVORITE ITEM IN MY SEXUAL TOY BOX: My vibrator and lube.

MOST PRIZED POSSESSION: My cell phone and my laptop.

HOBBIES: Hanging out with friends, and doing all the normal stuff.

PETS: I have a dog named Bruizer.

PET PEEVES: When someone chews with their mouth open. I can't stand that.

Tristan Mathews [PHOTO BY MICK HICKS, COURTESY ADONIS PICTURES]

Don't be nervous, have fun, and next position!

What was the best advice you were given starting out?

The best advice I was given was to fuck like there was no one in the room and do my best to please the fans out there.

What is the most aroused you have ever been on screen?

It was actually during a little shoot for a popular web company and my scene partner was just so hot I couldn't keep my hands off him, then we hooked-up again off camera. That was the only time I've ever hooked-up with a scene partner off set.

What things do you usually do to prepare for a shoot?

I just hangout with the cast and crew laugh and joke around and get comfortable with the surroundings.

And how do you usually spend the evening after a day of filming?

After filming I just go home take a shower and crash. Those are some long days.

XXX movies are notorious for putting guys in some crazy sexual positions for the sake of the camera. What's the toughest position you've had to assume?

I would say when I had to do like a back bend and get my face fucked.

Ouch. What movie was that?

It was for the movie *Hustle and Cruise* for Falcon Studios.

The things you do for your art. Where is the wildest place you've ever had sex?

The wildest place so far was on top of a trash can.

So tell me more ...

The trash can escapade was a blast and we had a good time. We were laughing at me sliding off the lid and cracking it in the end. It was great!

"It's so nice to be around people who love sex as much as I do."

Speaking sexually, very few guys are as skilled as me when it comes to ...

Sucking dick.

So what is your secret that makes your cocksucking so supreme?

I can deep throat and I use a lot of spit and let it hang from the tongue to the cock. It looks great on camera.

Describe your ideal romantic evening.

I'm not much into romance so I would have to say just hanging out at home watching a movie or going out to eat and then having a lot of sex.

Where do you hope this career takes you?

I really would love to stay in the sex industry and maybe do some producing. I love to write little scenes so hopefully one day I can put together a big story.

So you like stories as well. Hmm, give me the plot synopsis of a XXX movie you would like to star in?

I know there is a lot – but I would love to star in a fantasy cop role with whips and just total out of control mayhem.

When you mention wanting to maybe work behind the camera one day – what are the most important things you have learned in front of the camera that would come in handy behind it?

Be professional to the models, give them time to get what they need. Remember, they are fucking in front of a camera. Also just to have a good time and get the job done and have a great film when you're finished.

And going along with that if you were making a movie called Tristan's Orgy who would you want as your four costars?

Benjamin Bradley, Johnny Hazzard, Johnny Castle, and this boy I work with who doesn't really have a name in the industry – but boy he should.

How do you think the XXX experience has changed you?

It changed me in some ways – to be more comfortable with my sexuality, also it's so nice to be around people who love sex as much as I do, and to be open and naked in front of people.

What is the biggest example of bad behavior on a XXX set that you've ever witnessed?

I have never really witnessed any bad behavior on set.

So does the presence of a crew and people on set make sex difficult or does performing in front of people turn you on all the more?

It doesn't really bother me. I guess you can say it turns me on.

You've worked with lots of different studios. How different and varied is their treatment of models from one studio to the other?

They're actually pretty much the same, every one is very professional.

You mention the XXX food. What is a typical spread like on set?

Water, soda, sandwiches, energy bars.

Do you have any memory as a kid or young adult that you look back upon and think, "Yeah, that kid was destined to grow up to be a porn star"?

As funny as this sounds I'll always wanted to be in the adult entertainment industry, or a Chippendale dancer. When I was a little kid my mom had a Chippendale air-freshener hanging in the car.

If you were offered a role in a fetish film how far do you think you would go?

Like I always say I'm down for it all! The kinkier the better.

Do you think the industry has a responsibility regarding the use of condoms and/or promoting safe sex?

The companies I work with are all condom safe and promote safe sex. I also promote it as well. When you have multiple sex partners you should want to use condoms. I can't stress that enough.

If you could change one thing about the way the industry is currently run what would it be?

I actually think the industry is run well, I'm sure it has its flaws but I don't see them.

If a guy came to you for advice about getting into the business what would you tell him?

I would tell him being in industry you have to be somewhat talented to do what you do and to have a passion for it, and that you definitely can't be camera shy.

Porn sets are often the place of some surreal and hilarious incidents. Do you have any personal tale you would care to share?

I have two really funny moments one was talked about in previous questions when I had to fuck on the trash can and I was falling off and it was cracking and also when I was fucking on a chair and totally fell off it!

How do we get you in the sack and what do we do with you once we get you there?

Basically if you want me in the sack don't beat around the bush just tell me you want to fuck and boy be ready to handle me because I'm a freak in the sheets.

So just how are you a freak in the sheets? Can you give us some idea what to expect and what qualifications we'll need to satisfy you?

Well , behind the cameras I'm pretty much the same as in front, and you better be able to keep up with me!

When you pass a hot looking guy on the street what gets you to turn around and do a double take every time?

Well living in California I have to double take a lot. I love really muscular guys.

How would you describe yourself in a personals ad?

I'm very outgoing and love to have fun, go to the movies, dinner, hanging out at home, and all and all have a great time with someone like me.

What is the biggest misconception people have about you when you meet them?

This is a great question. I'm very honest with what I do and tell people when asked. Some think it's awesome and some think it's gross and I'm dirty and have no morals.

People often think of porn stars as these ideal specimens, but if you could change one thing about yourself through cosmetic surgery what would it be?

I would definitely change my chest and get pec implants. Everyone laughs at me, but that would be the one thing for sure.

Does your cock have a nickname?

Yes, it's pretty original I call him "lil man."

If you had to choose between sex and love, which would you choose and what are your thoughts about fidelity?

I would have to say sex of course! Love comes and goes.

How do you consider yourself a typical Capricorn?

I'm very ambitious and wild.

Describe your dream vacation.

Going to Italy. I have never been and would love to go. If anyone wants to take me, e-mail me. (Laughs.)

BO **MATTHEWS**

How did you get started in the business?

I've been fascinated by the idea of doing porn for years but had never really taken it seriously. While I was dating Brian Mills (director of production at Titan), I learned a lot about the behind-the-scenes aspects of the industry. A couple months after Brian and I broke up, I was at a sex party and had an experience where I was getting fucked in a sling and nearly everyone at the party stopped to watch. And I loved it! It was that day that I decided to give my best shot to getting into the industry. I worked out really hard at the gym for a couple months, got in the best shape of my life, and Brian agreed to take my first professional-quality nude pictures. I forwarded a couple of these to Adam Faust, who I knew from online, Adam forwarded them to a couple studios, and I got my first two movie offers the next day.

STATS

BIRTH DATE: July 11, 1971

SIGN: Cancer sun, Aquarius moon, Gemini rising.

HOMETOWN: San Francisco (not where I grew up – but home nonetheless).

HEIGHT: 5'10"

WEIGHT: 160 lbs

TWO BEST CHARACTER TRAITS: Honest and ethical.

TWO WORST CHARACTER TRAITS: I can be snobby in some ways and I'm a bit self-absorbed

FAVORITE MUSIC: How long of a list do you have time for? Music is my biggest passion. In general, underground/Indie rock, some electronic, some underground hip hop. My favorite albums of this year so far: Battles, Shining, Dalek, Of Montreal, Frog Eyes.

FAVORITE MOVIES: *Hellraiser; Memento; Crouching Tiger, Hidden Dragon; Borat; Seven; Requiem for a Dream; Pan's Labyrinth.*

FAVORITE MOVIES I'VE BEEN IN: *Link: The Evolution* and the as-yet-unnamed one I just did for Mustang.

XXX COSTARS I'D DO AGAIN IN A MINUTE: Tyler Saint and Nick Moretti.

IF I COULD MAKE ONE REQUEST ON A PORN SET IT WOULD BE: That the sex would be less scripted.

AS A TEEN I ALWAYS FANTASIZED ABOUT SEX WITH: The Soloflex man and Bob Paris. Guess my gaydar was better than I thought!

CURRENT FANTASY MAN: Alex Collack.

SEXIEST PART OF A MAN: His nipples.

THREE INGREDIENTS OF MY HOTTEST SEX FANTASY: A sling, at least four other hung studs, and a world where condoms are no longer necessary.

FAVORITE ITEM IN MY SEXUAL TOY BOX: My tongue.

MOST PRIZED POSSESSION: My CD collection.

HOBBIES: Camping, hiking, rock climbing, concerts.

PETS: None currently. Cats and snakes are my favorites.

PET PEEVES: Dishonesty; impatient drivers; bad dance music.

Do you recall your first film and the first bit of direction you were given?

My first film was *Mister Fister* for HotHouse. The first piece of direction I remember getting from director Michael Clift was to stop smiling and look a little more serious!

What was the best advice you were given starting out?

Unless you're the sort of jaw-dropping hottie who gets offered an exclusive immediately, this industry takes a while to break into. For a couple months after I did my first movie, I was finding it impossible to get any more work and it really bummed me out. A number of knowledgeable people told me to be patient and wait for the movie to come out. Sure enough, within a couple weeks of that I got two more offers. I'm now accustomed to the cycle of downtimes between shoots.

What is the general scenario of that casting cycle?

I should start by saying that this has just been my experience, and I'm sure it's worked differently for other guys in the industry. When I started out there was that initial rush of interest, I did my first movie and then I didn't work again for two months. My next two movies happened when the first one came out and I had fresh new pictures to send to studios. My fourth movie had already been scheduled for about the same time a couple months earlier, so I actually did three movies in one month. And then there was another long gap before I got my fifth offer – and again, this was a direct result of one of the earlier films being released. That second gap between shoots didn't freak me out as much, however. I'm now in a position where a couple of the studios I've worked with are contacting me to do another movie with them, so I feel like I've finally turned that corner and am an established name. I mentioned that cycle within the context of the advice I'd give to someone just starting in the industry, so just to reiterate: you've got to be patient and you've got to maintain a presence for the studios even when you're not working.

Bo Matthews [PHOTO BY KENT TAYLOR, COURTESY RAGING STALLION STUDIOS]

What are the best and worst parts about being a porn star?

The best parts for me are that I've truly killed a couple of my longstanding demons (more on that below), and I'm starting to accrue some social capital that I can spend however I choose. As a specific example of what I mean by that – I've been thrilled to appear at a couple fundraisers and channel my willingness to be mostly-naked in public and let people touch me into something a bit more meaningful. From the beginning it's been important to me that any recognition I get from doing porn is used for something more than self-promotion.

The worst parts ... to be honest, it's been a mostly-positive experience! It bums me out a bit that I haven't been able to share this exciting new aspect of my life with my parents (my siblings both know), but otherwise all of my friends and even my boss at my normal job have all been incredibly supportive. Also, I really think there's something to be said for doing this in my 30s (instead of at a younger age) – I've got a clear enough sense of who I am and what I'm about that I'm able to avoid falling into some of the more common traps I've witnessed snag other guys in the industry.

If you were making a movie called Bo's Orgy who would you want as your four costars?

Alex Collack, Jake Deckard, Brendan Davies, my boyfriend and my favorite fuck buddy. I know that's five, but a guy's gotta push the limits in this industry.

(Laughing). I like that. What is the most sexually aroused you have ever been on screen?

I had amazing chemistry with my scene partners in *Link: The Evolution* – Nick Moretti and Tyler Saint. We couldn't keep our hands and mouths off each other even when the camera wasn't rolling! Even after all the paces I was put through during that day of shooting (my first ever piss-play, getting fucked while all but standing on my head, long sessions of gagging on two big dicks, etc.) at the end of it I was able to cum almost immediately once we got around to cumshots. It was the fastest cumshot I've ever had!

Do you recall any episode or incident as a kid or young adult that you look back on today and think, "Yup, that kid was destined to grow up to be a porn star"?

I was pretty sexually unadventurous until I returned from four years in the Peace Corps in 2000. (There's something to be said for multiple years of near-celibacy as a motivator for sluttiness!) So no episodes or incidents. But my parents explained sex to me when I was five, and I vividly remember spending my childhood staring at men's crotches, and whenever the bulge was impressive I'd think "He'd be fun to go to bed with." Where does a six-year-old come up with something like that? So I think this die was cast a long time ago, it just took me a while to be true to my nature!

Do you have some fantasy you are just waiting for some director to ask you to film?

Two. On one hand I'd love to do a gang bang video and take on at least four other guys. And then on the flip side – I have yet to do a scene that involved anything as prosaic as a bed! So I'd love to do a more vanilla/romantic scene with a guy that I was really into physically. It'd be a real [change from] my current repertoire!

Have you ever developed a crush on any of your costars? Care to name names?

I wouldn't say that I've developed any crushes. But Nick Moretti (one of my scene partners in *Link: The Evolution*) is somebody who – if he didn't live on the other side of the country – I would definitely want to get to know better and spend more time with.

What things do you typically do to prepare for a XXX shoot?

I don't have any form of sex, including jacking off, for three days beforehand. I really monitor my diet and eat absolutely nothing after 6:00 p.m. for a couple days before. The day before, I don't go to the gym – I want to show up as rested as possible. The morning of the shoot, I very thoroughly douche. I don't eat anything that morning but will drink Gatorade throughout the day to keep my blood sugar up.

And how do you usually spend the evening after all day on the set?

I go home or back to my hotel room and crash! Porn shoots can be really exhausting. Though there was that one time where my scene partner(s) and I ... [censored] ... the evening after the shoot!

Where do you hope this career takes you?

Honestly, my top priority for doing porn is to have fun. It's an amazing opportunity that a lot of people will never get or never believe they could do. The extra cash on the side is great, but I have a full-time job as a professional scientist, so it's not something I rely on. I never went into this expecting to become a star so any amount of recognition I get for doing porn I'd like to translate into something more meaningful, whether it's helping with fundraising appearances, or using my upcoming website as a platform to talk about issues that are important to me.

Has making XXX movies been the fun you hoped it would be?

Absolutely. I love the atmosphere on a porn set – the freedom to be naked and sexual and a bit crazy. Not only does nobody bat an eyelash but it's actually the expected behavior. This isn't to say it isn't work. I'm almost always exhausted at the end of it. But there's a camaraderie between models, even if there's no genuine chemistry I've still consistently experienced an implicit common understanding of what's required to give a good scene. And I can honestly say that I've yet to meet anyone from behind the scenes (and I've now worked with five different studios) that wasn't a pleasure to work with.

If you were offered a role in a fetish film how far do you think you would go?

The funny thing is I've done more fetish(y) films than those that aren't! In *Mister Fister* I rode the largest object I've ever had up my ass. In *Link: Evolution* I engaged in my first ever piss play and got in a piss spitting match with one of my scene partners. And in the still-untitled movie I recently shot with Mustang, I'm caged, hung upside down, shackled, and all-around abused. Each of those films pushed my personal boundaries in some way, but I have to stress that it's always been my choice. Every director I've worked with has told me that they don't want me doing anything with which I'm not comfortable. And the fact is I'm doing porn as a form of fantasy fulfillment, and that makes pushing my own boundaries exciting and fulfilling. *Link* and the Mustang film are my two favorites so far precisely because of that aspect.

What about making XXX movies didn't you expect?

It can be incredibly unsexy! That doesn't mean I'm not having a good time, or that I don't have great chemistry with my scene partners – it's more about the constant stop and start, the fact that you're often taking direction in terms of what happens next. But what has also surprised me is how none of that stuff translates into the final product. One of my movies was a pretty rough shoot due to some less-than-engaged scene partners. However, the final edit looks fantastic and hot – you'd never know that we barely interacted when the cameras weren't rolling.

Porn is notorious for putting guys in some very uncomfortable positions for the sake of the shot. What is the most uncomfortable one you have ever had to assume in a movie?

I spent an hour on my back, legs in the air, with my ankles and wrists shackled in a single plane while Matthew Ford and Jake Dakota fucked the hell out of me for the as-yet-untitled movie I just did for Mustang. The shackles kept slipping off my boots and cutting into my shins, so between takes we'd keep sliding them back up. Besides sore shins, my lower back was killing me the next day.

Earlier you mentioned some of the pitfalls and problems younger people sometimes have in this business, can you give some examples?

I suppose in my answer to a previous question I shouldn't have limited this to younger guys. I also don't want to be overly stereotypical. I was referring to what happens in any of the entertainment industries when you've got somebody who's suddenly receiving a lot of exposure and attention for engaging in a venture which inherently has an expiration date. Very few guys have a career in porn that lasts more than a couple of years, and yet while it lasts it can be immensely exciting. So for me the advantage of doing this in my 30s is that I've already had some other significant life experiences (notably Peace Corps) that have contributed to my sense of identity. Not to say that I don't love being a porn model, but I'm not basing my entire sense of who I am on it. Whereas somebody in their 20s (and/or someone who maybe hasn't had any significant life experiences prior to this) could hardly be blamed for letting it go to their heads.

So I've heard plenty of stories of guys whose whole reality becomes being a porn star and then when the party's over they have a really rough spell because they're not getting the same kind of attention and don't have anything else in their lives to refocus their energy onto. The additional layer to that for porn models is that you can fall into this trap of thinking that your personal sex life has to somehow be a reflection of you as a porn star. As much as I've loved some of the crazier stuff I've done on video, I'm pretty clear that it was a fantasy I was fulfilling, and that it doesn't have to spill over into my personal sex life or sense of myself as a sexual being. There's also this idea that to be a good porn star you've got to somehow be a bad boy which isn't to say that a lot of the guys who are drawn to this industry weren't already in some way bad boys, nor do I deny that it's totally given me a way to indulge my own inner bad boy! But I've seen or heard of cases where somebody bought into this whole mental trip of "I'm a porn star so I should act like _" and that can lead to other problems. (I realize that's vague, but I'm trying to answer the question without resorting to overgeneralizations or being gossipy!)

What is the worst behavior you have ever witnessed on set or event from a so called professional?

To be honest, I've yet to have a negative experience on any of the five sets I've worked on or with any of my scene partners or studio employees. I've been consistently impressed with the professionalism in this industry. Even on the one shoot where I didn't have much chemistry with my scene partners, nobody was ever impolite or acted like a diva. In fact, the only example of unprofessional behavior I have to offer was my own. I was having a tough time with my cumshot on one film, and there was a guy on the crew who I was totally into. Even though it was explicitly against the rules I'd agreed to in my model release, I asked the director if I could have ten minutes alone with this guy to get my head into the right place, and they both agreed. Everybody walked away from that event having gotten what they wanted, so I think it was a justifiable lapse!

Do you think the industry has a responsibility regarding the use of condoms and/or promoting safe sex?

Absolutely. It's easy for those of us who live in progressive coastal gay populations to lose sight of the role porn plays in setting norms as well as creating fantasies for young gay men in less cosmopolitan settings. I'd be a hypocrite if I denied that I find some bareback porn very hot. But I'm a well-educated city dweller who understands the subtext, not a 16-year-old in some rural area who doesn't know any other gay people and is watching porn not just to get off but almost as a sexual primer. It's important to keep in mind that very few young gay men receive any direct guidance or support about their emerging sexuality.

Having grown up in a rural community myself, I remember how powerful an experience porn was for me initially, how it informed my fantasies and how I learned a few things about how men could be sexual with each other from it. I've often wondered if there could be such a thing as socially responsible bareback porn ... perhaps with a disclaimer at the beginning of the video—that you couldn't fast-forward through or skip—about the HIV status of the performers, or about sero-sorting ... whatever it took to contextualize the images.

Porn sets are often the place of some surreal and hilarious incidents. Do you have any personal tale you would care to share?

Working with Chi Chi LaRue is an experience every model in the industry should get to have. I've commented elsewhere that I'll be on my deathbed and still hear her voice yelling, "Fuck his face! Now take it out and

Bo Matthews [PHOTO BY KENT TAYLOR, COURTESY RAGING STALLION STUDIOS]

spit on it! Lick it! Shove it back down his throat! You fuckers are sick! This is so fucking fierce!" I crack up every time I think about it. The entire day spent shooting my scene in *Link: The Evolution* was one of the craziest of my life. I recently did a scene with Chad Hunt – who is either a bottom's fondest fantasy or biggest fear, depending on one's preferences and capabilities. Working with Chad is a pleasure. He's very relaxed and easygoing, and also knows how to be responsive to his bottom. We started out the scene with me riding him, and as often happens when I'm taking a really big dick, I bled a little. So the first couple times I lifted myself off his cock (mostly to give my aching quads a break – reverse cowboy is hard on the legs!) a bit of red-tinged lube would fall out of my ass onto his thigh. The grip brought over some paper towel to wipe it up, and Chad joked, "Does anybody have the toast, cuz I've got the strawberry jelly!" (Yes, I realize this is gross ... but then sex often is.) I turned around grinning and said, "This happens to you a lot, doesn't it?" He just sighed wistfully, "Oh honey ..."

Can you give me a typical scenario of when people usually recognize you from your films?

It's only happened once so far, and was probably not a typical scenario. I was at a bathhouse and when I mentioned to one of the guys I played with that night that I was in movies, his eyes got huge and I could see the light bulb go off over his head. Turns out he'd been jacking off all week to the Internet trailer of my most recently-released film, and he confided that I was the guy in the trailer he found the most hot. He claimed not to have recognized me when we were cruising each other because it was such a different context and given that he was able to describe the scene from the trailer in some detail, I believed that he'd actually seen it and this wasn't just some line he was feeding me. So we both made each other's night with that exchange (not to mention what happened afterward ...)

What is the biggest misconception people have about you when you meet them?

Probably that I'm a boring person! I can be very reserved and almost formal with new people. The other common misperception is when people meet me on the dance floor, they tend to think I'm rolling on ecstasy. I'm a pretty expressive and energetic dancer.

People tend to think of porn stars as these ideal specimens, but if you could change one thing about yourself through cosmetic surgery what would it be?

Funny you should ask ... I have a mild case of gynomastia, which is when a guy grows breast tissue. Ever since puberty my chest has been my largest physical insecurity; for years I wouldn't go shirtless in public places. This was only compounded by the fact that I was overweight for most of my 20s. I mentioned above how porn has helped me kill some of my demons, and this is exactly what I was referring to. A couple months before I decided to get into the industry, I actually went to see a plastic surgeon in San Francisco who specializes in correcting gynomastia to find out how much the procedure would cost. It was thousands more dollars than I could have afforded. But then something strange happened. I was working hard to get into shape, and was also newly single so was spending a lot more time out at bars or clubs, where I always go shirtless. Not to mention I was having a lot of sex! And I kept getting consistent complements on my chest! So over a couple of months that self-consciousness all but disappeared.

of compliments on a body part that I'd always perceived with dismay. At the personal level, all I can say is that I internalized those physical ideals at a really young age, and years spent trying to intellectualize them away only kept me persistently unhappy. It was only when I started working out and taking responsibility for what I wanted to see in the mirror, that I started shedding some of those self-

"Having grown up in a rural community myself, I remember how powerful an experience porn was for me initially, how it informed my fantasies and how I learned a few things about how men could be sexual with each other from it."

I hesitated to answer this question that honestly, but it's been interesting to realize just how many of my insecurities were self-imposed. I'm frankly glad that I was able to achieve peace with my body through other means than surgery. Even though it's not specifically what you asked me, your question does imply another issue that I think doesn't get discussed enough – the ways in which those ideals get created and internalized by gay men in the first place. It's a fairly common criticism leveled against porn that it contributes to poor body image among gay men because of what the industry standards are for models.

I can imagine some people reading what I just wrote about my own evolving relationship with my body and wishing that I could have reached that peace with myself without having to lose the weight or get a bunch

imposed burdens. The point is, you can only feel bad about yourself relative to what you see in porn movies, or advertising, or any other form of media. If you've internalized the images enough to make the comparison in the first place. And at a societal and historical level – lean muscular physiques have been the ideal for male physical beauty for centuries. There are powerful evolutionary reasons for this that persist even though human beings haven't been subject to the related natural selective pressures for thousands of years.

And finally, I think the diversification of gay porn into a bunch of niche markets is a really interesting and positive phenomenon. It reflects the diversity among gay men ourselves – our interests, our fantasies, our physical types. There might still be a dominant aesthetic, but I don't think you could make the case anymore for a single ideal specimen.

So you also mentioned being able to use your status for fundraisers and such. What are some of the things you have done in those areas?

So far I've appeared at two fundraisers in a relatively nearby city where they don't get many porn stars. The recipients in both cases were the local LBG film festival. I sold body shots, helped sell raffle tickets, and there was this rather amusing incident involving a cage. I'm also scheduled to help out with a couple fundraisers coming up in San Francisco. I'd love to achieve enough name/image recognition to contribute to ad campaigns for safe sex, anti-meth, etc.

Very admirable, and very necessary. Where is the wildest place you've ever had sex?

On film – undoubtedly the abandoned meat-packing plant where *Link: The Evolution* and the Mustang movie were both shot. In my personal life – in the backcountry of Yosemite National Park, not too far from the Tuolumne River and Glen Aulin Trail.

Speaking sexually very few guys are as skilled as me when it comes to ...

Building chemistry and having fun. Probably not the sort of answer you expected, but it's what I pride myself on. A lot of guys in the industry are very professional about doing scenes, and some are even mechanical. As much as possible given the circumstances, I try to really get into what's happening, develop chemistry with my scene partners, and make the shoot fun rather than work. I've been told on a couple occasions that I saved or stolen a scene.

How would you describe yourself in a personals ad?

Honest, genuine, intelligent, sexual, laughing, analytical, reflective, adventurous, and complex.

How do we get you in the sack and what do we do with you once we get you there?

I just started a new relationship, and even though neither of us is a monogamist at heart, we're both still in that honeymoon stage of wanting to establish the trust with each other that comes with time, so that when we eventually do open up the relationship it won't derail what we've got going. So the first thing you have to do is wait a couple more months. Next it'd be good if you were physically equally into me and my boyfriend and vice versa – we both love three-ways but have also both had the experience where it was really a two-way with an extraneous third, and that's not fun for anyone.

Now that we've cleared all the hurdles, I want you to be very sensual and oral. I love to fuck, but it's a stop along the path, not the total destination. I want your mouth and hands all over my body because mine are going to explore yours. Have fun and be relaxed, the fewer limits the better. Versatility is also an attractive quality. I'm really not into roles or any sort of sex play that feels like it's based on some sort of power relationship. Finally, don't be afraid of intimacy. Staring deeply into each other's eyes, being gentle with each other as well as rough, and even falling asleep together. None of these things means we're getting married. It's all about enhancing our physical interaction and exploration of each other.

If you had to choose between sex and love which would you choose and what are your thoughts about fidelity?

Love wins if I'm forced to choose, no argument. But of course it's a false dichotomy because I couldn't really be in love with someone with whom I didn't have a sexual connection. I think if we're going to talk about fidelity the first thing we need to do is detach that concept from monogamy because they're two different things. I have zero interest in monogamy. But I've never cheated in my life, and cheating on me is the one thing that I consider unforgivable. Clearly I'm not talking about sex here I'm talking about deception and a basic disrespect for our relationship and the parameters which we've defined together, whatever they may be.

When you pass a hot looking guy upon the street what gets you to turn around and do a double take every time?

Big arms, without fail.

Describe your ideal romantic evening.

Great dinner and a bottle of wine, during which lots of flirting and touching under the table and eye contact. Back to his place or mine, set the scene with candlelight and mood-appropriate music. Throughout there's good conversation. We learn something new about each other, share some laughter, build the kind of emotional intimacy that leads to awesome physical intimacy. Nothing is rushed. We might kiss for an hour before any clothing gets removed. We slowly explore each other's bodies (as they become increasingly revealed) with our fingertips and tongues. To reduce the evolution of our physical interaction to a list of activities and behaviors would be to minimize its intensity. Afterward, we fall asleep wrapped in each others' arms.

If you had to compare yourself to an animal what species do you think best captures your essence and why?

That's a tough one for me as a biologist – there are so many different animals that I love! But I've always had an affinity for cats ... independent yet still loyal; alternately fierce and playful; aloof with strangers but affectionate and tolerant with those I know and love.

If your life had a theme song what would it be?

Some of the lyrics of Following Through by the Dismemberment Plan come immediately to mind: "I could say I hope I'm not misread, but that's alright/I'm quite OK with losing that fight/I can do it anywhere with anyone at any time / Don't you forget this is my life and it's going to be good/ Don't you know?/Not a promise or a threat or an ultimatum, though I could do those too/I'm just telling you: I've got this life, I've just got to live/I'm just following through."

Does your cock have a nickname and if so how did it come about?

It doesn't ... but my *nom du porn* is directly related to one of my nicknames back in my fraternity days: "No-Ho Bo", a reference to my seeming inability to get laid. Fifteen years later the joke is on my frat brothers, cuz now Bo just is a ho!

How are you a typical Cancer?

I can be very nurturing, I'm inherently relationship-oriented (not just romantically but also in terms of taking my friendships very seriously) and I'm definitely in touch with my emotions. I think my emphasis on sensuality in my real sex life has a lot to do with seeking connection of whatever sort with my sex partners. All that said – my moon is in Aquarius and that's exerted an equally-large influence on my life. The fact that I'm doing porn is totally my Aquarius energy wanting to shake things up!

Describe your dream vacation.

I would love to have the freedom to take a year off and see the world with the man I love. I tend to gravitate more toward nature (seeing wildlife and appreciating landscapes), but if time and finances weren't an issue then I'd also want to experience a variety of cultures and learn as much as I could about their history. I'm a really active vacationer – only rarely do I want to just relax.

MARTIN **MAZZA**

How did you get started in the business?

My first experience before the cameras is a long story, I was basically involved in an orgy and someone filmed all the action, just thinking about it now makes me horny; it was wild. I had been trying to get into porn for a long time. I emailed Chi Chi LaRue a few times and one day I received a call and I was in. It was one of the best experiences of my life – working for Chi Chi.

What were you looking for when you got into it?

I wanted to change my life and have a new experience. I had been trapped in an office for five years after college and I was bored with my life. Now my life has made a 180 degree return. I get to travel, make money, to be on the guest lists of the hottest clubs and to top it off, I get to fuck with my idols. Everyone I have met in the porn industry has been great and so open minded. I wouldn't change my life even for that desk in the White House. (Laughing).

Do you recall the first movie you were in and the first bit of direction you were given?

The first movie I made was with Chi Chi LaRue. I was going to get fucked by two guys and was really nervous. I had never worked with a director before and didn't know what to expect. Was the director going to yell at me if he didn't like my work? I didn't know, but Chi Chi was incredible. He opened his heart to me and was so kind and professional. It all felt like family. I will always feel a great sense of admiration for Chi Chi and remain very thankful for all that he did for me.

What else about working with Chi Chi makes it so great?

I admire him as a person and a businessman. He can achieve anything he wants. In addition, when I worked with him he was always in control of the situation but still managed to create this family like atmosphere. I remember that he would write in his diary all the events he wanted to remember and I'm sure he must have lived through some unique experiences throughout his life. I also love it when he transforms into this phenomenal Drag Queen; he comes to life as do all around him. I have to say that I have a thing for drag queens. In fact, my ex boyfriend is Ankissyous a very well known drag queen in the London scene.

What about making XXX movies didn't you expect?

I didn't expect to have so much work to say the truth. I also didn't expect that it would have such an impact in my life. I thought that only a few people would notice but now it's like I have all these people talking to me and showing an interest. I would have never expected to have a fan club. I also never expected to find such great people in this industry.

What is the most aroused you have ever been on screen?

It is really hard for me to pick a scene. Each one has made me feel something different and new. Maybe it has been because of the co-stars, the direction, or the set. I can't really think of one time. I will tell you this though – I have been fucking aroused in all of my scenes.

Martin, is it difficult to be in the adult film industry when based in Madrid? Have you been tempted to move to the US?

Yes, some times it can be hard. I have to travel a lot and have visited the US many, many times. Some of the best studios are there, and I have really enjoyed working there. In the US you have great production, scripts, reputation, and great experience in practically everything. Moving to the US has crossed my mind many times. However, Madrid is home and it would be very hard for me to leave, but you never know what the future has in store.

STATS

BIRTH DATE: October 15, 1977

SIGN: Libra

HOMETOWN: Madrid

TWO BEST CHARACTER TRAITS: I'm loyal and honest. I never lie.

TWO WORST CHARACTER TRAITS: I'm not a good morning person and I am a true perfectionist. If things don't work out the way I want them to, I become really upset with myself.

FAVORITE MUSIC: House music. – DJ Disciple feat Dawn Tallman – work it out, Bob Sinclair – world, hold on) or all music like (Urban Cookie Collective) I love them and my best DJ Filippo Romano (he is like my brother) and Chi Chi LaRue, I love Chi Chi.

FAVORITE MOVIES: Scary movies or romantic movies.

FAVORITE MOVIES I'VE BEEN IN: *Bedroom Eyes*, *Aussiebums*, etc.

XXX COSTAR I'D DO AGAIN IN A MINUTE: Tony Mecelli

IF I COULD MAKE ONE REQUEST ON A PORN SET IT WOULD BE: I would love to have a scene set in a dungeon where I'm the prisoner. I would be blindfolded and I'd be gang raped by a group of merciless African-American muscle studs with huge dicks. They would spit on my face and ass and take turns fucking my hungry hole.

AS A TEEN I ALWAYS FANTASIZED ABOUT SEX WITH: With Marc Williams, a fucking gorgeous guy. His boyfriend will kill me when he reads this (Laughing).

CURRENT FANTASY MAN: Fucking and getting fucked in a session with many straight guys.

SEXIEST PART OF A MAN: The ass. For me a big muscular ass is the best thing a guy can have. A nice, big, smooth ass. That's when it comes to sex. Now for love, I would have to say the eyes.

THREE INGREDIENTS OF MY HOTTEST SEX FANTASY: A big smooth ass, a good kisser, and someone with dark and hot skin.

FAVORITE ITEM IN MY SEXUAL TOY BOX: A big dildo.

HOBBIES: To lie naked on my sofa with a sexy guy, watching a DVD. Being a go-go boy at some cool dance clubs, as well as being a DJ. I love music.

PETS: Right now I only have my small Chihuahua dog Joshua, but I love animals and have had at my home in Madrid, flamingos, fish, parrots, quails, among others.

PET PEEVES: It really gets on my nerves when people criticize others. I just cannot stand it when people try to point out flaws in others for no good reason. As soon as someone starts gossiping or ridiculing someone I lose it.

Martin Mazza [PHOTO COURTESY HOT HOUSE ENTERTAINMENT]

What things do you always do when you prepare for a movie shoot?

One week before the shoot I will go to the gym twice a day, I will take the sun and put special care on my skin (no one likes an unwelcome pimple). I also make sure that I have no sex before the day of the scene. I have a good dinner the day before and avoid drinking a lot during the day of the scene.

Martin Mazza [PHOTO BY KENT TAYLOR, COURTESY RAGING STALLION STUDIOS]

And what do you usually do when you get home from a busy day of filming?

I switch off my mobile, disconnect the Internet and get into a nice hot bubble bath. I then tuck myself into bed and rest. A day's shooting tends to wear me out quite a bit.

Are you a natural exhibitionist?

Before we start the show I just think Man, it's me on that fucking stage in front of all those people! And when the show begins my blood is boiling in my veins. I have performed in front of more than 3000 people!

If someone were to come to you for advice about getting into the business what would you tell them?

Today I may appear on some Spanish TV shows. I also have my profile on almost every website and I even have my own website (www.martinmazza.eu). Many people will tell me that they're really interested in getting into the porn business. They ask me about what they should do to get started. I myself do some castings for a few production houses such as Triga films, Lucas Entertainment, Collin O'Neal, HotHouse, among others. I was also doing castings during the Gay Porn Festival in Barcelona for the movies that are being shot right now in Spain. I have come across some stunning guys who want to get into the business but I always tell them is that they have to be 100% sure that this is what they want to do and that they have to be fully aware of what they are getting into. It is great to fantasize about being a porn star but you have to think if you see yourself in a set with a crew watching you having sex for hours. It's a great job if you like it but it's also hard work!

Have you ever developed a crush on any of your costars? Care to name names?

I did once. Very hot guy! However, he has a boyfriend who is also in the porn industry and lives in LA. In fact, his boyfriend is a very good friend of mine so while I wish that I get to do more scenes with him I will never try anything off camera. And, of course, I cannot reveal who he is for obvious reasons.

What is the best way to get Martin Mazza into bed ... and what do we do with you once we get you there?

I don't like being hunted. I much prefer being the hunter. When I spot something I like I know that I want it and I'll make sure I get it.

If that's the case what is your trick to seducing a man and getting him in bed?

I tend to go for really good looking guys – but muscles and looks are not enough. I then find out if the guy is nice. If that's the case I will really go for it. I will talk with the guy, listen to him, and try to win him over. I will also be very honest and tell him exactly what I think.

If you were to make a movie called Martin Mazza's Orgy who would you want for your four costars?

I would go for Matthew Rush of course and his boyfriend, I would also go for Marc Williams (he makes me fucking rock hard!), I also love Billy Brandt and did I say that I love people with dark skin?

You have worked for so many various companies Arena, Lucas, Raging Stallion, Falcon, Hot House to name just a few. Is there a lot of variation in how the different companies and different directors make porn?

You always want to make sure that there is a good vibe between the director, the actors and the rest of the staff. Before the scene I would always talk with the director and come to an agreement about what we can do to make the scene work out for the best. The variations between directors are more in terms of how much they want you to kiss, if they want you to fuck a lot, play more, be more oral. The degree of freedom that they give you to improvise also tends to vary.

How would you describe yourself in a personals ad?

Masculine and athletic guy with a clear mind. No lies; no funny business. I really do not care for lies since I don't like to waste time. I can be very horny – but not every day and every hour.

I have also heard that you are also from quite a noble background ... is that true?

I do have a noble background which comes from my mother's side. She is the Marquise of Fernandez de Alvarado. It comes from an ancestor who discovered Guatemala in the time of Christopher Columbus. In addition, my entire family keeps a close relationship with the Opus Dei and I attended one of their schools since I was a child. Despite everything that I do, I have a great relationship with my father's family. However, on my mother's side is a different story. I have a great relationship with her but the rest of her family refuses to speak with me. Regardless of what they say however, as an only child I will one day inherit the title of Marquis.

Where is the craziest or wildest place you have ever had sex?

"I tend to go for really good looking guys – but muscles and looks are not enough."

I was at a movie theatre in Sydney. I was bored in my hotel room and decided to go watch a movie. It was some romantic comedy (I can't remember which one right now for obvious reasons). There was this really hot guy sitting there on his own which I thought was very strange. Anyway, I decided to sit next to him and about fifteen minutes into the movie he got up and walked past me making sure he rubbed against me. He went to the back of the theatre and I followed. It was hot!

What would be your dream vacation?

To be in love and go off to a deserted island with my guy. Just the two of us walking naked on the beach without a care in the world but each other – just like in *The Blue Lagoon*.

NICK MAZZARO

What are your cats' names Nick?

Amando. It's a big, white, fluffy male cat.

How did you get started in the business?

Actually I was asked in the gym when I was taking a shower if I wanted to do porn when I was in LA on vacation. First of all I did not take it seriously, but then I was asked several times and finally I said yes.

What were you looking for when you got into it?

Well I am an exhibitionist and have done strip shows for years. I like to show off myself naked and the thought of having sex with other hot guys in front of the camera excited and horned me up very much.

What things do you always do to prepare yourself for a film shoot?

I get a lot of sleep, at least 12 hours sleep before a shoot and before that a good work-out in the gym. I want to look good and give my best when on set.

What is the first thing you do when you get home from shooting a movie?

First thing is to call my mom and tell her how the shoot was, she is very curious and wants to know every-

STATS

BIRTH DATE: August 13, 1974

SIGN: Leo

HOMETOWN: Stuttgart, Germany

HEIGHT: 6'1"

WEIGHT: 235 lbs

TWO BEST CHARACTER TRAITS: I'm patient and good natured.

TWO WORST CHARACTER TRAITS: I never settle for less and I'm always striving for perfection.

FAVORITE MUSIC: Janet Jackson and Diana Ross.

FAVORITE MOVIES: *The Bodyguard, Casablanca, Independence Day, Titanic.*

XXX COSTAR I'D DO AGAIN IN A MINUTE: Michael Solider.

IF I COULD MAKE ONE REQUEST ON A PORN SET IT WOULD BE: Better scripts and stories.

AS A TEEN I ALWAYS FANTASIZED ABOUT SEX WITH: A threesome with two hairy men over thirty.

CURRENT FANTASY MAN: Colin Farrell.

SEXIEST PART OF A MAN: His lips.

THREE INGREDIENTS OF MY HOTTEST SEX FANTASY: Barracks, nighttime, a dozen soldiers.

FAVORITE ITEM IN MY SEXUAL TOY BOX: Nipple pinchers.

MOST PRIZED POSSESSION: My large collection of science fiction books.

HOBBIES: Weight lifting, scuba diving, mountain biking, climbing, reading science fiction books.

PETS: Pussycats.

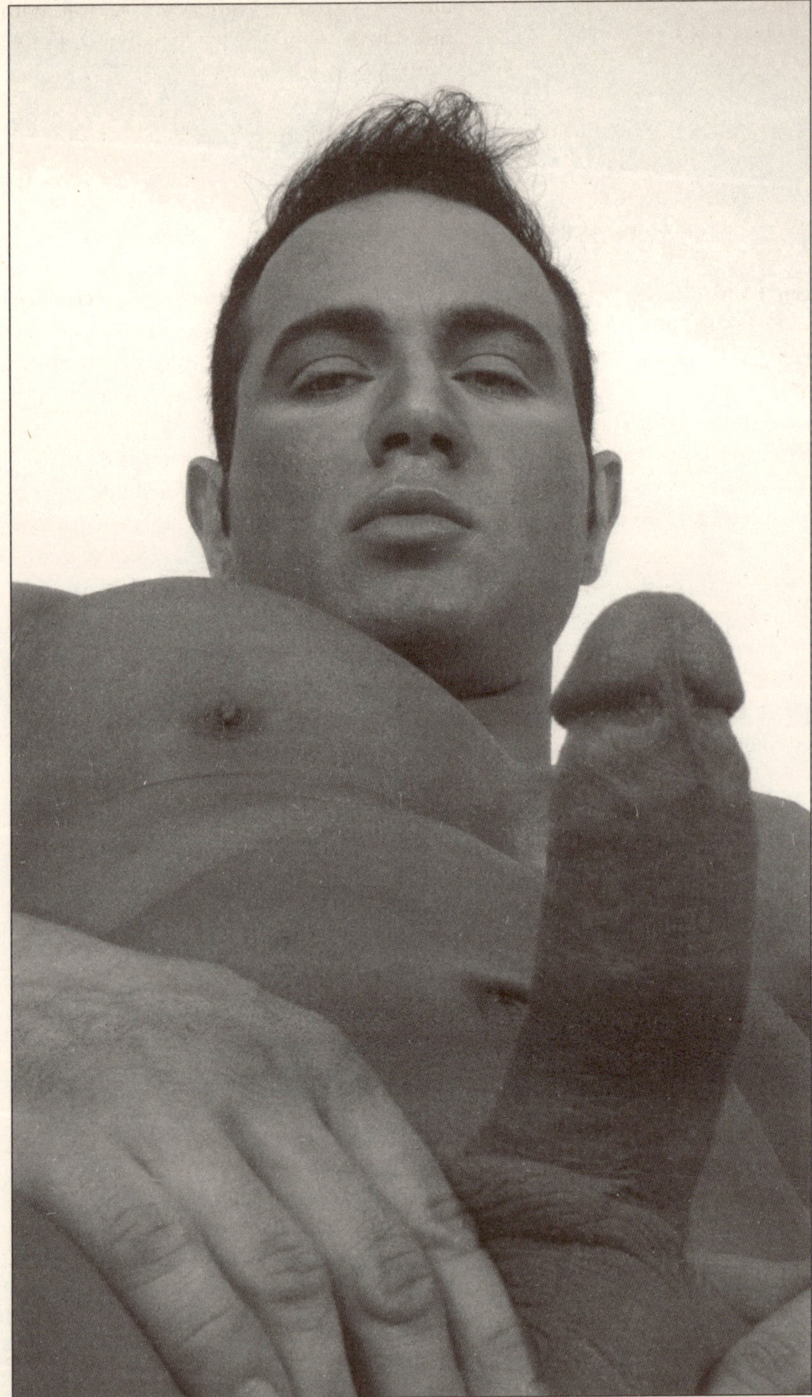

Nick Mazzaro [PHOTO COURTESY NICK MAZZARO]

thing. Besides this I take a long bath at least for an hour and listen to my favorite music.

I am intrigued that your Mom is curious about the shoot. Has she always been supportive of your career or has she come around in time?

Yes, my mom always supported me from the very beginning and she always asks for a copy of my movies. She has all my movies and is very proud of my work.

You mentioned wanting better scripts for XXX movies. What sort of genre porn movie do you think it would be the most fun to make?

Well, what the whole porn business is about creating illusions and fantasies and this is what the viewers want to see. They want to indulge themselves in a fantasy world and escape for a while from their everyday lives. I think there should be a story in a porn like they do it in some straight porns. A mixture of soft and hardcore version. We are overwhelmed with porn from all over but not with sensuality, I think this is the key to a successful adult movie.

If someone came to you asking for advice about getting into the business, what would you tell them?

Stick to your principles and don't do things you don't like to do. Believe in yourself and in what you are doing, always give your best and behave yourself professionally. Stay away from drugs!

Is it fun, uncomfortable, or interesting to watch yourself have sex on screen?

Actually I am very critical with myself and always looking for things I did that looked good on screen in order to do them better next time. I don't concentrate on the movie or the other actors I just concentrate on myself – how I look, what I do, and what I can do better next time.

Have you ever developed a crush on any of your costars?

No, but on one of my directors. I will not tell you who. He is happily partnered.

If you were making a movie called Nick Mazzaro's Orgy who would you cast as your four costars?

Oh, my God, there are so many hot guys in the business I would definitely like to work with. I had the pleasure to work with Michael Soldier and Michael would definitely be one of them. When we met this year at the GAYVN Awards in LA we had hot raunchy sex in the restrooms. Who cared about the awards anyway?

Do you think the industry has a responsibility regarding the use of condoms and/or promoting safe sex?

Yes absolutely, the porn industry should promote safe sex.

If you could change one thing about the way the industry is currently run what would it be?

Monthly compulsory HIV/STD tests and no drugs on set.

Do you have some best example of bad behavior on a XXX set you would care to share?

Yes I do, but I would not say bad behavior. I have worked with some porn companies which were completely disorganized. You come to the set and there is no schedule at all nobody knows what he is supposed to do and everybody is waiting and waiting. I hate this!

Porn sets are often the place of some surreal and hilarious incidents. Do you have any personal tale you would care to share?

Oh yes, once when I was waiting for my fluffer before the shoot, somebody from the team ordered pizza, the pizza boy came in and I thought he was the fluffer, I grabbed him and pushed down his head to blow me, in the beginning he was confused and then he got mad at me. I was so embarrassed and apologized.

Nick, people often consider XXX stars to be these specimens of physical perfection, but if you could change one thing about yourself with cosmetic surgery what would it be?

I've already had everything done, nothing else needs to be done at the moment.

What factors do you think have been the greatest contribution to your success as a XXX star?

I think the ability to be flexible and easy to work with and my looks of course.

So can you give me a quick run down of the typical casting process according to your experience for adult films?

Well, all the castings I had for adult movies were definitely not made on the couch. I think this is due to the fact that I have mostly worked with major production companies. Its is usually a lot of talking and filling out papers and sometimes taking off my clothes to show myself naked and have pics taken.

Is stripping (the tease, but live) or making porn (actual sex, but on film) a bigger thrill for you as an exhibitionist?

Yes, stripping is a greater tease. There is an interaction between me and the audience. I can tease and play with them, see how they react and adjust my show to their reactions.

Which sex profession have you enjoyed the most and why: stripper, escort, or porn star?

Definitely escorting. It's amazing how many different interesting guys one can meet in this kind of business and from all over the world. My favorite ones are the straight, married men who are looking for usually their first, sexual experience with another man. When we finish I very often hear them telling me "I know now what I have been missing all those years" or "girls don't know how to blow." And these are usually the guys who hire me on a regular basis.

If you weren't working in the porn industry how do you think you would be earning your living?

Well, actually I have a masters degree in sports and I'm also a certified personal trainer. I used to do a lot of personal training before. During that time, I was asked very often if I would do more than just personal training and this is how everything started with escorting. So I guess I would go back to personal training, although I still do it part-time.

When stating your favorite sexual fantasy you mentioned wanting a dozen soldiers, barracks, and night-time. Would you care to take that one step further and tell me how it all comes together?

Imagine – me in a foreign country somewhere in the Middle East. I am driving at night and get lost somewhere in the desert. My car breaks down. I am frustrated, tired and thirsty. I leave the car somewhere trying to get somewhere by foot in order to get some help. My clothes are ripped and dirty. I take off my shirt. Sweat rolls down on my muscular body. I am desperate. My body is filthy with dirt. Finally I see some lights far away. I am so happy and try to get there as fast as I can.

When I finally get there, a lot of soldiers are there having a party – all muscular good looking ones. They talk to me but I don't understand them. I don't speak their language. They stare at me – examining every inch of my body. They rip off my clothes and throw me on the floor. They start laughing at me, pouring water on me. I am in the middle on the floor and they are all around me. They are already topless. They open their pants slowly, take out their cocks, and start jerking off. They turn me around and slap my ass. One of them is holding my hands another my feet. They kiss me. They touch me all over. Well you can imagine their rest of the story!

Where is the wildest or most unusual place you have ever had sex?

That was when I was eighteen years old with a young priest in the backyard of church.

What is the kinkiest thing you've ever done?

Well, as an escort too, I had several clients who were into kinky stuff. The kinkiest stuff a client wanted me to do was to have him bound to a tree, legs up, head down and tickle him until he shot his load. In the beginning it was weird for me but I had a lot of fun doing it.

"My favorite [escort clients] are the straight, married men who are looking for usually their first sexual experience with another man."

When it comes to seducing a man I've found nothing works better than ...

Looking deep in his eyes and undressing him with the eyes.

Speaking sexually, very few people are better than me when it comes to ...

Rimming an ass! I love to rim big, tight, bubble-butt asses. Watch me in *A Rim with a View: Part II* from Not Into Bush Productions and you will see what I mean.

How do we get you in the sack and what do we do with you once we get you there?

Just be nice and you can get me in the sack very easily and you can do whatever you want I am very flexible and very very easy-going and as a European very open-minded.

When you pass a sexy guy on the street what is it about him that makes you turn around and do a double take?

The aura, I can sense it very easily if someone has a negative or positive one. If I can sense he has a positive one I will definitely turn around to look at him again.

What is the biggest misconception people have about you when you meet them?

A lot of people think that I am arrogant or hard to deal with which is not true.

If you had to compare yourself to an animal what species do you think best captures your essence and why?

Leo the lion would be the right one for me – always fighting to achieve goals in life, very proud of the achievements, and emotionally very sensitive.

In what ways do you think you are a typical Leo?

Oh, yes, I am very typical Leo, I always want the best, never settle for less, I am very proud and get hurt very easily. Sometimes the others think I am arrogant but I am not, I would say I am more reserved when I am among people and usually stick out because of this. I am also too proud to ask somebody to help me if I need something or have a problem. I try to resolve it myself.

Describe your ideal romantic evening.

A romantic evening for me would be in a swimming pool – just me and the other person, not much light if any at all watching the stars, with no noise at all, just listening to the silence of the night.

Nick Mazzaro [PHOTO COURTESY NICK MAZZARO]

If you had to choose between sex and love which would you choose and what are your thoughts about fidelity?

I would choose love – no doubt about this. I am monogamous when in a relationship and expect the same from my partner. This may sound old-fashioned but to be true to each other in a relationship is very important to me. I have zero tolerance for open relationships.

Describe your dream vacation.

Would be in Iceland. I've never been there but would love to visit sometime. I am fascinated by the natural beauty of this country. I guess it's like being on another planet.

BLAKE **NOLAN**

How many dogs do you have and what are the breeds and names?

I have two mutts, one is a terrier mix named Mona that I found in Puerto Rico while on vacation and the other is a big lug Doberman Shepherd mix named Buddie.

So Blake, how did you get started in the business?

I looked and felt the best of my life so I wanted to have something for posterity. I was too nervous to do a guy on guy scene, but I found a company looking for solo performers. I sent in some pics and the rest is history.

What were you looking for when you for into it?

I really wanted to have the experience, discover what it was all about and see if it was something I could do. Previously I had been very uptight about sex (former Catholic here) and I wanted to do something to really embrace my sexuality.

Do you feel that making XXX films has helped you embrace your sexuality?

STATS

BIRTH DATE: May 17

SIGN: Taurus

HOMETOWN: Boston

HEIGHT: 6'2"

WEIGHT: 235 lbs

TWO BEST CHARACTER TRAITS: Loyal and a good sense of humor

TWO WORST CHARACTER TRAITS: Impatient and stubborn

FAVORITE MUSIC: Alternative: Audioslave, Muse, Killers, She Wants Revenge

FAVORITE MOVIES: *American President, Death Becomes Her*

FAVORITE MOVIES I'VE BEEN IN: *Centurion Muscle Alpha, Lords of the Jungle*

XXX COSTAR I'D DO AGAIN IN A MINUTE: François Sagat (again and again ...)

IF I COULD MAKE ONE REQUEST ON A PORN SET IT WOULD BE: Play sexy music, like Nine Inch Nails or Depeche Mode, but then you might not hear the director.

AS A TEEN I ALWAYS FANTASIZED ABOUT SEX WITH: Lee Horsley, the Matt Houston guy. Woof!

CURRENT FANTASY MAN: Ben Roethlisberger, Steelers QB.

SEXIEST PART OF A MAN: Smile, especially if he has a slow, devious grin, drives me nuts

THREE INGREDIENTS OF MY HOTTEST SEX FANTASY: The Navy Seals, a deserted island and of course, me.

FAVORITE ITEM IN MY SEXUAL TOY BOX: I don't have a toy box. Damn, I am vanilla. I am going to have to explore that a little more.

MOST PRIZED POSSESSION: My dogs.

HOBBIES: Reading, tennis, bodybuilding, travel.

PETS: Two of the sweetest, most lovable pain in the ass mutts.

PET PEEVES: Bigotry, cruelty, indifference, duplicitous people and, oh yeah, *Deal or No Deal*. What the hell is that all about?

Definitely. I used to feel I still had a long way to go when I compared myself to others in the industry, but when I instead compare myself today with how I was a few years ago, I realize I have come a long way and I am really proud of that.

Blake, were the people who knew you surprised when you started making movies?

None of my close friends were all that surprised. They knew it was always something I wanted to do. I think they would be surprised if I quit my day job to pursue porn full time.

Do you recall your first movie and the first bit of direction you were given?

The first movie I ever did was a solo, so there was little direction. Probably things like, "OK, now finger your hole" or "tug on your nuts."

What about making porn didn't you expect?

I really didn't expect it to be such a huge industry with so many similarities to mainstream entertainment venues. Award shows, gossip columns, agents, exclusivity deals. There are so many people involved that I never knew existed in porn.

What things do you do to help your prepare for a shoot?

Eat little to no carbs. To prepare mentally, if I can spend some time with the person I am going to have a scene with, that usually helps a lot. I realize this can backfire, but I have been pretty lucky so far. There are certain things that will shut me down, so I like to warn a scene partner ahead of time and find out what they like and don't like as well.

What is the most turned on you have ever been on screen?

In *Centurion Muscle Alph*a, I was eating François Sagat's ass while he sucked my dick. I was so amazingly turned on, I forgot I was in a studio and doing a scene.

If you were offered a role in a fetish film how far do you think you would go? And do you think you would be more likely to go further for the cameras or in the privacy of your own bedroom?

If it were for a director I liked and trusted, I might explore a little bit beyond my repertoire, but I would definitely explore further in the privacy of my own bedroom.

If you were making a movie called Blake's Orgy who would you demand as your four costars?

Only four, that's not fair. There are so many hot men in the industry. Can you clone Collin O'Neal? That would work.

So what about Collin O'Neal makes him your ideal XXX costar?

He is so many things in one person. He has a boyish charm, but also a rugged masculinity. If you look into his eyes, there is just so much going on in there. You can see he is a deep, intellectual person, but he can also be the social, party guy with an amazing sense of humor. And on a more superficial level, he is amazingly handsome, has a beautiful ass and a perfect dick.

What is the first thing you like to do when you get home from filming a XXX flick?

Eat pizza and have hot monkey sex with my partner.

Is it tough having a partner and making porn? What are some of the keys to making that work?

I think it can be tough, but my partner is an amazing man. We have been together more than 11 years now. We were monogamous for much of the relationship, but the partnership evolved over the years and we were able to evolve with it. We have always been honest with each other and trust each other completely. I think that is what makes it work.

So what about your partner made you realize he was the one when you guys got together 11 years ago?

We had been chatting on AOL and then the phone for weeks before we met. Back then, nobody had pictures available, so we only had descriptions to go by. I knew I loved who this man was as a person and wanted him in my life, but when we met and there was this amazing physical chemistry as well, I knew he was the one.

Blake Nolan [PHOTO BY KENT TAYLOR, COURTESY RAGING STALLION STUDIOS]

If someone were to come to you for advice about getting into the business what would you tell them?

Have fun with the experience and don't make it your life. This way anything you do is based on your desires and not making the rent.

Do you have some grand fantasy that you are just waiting for some director to ask you to film? Lately,

I have been fantasizing about having sex with one or more young, smooth guys. Not twinks, but a young athletic jock type like Brad Star or Erik Rhodes. Most of my scene partners are rugged, hairy men, which I love, but such a contrast would be very hot.

Do you think the industry has a responsibility regarding the use of condoms and/or promoting safe sex?

Absolutely! I think it is up to the industry to show how hot sex can be even while playing safe. The more people see it, especially the younger, more impressionable fans, the more it will become second nature for them to throw on a condom or ask someone to put one on.

Have you ever developed a crush on any of your costars? Care to name names?

Not really a crush, but I did meet someone who I connected with physically and mentally

so it was great to have them around. They made me feel very comfortable being away from home.

Do you have a favorite overall scene from a XXX movie and if so what scene and for what reason?

There is a scene I remember I used to watch over and over. It's an old pre-condom movie (I don't even remember the name of it) with Tom Brock and Jim Pulver. Jim Pulver fucks the snot out of Brock on a subway. It was just such a hot, animalistic fuck and Brock was my dream bottom.

Do you have any childhood or adolescent memory that you can look back upon and say, "Oh yeah, that kid was destined to grow up to be a porn star"?

When I was five, my mother said I ran away and she couldn't find me anywhere. She was a total wreck when the phone rang and the police called to tell her I was down at the precinct. She said when she got there, I was sitting on one policeman's lap, eating an ice cream cone and talking a blue streak to the rest of the squad who were standing around in a circle chuckling in amusement. I knew where to go alright!

Have you experienced any real life repercussions from appearing in XXX films?

Not yet, but I think about it sometimes. I did get my teaching certification and if I ever decided to pursue that, I would worry about it some.

If you could change one thing about the way the industry is currently run what would it be?

I would like to see more romantic porn. I mean I like the hard fucking nasty shit too, but it would be good to see more passionate sex showcased.

"The more people see [safe sex], especially the younger, more impressionable fans, the more it will become second nature for them to throw on a condom or ask someone to put one on."

Do you have some best example of bad behavior on a XXX set you would care to share?

I have been very lucky in my experiences. I have always worked with complete professionals. Everyone has always treated me with great respect. I can only give a word of advice to bottoms out there: please douche thoroughly.

Speaking sexually, very few guys are as skilled as me when it comes to ...

Kissing (we are talking knee weakening).

How would you describe yourself in a personals ad?

A little information about me – masculine, muscular, healthy, physically and mentally fit guy. Priorities in my life include family, friends, my dogs, work, and taking time out to have fun;

Blake Nolan [PHOTO BY KENT TAYLOR, COURTESY RAGING STALLION STUDIOS]

interests include working out, hiking, tennis, books, new restaurants, movies, and traveling. Tend to be attracted to guys who are masculine, in good shape, honest, self-assured, goal-oriented, and can make me laugh.

Where is the wildest place you've ever had sex?

Once, when I had been traveling for a couple of weeks, my partner and I couldn't wait to have sex, so we did it in the airport parking garage next to our car.

When it comes to seducing a man I've found nothing works better than ...

Making them feel special. Listening to what they say. Giving them your total attention and flattering their attributes. Making them laugh goes a long way too.

When you pass a hot looking guy on the street what gets you to turn around and do a double take every time?

A nice pair of legs will get me to turn around to check the ass, but a slow, sexy grin gets me every time.

What is the biggest misconception people have about you when you meet them?

I think the biggest misconception is that I am unapproachable. I love meeting new people, especially fans of my work. I am pretty imposing at 6'2, 235, but I am one of the friendliest down to earth people around.

How do you think you are a typical Taurus?

Mess with the bull, you get the horns.

If you had to compare yourself to an animal what species do you think best captures your essence and why?

I guess I would say a bear, not just because I am big and furry, but because when left alone or treated well, I am a friendly passive guy, but come shit in my territory or screw with me or a loved one and I will rip you to pieces.

Describe your ideal romantic evening:

Getting dressed up, going to a nice restaurant, good food, wine and conversation. A lot of kissing and foreplay in the hot tub before things really get started.

If you had to choose between sex and love which would you choose and what are your thoughts about fidelity?

I have always been able to separate sex and love and I think that is why I am able to work in the adult industry. To me fidelity is where you put your heart, not your dick. It would be more upsetting to me if someone I loved shared their hopes and dreams with someone else, rather than sharing their bodily fluids.

Describe your dream vacation.

I would love to explore Central Europe. It would be great to explore the history and architecture of Prague and Budapest. And the men there are amazing.

Where do you foresee this career taking you?

Not far. Really, I have already accomplished more than I ever imagined. Working with Colt and Falcon, making the cover of Unzipped, being made an exclusive with Raging Stallion, meeting Chi Chi LaRue. I hope one day to meet Steven Scarborough because I really respect him a lot and I love his movies.

MATTHIEU **PARIS**

What's your dog's name and breed?

His name is Brisco. If he had been born a year later he would have been named Crisco! He's a German Pointer.

How did you get started in the adult film business?

It was my dream to be in the porn business. When I arrived in Paris I met a guy very aware of the business who gave me all the addresses of where I needed to go to be cast. Then by chance I chatted with Mo Duran, from Raging Stallion, on the Net and my career was launched. I will always be grateful to Raging Stallion Studios.

What were you looking for when you got into it?

At the beginning it was just accomplishing that dream I had to be in a porn movie, but little by little I got caught into wanting to shoot more and more movies.

So what about making XXX movies made you want to keep making more and more of them? What were you getting out of the experience?

I'm so excited when the cameras are rolling. It's like an addiction. It's not the sex because I've had better sex without camera on me. But the

STATS

BIRTH DATE: June 17, 1976

SIGN: Gemini

HOMETOWN: Paris, France

HEIGHT: 6'2"

WEIGHT: 198 lbs

TWO BEST CHARACTER TRAITS: I'm nice and open-minded.

TWO WORST CHARACTER TRAITS: I'm jealous and sometimes have a bad temper.

FAVORITE MUSIC: Progressive music.

FAVORITE MOVIES: *Moulin Rouge, Amelie.*

FAVORITE MOVIES I'VE BEEN IN: *Mister Fister, Arabian Fist, Fist and Shout.*

XXX COSTAR I'D DO AGAIN IN A MINUTE: Dirk Jager or Huessein.

IF I COULD MAKE ONE DEMAND ON A XXX SET IT WOULD BE: I would like shootings to flow, so no stop and go.

AS A TEEN I ALWAYS FANTASIZED ABOUT SEX WITH: Not as a teen, but I wanna shoot with Adam Faust and Arpad Miklos.

CURRENT FANTASY MAN: Big muscles, big arms, hairy men.

SEXIEST PART OF A MAN: The armpits

3 INGREDIENTS IN MY HOTTEST SEX FANTASY: Odors, exciting place, hairy men.

FAVORITE ITEM IN MY SEXUAL TOY BOX: My dildo "Bam" – black and realistic.

MOST PRIZED POSSESSION: My boyfriend.

HOBBIES: The Internet, the porn industry, sex parties.

PET: My dog

PET PEEVES: Queenie men, and drinking from someone else's glass (or eating from someone else's silverware) – yikes!

Matthieu Paris [PHOTO BY KENT TAYLOR, COURTESY RAGING STALLION STUDIOS]

idea that guys will get off watching me makes me very horny.

What was the best advice you were given starting out?

My friend Pascal, who helped me get started, has always had good advice for me. I often talk to him about where I want to go with my career. If I should accept such and such a project. He helps me stay grounded.

And if someone came to you for advice about getting into the business what would you tell him?

I often advise beginners who ask me that very question. I tell them to know exactly why they want to get into it, what kind of movies they want to make, and what kind of career they expect. For me it's important to have a guideline to follow.

What is the most aroused you have ever been on screen?

I loved the scene I did with Kent North in *Mister Fister*, but I think the biggest turn-on was during my scene with *Violator* and Butch Grand in *Fist and Shout Part 2*. Big men with big hairy arms – Woof! I also have fond memoirs of the shooting of *Arabian Fist* with Dirk Jager.

You mention Kent North whose passing was so sad. Is there any memory of working with him you would care to share with readers?

During our scene we were just very close, totally on the same wavelength. He was such a nice person in real life and a great partner.

How did you get into fisting?

Until the age of 25 I was a top only. But I met a partner when I was living in the center of France who started to want to insert dildos in my hole and other strange objects – like cucumbers and eggplants. Then he started fisting me and that was it. I had found my calling.

What is a common misconception about fisting that people have?

Some people think it's dirty. I say "If you can put your dick in this hole, why couldn't you stick your hand in, too?"

What do you feel is the secret to making fisting a pleasurable experience?

For the best experience possible it needs to be done in good conditions – and especially not done quickly! But the most important thing is the connection between partners. The trust has to be there for sure. Fisting is the most pleasurable and incredible sex act, and once you get started I can assure you that you will never look back. It's addictive.

What things do you usually do to prepare for a day of filming?

During the days before the shoot I'm always very nervous and anxious, so I try and relax alone – read, eat, etc., to free my mind and stay focused on giving my best to the director.

And how do you usually spend the evening after a day of shooting?

Two possibilities: Either I grab something to eat and take a nap if the shooting has been exhausting or I keep on fucking all night long! I'm a pig you know.

If you were making a movie called Matthieu's Orgy who would you demand as your four costars?

Adam Faust, Sean Harris, Huessein, and Joshua Adams.

Do you have any amazing fantasy you are just waiting for some director to ask you to film?

I had the fantasy of getting my hole totally lubed up with a funnel, and that's been done. Now if someone would propose me a gangbang close to a rape but in a very familiar setting – a real-life situation not in a studio – I'd be very happy.

So what would your setting be?

I think it would begin in the street, where a bunch of guys would follow me to my apartment building, then force me to the cellar or the parking lot and have their way with me. It would have to look very realistic, almost brutal at first, before turning very sexy.

Is it painful, educational, arousing, or hilarious to watch yourself on screen?

At the beginning I hated watching myself on the screen. I could only see what was wrong, and was very critical of my performance. With time I learned to watch my movies as a whole, not just through my performance or through my own vision. But I don't get off looking at me on a big screen.

Do you have any long term ideas or plans of where you want this career to take you?

I'm hoping to have the longest career possible. I don't want to shoot only fisting movies and I want to work with different studios, even if I am happy being a Raging Stallion exclusive. In the long run I want to direct my own line of fisting movies. I have a few ideas I want to see on the screen and why not create my own studio in Europe in a few years.

So what have you learned in front of the cameras that is going to come in handy when you move behind them?

I know exactly what would look good on camera and I know what hard work it is. I'd be very kind with performers, but I'd want them to give me 110%.

People often consider porn stars to be these ideal physical specimens, but if you could change one thing about yourself through cosmetic surgery what would it be?

People tell me I have a big dick, but if it were fatter and longer I wouldn't mind. I'd also love to have more hair on my chest, so I'd go for hair implants there!

Do you have some childhood or young adult memory that you can look back upon and say, "Yep, that kid was destined to grow up to be a porn star"?

As far as I can remember I always wanted to be on film and sex is my favorite thing to do – so yeah, I was doomed from the beginning.

XXX Movies are notorious for putting models in some very uncomfortable positions for the sake of the shot. What is the most uncomfortable one you have ever had to assume?

No position is too uncomfortable for me. In fact, I'm the first one to ask the director if I can switch positions very often. I've been seein getting fisted standing up, upside down. In the last movie I was in, *Fistfracht* for Wurstfilm, I was in excruciating pain because I had hurt my back just before the shoot. I hope it doesn't show.

If you could change one thing about the way the industry is currently run what would it be?

Each company has its own way of doing business that fits its style, with its own niche. There's room for everyone, I think, but I'd make sure all the models were well treated. Without performers there would be no industry.

Do you have some best example of bad behavior on a XXX set you would care to share?

Porn is hard work and I never really experienced anything bad on the set, except for performers who think they are better than the others. The diva attitude has to go (because it shows on the screen anyway).

Do you think the industry has a responsibility regarding the use of condoms and/or promoting safe sex?

I think the industry exists for people to get off and get excited by whatever fantasy they want to see on the screen. In no way should there be a censor to decide what people should watch or do in their own bedroom. There are other ways to do that. It's a free world, as long as everyone is honest.

What is the biggest misconception people have about you when you meet them?

People who don't know me often think that I'm cold and very intimidating when in fact I'm quite outgoing and fun.

How would you describe yourself in a personals advertisement and what

sort of man would you be advertising for?

I'd probably look for a muscle man, and most importantly hairy. It would look like – GWM, 31 y.o. 6'2" `198 looking for hairy muscle stud for hot and kinky adventure.

If you had to choose between sex and love which would it be and what are your thoughts on intimacy?

Fidelity? Hmmm. I believe in fidelity of feelings. I've been married to the same man for ten years. He has all my heart and soul but he knows that sexually I have a very big appetite.

"I say 'If you can put your dick in this hole, why couldn't you stick your hand in, too?'"

So we decided that sexual jealousy wouldn't be part of our relationship. I don't need to choose between love and sex. I have both.

When it comes to seducing a man I've found nothing works better than ...

A naughty gaze.

What is the best pickup line you have ever used or fallen for?

I don't usually fall for that kind of language. But one night, while I was working at the Depot, a sex-club in Paris, a guy said to me very directly: "I just want you – right here, right now." Of course I couldn't right away, but it gave me a hard-on for the rest of the night.

When you pass a hot looking guy on the street what causes you to turn around and do a double take every time?

I always do a double take on the street! But with a nice muscled guy with hairy arms I change directions!

Describe your ideal romantic evening.

Ooh la la! I don't think a romantic evening is made for me, but why not start with a night at the Moulin Rouge with dinner and a show. For the rest, actually I prefer to be surprised. I'm more touched by the unexpected than the romantic.

Where is the wildest place you've ever had sex?

I don't usually go out to sex clubs or big meetings, but I think the city where guys are the most sex-crazed is Berlin. That town has the most hardcore and hottest guys I've ever met.

How do you think you are a typical Gemini?

I think I can be very diplomatic. I have a hard time saying no. I'm generous and usually a very nice person, but when a situation pisses me off, I can be very brutal, abrupt with words, and it could even get physical.

If you had to compare yourself to an animal what species do you think best captures your essence and why?

I'd be a predator, always looking for flesh. Or an ostrich with it's butt sticking in the air (Laughs).

Describe your dream vacation.

I have to admit that while we were

shooting *Mirage* and *Arabian Fist* finding myself around swimming pools and Jacuzzis with the biggest porn stars of our time was totally my idea of a perfect vacation.

Does you cock have a nickname and if so how did it come about?

I never named my cock, but my ass is what people are talking about – maybe The Tunnel!

Matthieu Paris [PHOTO BY KENT TAYLOR, COURTESY RAGING STALLION STUDIOS]

ZACKARY **PIERCE**

How did you get started in the business?

I went to meet Matthew Rush at Bourbon Street in San Diego one night. Got stinking drunk. Went home with my roomie Josh and said I want to be in porn. Snapped some photos, filled out Falcon's questionnaire, and woke up the next morning to them calling. Before you knew it was flying to San Francisco and then Hawaii!

What were you looking for when you got into it?

Fun!

Do you recall your first movie and the first bit of direction you were given?

Filming *Iron Works*, the director told me, "Keep this up, and you will be a huge star before you know it!"

You mention getting bored easily, what about making XXX movies is the most boring part of the day?

Waiting. Waiting for amateurs to cum. Waiting for the sets to be just right. Waiting for the makeup artists to get your makeup right (They never do). Waiting for this and waiting for that. Hurry up and wait. Thought I

STATS

BIRTH DATE: June 11, 1981

SIGN: Gemini

HOMETOWN: Chicago, IL

HEIGHT: 5'9"

WEIGHT: 170 lbs

TWO BEST CHARACTER TRAITS: Common sense and the ability to win the admiration of others.

TWO WORST CHARACTER TRAITS: I have a need for constant mental stimulation and a need for variety in life. I get bored easily.

FAVORITE MUSIC: Dance

FAVORITE MOVIES: Comedies

FAVORITE MOVIES I'VE BEEN IN: *The Road to Temptation* (Hot House), *How to Seduce a Straight Man* (Red Devil), *Little Big League 2* (Unzipped).

XXX COSTAR I'D DO AGAIN IN A MINUTE: Eddie Stone

IF I COULD MAKE ONE REQUEST ON A PORN SET IT WOULD BE: No whining

AS A TEEN I ALWAYS FANTASIZED ABOUT SEX WITH: Teachers

CURRENT FANTASY MAN: Chris Wilde, Michael Brandon, Francois Sagat

SEXIEST PART OF A MAN: His torso

THREE INGREDIENTS OF MY HOTTEST SEX FANTASY: Muscles, sweat, passion

FAVORITE ITEM IN MY SEXUAL TOY BOX: Underwear

MOST PRIZED POSSESSION: My condo in San Diego

HOBBIES: Cruising for sex

PETS: None

PET PEEVES: Uncleanliness

was in the military again!

You also mention "no whining" as the thing you would like to change most on a XXX set. What is the whining usually about?

"Oh that hurts. Wait. I need a break." If you are a bottom be good at it. I am a top and I am good at it. If you are a bottom I expect you to do your part. Otherwise maybe porn ain't for you. And, as for those dirty bottoms? I needn't say more.

If you were to make a movie called Zachary's Orgy who would you want as your four costars?

Michael Brandon, Chris Wilde, François Sagat, Francesco D'Macho.

Speaking sexually, very few guys are as skilled as me when it comes to ...

Hitting that spot just right. I am better at doing this off film. Because with film you have to do it to the side. Do it this way or that so it looks good. But when I am just having

Zachary Pierce [PHOTO COURTESY HOT HOUSE ENTERTAINMENT]

Zachary Pierce [PHOTO COURTESY HOT HOUSE ENTERTAINMENT]

"If you are a bottom I expect you to do your part. Otherwise maybe porn ain't for you."

great sex it's a whole different story.

So if cruising for sex is your hobby how do you usually cruise? Can you give me the usual scenario?

Gym (not a gay one) and intense eye contact from across the room.

Where is the wildest place you've ever had sex?

Somewhere between Baker and Vegas. Driving home and sitting in traffic, bored, horny. Pulled off and got off!

Describe your ideal romantic evening.

Orgy! The more the merrier!

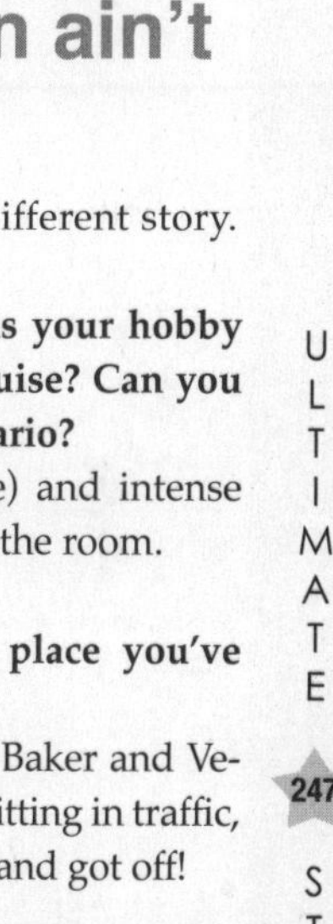

AKOS **PIROS**

How did you get started in the business?

It was my desire to make porn beginning from my youth. I started late, when I was at the end of my thirties. I wanted it though so I searched for contacts, I found contacts, and I got started. Whenever I intensely want to do something I do it. I find a way to do it, sometimes without success and sometimes with success. In porn it worked out well.

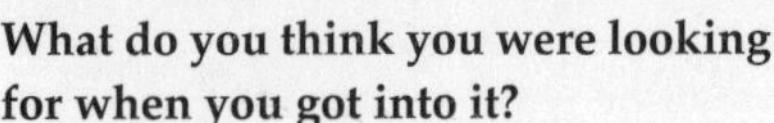

What do you think you were looking for when you got into it?

I am exhibitionist. It makes me totally horny when I see or imagine others turned on by watching me being naked and showing off and enjoying pure sex.

What things do you usually do to prepare for a film shoot?

I like to be prepared by the director. I want to read the story or the script. I want to know the goal (objectives, target) of the film we shoot together. I want to learn the dialogue and lines (some directors don't send it, unfortunately) because I want to do my job as well as possible and because I want to be prepared mentally for the role I have to play in the film. The better we actors are at playing our roles the better the film will be for our fans and the gay community (and of course the business results will be better for the producer!).

What is your favorite thing to do sexually?

I will tell you three favorites because I can't decide – all three are on the same level:

a) To be a very consensual top/master over one or more boys/men.

b) To be the best slave/bottom pleasing and obeying (including suffering and being humiliated) a real man with the goal that he will be proud of me and being totally satisfied with that.

c) To have very sensitive romantic sex with one male-partner (that means not a feminine kind of boy, but a real man). It would include good foreplay, a lot of time (a long scene), licking, stroking, fucking and/or being fucked.

You mentioned your prized possession was your books. What sort of things do you like to read?

I read German, Hungarian and English written books (it's necessary to save the language-skills). I like management-books (about leadership) and books about rhetoric (these kind of books I need for my main profession); I read a lot of biographies and autobiographies because I can learn a lot from other men and their lives; and I like novels because they show a lot of characters and they describe life with all its wonderful and hard sides. Well written novels develop my emotions and sensitive feelings toward others and motivate me in hard times to fight for my future or for others I like or love.

My favorite writer is the Norwegian Nobel-Prize winner Knut Hamsun. And I like to read about history and documentations about political/economic topics. I need a lot of space for my books to save them all in my flat. Of course, it is often a question of time. But I decided to read in the gym during training on the Laufband/running machine – I don't know the English word for the machine. You use it in gyms for running.

A treadmill.

Yes.

Describe your ideal romantic evening.

Oh, Owen, it's a wonderfully important question, but hard to answer. I want to say: I can't plan the ideal romantic evening because what does romantic mean in my mind? The spring of any romance is love or falling in love with each other. And the romantic hours just happen. In my life it has always been a gift, a wonderful surprise. Whenever I have planned some kind of romantic get together – uh-oh ... in these things I am a bad planner, In my profession planning tasks is very important for me. But not in romance. In romance when I plan it, I want to be successful and see positive results, but that mental focusing destroys romance!

So, I won't describe my plan, I'll describe the most ideal romantic afternoon I've had in my life. It happened just a few weeks ago with a Chinese man of my age I had gotten to know in a Turkish-thermal-bath in an Eastern European capital. He lives in that capital in a small one-room-flat. He

STATS

BIRTH DATE: August 26, 1962

HOMETOWN: Vienna, Austria, EU

HEIGHT: 1.80 m

WEIGHT: 91 kg

TWO BEST CHARACTER TRAITS: I'm very reliable and sensitive.

TWO WORST CHARACTER TRAITS: I'm impatient when stressed and stubborn.

FAVORITE MUSIC: Johann Sebastian Bach; jazz.

FAVORITE MOVIES: Thrillers.

FAVORITE MOVIES I'VE BEEN IN: *Hostile* (Colt), *SexKlinik* (Cazzo), *UncutSexClub* (Lucasentertainment)

XXX COSTAR I'D DO AGAIN IN A MINUTE: Marc Williams

IF I COULD MAKE ONE REQUEST ON A PORN SET IT WOULD BE: Good fresh air, please!

AS A TEEN I ALWAYS FANTASIZED ABOUT SEX WITH: A group of athletic men and boys outdoors.

CURRENT FANTASY MAN: He's huge, rough, and muscular.

SEXIEST PART OF A MAN: A hard cock.

THREE INGREDIENTS OF MY HOTTEST SEX FANTASY: In front of people with more than two men, a lot of sperm and pee or just the opposite: very lovely and romantic sex with one loved man/friend.

FAVORITE ITEM IN MY SEXUAL TOY BOX: My tit clamps.

MOST PRIZED POSSESSION: My books.

HOBBIES: Sports, reading, cinema, walking around (nature).

PETS: (If you mean animals) I love pets but I don't have any. They would suffer since I am traveling a lot.

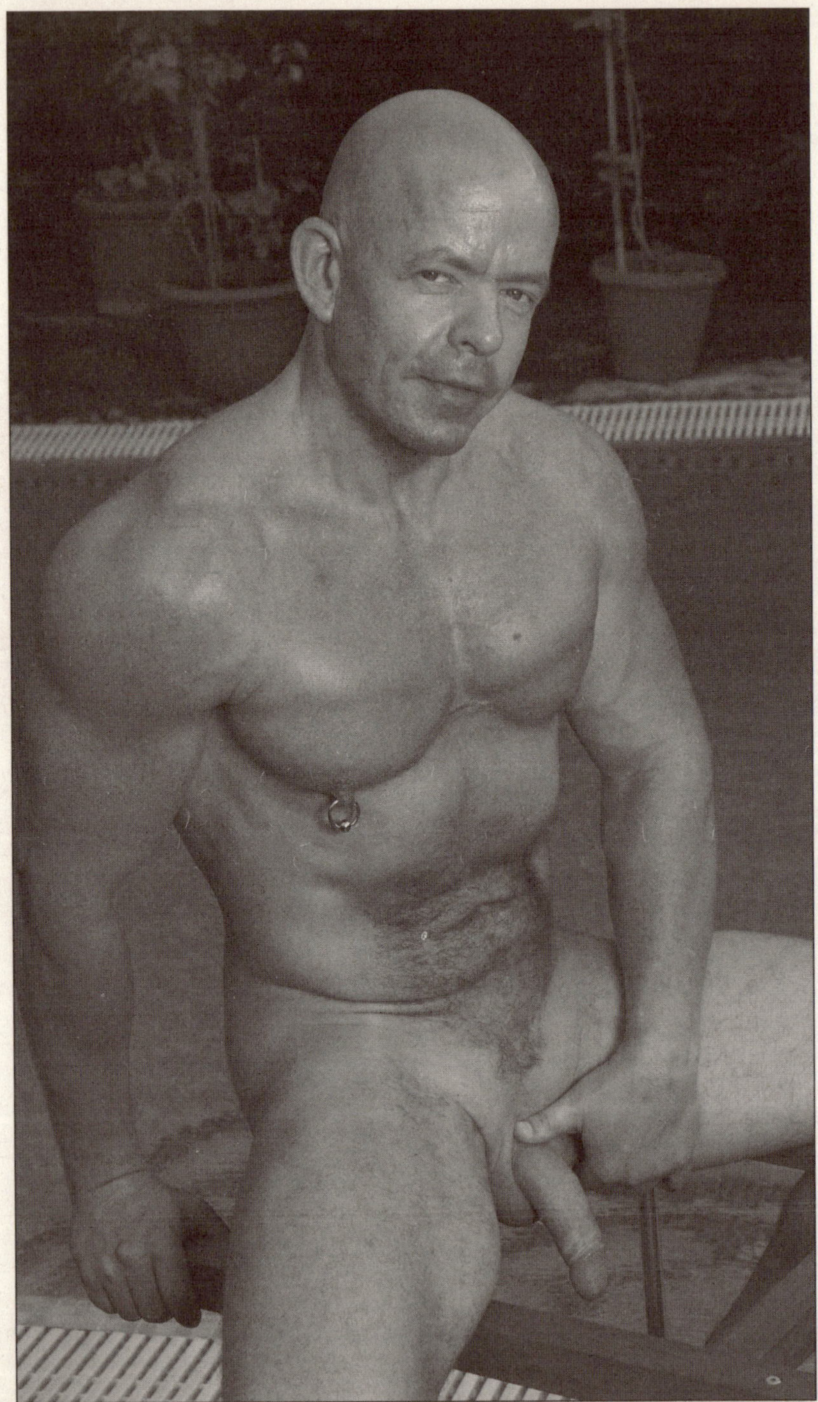

Akos Piros [PHOTO COURTESY LUCASENTERTAINMENT.COM]

invited me over. I was so glad to meet him again and he felt happy being with me. When I came in we hugged each other and I stroked his head, we kissed and we felt incredible. He made a wonderful Chinese tea, we drank it, ate some cakes, we talked a lot of our weeks since we met last time before.

Romantic? Yes because of atmosphere, the emotions, and the feelings. We held hands, talked seriously, joked, and laughed a lot. Loving and laughing is a wonderful combination. That afternoon I had only one interest and one goal – to do whatever he wanted to do. I did not want to waste time since we had so little together. I asked him, What do you want to do this afternoon? He smiled and replied, he would like to have a little nap now-so we did. We took off our clothes and shared his bed, a small one, but when we were very close to each other. It was enough space for both of us. I felt his skin. We did not start to have sex at that moment, we enjoyed lying together very close. He stroked me and I stroked him in a very sensitive and tender way. It was so fantastic for me. I never felt like I did that afternoon.

There were only good feelings, loving, being totally relaxed–soul and body–and being thankful for each other. That, combined with a lot of time (no watch, no stress, only us being together). His butt, his body, his skin, his face, his lips, his tongue. It was not cock-centered sex. It was body-to-body, skin-to-skin, nose-to-nose, head-to-shoulder, face-to-face and much more: heart-to-heart. Later on he began to sleep, his head resting on my shoulders. I absolutely don't like the noise of snoring (I have been a soldier for twelve years sharing tents and rooms with a lot of men in missions abroad so I've had enough of snoring for my life). His snoring I really loved! Yes, it's crazy, but it's one of the signs of that romantic afternoon. I did not mind his snoring, but it felt so good seeing and hearing him being totally relaxed. When he awoke we continued our touching and stroking and kissing each other. It developed and then we began to blow each other with unbelievable intensity and tenderness. You can imagine the following minutes and hour. It was so wonderful and romantic.

That's really lovely. Can you describe your dream vacation?

A silent quiet place in nature, but close to city with a lot of people there, time and somebody to share the vacation with – somebody meaning a real friend ...

What are you the most grateful for in your life?

I am most grateful to be alive. It sounds strange, but I have been in danger sometimes in my life (in real danger) – and I am really glad for the simple luxury of living!

What do you hope to be doing five years from now?

I hope to be healthy and doing my jobs, still being able and willing to do it well and to earn that money I need for economical stability. In private life I hope to have a man whom I love and he loves me and that the circumstances of our lives allow us to live together. It's my greatest desire at the moment. It's not possible with my Chinese man I told you about. He has to go back home very soon, unfortunately.

What about making XXX films surprised you?

Most of the colleagues are very friendly, there is no negative kind of competition or fighting among porn stars. Even though of course everybody wants to be the best. We all know that a film is well done only with good teamwork!

ever forget the goal of each film: the viewer (your fans!) should enjoy all details of your acting!

4. Be a good porn star for your fans: Answer all e-mails you get in a friendly way and as soon as possible! It is our way of customer care!

5. Do a good marketing job for

"In last months, when I go to gay club or gay sauna, fans are asking me to wank off and cum onto their hands and they use it as lotion on their skin. It's strange, but they love it."

If a young man were to come to you for advice about getting into the adult film business what would you tell him?

1. Welcome, colleague, into our business! I wish you great success!

2. Why do you want to do it? Do it only when you are sure you want to do it, when you are enjoying doing sex work on the set or on the stage (and not only because you need quick money)! When you enjoy it you will be a good porn star.

3. The porn business is a normal business. Therefore be a good worker like in all other jobs: be on time; be friendly; do all which is good for the company you are still working for; obey (not in a stupid way, but using your brain proactively and feeling responsible for your part as part of the whole thing) the director; be a good team player in cooperating with your colleagues; be patient (oh, sometimes you have to wait so long); be prepared (mentally for your role, learn your lines); negotiate all details which are important for you days before shooting, never on the set. Don't

yourself! If you don't know how and what that means in detail, feel free to ask me. Without marketing you will get no jobs and nobody is really waiting for you.

6. Take care of your health!

7. Be proud of your job and yourself! This also means, don't let anybody abuse you. You should be used in a good professional way, of course, but never abused by those who only want to make quick money for themselves by showing you off. Sometimes we have to say no, when jobs are offered. If you are not sure phone me or another colleague, I shall listen to you and your story and we will try to make a good decision!

8. Please don't take any drugs. It's so sad to seeing a lot of colleagues being on drugs. Perhaps they feel better during hard shoots, but we are more successful for longer times (period), when we are fit and healthy and free!

9.When you do your porn job professionally, feeling responsible for the business behind it, as a good colleague and as a good member of the director's team, keeping your body healthy and in good shape – then you have the chance for good jobs for a lot of years. We men have more chances than women. We get more interesting as we get older and mature – that could be your future, too! I wish you the best!

10. Life has its risks. A porn job's greatest risk is that we can loose our job suddenly by getting sick or by accident or by others (new love, real love?) or by political changes (new laws). Keep your original job skills active, update your knowledge in your other profession(s), be ready every time for working outside of porn, keep independent and free! The best way is not to work exclusively in porn. It is better to do it as a side-job.

How do you usually spend the evening when you get home from shooting/filming an adult movie?

When the next day is free from shooting, first I go to gym and a steam sauna. Then I love to eat some good foods, hopefully not alone, but with a good friend. Or simply laying on the bed and watching TV or a good film. And then sleeping very well. Oh, it is a fine feeling when a job is done well! And when I am not lonely: a good sex-session without the goal of success like in a job is very fine, too! Sex only for enjoyment and satisfying horny lust!

You probably have many fans who request various things from you. What is the most unusual or memorable thing you have ever been asked by a fan?

A new trend has developed it seems. In last months, when I go to gay club or gay sauna, fans are asking me to wank off and cum onto their hands and they use it as lotion on their skin (chest or face or just hands). It's strange, but they love it. When I am ready, I do it. Sometimes I am not ready. I call that "Operation SpermAkos". Those who ask me via e-mail living far away from me, mostly want to have (in a traditionally way) pants or thongs with my sperm in it. I sell it, of course, when they want to have it. Of course with freshly produced SpermAkos! Just ask akos@akos-piros.com.

So do you have to cum a lot to keep those fans happy who want all your sperm? Do you have any tricks for ejaculating a big load?

Oh, yes, I have to cum a lot, and I like it very much! The men who want me to cum for them, the men I always see, they are really happy to have my white sperm as lotion for their skin. The only big-load trick I know is to go without cumming one or two days to ejaculate a big load. So because I cum each day two to four times, I seldom have really big loads. I need a special task or mission to produce a big load! Owen, if you know another trick, please tell it!

When people recognize you from films do they treat you differently?

Mostly I am very surprised, when somebody asks: Are you Akos Piros? It happens sometimes in a coffee shop or in the metro (tube, underground) or when I walk through a city. The last time it happened in Las Vegas, even though I am from Austria!. I enjoy it very much, and when we have time we go for a quick drink to talk with each other.

What are the best and the worst parts of making a living in the sex industry?

The best is traveling around and getting a lot of cute colleagues and fans. The worst part is to working sometimes with straight guys in gay porn (Eastern Europe).

So what is the worst part about working making adult films with straight men?

I prefer to have good sex with those who like sex with men too. I am far from being a rapist. I like to rape somebody as a part of role play (in S/M-sessions for private, or in films). But during film shooting: I must work against my own nature and sexual feelings. When I know: this guy is straight and he is having sex with me only because of money – I get used to it, but I try to switch off my brain when it begins to disturb me mentally.

Do you enjoy watching yourself on film or does it make you embarrassed or uncomfortable?

Watching myself is as strange for me as listening my own voice recorded. I am too critical towards myself. I am not embarrassed, but I feel uncomfortable.

Where is the wildest or most unusual place you have ever had sex?

My wildest place? It was a nudist area on Balaton Lake in Hungary in front of many others. We only took care that there were no children there. Many watched and nobody had any problem. Some gave us a great applause after cumming. It was great!

What are your secrets for seducing a man you are interested in?

You asked using the right word: secrets. It is still my secret. And who knows – perhaps I get interested in you, when I personally get to know you, Owen! What would I do without my secret if I tell it to you here?

OK, if you won't tell me how you seduce men than can I know what is the secret to arousing or seducing you?

Owen, You never give up! It's a good question, and very important for me. You deserve my answer! The secret is: When I see and feel that you really like me, and you enjoy my body, and when I feel you are a man with a body (it means strong hands, too. I check out everybody when shaking hands!), brain. and soul. When that is all together you are on your way to arousing and seducing me. How can I feel it and see it? With my eyes and in my heart. They are very sensitive and directly connected with my cock.

Akos Piros is a very nice lyrical name. Is it your real name? If not, how did that name come about?

My very first film made in Hungary was shot for an US-company; I was not asked which stage name I have. The director wrote the US producer: "Call him Chad Thomas". During shooting for Cazzo Film/ Berlin (*Sexklinik*) the producer asked me to find a better name because I am a European and Chad is more an American name. I decided to take my real second Christian name Ákos. It is an old Hungarian name. Cazzo-Producer said: You need a second name like a family name. I could not find the right name for me. So, he chose "Fehér" because this name was

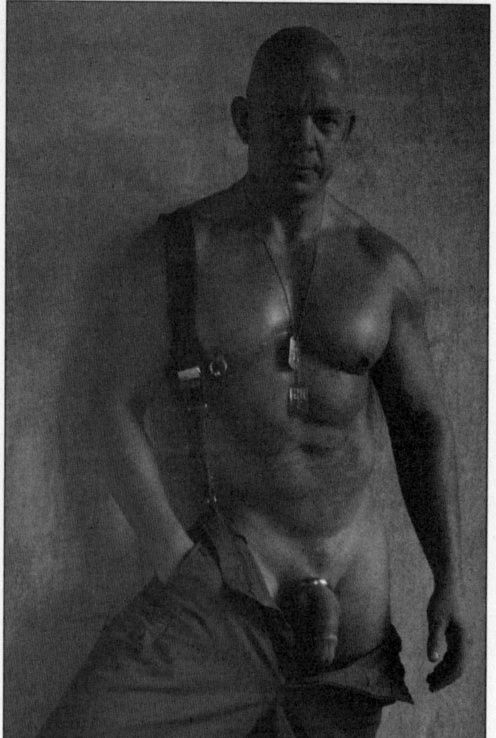

Akos Piros [PHOTO BY RAYMOND AUPELES, COURTESY AKOS PIROS]

the name of one of his good school fellows. I knew: nobody could pronounce it. Fehér means is the color white. So I decided quickly: Piros. It sounds good as well as second name after Ákos (lyrical!). Piros means red, the color of blood. It is life (in the ancient way of thinking), it is temperament, and it is what we need to make our cocks rock hard to enjoy others and ourselves.

What are a couple of your favorite XXX DVDs?

My favorite XXX DVDs are Cazzo-Film, Colt, Raging Stallion, Titan and MackProd (Mack Manus, France). I like the good bodies of real men, their rough and natural sex, and the work of these directors and cameramen.

How do you think being involved in their sex industry has changed you?

I shall ask friends of mine who know me very well. I am not sure how has it changed me? At the moment I know only one way – because I need my fit and well shaped body I thank God every day before sleeping for taking care of me and protecting me. Before porn work I did not feel how important it was for me to be healthy. I did not think of it, so I was not glad about being healthy! I do everything to keep myself healthy and I pray every night to be protected the following day, too! If one day my body becomes sick I was protected for so many years! Whatever will come I will be able to look back and be glad for what was given to me before. I will be proud of all I did with my body, too!

STEVEN **PONCE**

Steven, how did you get started in the business?

I started doing movies for a website, I went to the shoot only to look and the bottom didn't show up, so I they begged me to do the scene. The next thing I knew I was in the movie. Then later I met Michael Lucas in a live presentation in West Palm Beach. My friend, now my agent, introduced him to me. After a short talk, he asked me if I wanted to do movies with his company and the rest is history.

What were you looking for when you got into it?

Money and fame.

Do you recall the first movie you made and the first bit of direction you were given?

Don't look at the camera!

What about making XXX movies didn't you expect?

That it's really hard work and not just sex.

What things do you usually beforehand do to prepare for a film shoot?

Take a good nap and don't have sex or jerk off for four days.

And how do you usually spend the evening when you get home after a

STATS

BIRTH DATE: July 14, 1980

SIGN: Cancer

HOMETOWN: Fort Lauderdale FL

HEIGHT: 5'6"

WEIGHT: 150 lbs

TWO BEST CHARACTER TRAITS: Honesty and my good sense of humor.

TWO WORST CHARACTER TRAITS: Lack of patience, and sometimes I'm very naïve.

FAVORITE MUSIC: Music of the '80s and '90s.

FAVORITE MOVIES: *Star Wars*

FAVORITE MOVIES I'VE BEEN IN: Michael Lucas' *The Bigger the Better*

XXX COSTAR I'D DO AGAIN IN A MINUTE: I love them all, I don't know how to choose.

IF I COULD MAKE ONE REQUEST ON A PORN SET IT WOULD BE: More water please!

AS A TEEN I ALWAYS FANTASIZED ABOUT SEX WITH: Lucas Ridgeston and Alec Martinez

CURRENT FANTASY MAN: Brent Everett. I found him really hot!

SEXIEST PART OF A MAN: Chest, eyes andlips

THREE INGREDIENTS OF MY HOTTEST SEX FANTASY: I'm into the romantic stuff: a fireplace, nice baskets of fruits, and a big couch!

FAVORITE ITEM IN MY SEXUAL TOY BOX: My inflatable butt plug

MOST PRIZED POSSESSION: My life and my *Star Wars* memorabilia.

HOBBIES: Watching cartoons, the gym, and playing video games.

PETS: A tarantula and a fish tank.

PET PEEVES: When people are not polite!

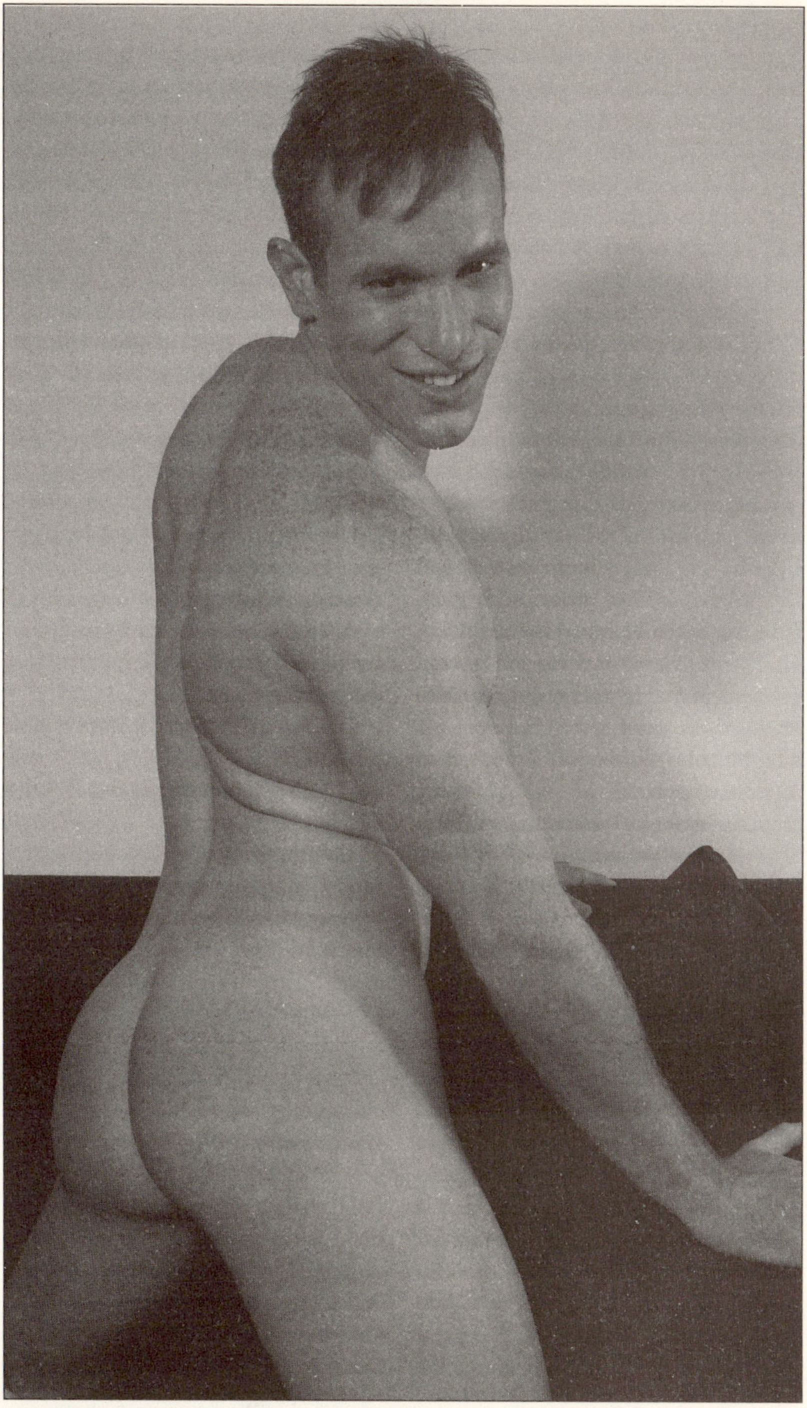

Steven Ponce [PHOTO COURTESY LUCASENTERTAINMENT.COM]

long day of filming?

Just watching a good movie, some fattening food, and with a nice drink

If you were to make a movie called Steven Ponce's Orgy who would you want as your 4 costars ... I know, that's kind of a tiny orgy?

Rafael Alencar , Brent Everett, Alec Martinez and Jonathan Vargas.

If a guy came up to you and asked for advice about getting into the adult film industry what words of wisdom would you give him?

Take it only as temporary job and make sure if you want to do it. Once you do a film there is no turning back.

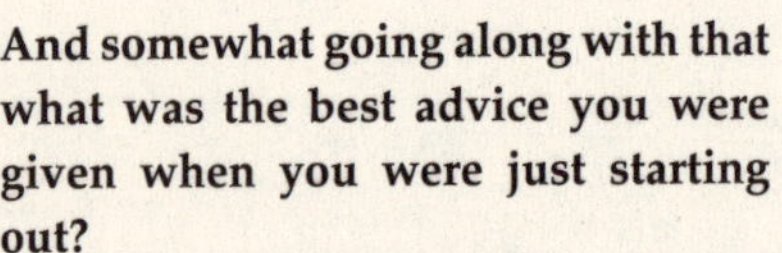

And somewhat going along with that what was the best advice you were given when you were just starting out?

I don't know. The only thing I remember is that they asked me if I was sure if I wanted to do it.

Speaking sexually very few guys are as skilled as me when it comes to ...

Kissing and giving head.

People oftentimes think of porn stars as these perfect specimens, but if you could change one thing about yourself through cosmetic surgery what would it be?

I want perfect abs.

Steven Ponce [PHOTO COURTESY LUCASENTERTAINMENT.COM]

How would you describe yourself in a personals ad?

Nice, honest cute red haired Puerto Rican boy.

Describe your ideal romantic evening.

A nice diner with candles, a good wine and then, a good movie ... knowing that I probably won't watch it anyway.

MICK **POWERS**

How did you get started in the business?

Oddly enough, I was asked. Teddy at ButchBear saw some pics that 100% Beef rejected by saying I was not porn material and he immediately called me.

What were you looking for when you got into it?

Just a change. I was recently single.

Were the people who knew surprised when you got into the business?

Yes, because I am shy.

Do you recall your first film and the first bit of direction you were given?

Muscle Bear Motel by ButchBear. The first thing I think Teddy said was "Boys, go slower. please!"

Do you think the industry has changed you and if so in what way(s)?

It made me get everything in writing.

STATS

BIRTH DATE: April 3

SIGN: Aries

HOMETOWN: Columbus, OH

HEIGHT: 6'

WEIGHT: 240 lbs

TWO BEST CHARACTER TRAITS: My smile and my open heart.

TWO WORST CHARACTER TRAITS: I'm gullible and a spendthrift

FAVORITE MUSIC: Right Now, the Dixie Chicks Long Way Home and the soundtrack to *Avenue Q*.

FAVORITE MOVIES: *Notting Hill* and *Kill Bill Volume 1*. Favorite porn would be *Arabesque*.

FAVORITE MOVIES I'VE BEEN IN: *Muscle Bear Motel* and *Centurion Muscle III: Omega*.

XXX COSTAR I'D DO AGAIN IN A MINUTE: Blake Nolan, Jake Dakota, and Huessein.

IF I COULD MAKE ONE REQUEST ON A PORN SET IT WOULD BE: Hold the damn lunch trays until the guys filming can eat! And can you put us in a hotel where it doesn't cost $40 to get to the bars in a cab.

AS A TEEN I ALWAYS FANTASIZED ABOUT SEX WITH: Lee Majors and Jake Tanner.

CURRENT FANTASY MAN: Jake Deckard or Cal Reynolds or Alex Collack or Johnny Hazzard.

SEXIEST PART OF A MAN: His eyes

THREE INGREDIENTS OF MY HOTTEST SEX FANTASY: Jake Deckard, Alex Collack, and a tube of Gun Oil.

FAVORITE ITEM IN MY SEXUAL TOY BOX: A vibrating butt plug.

MOST PRIZED POSSESSION: Carved wooden box made by a friend.

HOBBIES: Cooking and fencing.

PETS: Hank and Kurt, two big cats

PET PEEVES: Bar owners who screw up personal appearances and then try to blame the studios. Also, Colt models who invite you to visit but conveniently forget to mention their boyfriend until he walks in the door unexpectedly.

Mick Powers [PHOTO BY KENT TAYLOR, COURTESY RAGING STALLION STUDIOS]

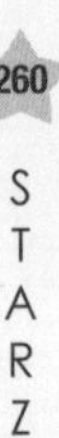

you are having fun. If it becomes something you must do, get out.

If you were making a movie called Mick's Orgy who would you want as your four costars?

I will limit this to people I have not filmed or had sex with: Jake Deckard, Alex Collack, Parker Williams, and Carlo Masi.

What is the first thing you do when you get home from a XXX shoot?

Lay on the bed eating ice cream and petting my cats.

Speaking sexually, very few guys are as gifted as me when it comes to ...

Trash talking!

"Talk to me intelligently. I do have several college degrees after all. Then, we can fuck like bunnies."

Where is the wildest place you've ever had sex?

The back of a police car.

I must hear more about the sex in the back of the cop car.

Let's just say West Virginia cops are easy.

What things do you always do to prepare for a XXX shoot?

Save up for five days ahead of time and read erotic friction.

If a guy was to come to you for advice about getting into the business what would you tell him?

Think twice, but do it as long as you are having fun. If it becomes something you must do, get out.

So what is the key to dirty sex talking?

Believing in what you are saying.

Have you always been a filth talker or did something happen that sparked that tendency?

It just comes naturally.

When you pass a hot looking guy on the street what gets you to turn around and do a double take every time?

Eyes and a cute ass ... and yeah, why not?

How do you see yourself as a typical Aries?

I have a bit of a temper.

You list one of your worst qualities as being gullible ... so if that's the case what is an example of an instance where you were extremely gullible?

Let's just say a Colt model who used to live in Alabama invited me down to visit and somehow forgot to mention that he had a boyfriend. The boyfriend found out and the jerk tried to blame me! It was the worst experience of my whole adult life.

Those pet peeves to sound awfully specific ... Care to name the Colt model or at least more details?

No, let's just say his dick is Photo-

Mick Powers [PHOTO BY KENT TAYLOR, COURTESY RAGING STALLION STUDIOS]

Shopped in all his pics.

Have you ever developed a crush on any of your costars? Care to name names?

How can you not fall just a little bit in love with Blake Nolan. His mate is so lucky.

What is the craziest bit of drama you have ever witnessed on a XXX set?

My scene partner had a nervous breakdown and we had to start over with someone else. And no, I will not name the person, the studio or the film!

How is your XXX persona Mick Powers different from the real you?

Mick is much more outgoing than I am. He also is a lot more open sexually than I normally am. I am quite shy.

Have you ever done anything sexually on screen that you would never do in real life?

I've done more than one threesome. I am a one on one type of guy normally.

How would you describe yourself in a personals ad?

Boring, quiet cat lover with unusual side job seeks Steve Kelso.

Mick, how many cats do you have and what are their names?

My ex and I wanted guy names for our cats so my cats are named Hank (after Hank McCoy, Beast in the *Xmen*) and Kurt (after Kurt Wagner, Nightcrawler in the *Xmen*) because they are blue and black, respectively.

How do we get you in the sack and what do we do with you once we get you there?

Talk to me intelligently. I do have several college degrees after all. Then, we can fuck like bunnies.

What city or place always takes your breath away and why?

New York City. Times Square of course. How can you top that?

Describe your ideal romantic evening.

Me and a nice furry guy with a copy of *Notting Hill* and the cats for a snuggle.

Describe your dream vacation.

Jake Dakota, a tent, and a bottle of Gun Oil.

ZACK RANDALL

How did you get started in the business?

I answered an ad in the school newspaper! It was a daily publication at my university and in the classifieds there was an ad searching for a male model not too shy to jack-off in front of a camera. I answered it and decided that porn was a really easy way to make money.

What were you looking for when you got into it?

Just the money. I never thought I would be famous or be in a magazine. I just wanted that little bit of extra cash so I could have fun while I was in college.

Were the people who knew you surprised?

Pretty much everybody thought it was awesome! All of my friends started calling me "Porno Man" but it was in a respectful way. They knew my academic and social history and were more impressed with my open-mindedness than shocked at the nature of my job. My parents weren't so cool with it.

So tell me a bit more about your parent's reaction when they found out?

Well, it all started when I went home for winter break my junior year of college. My parents and I were in the living room that evening, and my mom popped the question, So, who's Zack Randall? I gave a start and said, "Huh?" "I was trying to get in touch with you," she continued, "so I decided to try Myspace.com and I found pictures of you with a different name." Apparently she had input my age, zip code, and other info into the search and Zack Randall popped up. Obviously, she recognized me. On my site at the time, I had alluded to some of the shoots I had done, including the Playgirl magazine, which had come out the month before (November 2006.)

"So, where is it?" she asked. "The magazine."

I had no choice but to show my parents the Playgirl and watch as they skimmed through eight pages dedicated to my naked self. Needless to say, they were less than pleased. I was told to get out of the business as quickly as possible and without reaching any level of recognition. They still don't approve of what I do, but then, when has parental consent ever been a prerequisite for my actions?

Do you recall your first movie and the first bit of direction you were given?

My first movie is no longer out. It was for a Website that only lasted six months or so. I recall it being very straight-forward: "Pretend you were

STATS

BIRTH DATE: April 19, 1985

SIGN: Aries

HOMETOWN: Seattle

HEIGHT: 5'11"

WEIGHT: 145 lbs

TWO BEST CHARACTER TRAITS: My intelligence and my ambition.

TWO WORST CHARACTER TRAITS: I can be impatient sometimes, though usually only with myself. I can also never be satisfied. I always tirelessly need to improve the world around me.

FAVORITE MUSIC: Jazz. The real stuff, from Duke Ellington to Charlie Parker up through Miles Davis, John Coltrane, and Stan Getz.

FAVORITE MOVIES: I like older movies. I grew up on comedies from the '30s (The Marx Brothers) through the '70s (*The Pink Panther* series) with a lot of Mel Brooks and miscellaneous science fiction movies, too.

FAVORITE MOVIES I'VE BEEN IN: I wouldn't' know, as I haven't watched any of my movies. The ones I feel I have performed up to my own standards would have to be *The Intern* or *Gigolo*.

XXX COSTAR I'D DO AGAIN IN A MINUTE: Derek Rivero would have to be my favorite.

AS A TEEN I ALWAYS FANTASIZED ABOUT SEX WITH: My peers. I would fantasize about the hot people in my high school. I never got into mainstream media (music, movies, TV) so it never really occurred to me to be obsessing over millionaires who live in L.A.

SEXIEST PART OF A MAN: I would have to say the abs. More than anything, good abs seem to be the universal sign of fitness.

FAVORITE ITEM IN MY SEXUAL TOYBOX: I actually don't have any sex toys. I never needed them. Not even lube.

MOST PRIZED POSSESSION: My saxophone.

HOBBIES: Philosophy, rock climbing, jazz saxophone, working out, reading, and hanging out.

PET PEEVES: Ignorance, stupidity, close-mindedness, etc. Anything that involves lack of tolerance or respect can irk me.

making a masturbation video for your girl/boyfriend because you are going on vacation for two weeks and don't want them having sex with anyone else." I acted towards the camera as if I wanted my significant other to use the video for a fortnight without getting bored. It seemed to work well.

What about making XXX movies most surprised you?

I was surprised at how laid-back even the most professional set is. The most experienced performers have the same difficulties as novices sometimes, and directors learn how to put up with the time it takes to shoot a scene. Waiting is usually the most time-consuming task, contrary to prior belief. The personability of the actors was another surprise. Big mean-looking porn stars can be incredibly friendly in person.

What things do you typically do to prepare yourself for a film shoot?

A week before the shoot I start jacking off 3-4 times a day to build up my ejaculate and then cease 24 hours before I need to perform. On the morning of a shoot I do 50-100 diamond push-ups and a couple hundred sit-ups to engorge my muscles. As for food, I was raised on organic foods, so I consider my diet to be an integral part of my looks. You are what you eat, so eat lots of protein, few carbs (never any candy or excess sugar), and keep the fat to the minimum. I usually don't eat the morning of my scene. I get energy from drinking juice or eating an energy bar if I need it, and then afterwards I like to eat a steak to replenish my supplies.

And how do you usually spend the evening after a day of shooting?

Usually at the bar with Tanqueray

martinis (dry martinis, of course) or a nice bourbon on the rocks (Maker's or Knob Creek are my favorites.)

What is the most aroused you have ever been on camera?

Probably one of the times I made a home video of myself on a Webcam. When there are no other distractions I can really relax. Everything else is pretty much just good acting. There was, however, a lot of chemistry with my fiancé; I almost ejaculated prematurely (i.e., before the director told me to) in our scene when we first met.

What about your fiancé Derek Rivero makes him the perfect partner for you?

Pretty much everything! He's ambitious, sexy, cute, and intelligent. We both find no limits in our desires to succeed, and we both want what is best for each other. I have never loved anyone as intensely as I love Derek. The perfect partner is someone who can grow with you over time. I feel we can both learn from each other in reciprocating aspects of life and do very well with solving problems together.

Are you planning a legal wedding or union?

We have not planned anything yet, but I'm hoping for a legal wedding.

Porn sets are often the setting for some unintentionally hilarious behavior. Care to share any funniest or most shocking thing you've witnessed or had happen on a XXX set?

There was one particular event that stands out, and that was when I was topping in a three-some. There was only one bottom, and he decided he wanted to try to take both of us at once, so we played around for a while trying to find a position where it was physically possible, and hopefully a little bit comfortable as well. After trying for a half hour or so, the bottom asked for anal-ease, or in our case, this topical analgesic that had Lidocaine in it. We lined up to take our shots again and unfortunately, the cream got on my dick, instantly and painfully killing my erection. Again, a half-hour had to pass, this time because of my

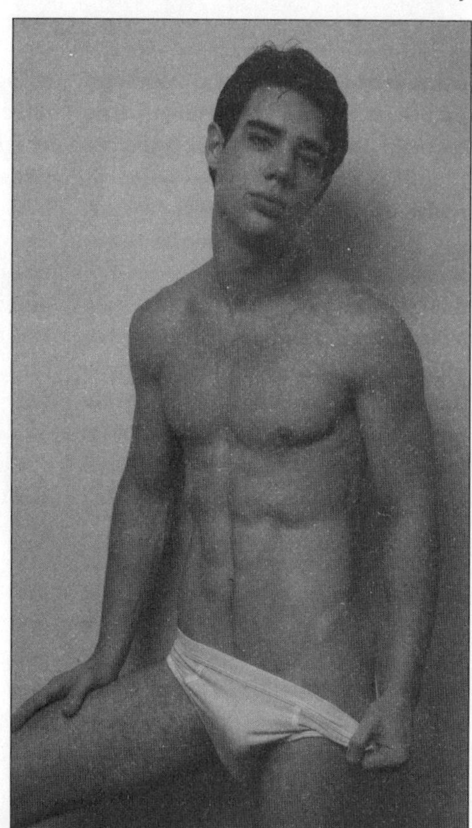

Zack Randall [PHOTO COURTESY LUCASENTERTAINMENT.COM]

malfunctioning member and a crew that could barely hold their sides in as I was trying to regain my dignity. Lesson learned: Keep Lidocaine off your privates!

XXX movies are known for putting guys into some very uncomfortable positions for the sake of the shot. What is the most uncomfortable sex angle you've had to assume on film?

I had to hold myself on the edge of a bathtub once, which was pretty uncomfortable. I've also been fucked standing up in the shower, which can also be difficult.

"Keep Lidocaine off your privates!"

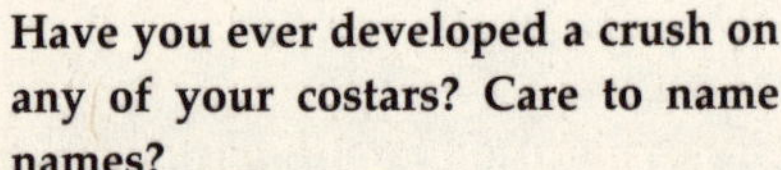

Have you ever developed a crush on any of your costars? Care to name names?

The only guy I've worked with that I developed a crush on is my fiancé, Derek Rivero. We met on the set in Walla Walla, WA, of all places.

If you were making a movie called Zack's Orgy who would you want as your four costars?

Derek Rivero, D.O. (a Black Scorpion exclusive at the moment), Brent Corrigan, and Blair Mason.

Do you think XXX movies have a responsibility to promote and depict safe sex in their movies?

Yes and no. On the one hand, unsafe sex can cause many problems in our society that I feel can be prevented by the teaching of safe methods to enjoy sex, and of course porn is where most people see what is to be emulated. This influence makes porn unique in our culture as the one thing that could easily teach the majority of the populace. On the other hand, why should we put the responsibility of teaching youth about safe sex on the companies who sell sex for entertainment? That's like James Bond putting on his seatbelt when he jumps into his car or hip hop songs singing about going to college. Just as it is up to driving instructors to teach us to drive safely, it is up to schools and parents to adequately portray sex in a realistic sense that will lead to responsible actions. Porn is entertainment, not reality, and people need to be intelligent enough to understand that even though not wearing a condom can be more sexually stimulating (both visually and tactilely), it is not necessarily the best thing to do in real life.

Do you have some amazing sexual fantasy you are just waiting for some director to ask you to film?

I hate to be boring and say "not really," but not really. Maybe add a few people to my orgy like Benjamin Bradley and Brent Everett and have us spend a week on an island with a lot of alcohol. Reality-style fantasy island sex. Ooh yeah!

Any tales of bad behavior on a XXX set you would care to relate?

I can recall a time where one model tattled on the others for underage drinking on the set. He was just a diva that didn't get things his way.

Where is the wildest place you've ever had sex?

On the floor of a 19th century pew-

Zack Randall [PHOTO COURTESY LUCASENTERTAINMENT.COM]

ter shop about 20 miles from Woodstock. I've also done it in classrooms on campus, the tennis courts, and study rooms, but I'm sure a lot of people have. I masturbated in art class once without anyone finding out because we were wearing aprons while painting. Ah the memories!

Speaking sexually, very few people are as skilled as I when it comes to ...

Kissing. If that's not sexual enough, I've also been told I'm very good at topping.

Describe your ultimate romantic evening.

A perfectly romantic evening would include but not be limited to: Dinner at an Italian restaurant with a fine bottle of wine, followed by a relaxing walk through a moonlit park, and then back home for a romantic comedy and popcorn on the couch. Substitutions and addendums can be made, but that's a pretty good formula.

Where do you hope or want this career to take you?

I am in the process of raising my personal expectations as an actor and an individual. My goals now include opening up my production company (Randall/Rivero) and producing porn for my own Website and DVDs. In time, I hope to grow internationally and win awards for both my performances and productions.

So tell me about the steps you are planning to take in starting your own production company?

At the moment I'm looking for people to film. I want to get a lot of content shot and edited before launching the site. Everything else is already taken care of. Once the site is up, it will just be a matter of continuing what I've been doing.

What things do you think you have learned in front of the camera that is going to come in handy when running your own production company?

I have an actor's perspective, so where some directors have been behind the camera for their entire career, I can very much relate to the models and help quash any problems they might have. Working with so many companies in such a short span of time has allowed me to experience many different ways to shoot, direct, and edit as well, and I'm planning on putting that knowledge to good use too.

Describe your dream vacation.

It would definitely have to be tropical, have a beach, amazing weather, and as much time to relax as I want.

ERIK **RHODES**

How did you get started in the business?

I was escorting a lot and at the time was pretty hard up for cash and said what the fuck. I figured it was basically what I was doing anyway, plus it would be with hotter guys, so I felt it was a win win solution.

What is they key to being a good escort?

Make sure you tell them what they want to hear. Don't give attitude or think you are better than them. Try to have fun or at least, look like you are having fun. Easy.

What were you looking for when you got into XXX movies?

Basically money, I never knew I would have fans. I never thought porn would take my life away like it has.

STATS

BIRTH DATE: February 8, 1982

SIGN: Aquarius

HOMETOWN: Long Island, NY

HEIGHT: 6'3"

WEIGHT: Last I checked – 230 lbs

TWO BEST CHARACTER TRAITS: "Good time Charlie," a porn star without the attitude and big head.

TWO WORST CHARACTER TRAITS: Body dysmorphic (distorted body image disorder) and depression/temper.

FAVORITE MUSIC: Hardcore, post hardcore, emo, screamo, basically anything you can kick someone's ass to.

FAVORITE MOVIES: *Natural Born Killers* or anything by Quentin Tarantino

FAVORITE MOVIES I'VE BEEN IN: *Heaven to Hell, The Velvet Mafia Part 1.*

XXX COSTAR I'D DO AGAIN IN A MINUTE: Don't get me wrong, I like everyone I have worked with (except Billy Brandt), but I'd rather work with new people. If I kept doing the same guys over and over it would be boring to the viewer.

IF I COULD MAKE ONE REQUEST ON A PORN SET IT WOULD BE: One thing – to have 24 oz. Rockstar energy drinks!

AS A TEEN I ALWAYS FANTASIZED ABOUT SEX WITH: Trent Reznor.

CURRENT FANTASY MAN: I'm with him, Danny Dias from *Road Rules Extreme* .

SEXIEST PART OF A MAN: The yummy muscle or in other words the V shape between the mans lower abdomen and legs.

THREE INGREDIENTS OF MY HOTTEST SEX FANTASY: Crisco, rubber gloves, unlimited dildos, a sling, a fuck machine, poppers and some crazy hardcore porn playing in the background and I'm set to go!

FAVORITE ITEM IN MY SEXUAL TOY BOX: What I call mega dong (just a dildo that has treated me well when no one has been around).

MOST PRIZED POSSESSION: My isolation.

HOBBIES: Attending concerts, fighting, drinking, most the shit college kids do that for some reason still have not gotten over.

PETS: None at the moment.

PET PEEVES: Liars, stereotypical queers, hypocrites, young know it all twinks in the porn world the list go's on ...

Erik Rhodes [PHOTO COURTESY STUDIO 2000]

I am also curious. When fans do talk or email you or whatever what is it they usually comment about or say they like about you as a porn star?

Well they say they love my movies and that they think I'm the best thing in porn, I'm the hottest guy out there ... blah blah blah. It's just hard to believe. There are so many hot guys out there. I just feel like a normal guy. It's still so weird to me.

Erik, I am sure you get asked a lot of things. What is the craziest and/or most usual request a fan has ever made of you?

I have been asked so much crazy shit it's hard to remember everything. But just recently I have been asked to shit in a pair of underwear and mail it to some dude. According to him he's not into scat but really would get off with a pair of my shitty underwear. I don't believe him. The guy probably has a trophy wall of porn star scatted up bundies. (Laughing). I said just send me a check for a postage paid envelope and you can have me.

What about making XXX movies surprised you?

How professional it is. I thought it would be a very sleazy job, but I have now realized it's a job like anything else.

What is the most aroused you have ever been on screen?

Twice, Matthew Rush fucking me doggie style in *Heaven to Hell* and Brent Corrigan riding my dick in The *Velvet Mafia Pt. 1.*

I couldn't help noticing that you mentioned all your costars being OK except for Billy Brandt. Could you elaborate?

On a porn set you try to make friends with the people you are going to work with and with Billy there was nothing to like. He was totally unprofessional and completely disgusting.

Is it impossible, uncomfortable, educational, funny, or arousing to watch yourself in a movie?

I find them funny and don't normally watch them. But I do view them once when they are released to see if they came out alright and to see if there is anything I can improve.

So what are a couple things about your sexual performance you have noticed that you have worked to change or improve for movies?

Well basically I only watch to see if I looked stupid in certain positions and try to avoid them for next time. I also watch how my body looks and see what I need to improve on.

The XXX business you guys also get put into some pretty extreme sexual positions for the sake of the camera. What's the most uncomfortable sex/contortionist position you've ever had to assume for the movies?

Any time you see me riding dick, just assume it was pure torture for me. My knees where not made for that shit.

If a guy came up to you (and they probably do) asking about getting into the business what advice would you give them?

I would tell them to watch their back. This industry is looking to cash in on you. You need to cash in also.

Think of yourself first. But at the same time don't be a fucking know it all, unless you do.

If you were offered a role in a fetish film how far would you go for the camera? In other words, what are your limits?

Besides safe sex, I don't have limits. Falcon does. I guess when they start getting really hardcore I'll be in the center of it all.

Have you ever done anything sexually on screen that you would never do in your personal life?

Never, I think I do more in my personal life then I do on screen.

I first realized I was a porn star when …

I found my name on Wikipedia.

If you could change one thing about the way the industry is currently run what would it be?

I would have the companies stop filling the talent's heads with tons of bullshit. I think each model should get a form with the statistics. How many porn stars end up drug addicts? How many models end up with deadly diseases? How many models commit suicide? How many models make it out of this industry unscarred? So they have the choice to run away as fast as they can.

Hey, but I'm in this industry already so how can I bitch? Something I would also change is to not call everyone a porn star. Not everyone is a star. I call these people porn filler. The movie needed an extra cock and ass and that's you! So many of these newbies do one porn and think they are a star. Pay your fucking dues, make a name for yourself and then maybe you can be a star, but for now your just filler!

Do you have some best example of bad behavior on a XXX set you would care to share?

Well, I'm not as big as a train wreck as some people think. I take great pride in my scenes and will not compromise how I look during a movie for anything so normally when I walk on set I should be top notch. As far as bad behavior, the worse thing I can think of off hand, is making fun of a model I was working with during our scene behind his back because he couldn't understand English every well.

Porn sets are often the place of some surreal and hilarious incidents. Do you have any personal tale you would care to share?

All I can think of is working with Billy Brandt on *From Top to Bottom*. He was all high and retarded, farting like crazy making everyone sick, and then of course, I am the one who needed to eat his ass. Personally I wanted to kill him for his unreal lack of professionalism but I kept my mouth shut till the movie was over and released. If I saw him on the street now, and he wasn't high, I'd break his face.

Do people usually treat you differently when they recognize you or discover that you've done XXX movies?

Yeah, either they love me and can't wait to talk to me and take pics or they stare and give nasty looks while whispering to there friends saying "He's a porn star, he must be positive." I find it funny that I'm considered the whore when what I do isn't far off from what most fags do every Friday or Saturday night. Stop judging me and judge your own motherfucking self.

How do you think the entire experience of making XXX movies has changed you?

I have really become more of a recluse because of it. It has honestly showed me what ugly hypocrites some gay men can be. The rumors and all the bullshit has really torn me apart.

What are your thoughts about fidelity?

If I don't say love I might not get any sex from my boyfriend. But in all honesty if I didn't get sex my love life would be miserable. Shit, if it wasn't for some intense sex now with my boyfriend we would want to kill each other on a regular basis. So for me – sex all the way! As for fidelity, it is possible even if you are a porn star?

What is the key to turning you on or what gets you hotter than anything?

"I find it funny that I'm considered the whore when what I do isn't far off from what most fags do every Friday or Saturday night."

Ass play. An open sloppy hole drives me crazy.

Do you think the industry has a responsibility regarding the use of condoms and/or promoting safe sex?

Not at all. I think it's the people's choice. Whether on camera or in your on own free time, if you choose to not use a condom, by now you should know what your getting into. I'm sorry you can't play stupid with this one. You can't blame anyone but yourself if you get something.

Are you a natural exhibitionist?

No, I am very shy and I have always been. I am very self-conscious.

Where is the wildest place you've ever had sex?

Shit, I don't know, I have had sex everywhere and I assume there are a lot better places than I can't even think of because I was drunk when it happened.

If you had to choose between sex and love which would you choose and

When you pass a hot looking guy on the street what about him makes you turn around and do a double take?

I normally don't pay attention to people on the street. I put my iPod on and my hoodie up and I try to hide from the world. If I notice someone hot I will do a double take but only sometimes, if they are really worth it, if not I'll just keep my head down and keep trucking.

When it comes to seducing a guy I want I've found that nothing works better than ...

Just being myself. I leave a lasting impression and it always has them coming back.

What's your favorite method for driving men crazy in bed?

I guess just being totally versatile is a good thing?

What is the best pick up line you have ever used or fallen for?

I really don't use pick up lines and trust me I don't fall for them. I did use one once totally to my embarrassment which went something like "Why are you going in there when all the fun is out here."

If your life had a theme song what would it be?

If you're thinking of like a TV show theme song – I would say the theme song to *M.A.S.H.* I would be living in my own personal hell. If not a TV theme song, I would say my life can be summed up in anything by Nine Inch Nails. I think the song "Terrible Lie" would work pretty perfectly.

Does your cock have a nickname and if so how did it come about?

Ant Eater thanks to a bunch of naive circumcised porn stars. (Laughing). Personally, I like Johnny Sloppycock a whole lot better.

If you had to compare yourself to an animal what species do you think best captures your essence and why?

Wow, what a cliché question to ask a porn star. I will not answer this question with the typical "oh definitely a Lion or Tiger" bullshit. But I will answer it, so if I had to say what animal capture my essence it would def be a Hippo. I'm lazy as shit and if you annoy me I'll seriously fuck you up.

Your MySpace message this Xmas was: "Fuck Christmas, I hope your Christmas tree bursts into flames and destroys your holidays. XOXO" Are you bullshitting or are you a Scrooge?

I hate Christmas, it's totally much more stress than I feel like dealing with. So yes, I am Scrooge.

Where do you hope this career takes you?

To be honest, I don't have high hopes. I feel like my five minutes will end pretty quickly and this whole ride will lead to an early grave. Come on, let's be honest, I ain't going to pretend that I can sing like some of these retired porn stars. That shit is fucking ridiculous and pathetic if you ask me. So fuck it, die, while some one still cares and you live forever!

Describe your ideal romantic evening.

I don't think I have a romantic bone in my body. Sorry sissies. If you want my idea of a good evening out – lots of beer and drunk sex is cool with me!

Describe your dream vacation.

London, with no schedule.

What is the biggest misconception people have about you when you meet them?

That I'm big asshole. I'm still very humble. But just don't step on my toes, I'm still human and you can still get punched in the face. If you can see past me being a piece of meat, then you're cool in my book.

Do you have any childhood or adolescent memory that you can look back upon and say, "Oh yeah, that kid was destined to grow up to be a porn star"?

Not at all. I was always very shy and still am. I guess turning into a big old whore bag slut of a porn star was my way of dealing.

DAMIAN **RIOS**

Damian, how did you get started in the business?

I sent out some pictures to Channel 1 Releasing and Chi Chi contacted me and told me to meet up with Doug Jeffries who was going to be in Miami. Two months later I was on the set filming my first two movies.

What were you looking for when you got into it?

I had to do it, I didn't want to let time go by and regret not knowing what it would have been like.

So you mention Tommy Blade making you comfortable during your first shoot. What did he do that took the edge off that day?

Tommy is one of the sweetest people you could ever meet. He captures everyone's attention and makes you laugh. He's gorgeous, that helps, too.

What about making XXX movies didn't you expect?

Feeling as nervous as I did once I got on the set.

Do you consider yourself a natural exhibitionist?

Of course I do. I've been stripping for a little over eight years.

Does your porn persona Damian Rios different from you? If I came up to you and expected to meet that character how would you and he differ?

No, we're both exhibitionists, we love the attention and enjoy seeing

Damian Rios
[PHOTO BY GEOF TEAGUE, COURTESY RAGINGSTALLION.COM]

others enjoy themselves.

Do you think being in XXX will expand your sexual horizons and if you do how so?

It already has. I've realized how much of a power bottom I am.

Do you have a favorite all time scene or XXX movie?

Soaked. The scene where Brent Everett rails Roman Heart's ass.

Since your boyfriend is in the business is there any competition between you and your current BF? And who is it?

Sometimes I do, but I think it comes more from jealousy that he doesn't want anyone else deflowering me or at least that's what I tell myself. My boyfriend is Scott Tanner.

Is he supportive and do you foresee it as difficult to make XXX movies while being in a relationship?

No, not really. He has been doing it a little longer and wants me to just work my day job. We met on the set of my first movie so I don't know why he isn't more supportive. But, I still love him!

Were the people who knew you surprised when you took the plunge into adult films?

STATS

BIRTH DATE: March 28, 1979

SIGN: Aries

HOMETOWN: As I was growing up my family traveled everywhere, but I guess I would have to call Tampa Florida my home.

HEIGHT: 5'10"

WEIGHT: 180 lbs. on a good day.

TWO BEST CHARACTER TRAITS: My charm and ability to open up and communicate with everyone.

TWO WORST CHARACTER TRAITS: My temper and my quickness to judge.

FAVORITE MUSIC: I'm into all types of music, but my heart has got to go out to freestyle. I've been listening to this type of music all the way back to fifth grade.

FAVORITE MOVIES: Right now I am in love with *Dream Girls*. I can't get enough.

FAVORITE MOVIES I'VE BEEN IN: Since I just started out a few months ago and there's only movie that's out right now I would have to go with *Two of a Kind* directed by Doug Jeffries.

XXX COSTAR I'D DO AGAIN IN A MINUTE: Tommy Blade. Being on the set for the first time can be difficult and from the start he made sure I was comfortable.

IF I COULD MAKE ONE REQUEST ON A PORN SET IT WOULD BE: To fuck my man, Scott Tanner! Have you seen his ass? And he loves getting it pounded regardless that he doesn't like to show it on video.

AS A TEEN I ALWAYS FANTASIZED ABOUT SEX WITH: The men in my mom's Fredericks of Hollywood catalogs. I could stay in the bathroom for hours lusting over those guys.

CURRENT FANTASY MAN: Pavel Marek hands down. He was amazing in Titan Media's *Farm Hands*.

SEXIEST PART OF A MAN: A guy's waistline, right where the V shape forms.

THREE INGREDIENTS OF MY HOTTEST SEX FANTASY: The scenery for starters, then one man on my hole, and the other man taking care of any other desire. How about going down on my cock?

FAVORITE ITEM IN MY SEXUAL TOY BOX: Chad Hunt's dildo.

MOST PRIZED POSSESSION: My Nissan 350Z

HOBBIES: Working out.

PETS: I'm working on getting myself a Teacup Yorkie.

PET PEEVES: Liars!

No, they all knew I would end up doing something extreme so it's not something that shocked them.

Has making XXX movies been the fun that you anticipated and going along with it what is the most fun about it?

Even more than I imagined. Everyone on the set is amazing, they treat you like your family. The crew made it fun.

If someone were to come to you for advice about getting into the adult film industry what would you tell him?

Have fun and enjoy it or don't do it.

If you were to make a movie called Damian's Orgy who would you want as your four costars?

Pavel Novotny, Pavel Marek, François Sagat, and Johnny Castle.

Do you have some amazing sexual fantasy you are just waiting for some director to ask you to film?

I have recently found it very interesting to be manhandled by my boyfriend and sometimes ask him to just take it from me regardless if I'm not into it. I always am, so it's pretty hard to catch me off guard, so I ask him to rape me! I would love to be in a gang initiation where all the members have to fuck me before I can get in.

Have you had the experience of seeing yourself in a movie yet? If so is the experience educational, uncomfortable, unbearable, or arousing?

No, not yet. I live down in Key West and everything gets here a few months later than anywhere else. I'm curious though as to how it turned out.

So many people consider porn stars to be these ideal specimens but if

"I would love to be in a gang initiation where all the members have to fuck me before I can get in."

you could change one thing about yourself through cosmetic surgery what would it be?

This is such a vain question, but if I had to do something I would love to have my lips fuller.

Do you think the industry has a responsibility regarding the use of condoms and/or promoting safe sex?

Yes, with all the STDs I don't think companies should be endangering other lives for the sake of making a few dollars. It's too risky and not worth a life. I am pleased to say that all the companies I have worked for have made me use a condom even when I was making a film with my boyfriend.

Do you have some measure of success you are looking for in the XXX industry? In other words, how are you going to know that "you've made it"?

I decided to do this because I wanted to try out something a little more fun than my current day job. I've always wanted to do it since I went through my dad's collection of bi films as a little boy. I don't think I have made it yet but, the fact that you

already know who I am and I barely have one movie out is a good sign of things to come.

Do you have any long term plans of where you want this career to take you?

I just want to have fun with this, as soon as I think of it as a job than I'll stop. Right now I'm just trying to enjoy it.

If you were offered a role in a fetish film how far would you go?

I might let someone tie me up and spank me a little but that's about it. I'm not really into fisting or hot plates.

If you could change one thing about the way the industry is currently run what would it be?

To pay more!

Do you have some best example of bad behavior on a XXX set you would care to share?

Coming to the set high. I haven't witnessed anyone but I have heard of it happening. You can't get anything done.

Do you have any childhood or adolescent memory that you can look back upon and say, "Oh yeah, that kid was destined to grow up to be a porn star"?

I was always very curious about sex even at the age of three. I could remember doing things with other guys way before I was even going to school, how that was happening I don't know but it did.

How would you describe yourself in a personals ad?

Power hungry bottom with insatiable hole seeking giant cock!

When you pass a hot looking guy on the street what is it about him that gets you to turn around and do a double take every time?

Exotic men, not to into a guy that blends in with the crowd. Nice body, beautiful smile. I want to see his confidence but not his ego.

Speaking sexually very few guys are as skilled as me when it comes to ...

Giving head. I just don't understand why some guys think that teeth feel good. I'm also a passionate kisser, I can't stand someone who can't kiss, it's a huge turn-off.

What gets you hard faster than anything?

Passion and chemistry. On my back watching the other person fuck me and seeing them enjoy my hole.

When it comes to seducing a man I've found nothing works better than ...

Showing my ass.

What gets you hard faster than anything?

Getting gang raped – just kidding. I don't know, I guess it has to depend on where I am and who I am with or who I want to be with.

Where is the craziest/hottest place you've ever had sex?

It wasn't sex but it was hot. I was in my early years of high school and I was still in the closet. I had gone out with my straight friends and the club we happened to go out to was gay friendly. Towards the end of the night I went to the bathroom when some random guy pushed me into the stall, pulled down my pants and took charge of my cock. He blew me and let me cum in his mouth. I can't remember ever having such an intense orgasm. My friends outted me that night as they saw me walk out the stall with him.

How do you think of yourself as a typical Aries?

Fearless and courageous. I will fight passionately for what I want but sometimes I can be impatient.

What is the biggest misconception people have about you when you meet them?

If they know I do films than they automatically think I am an escort. I'm not!

If you had to choose between sex and love which would you choose and what are your thoughts about fidelity?

Now that I am in a relationship all I want is love. Sex is good for the first time or a one night stand. I don't like to get my feelings and emotions involved when I know it's not going to go anywhere. I've been played twice in my life and it feels horrible. I wouldn't want to put my boyfriend through that nor do I want to go through that again.

Describe your ideal romantic evening.

I love staying at home with my man. He loves to cook. Then watching movies lying on the same couch on top of each other.

Describe your dream vacation.

Back on the beaches of Sicily with my friends. I lived there for almost four years before coming to Key West and I would love the opportunity to go back.

Damian Rios [PHOTO BY GEOF TEAGUE, COURTESY RAGINGSTALLION.COM]

Where do you want your life to be five years from now?

I want to have received my degree and working in the E.R. living with my man in our house with our two dogs.

DEREK **RIVERO**

How did you get started in the business?

My first film was actually a dare. Being the kind of person that I am, I never turn down a dare and before I knew it I was sucking dick and fucking.

What were you looking for when you got into it?

Nothing, but I found so much more, like my fiancé Zack.

What was the best advice you were given starting out?

The best advice given to me was to never trust anyone. Especially greedy companies, producers and agents who think they are God's gift to gay porn. You must stay grounded because it's all just an illusion. Being of the moment is everything but just as quickly as you come up you can fall down.

Do you recall your first film and the first bit of direction you were given?

Yes, it was with a very talented twink who managed to suck himself off while I fucked him. That was hot!

So as someone who is just 18, did you have plans for doing this for a while and have to wait around until your birthday?

I've always had a passion for boys.

Do you think you are treated a bit differently since you are so young?

No. Actually people seem to be more intimidated at the fact that I'm 18 and already run my own studio.

So why don't you tell me a bit about your studio and the type of films you are interest in making?

We have been shooting movies with some of the top caliber models in the industry, and so far all I can say is I'm really excited to show the world my work.

What was your initial motivation for starting your own studio?

I think the timing was right, and the money was there, and we decided to invest it instead of traveling the world or something like that.

What was the most difficult part about getting the studio started?

Finding hot guys that can keep it hard.

Does having Zack in the industry even cause problems regarding jealousy of one sort or another?

No, this is just our job and we know that none of it is real. Porn sex is like a Banana split without the Banana and anyone who's a porn star would understand.

So how did you and Zack meet?

We met on the set of a Black Scorpion production in Walla Walla, WA. He was my scene partner and we had crazy amounts of chemistry flowing between us. At one point we stopped kissing and realized all the cameras had already left.

Is having a partner also in the industry a plus? If so in what ways?

Absolutely! People tend to think that being in the adult entertainment industry you are unable to commit or you must be emotionally unavailable, that's bullshit. Our jobs have nothing to do with our personal lives and dating someone else in the industry allows you to escape obsessive jealousy and a potentially unhealthy relationship. In love, it's essential to understand each other's needs and personally I don't think it's possible for someone who works as a teacher for example to understand the demanding requirements of being a porn star or porn producer. There will be conflict.

Does it have drawbacks as well?

When it comes to love there are no drawbacks.

Do you have some great sexual fantasy you are just waiting for some director to ask you to film?

I no longer work for other studios, but I am anxious to shoot a movie with Zack and Brent Everett.

If someone were to come to you for advice about getting into the XXX business what would you tell him?

I would tell him to stay as far away as possible from agents. They just complicate an already easy casting process and then screw you out of the cash. Be smart and manage yourselves that's the easiest way to climb to the top and take charge of one's career.

STATS

BIRTH DATE: April 11, 1989

SIGN: Aries

HOMETOWN: Manhattan

HEIGHT: 5'10"

WEIGHT: 135 lbs

TWO BEST CHARACTER TRAITS: Ask someone I know.

TWO WORST CHARACTER TRAITS: I'm crazy about cleanliness, and sometimes and I can be a bit stern.

FAVORITE MUSIC: I usually listen to pop, rock, and a lot of trance.

FAVORITE MOVIES: I tend to like comedies because I believe humor is the cure to everything.

FAVORITE MOVIES I'VE BEEN IN: *Little League 3: Bottom of the Ninth*

IF I COULD MAKE ONE REQUEST ON A PORN SET IT WOULD BE: Fiji water! You can never have enough water.

AS A TEEN I ALWAYS FANTASIZED ABOUT SEX WITH: Justin Timberlake.

CURRENT FANTASY MAN: My fiancé Zack Randall, no one gets me hard/off quicker.

SEXIEST PART OF A MAN: Masculine arms and hands really turn me on.

THREE INGREDIENTS OF MY HOTTEST SEX FANTASY: Zack Randall, Brent Everret and I ... Sounds delicious.

FAVORITE ITEM IN MY SEXUAL TOYBOX: I don't have one.

MOST PRIZED POSSESSION: Everything. If I bought it, I love it.

HOBBIES: Tennis, clubbing, shopping and shooting porn. I couldn't live without these things.

PETS: None for now, owning your own company doesn't exactly give you time to spare.

PET PEEVES: When Zack leaves his towel on the floor. (Laughs). Love you babe.

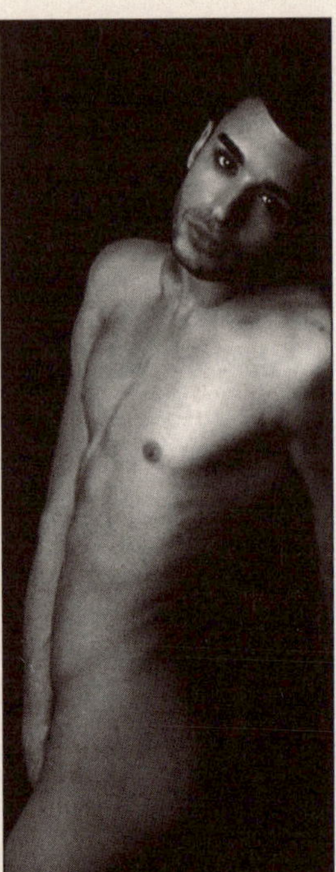

Derek Rivero [PHOTOS BY ERIC GREGORY PHOTOGRAPHY]

"I'm living most 18-year-old boys' dreams and I love it."

Is it humorous, educational, painful, or arousing to watch yourself on screen?

All of the above.

How do you think your experience in XXX films has changed you?

I don't look at anything the same anymore. Imagine turning 18 shooting three porn movies and then retiring five months later and opening your own studio. I'm living most 18-year-old boys' dreams and I love it.

What do you always do to prepare for a shoot?

I eat lots of pizza and candy. It's one of the advantages of being 18.

And what do you do evenings after a long day of filming?

After a long day of filming nothing is more appropriate than a big fat Long Island Iced Tea.

What is the craziest thing you have ever witnessed on a XXX set?

I once saw one of the guys from my movie injecting his cock with something to make it stay hard. I couldn't believe it. Not only was I in shock but really rather appalled. I personally prefer the conventional Viagra or Cialis if any erectile problems arise.

People often consider porn stars to be these ideal physical specimens, but if you could change one thing about yourself through cosmetic sur-

gery what would it be?

I have no idea. I like everything just as it is I guess.

How do we get you in the sack and what do we do with you once we get you there?

Sorry, I'm engaged.

If you had to choose between sex and love which would it be and what are your thoughts on fidelity?

Love. And fidelity is just a coward expression of one's own sexual repression.

Describe your dream vacation.

Fiji

Speaking sexually very few guys are as skilled as me when it comes to ...

Oral sex, I rock!

Describe your ideal romantic evening.

It would start off with a romantic candle lit dinner, followed by a few drinks and a short ride back to my place for some serious fucking!

TROJAN **ROCK**

So first off I want to hear how the name Trojan Rock came about.

I used to play Rugby, and we all had warrior names: As one of the largest members of the team I was able to create diversions allowing other team mates to break through the oppositions defenses. Trojan was the name given to me.

How did you get started in the business?

I got my start in porn when Carlo Cox asked me to join him for a movie while I was on holiday in Brazil. How could I turn down such an opportunity!

What do you think you were you looking for when you got into it?

I love showing off sexually and performing, and I love sex with great looking men. I thought it would satisfy both of those desires ... and it does for sure.

Do you recall the first movie you did and the first bit of direction you were given?

The first movie I made was for Marco Studios in Brazil. I didn't speak Portuguese then, so I am not sure what the director was saying, but I have a feeling it was ... relax and do what comes naturally!

How did you and Carlo Cox get together?

We met on-line, and then by chance at a party of a mutual friend. It was definitely "Get your rocks off" at first sight!

Did Carlo give you any advice getting into making XXX movies?

Yes, he told me to follow my own instincts, and he was right. Before my first movie, he reminded me, we were just going to be doing what we did already in clubs and at home ... but this time there was a camera. He also told me not to take any of it too seriously, and to have a great time fucking!

Do you think it helps being in the business and having your partner be in XXX as well?

Yes, for sure it helps. We understand the nature of what we are doing. That sex is fun and that is why we are doing it. We also know the reality of how hard, and at times exhausting it can be. Also, I love watching my partner in movies, and get off knowing what pleasure he is having.

What about making porn came as a surprise to you?

That I would enjoy it so much (Laughing). I guess also, the only surprise to me was that sometimes it can be like a major workout (it is physically demanding) or an incredibly long yoga session (all those positions), but

STATS

BIRTH DATE: September 1964

SIGN: Libra

HOMETOWN: London/Rio

HEIGHT: 6'2"

WEIGHT: 94 kg/ 210 lbs

TWO BEST CHARACTER TRAITS: I'm honest and generous.

TWO WORST CHARACTER TRAITS: I'm honest and impatient.

FAVORITE MUSIC: Any contemporary Brazilian or Madonna (I am gay after all!)

FAVORITE MOVIES: Porn movies – *Eruption* (Titan) the scene with Eduardo with Dean Coulter. Main stream – *Before Night Falls* directed by Julian Schnabel. You cannot watch this and not be moved to tears.

FAVORITE MOVIES I HAVE BEEN IN: *Out in the Open* for Alpha Male Media.com the scene with Adriano Marquez and *Centurion Muscle* for Raging Stallion, my scene with Xerxes and Eric Hunter.

XXX COSTAR I'D DO AGAIN IN A MINUTE: Carlo Cox

IF I COULD MAKE ONE DEMAND ON A PORN SET IT WOULD BE: Not to work with gay for pay – ever! It ruins the chemistry and chemistry is everything!

AS A TEEN I ALWAYS FANTASIZED ABOUT SEX WITH: Tom Selleck – yes, it's true!

CURRENT FANTASY MAN: Steve Cruz

SEXIEST PART OF A MAN: His eyes, for sure! And of course a juicy, hairy butt!

THREE INGREDIENTS OF MY HOTTEST SEX FANTASY: Hairy beefy butts, thick cocks, and great smiles – therefore a session with Steve Cruz and Jake Deckard.

FAVORITE ITEM IN MY SEXUAL TOY BOX: My man Carlo Cox

MOST PRIZED POSSESSION: My home in Rio de Janeiro.

HOBBIES: Performing in and producing porn.

PETS: Sam, my Irish setter.

PET PEEVES: Dishonesty, guys who aren't honest with their partners and play behind their backs!

what can be better than fucking for hours with hot guys!

Do you have some amazing fantasy you are just waiting for some director to ask you to film – care to share?

I love sex outside, so to do an orgy scene, or a one on one somewhere wild and exotic would be amazing. I loved watching early Titan movies, like *Eruption* or *Island Guardian* ... and would love to be in a scene in such glorious natural surroundings. A big tribal orgy *al fresco*!

Speaking of that – if you were to make a movie called Trojan Rock's Orgy who would you want as your four costars?

Steve Cruz, Jake Deckard, Ben Jakks, Blake Nolan

Porn movies are notorious for putting you guys in some very uncomfortable positions for the sake of the camera. What is the most difficult position you have ever had to have sex in for a movie?

No position is too difficult if you are enjoying the action, but working in Berlin, I had to work in an old abandoned distillery basement in zero degrees, freezing my bollocks off. Now that was uncomfortable!

What do you usually do to prepare for a film shoot?

To get ready for a shoot – I eat well, exercise a lot, and try to rest. Also, I won't have sex for at least a day before hand.

And what is your typical evening like when you get home from a day of filming?

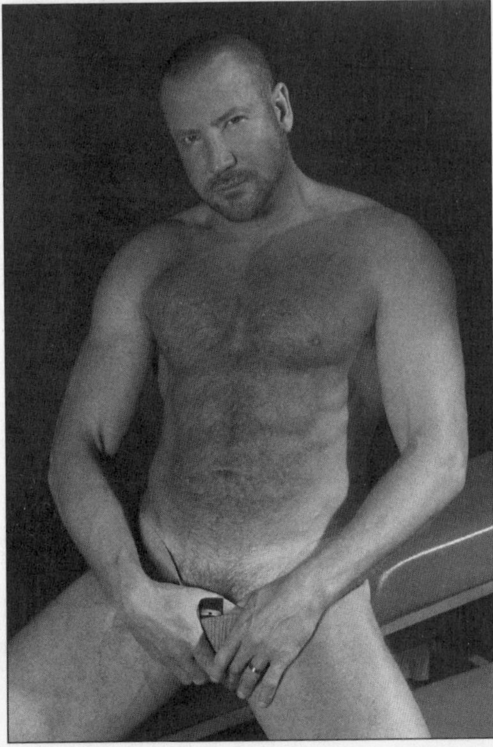

Trojan Rock [PHOTO BY KENT TAYLOR, COURTESY RAGING STALLION STUDIOS]

That depends. If you are lucky enough to have a short day and finish early, I may go to dinner with another actor or a group of us will go out together. Sometimes, you might end up continuing some of the action back at the hotel. There is nothing typical after a shoot.

If someone came to you for advice about getting into the business what would you tell him?

Do it, enjoy it, but don't take it too seriously. Only do it if will be fun.

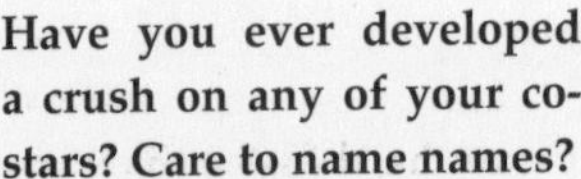

Have you ever developed a crush on any of your co-stars? Care to name names?

I think that everyone I have worked with, except the gay for pay guy, and I have had great chemistry with and of course, have had a small crush on – that what makes the work so cool!

Have you ever done anything sexually on screen that you would never do in your personal life?

Had sex with a supposedly straight man! Why the hell would I have sex with a straight guy, when there are so many hot and horny gay guys out there?

What is the most drama you have ever experienced on a set?

I once was put in the unfortunate position of working with an actor who was supposedly gay for pay. I would never want to do that again. There is no need for this in this industry as there are so many guys who love what they do and are proud of who they really are and what they are doing. Enough said.

Porn sets are often the place of some surreal and hilarious incidents. Do you have any personal tale you would care to share?

OK, recently I was still on set while a couple of guys were shooting a scene. Unfortunately, the chemistry between what should have been a blow away couple died out. The director came into the dressing room swearing and saying, "Oh fuck, they can't fuck ... I need a stunt cock." You would never know it was me, but, I had to step in and fuck one of the guys so the director could get a penetration shot, and then the guy could come while being fucked. I wasn't going to complain. The guy was so hot and the scene needed to be completed!

Do you have any childhood or adolescent memory that you can look back upon and say, "Oh yeah, that kid was destined to grow up to be a porn star"?

Well, I started fantasizing about being filmed as early as I can remember seeing my first porn film, but I would never have thought it would become a reality!

So as a natural exhibitionist do you have an ultimate exhibitionist fantasy?

Fucking and being fucked on a terrace overlooked by as many who would care to view, rear window style! Woof!

Do you think of watching yourself in a movie is arousing, uncomfortable, unbearable, or educational?

I remember watching the tape of Adriano Marqeuz and myself in *Out in the Open* as highly arousing. It's better than just a memory of a great sex session because you can relive it second by second, or frame by frame ... that's so damn hot.

When people recognize you from your film work do they treat you differently?

It is always great and exciting when people recognize you. I hope they don't treat me any differently. They find me approachable.

You must have many fans. What is the most unusual request that a fan has been made to you?

I think the strangest is the request for marriage which is also, at the same time, ironically, the most flattering.

"Why the hell would I have sex with a straight guy, when there are so many hot and horny gay guys out there?"

Though you aren't single, how would you describe yourself in a personals ad.

Bloody gorgeous.

What gets you hard faster than anything?

A hairy bubble butt, ready to be eaten.

What is the best pick-up line you have ever used or had used on you?

The best pick up line is no pick up line. Let the eyes say it all. Words are never needed.

How do we get you in bed and what do we do with you once we get you there?

A cheeky smile, bright eyes, no attitude, the right chemistry and I will be there! Once you get me there anything can happen. The exploration never ends.

Where is the most unusual place you've ever had sex?

On the terrace of a hotel room in Barcelona where the whole world could watch, or in fact probably did.

So as a natural exhibitionist what is the wildest sexual experience you've ever done in front of someone?

The wildest sexual experience was performing a live sex show in a sex club in Nice, to release the DVD of *Cowboy Stories* by Mack Studios. All the stars were on stage in front of 300 people doing what came naturally. The audience went wild and so were we!

People tend to think of adult film stars as these perfect specimens, but if you could change one thing about yourself with cosmetic surgery what would it be?

That's funny! None of us are perfect but I am really at the stage in my life where I don't want to change anything. The only thing I would change would be time. I wish I had reached the conclusion that we are as we are many years ago and not wasted so much time worrying about how I looked or what I could change! OK, give me bigger legs, and my toes need straightening ...

What things do you think have been the greatest help in your success as a XXX star?

Loving men and sex would be the main thing. There is nothing more exciting than getting on set and fucking with horny gorgeous men. Another thing, would be not relying on the industry for my main career. I think because I do it for fun, it means I am more relaxed and can enjoy it more than those who do it just for the money. One other thing – having a partner who is in the industry has been a great help. We understand what is going on set and what the work entails, so there is no jealousy, just support and encouragement.

What is your favorite all time XXX film?

I actually have two favorites: One is *Conqueror* with Billy Harrington, directed by Chi Chi LaRue. Billy is such a hot stud. And the other is Titan's *Island Guardian* – the scene with Adriano Marquez and Brad Michaels always blows me away. I think I have worn out the part on the DVD where Brad unbuttons Adriano's shorts. Wow!

Do you think the industry has a responsibility regarding the use of condoms and/or promoting safe sex?

If the safe sex message is not getting through, then it needs to be rethought as to how it is being communicated. I don't think you can put the responsibility of safe sex at the doors of the porn companies.

Describe your ideal romantic evening.

At home, with Carlo Cox, and our dog, a dinner in and watching a good movie together, and then sex. Simple.

If you had to choose between sex and love which would you choose and what are your thoughts about fidelity?

Well luckily I have the perfect combination being married (legally) to a porn actor. Fidelity, for us is less related to monogamy, but more to respecting each other's well being, and allowing each other to grow. I would always choose love above sex. Love is constant.

What is the biggest misconception

Trojan Rock [PHOTO BY KENT TAYLOR, COURTESY RAGING STALLION STUDIOS]

people have about you when you meet them?

That I am serious and gruff. I am really a pussycat!

If you had to compare yourself to an animal what species do you think best captures your essence and why?

A Lion. I have one hell of a roar when I have a thorn in my paw. I am powerful, protective and can be gentle.

Describe your dream vacation.

Somewhere with wild beaches and scenery, where I can have sex on the rocks as the water is crashing nearby. The Seychelles is perfect for this!

Do you have any ideas where you want your life to be five years from now?

More of the same please, and also, I would like to see my porn studio www.alphamalemedia.com become the best studio providing real men and real sex. All chemistry and no faking it here!

FRANÇOIS **SAGAT**

François, how did you get started in the business?

I was discovered on a French gay magazine cover called *Gay Video*. At that time, I was already thinking about working in the US, with TitanMen as my first choice.

What were you looking for when you got into it?

Of course, to have the feeling of being appreciated for my sex appeal and to record the way my body is when I'm still working out at the gym. (Laughing). But I got into it mainly to do great scenes, with a lot of work on building my image. And I love the fact that I can meet so many beautiful and interesting guys from every culture and country. Pictures are really important for me ... I love working on it; every day is building on myself and the way people look at me. Of course, I'm making all the mistakes somebody young and not really prepared is susceptible to doing, but it's really good to learn for the future. Being smart is key if you want to think about a career.

STATS

BIRTH DATE: June 5, 1979

SIGN: Gemini

HOMETOWN: Cognac, France

HEIGHT: 5'9"

WEIGHT: 185 lbs

TWO BEST CHARACTER TRAITS: I'm nice and I'm a dreamer.

TWO WORST CHARACTER TRAITS: Probably that I'm innocent and stolid (a bit cold, too).

FAVORITE MUSIC: Neptune's, Timbaland, Dr. Dre, Madonna, Justin Timberlake, Marilyn Manson, R&B, electro, pop, rock

FAVORITE MOVIES: I love John Waters' cinematography, and especially *Serial Mom*. Also George Romero's *Living Dead* movies, superhero movies, anything by David Lynch and Gus Van Sant

FAVORITE MOVIES I'VE BEEN IN: TitanMen's *Breathless* (it's a strong movie directed by Bruce Cam – really nasty and beautiful natural settings).

XXX COSTARS I'D DO AGAIN IN A MINUTE: Francesco D'Macho and Dred Scott

IF I COULD MAKE ONE REQUEST ON A PORN SET IT WOULD BE: Diet Coke everywhere! Oh, and no queens or sissies for sex partners.

AS A TEEN I ALWAYS FANTASIZED ABOUT SEX WITH: Brad Pitt and Supergirl.

CURRENT FANTASY MAN: He's another porn actor – a beautiful Italian man ... I'll leave it at that.

SEXIEST PART OF A MAN: From the face down to the neck.

THREE INGREDIENTS OF MY HOTTEST SEX FANTASY: Outside during the summer with lots of sweat and rain.

FAVORITE ITEM IN MY SEXUAL TOY BOX: No accessories necessary, except a leather belt.

MOST PRIZED POSSESSION: My gold necklace from my baptism, with a medallion of St. Nicholas.

HOBBIES: Illustration, taking and retouching photos, and movies

PETS: I love cats, but I don't have any anymore. I also think snakes are beautiful.

PET PEEVES: Insects and spiders.

I'm not really smart when it comes to myself but I am able to grow. Some experienced people are here to give me direction sometimes and that's good ... I just have to be more confident!

What is the first thing you do when you get home from a day of shooting?

Usually, after every shoot, even if I'm really dead, I take my protein shake and I go straight to the gym.

"Speaking with [my co-stars before a scene] is a big mistake. Talking about the weather or about *The Devil Wears Prada* breaks the good chemistry!"

What is the most aroused you have ever been on screen?

Recently, the fact that I can make people believe that I have a blast during my three-way with two big, beautiful, amazing straight guys from Hungary who hate to lick my ass! (Laughing). I adored the fact that my director took a certain pleasure with the idea of giving them orders, and that's what happened. It was memorable! It was also funny because I didn't feel desirable but the results of the scene on screen are so beautiful. Everybody (including myself) loves this scene already.

What things do you always try to do to prepare for a XXX shoot?

Generally, no sex or jerking off for two or three days before ... no perfume, no deodorant, a super, super, super cleaned out ass (of course!), a breath mint and two or three aspirins. On the set, getting hot with my other partners: smelling, sucking, kissing, and touching each other for a few minutes before starting. But just a teasing touch to get in the mood. Speaking with them is a big mistake. Talking about the weather or about *The Devil Wears Prada* breaks the good chemistry!

If a guy came to you for advice about getting into the business what would you tell him?

I would tell him that he will have to give a lot of himself because people and fans are really demanding. He will have to be on all the time. He will need to keep his regular job if he has it. The most important thing I will tell him is that there is no going back to the past ... and that every choice – company, filming, sexual preferences and practices, choice of partners and directors – is crucial ... in a good or bad way. Getting into the business is like putting tattoos on yourself. You belong to it and it belongs to you forever, so be ready psychologically and physically. Then I will tell him that he must do the best to have fun and enjoy while it he's working ... it can be a lot of fun!

Speaking sexually, very few guys are as skilled as me when it comes to_.

Kissing!

Where is the wildest place you've ever had sex?

It was in summer, in a plumbing truck with a beautiful young worker under a violent rainstorm in Saint Germain Des Pres, Paris.

François Sagat [PHOTO COURTESY TITANMEN.COM]

How do we get you into bed and what do we do with you once we get you there?

It's really easy to get me into bed if you are somebody really simple and demonstrative. And if you want to take care of me and see me again and again (if you are a crazy pig and romantic at the same time you are welcome). If you just need to have sex with me to put me on your porn star list, you're making the wrong decision and I can always easily tell. I love one on one sex, both vanilla and more violent, with kissing, kissing and more kissing and cuddling. Of course, I can be really nasty!

François Sagat [PHOTO BY KENT TAYLOR, COURTESY RAGING STALLION STUDIOS]

So in your sexual toy box you listed a leather belt, and just what do you plan on using that for?

I tried it in *Breathless*. They strangled me with it; it was amazing, really sexual. The Breathless belt disappeared in the Czech Republic (Laughing). My last private sex partner used his belt to attach my arms behind my back while he was fucking me – hot hot hot ... I wanna do it again.

In your hobbies you list photography and I was wondering if that and your interest in film hint that you may possibly move behind the camera one day in the adult film industry?

It would be great, but I still feel ill at ease thinking about taking care of a team. But my creativity is still full and here. I have to work on it but somebody would have to help me and believe in me. It's not my priority at the moment, though.

Describe your ideal romantic evening.

I had it in Paris a few days ago. The hotel and all the streets and restaurants around, the Champs Elysees, in bed with a good horror movie with an amazing man I've known

TYLER **SAINT**

How did you get started in the business?

I had been approached several times by various people to do porn or layouts, I guess the timing was never right until I was approached by my current agents John Tegan and Andrew Rosen to work on some projects.

What exactly are the perks of having an agent in the XXX world?

The perks of having an agent are considerable. They handle all the legwork involved in setting up video shoots, photo shoots, personal appearances and any other function that may arise. They are the go between for dealing with film studios and production staff. It certainly makes my life much easier.

Were the people who you knew surprised when you started making XXX movies?

Actually, no. My friends know I am a pretty sexual guy, so it was no surprise at all to them. I am also quite amazed at how supportive they all are – continually asking when new releases are going to be out so they can go buy them.

What were you looking for when you got into it?

I really had no preconceived opinion of the biz; I simply wanted to see how far I could go with it. So far so good!

Do you recall your first movie and the first bit of direction you were given?

My first movie was *Workload* by Jetset, directed by Andrew Rosen. My first scene took place finding Eddie Stone tied up in a closet – my first bit of direction was to rub my crotch and make it hard.

So what makes Jason Ridge such an awesome co-star – details please!

Not only is Jason Ridge as handsome as they come, he is also an incredibly nice guy as well. We had an immediate connection from our first meeting. We had a lot of down time between scenes so it allowed us time to really get to know each other. Jason is a seasoned pro which made our scene effortless and extremely fun. As for juicy details, let's just say our scene extended into our off time.

XXX is known for putting the guys in some rather difficult positions for the sake of the shot. What is the toughest position you have ever had to assume for the good of the movie?

I wouldn't say any scene I have done to date was that difficult. There are several things that are always issues like staying hard for hours on

Tyler Saint [PHOTO COURTESY HOT HOUSE ENTERTAINMENT]

STATS

BIRTH DATE: March 3

SIGN: Pisces

HOMETOWN: Born and raised in Vermont. I currently reside in West Hollywood, California.

HEIGHT: 5'8"

WEIGHT: 180 lbs

TWO BEST CHARACTER TRAITS: I'm dependable and loving.

TWO WORST CHARACTER TRAITS: I'm a procrastinator and overly trusting.

FAVORITE MUSIC: Dance music to workout and classical to relaxing.

FAVORITE MOVIES: *Little Miss Sunshine, The Color Purple, Big Business.*

FAVORITE MOVIES I'VE BEEN IN: *Link 5, Folsom Leather.*

XXX COSTAR I'D DO AGAIN IN A MINUTE: Jason Ridge – again and again and again.

IF I COULD MAKE ONE REQUEST ON A PORN SET IT WOULD BE: A perpetual erection.

AS A TEEN I ALWAYS FANTASIZED ABOUT SEX WITH: Bo and Luke Duke from *The Dukes of Hazard.*

CURRENT FANTASY MAN: Jake Tanner

SEXIEST PART OF A MAN: Although I am a leg man at heart, I really like lower oblique, (I call them Cum Gutters).

THREE INGREDIENTS OF MY HOTTEST SEX FANTASY: The outdoors, ten or so men, and lots of lube.

FAVORITE ITEM IN MY SEXUAL TOY BOX: I really like leather gear.

MOST PRIZED POSSESSION: My health

HOBBIES: Gym, e-baying, hiking, and traveling.

PETS: I have two cats – Charlotte and Phoebe.

PET PEEVES: Ignorance and disrespect.

end, extremes of heat or cold, or having sex on hard surfaces. As an actor, you just overcome these things and do whatever it takes to get the shot.

What things do you usually do to prepare yourself for a film shoot?

Mentally to prepare for a shoot really involves nothing, I am a bit of an exhibitionist and really enjoy sex. Physically, I have to make sure I go to the gym everyday, eat right, shave the necessary parts and get whatever props or special clothing needed for the shoot.

How do you usually spend the evening after getting home from a day of filming?

I am generally exhausted after a day of filming. I like to take a nice long bath, order take out, veg in front of the TV and drift off into a deep sleep.

As a natural exhibitionist do you have a first memory of when you realized that "Yeah, you like to show off."

I would have to say my first experience kind of happened on its own. In high school junior year gym class we all had to shower for the first time after class. I was never naked in front of other guys before, so it felt a bit awkward. Little did I know that my equipment was rather large for my age. I was teased a bit by my gym classmates, but in a good way. Any awkwardness was soon gone, replaced with an incredible confidence. Yeah I have a big dick – look at me!

So as a workaholic in this business can I assume you have some adult industry goals? Care to share?

I would like to someday write and direct my own video(s). My immediate goal is to become a production assistant and then a producer. Learning the business from every aspect is crucial in making a good product. Currently being an actor, I already know what the dynamics are for shooting

As an actor what have learned in front of the camera that will come in handy later when you are at work directing and or producing?

First of all camera angle – always having to have the perspective of the person watching the video. Secondly, being on set has allowed me to see the entire process from start to finish – i.e. dealing with actors, set location, lighting.

If you were going to make a movie called Tyler Saint's Orgy who would you want for your four costars?

Why limit it to four? I guess if I had to have that few, I would have to select guys I already have done scenes with since I know there is already a connection. I hate to single out four specific guys so I will be diplomatic and say that I enjoyed every scene I have done thus far, so any of the guys you see me paired with in my videos would certainly be welcome in a Tyler Saint Orgy.

What is the most aroused you have ever been on screen?

In a scene I recently did with Alex Collack and CJ Knight. A locker room scene with jock straps and two of my all time favorite porn stars made it incredibly arousing!

How do you think the XXX experience has changed you?

It has made me a bit more humble. It is a very humbling experience to know that people are watching and getting off looking at you.

People often think of XXX stars as these perfect specimens, but if you could alter one thing about yourself physically through cosmetic surgery what would it be?

This may sound kind of silly to some, but I really hate my toes. And now after reading this people will all be looking to see what I mean. As a kid I grew up on a horse farm in Northern Vermont. I was goofing off with a friend, long story short, my left foot got run over by a tractor which broke three of my toes. They have been a bit crooked since then.

Is it tough, interesting, unbearable, educational, or arousing to watch yourself on screen?

I am very hypercritical of myself. I watch my scenes basically to teach myself what I can do better on my next shoot. I can honestly say I do not find watching myself erotic in any way.

I'm curious. You mention watching your films to see places of improvement. What was something that struck you right away that you wanted to do better on film?

Nothing – that I need to be better. I am finding that I have this odd yet determined look on my face all the time. I kind of stick out my lower jaw. I want to try to stop doing that as it looks a bit silly to me.

If someone were to come up to you ask for advice about getting into the business what would you tell him?

Try not to be too naïve, enjoy the experience, maintain your professionalism. and most importantly, stay humble.

Are you harboring some wonderful secret fantasy you are just waiting for some director to ask you to film?

I am into group sex, so I would have to say I would love to have ten or so hot guys in a group all lined up while I do whatever I want to them. At the end, every guy unloads all over me!

So what are some of the things you would do to that group of 10 guys in your sex fantasy?

Although I play a top on screen, I am actually quite a versatile guy in real life. So just going crazy and doing whatever feels good is what makes it a fantasy for me. As long as I get to be showered with all ten loads, whatever else happens is just icing on the cake (so to speak).

You mention loving group sex. What is it about that experience that pushes all your buttons?

I am a very visual person, so as much stimulus I can surround myself with is always amazing. I really get into being the voyeur, even when I am involved in the group. Sometime just sitting back and watching the group can be just as fun as participating in it.

Have you ever done anything sexually in a film that you would never do off camera in your personal life?

Not yet.

Do you think the industry has a responsibility regarding the use of condoms and/or promoting safe sex?

I do, however, everyone should educate themselves to the repercussions of unprotected sex. Never trust anyone to disclose their status to you. In my life, I assume everyone is positive so there isn't room for doubt.

If you could change one thing about the way the industry is currently run what would it be?

It really bothers me that the industry chooses to use straight guys in gay porn. Many of them make it uncomfortable for the gay men to perform. Having to watch some dude who is about to fuck you jerking off to girlie magazines is a bit degrading. Just my opinion.

Do you have some best example of bad behavior on a XXX set you would care to share?

The most prevalent example of bad behavior that comes to mind are the attitudes of some of the actors who think they are God's gift to porn. Ego and bitchyness are not always present on set, but when it does rear its ugly head, it can make filming a bit tense.

Porn sets are often the place of some surreal and hilarious incidents. Do you have any personal tale you would care to share?

The first thing that comes to mind is a scene I did with a really hot LA porn actor -I was topping him and we were really into each other sexually. We were getting a bit rough with slapping and dirty talk – when all of a sudden he turned back to punch my chest and ended up clocking me in the jaw. It was quite a surprise to say the least – but in retrospect was so funny the entire crew burst out it laughter.

Do you have any childhood or adolescent memory that you can look back upon and say, "Oh yeah, that kid was destined to grow up to be a porn star"?

I used to draw circles around my nipples and penis with magic marker when I was only five. I also liked to take pictures of myself cumming later in my teens when I discovered the fine art of masturbation. I also liked to be naked as much as possible, preferring nudity to wearing clothes.

"Although I play a top on screen, I am actually quite a versatile guy in real life."

Those are some very telling pastimes. When you pass a hot looking guy on the street what about him gets you to turn around and do a double take every time?

I am a rather avid leg and butt man. When I pass a hot looking guy on the street, and his legs look good, I am always curious as to what his ass looks like as well. I generally end up getting caught checking him out – which in some cases works to my benefit.

Where is the wildest place you've ever had sex?

The wildest place I have ever had sex would have to be in the DJ booth at Palladium in New York City. Three of us going at it while hundreds of people were dancing just below us on the dance floor was truly amazing and very erotic.

Speaking sexually, very few people are as skilled as me when it comes to ...

Bringing out the inner pig in my partners.

When it comes to seducing a guy I've found nothing works better than ...

A simple sly smile.

Describe your dream vacation.

My dream vacation would be to sail around the world with a few close friends. How could it get any better seeing new places than to share the experience with special people in your life?

How do we get you in the sack and what do we do with you once we get you there?

Finding down time to get me in the sack is a difficult thing. I am a consummate workaholic. If by chance you catch me with some spare time then talking a little dirty to me gets my motor going. Once in the sack allow me to explore your body with my hands, mouth and tongue. I am very unselfish when it comes to sex. I enjoy pleasing my sack partner which in turn gets me off.

How would you describe yourself in a personals ad?

Well, I will take an excerpt from an actual ad I have: I'm just a regular guy, mellow, humble, caring – a kind of guy who doesn't judge someone on the way they look, what they wear or what they drive. My motto and way of living follows the simple rule – "treat everyone as you would like to be treated" Looking for honest guys with good values and integrity. Prefer men who are working on more than just their bodies ... interested in guys who are also working on their inner life. Perpetual Piscean, lover of life, either hyper or in a coma, love to have a memorable experience, moderately social but love my alone time, usually wind up in weird experiences but always land on my feet. I like traveling, learning a new point of view, being with friends, meeting new friends, reconnecting with old friends, analyzing myself, having others analyze me, asking questions, riding my motorcycle after dusk, eating dark chocolate, learning dirty phrases in foreign languages, laughing hard ...

So this makes me wonder ... what was the worst predicament an over trusting kid from Vermont who is in XXX had upon moving to West Hollywood?

Not really any predicaments to speak of.

What is the biggest surprise people have about you when you meet them?

That I am actually a very humble and gracious person. I always believe that staying grounded makes your fans relate better to you.

If you had to compare yourself to an animal what species do you think best captures your essence and why?

I am best compared to a cat. I require a lot of love, can be very independent, and love my afternoon naps.

If your life had a theme song what would it be?

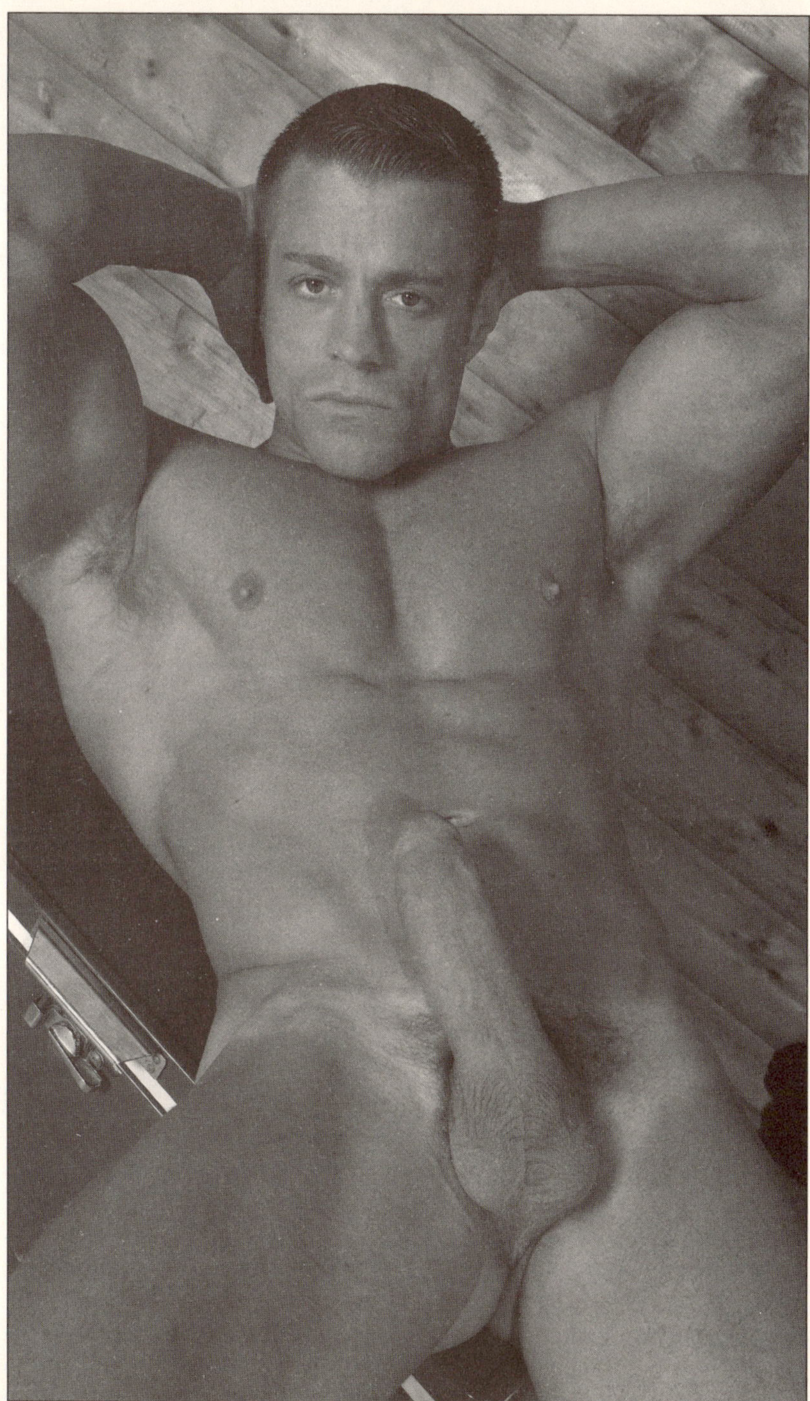

Tyler Saint [PHOTO BY KENT TAYLOR, COURTESY RAGING STALLION STUDIOS]

"Naked Fame."

If you had to choose between sex and love which would you choose and what are your thoughts about fidelity?

I believe that sex is a crucial part of love, so I would have to say both. Fidelity is a big deal for me – the thought of someone doing with my boyfriend what I consider special and sacred between the two of us would devastate me.

Describe you ideal romantic evening?

Being a Piscean, I am a hopeless romantic. My ideal romantic evening would consist of making a nice dinner followed by a candlelit bubble bath where I would wash and caress my date. Following the bath, a nice full body sensual massage with plenty of soft kisses and licks in certain places that need special attention. After the massage I would grant my date with any sexual desire he wanted!

ALLEN **SILVER**

How did you get started in the business?

The first video work I did was for Tom Bianchi in 2004. I had done some modeling for him prior to that and the idea of doing video thrilled me. I had fun with him.

What were you looking for when you got into it?

I wanted to know myself as I truly am. This was a way of really jumping into that. I wanted to see myself through other's eyes. Plus I love being seen.

When you say you want to see yourself as you truly are ... What have you seen? How have you seen yourself objectively?

I have my place in the spectrum of sexiness. We tend to often see ourselves either as awful or overstate our beauty. It has been an ongoing process to see where I fit in, what ways I am beautiful without being egotistical about it. I am at place where I love myself, but don't think I'm better than anyone else. I find confidence (but not arrogance) very sexy.

STATS

BIRTH DATE: July 19, 1961

SIGN: Cancer, Scorpio rising

HOMETOWN: Lubbock Texas

HEIGHT: 6'

WEIGHT: 190 lbs

TWO BEST CHARACTER TRAITS: Openness, presence, and integrity

TWO WORST CHARACTER TRAITS: I have a need for everything to be peaceful, to avoid conflict, and for holding onto resentments.

FAVORITE MUSIC: Currently am I wearing out *Beauty* by Vargo (cool centering music), All time favorite song is "Brown Eyed Girl" by Van Morrison (pure joy), best gay themed love song is "I Confess" by Mark Weigle (says everything about what it is like to love somebody you can't have).

FAVORITE MOVIES: *Meet Me in St. Louis, The Fifth Element, Enchanted April.*

FAVORITE MOVIES I'VE BEEN IN: *Dad's Automotive* (Pantheon), *Jonny's Place* (Ray Dragon), *Barn Storm* (Titan)

XXX COSTAR I'D DO AGAIN IN A MINUTE: Bo Matthews (a self-assured horny instigator) or Mick Powers (makes me laugh as well as being a hot fucker.)

IF I COULD MAKE ONE REQUEST ON A PORN SET IT WOULD BE: I want the entire crew naked. (Got them to do it once).

AS A TEEN I ALWAYS FANTASIZED ABOUT SEX WITH: Staying in the same tent as one my scout troop staff. I was hypnotized by his muscular legs and impossibly short cutoffs, ah the 1970s.

CURRENT FANTASY MAN: Bo Ladashevska

SEXIEST PART OF A MAN: Ass!

THREE INGREDIENTS OF MY HOTTEST SEX FANTASY: Spontaneous, shameless and intense.

FAVORITE ITEM IN MY SEXUAL TOY BOX: Rubber nipple compression rings.

MOST PRIZED POSSESSION: My Volkswagen Cabrio "Punkin." Been to Burning Man three times, what a trooper.

Have you always been an exhibitionist?

No. That came somewhere in my thirties, although I was always the kind of kid that flourished with praise. Getting older, I had to get over my I'm not good enough crap. Again, one of those things that took a while to change. I am still terrified to speak in front a group, but ask me flash my ass and I'm there.

Going along with that how does you lovemaking vary at home to that on the screen. If you are an exhibitionist, do you play it up a bit for the camera?

At home it's more relaxed and unstructured. Sometimes it's a hot spontaneous five minute brutal fuck (Mmm), other times lots of caressing and kissing etc. for a whole evening. When the cameras are rolling there is an agenda. I seek to ignite that passionate lust with my scene partners, but you gotta pace yourself as well since the filming involves a lot of stops and starts.

What about making XXX movies surprised you?

How you can't predict what the energy is going to be like on he set of any given shoot. There are so many factors in how the connection is going to feel and how many things have to be in place to make the shoot a breeze. You might be all over each other and done in a couple of hours, or there for a very long day of stops and starts. You have to be ready for anything.

Do you recall your first film and the first bit of direction you were given?

I can still hear Tom telling me, "OK, I need you to get hard now." Getting used to posing carefully while still being in a sexual state is a challenge. Fortunately, I get a buzz from being in front of the lens so that helps.

Do you consider yourself a "Daddy" type and if what physical and personality characteristics make you so right (or not right) for the role?

Yes, I tend to be the loving Daddy type rather than the vengeful angry kind. I think I have the look that a lot of guys hold as the image of Daddy. I'm blessed with a good body hair pattern that includes more than a little silver in it. I like to think that I hold both the power and kindness that makes a good dad.

This sounds like a lot of guys' fantasy ... tell me your tale about getting the entire crew naked on a XXX set.

I credit Bill Justeson with that. *Built to Last* was my first hardcore video and I was more than a little nervous. It was small crew, a director and a cameraman. Bill suggested that the crew get naked and Chris Roma was willing to go along. He uses the same cameraman for every shoot I've done with him who is a great playful lusty guy and Chris is quite a beauty. They both got turned on in the process and the shoot became very playful and intense for me as a result. I will always be grateful to Bill Justeson for his creativity in this.

What is the most aroused you have ever been on screen?

Built to Last with Bill Justeson. We were so into each other. We fucked for two more hours after the shoot was over.

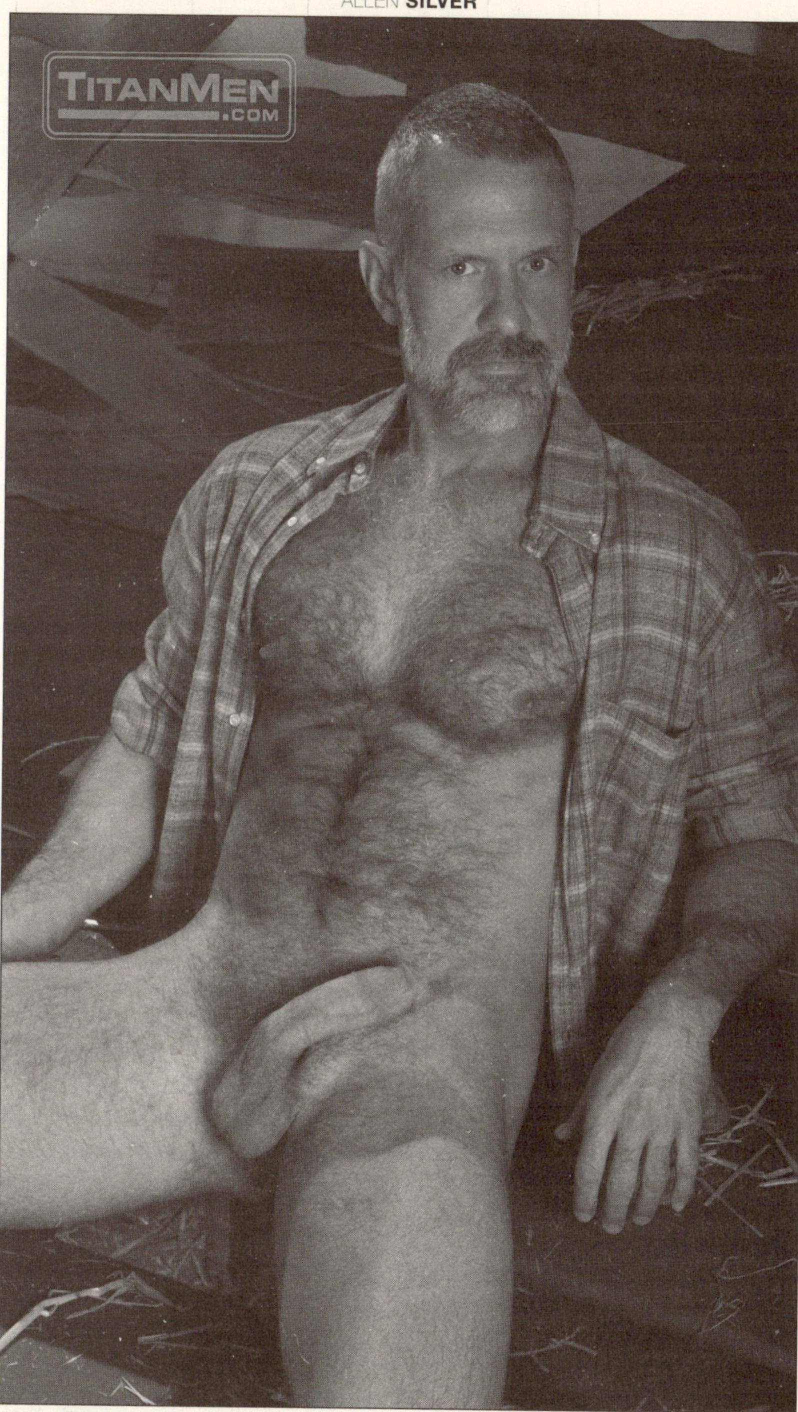

Allen Silver [PHOTO COURTESY TITANMEN.COM]

What things do you usually do to prepare for a film shoot?

Have a quiet evening before with lots of rest, eat well, that sort of thing.

And how do you spend the evening after a full day of filming?

I'm really a homebody so I like to soak in the tub and snuggle after a full day of video.

If we were to make a movie called Allen Silver's Orgy who would you want as your four costars?

I want to go with my classic fantasy men: Lance Gear, Blake Harper, Jason Branch. Think we could coax them out of retirement?

Do you think the industry has a responsibility regarding the use of condoms and/or promoting safe sex?

Yes. I was happy to see Bruce Cam take a stand in reference to the David awards. Of course it would be more fun to not use condoms. We all have freedom to have the kind of sex we want (as long as it's consenting) but we should make smart choices.

Watching bareback vids is a powerful fantasy, and that's cool as long as it remains a fantasy, but I think it's a lot easier to blow off putting on a condom when your head is filled with images of cum filled asses. Also, I do think many people hold porn performers in an idealized way. Therefore, ideal sex may seem to have to be sex without condoms. Hot, sweaty, heart to heart eye to eye full connection sex has less to do with whether there's a piece of Latex between us and more to do with how willing you are to go to that intense place together. I get messages from some very young fans. I think it would be irresponsible to give the message to some kids with their sex lives all ahead of them that barebacking is the way to go.

"Sexual fidelity with a partner just isn't for me."

If someone were to come to you for advice about getting into the business, what would you tell them?

Treat it a an experiment. See what is and isn't a match for you in doing adult films. I'd ask them about their experience in front of the lens (I think you need to be jazzed by having a camera pointed at you). Don't take any of this too seriously, you are playing to the camera which is different than how you behave in making love one on one. Be prepared for that.

Is it tough, impossible, arousing, or educational to watch yourself on screen?

Yes, no, yes, and yes. I think I have gone through three stages with this. I had a hard time watching myself after the first couple of movies. I do get turned on watching the videos, there was some hot love making in there! I wanted to see myself as I truly am, well the camera doesn't lie. I like the place I have in the spectrum of sexiness/beauty. Ray Dragon helped me a lot with getting over feeling weird about watching myself. He's a practical and grounded man who models inhabiting oneself fully in such a beautiful way.

Where is the wildest place you've ever had sex?

On a hill next to a rest stop in the Sierra Nevada's. My boyfriend and I were overcome with lust, pulled over, found the spot, yanked our pants down and fucked like dogs. We were not far from cars and families parked to take a rest. Still get turned on thinking about it.

Speaking sexually, very few guys are as talented as me when it comes to ...

Ejaculation control. Once the motor is running I can pretty much shoot on command.

When it comes to seducing a man I have found that nothing works better than ...

Eye contact and allowing the attraction to happen. Again, it's the confidence thing.

How do we get you in the sack and what do we do with you once we get you there?

Grow a beard and be a good kisser. Then once we're making love, I want all of your attention on what we are doing together. I will touch your body as if it were the most fascinating thing on earth (in that moment it will be). I want you to touch me in that same way. A good ass eating will put me in a trance as well.

How would you describe yourself in a personals ad?

More of Everything. Evolving, mature, beautiful man seeking other men groping their way upward. Let's look each other square in the eyes and dig in. Connecting on all levels is what makes life worth living. Meet me there.

What is the biggest misconception people have about you when you meet them?

I often get told that people are surprised that I don't have a lot of attitude. I don't know what they have encountered in the past. I'm always happy to talk to anyone that treats me respectfully. I'm not any better than anyone else.

If you had to choose between sex and love which would you choose and what are your thoughts about fidelity?

There's a lot of assumptions in that question, but I'll go along with your approach: Love is the thing that guides our humanness when we are at our best. There are many many different kinds of love. The best experiences of sex always involve a form of love, even if that only lasts five minutes, in fact sometimes that is the hottest! If you are talking about romantic love, that always has to segue into something deeper than that for a relationship to endure. Sexual fidelity with a partner just isn't for me. Different people are wired differently, so I can't speak for them. What matters most to me is trust in a relationship. A good relationship has to be built on it, everything else is secondary.

People so frequently consider porn stars these ideal specimens, but if you could change one thing about yourself through cosmetic surgery what would it be?

I love my body, but I have never been as slim around my back as I'd like. There's a little bit of love handles there. But I'd be hesitant to go under the knife even if money were no object.

Describe your ideal romantic evening.

Cooking dinner together we increas-

Allen Silver [PHOTO COURTESY TITANMEN.COM]

ingly find out how much we have in common and how deeply we are in sync. Suddenly, conversation stops as we fall into each other in front of the stove. The spontaneous sex is followed by almost uncontrollable laughter on both our parts. We finish making dinner and the conversation continues. After a walk outside to enjoy the breeze we spend the rest of the night making love more slowly and sleep wrapped in each other. In the morning – pancakes!

If your life had a theme song what would it be?

"Through Your Hands" by John Hiatt. Actually, I think that's everybody's theme song.

Does your cock have a nickname and if so how did it come about?

A couple of years ago my partner and I did a fun thing at Burning Man where we photographed people's genitals with a Polaroid, had them swap them with another person (best if they were the opposite gender) and had them wear their new genitals over the old ones. We called it a gender exchange program. In the process you had the opportunity to name your genitals. Mine is named "Lucky" ... and it is.

Describe your dream vacation.

I have always fantasized about sailing on a wind powered ship around the southern seas. I'm a big fan of Joseph Conrad and Jimmy Buffett. My dream vacation involves helping pilot a sailing ship around some tropical islands. I love being near the water.

Do you have any childhood or adolescent memory that you can look back upon and say, "Oh yeah, that kid was destined to grow up to be a porn star"?

No, I never imagined I'd be doing this, especially at this age.

RICKY **SINZ**

a.k.a Ricky 'The Hammer' Sinz

Hey Ricky, so how did the aka "The Hammer" come about?

I was a former pro Muay Thai fighter and had one of the most vicious right hooks and right elbows in the business I was flown to Thailand to compete in a bare knuckle title fight many years ago. I fought three fights and I won all three by knockout in the first round.

This whole combat thing is a big fantasy for a lot of men. Was combat a sort of sexual encounter for you. Was it ever arousing or erotic to you?

I served time in real combat so there is no sexual turn ons when it comes to mind, but aggressive sex and the feeling of loosing total control or even having total control is hot when you add the combination of strength, aggression, muscles, a dominant voice, and a vicious presence – you have an interesting experience.

Congratulations on reently being named a Raging Stallion exclusive. What are the perks that come along with a title like that?

Raging Stallion is the best of the

STATS

BIRTH DATE: November 12, 1980

SIGN: Scorpio

HOMETOWN: Chicago

HEIGHT: 6'

WEIGHT: 177 lbs

TWO BEST CHARACTER TRAITS: I'm loyal and sensual.

FAVORITE MUSIC: Reggae and house

FAVORITE MOVIES: *Spun, Lock Stock and Two Smoking Barrels*

FAVORITE MOVIES I'VE BEEN IN: *Grunts* and *Mission Sexploitation*

XXX COSTAR I'D DO AGAIN IN A MINUTE: Roman Ragazzi or Trey Casteel or both at the same time – some double dip action never hurt.

IF I COULD MAKE ONE REQUEST ON A PORN SET IT WOULD BE: To see the outtakes.

AS A TEEN I ALWAYS FANTASIZED ABOUT SEX WITH: Brad Pitt; he needs to bottom.

CURRENT FANTASY MAN: There are so many, it's hard to pinpoint just one.

SEXIEST PART OF A MAN: Hands down, the eyes.

THREE INGREDIENTS OF MY HOTTEST SEX FANTASY: Water sports, leather, and hardcore aggression.

FAVORITE ITEM IN MY SEXUAL TOY BOX: Anal beads.

MOST PRIZED POSSESSION: My health.

HOBBIES: Weight lifting, watching Adult Swim, building hot rods and import tuning.

PETS: Two dogs – a German Shepard/Rottweiler mix named Savannah, and my Brindle Pitbull named Killer, and a Vietnamese pot bellied pig named Bacon – he's smarter than both dogs put together.

PET PEEVES: Obnoxious people, slow drivers, egos, lazy people, and George Bush.

best in the business, they treat you like family, it is an honor to stand shoulder to shoulder with their models, and to be mentored by Chris Ward and Michael Brandon – they are true living legends. They have been like parents to me. They treat me with total respect and always keep an eye out for my welfare and well being. I am honored to hold the title Raging Stallion exclusive.

How did you get started in the business?

David Daju from Corkscrew Media Group and legendary director Toby Ross guided me into the business I replied to an ad that they had sent out and we have been the best of friends ever since they were there every step of my career and have been guiding me since.

Do you think the people who knew you were surprised by this career choice?

Not at all. I was always a wild one when I was younger so now when I see people that I went to grade school with they say we saw that coming.

I notice you have had a lot of mentors and men to guide you in your career thus far. Is that important to you ... and what has been the best bit of advice you have been given?

Having someone to turn to ask for advice is always important especially when they know what they are talking about. I know I don't have all the answers and I am a person who seems to learn the hard way so if I can cut out the downfall by just asking than I'll ask.

What is the best advice you were given starting out?

The best piece of advice was given to me by my parents when I told them I was entering the porn field. They told me they don't approve of what I'm doing but they will stand behind me in my choice and support me and that I should be safe and be myself.

If a guy were coming to you for advice about getting into the business what would you tell him?

I would explain my experiences and offer guidance. I have brought a lot of people into this business some have become very successful, some were too greedy and hard headed, it's a good business but you have to protect yourself.

What were you looking for when you got into XXX work?

I was looking to explore more of my sexuality and to cater to my exhibitionist side, and now I'm just holding on for the wild ride that lies ahead.

What things have you discovered so far?

I have discovered I am a total voyeur, exhibitionist, and I have discovered that a lot of people are to some extent.

So if porn caused you to discover some things about yourself sexually, do you think it also changed you somewhat and if so, how?

It allows me to be more open and it allows me to meet people who are into the same sort of kink that I am into.

So if you were offered a role in a fetish film how far do you see yourself going?

All the way

Ricky Sinz [PHOTO BY KENT TAYLOR, COURTESY RAGING STALLION STUDIOS]

When you say "all the way" is as far as you would go if offered a role in a fetish film, then what would be your ideal kink/fetish place?

I really want to do a medical fetish scene with someone strapped into a gyno chair and I want to just go to town electricity, tools, power tools, you name it I'll do it. I'm very open to trying new things and there is so much I haven't experienced so I'm down for whatever creams my twinky or someone else's for that matter.

I bet you have a lot of fans ... what is the most interesting request any of them has made of you?

I had a fan take my pictures and send them to a studio saying that we were a couple. They hired what they thought was me and my lover and they got my stalker. I found out about the incident three months after. I get a lot of requests for items off set, and autographs. Nothing too weird.

Have you ever made any fan's dream come true ... of sex with you that is?

I honestly can say that I haven't but that doesn't mean it won't happen.

Do you have a favorite fan encounter?

I have really enjoyed most of them. I have met a lot of really cool people and I continue to meet more everyday. I value all the support they give me so I try to let them know that I appreciate their support every chance I get

XXX movies are notorious for putting guys in positions that are pretty uncomfortable for the sake of the camera shot. What is the toughest sex position you have ever had to assume on screen?

Holding up Roman Ragazzi's legs while squatting down topping him, he has an awesome body and his legs are about as big as my chest so my legs were cramping pretty bad from holding all the weight.

Is it hard, educational, or arousing to watch yourself in a movie?

I tear myself apart when I see myself and pick out all the things I could have done better.

"My dick can get hard from a gentle summer's breeze."

Do you recall your first movie and the first bit of direction you were given?

Yes, *Mission Sexploitation.* It was really good direction from Toby Ross and David Daju. They explained to me how to get my point across on camera and then they let me be really creative. They are awesome to work with.

What is the most turned on you have ever been on screen?

I'm always turned on. When the camera rolls my junk is ready to rock and it all just comes out. I totally loose control and let the emotions flow.

What about making XXX movies came as the biggest surprise to you?

Honesty, nothing surprises me about this business.

What things do you usually do to prepare yourself for filming?

I try to get some good sleep. I work out, and I stop having sex for one week prior to the shoot.

And what do you do when you get home from a long day on the set?

I eat a big meal and go to sleep.

You seem like the kind of guy with some pretty intense sexual fantasies ... care to give me a taste of one?

I want some domination on a medical exam table, fisting, water sports, bondage, strobe lights, and I want it hardcore.

Where is the wildest place you've ever had sex?

I have had sex everywhere – rooftops, cars, forest preserves, parking garages, on the highway in my Porsche at 85 mph with the top down, on a go-go box at the club. Whenever I'm in the mood, its on.

What are the main things that tend to be the triggers that get you in the mood?

Flirting, and visuals.

So if visuals are one of the things that gets you going ... what are some of those visuals that get your dick hard?

Asses, eyes, big cocks, muscles, ink, fetish shots. My dick can get hard from a gentle summer's breeze.

People think of porn stars as these ideal specimens, but if you could change one thing about yourself physically through cosmetic surgery what would it be?

I wouldn't change anything, I'm happy with the body I have.

How would you go about describing yourself in a personals ad?

I would describe myself, as kind, loyal, down to earth, likes to have fun, responsible, loves dancing and Adult Swim, looking for same.

And if you were to take out a personal seeking someone what would

Ricky Sinz [PHOTO BY KENT TAYLOR, COURTESY RAGING STALLION STUDIOS]

your list of wants and requirements look like?

I would want someone honest, loyal, fun, normal, successful, mature and funny.

When you pass a hot looking guy on the street what is something that gets you to turn around and do a double take every time?

Muscles, eyes and tattoos.

Speaking sexually, very few guys are as skilled as me when it comes to ...

Verbal domination.

So can you give me a taste of verbal domination?

When I'm in my zone it just comes out, for example a bottom will be talking and I'll say something like I can't understand so shut the fuck up and fill your mouth full of cock.

Describe you ideal romantic evening.

Hmm. Romance, what is that? Just kidding. A romantic evening would have to include, a good dinner, some dancing, shopping a long walk somewhere nice and some fierce first date sex.

Describe your dream vacation.

The French Polynesian Islands.

Where do you hope this career takes you?

I don't really hope it takes me anywhere – if I have no expectations then I have no disappointments.

JT SLOAN

How did you get started in the business?

Some military buddies sent a naked picture of me into a gay magazine as a joke, and one thing led to another, and I was asked to do videos.

So based on your experience, how gay was the military?

The military is not "gay," but the Canadian military from my experience is very understanding.

What were you looking for when you got into porn?

Fun, sex with hot guys and a fun vacation.

What about making XXX movies surprised you?

How for most scenes the cum shot is done first.

What was your biggest fear getting into the business?

None. I believe that if you fear anything it controls you.

Are you a natural exhibitionist?

Yes.

STATS

BIRTH DATE: September 25

SIGN: Libra

HOMETOWN: Edmonton, Alberta, Canada

HEIGHT: 5'8"

WEIGHT: 190 lbs

TWO BEST CHARACTER TRAITS: Honest and dependable

TWO WORST CHARACTER TRAITS: Too honest and hard to say no

FAVORITE MUSIC: Anything mixed by Manny Lehman or Mike Dueretto

FAVORITE MOVIES: Anything with hot men

FAVORITE MOVIES I'VE BEEN IN: *Raw Hide, Bull's Eye, Man's Country*

XXX COSTAR I'D DO AGAIN IN A MINUTE: Chad Connors

IF I COULD MAKE ONE REQUEST ON A PORN SET IT WOULD BE: Lots of naked men having heavy sex and let's shoot it all no cuts.

AS A TEEN I ALWAYS FANTASIZED ABOUT SEX WITH: Any hot blond guy with a huge cock ... Kevin Williams.

CURRENT FANTASY MAN: Randy Spelling

SEXIEST PART OF A MAN: All of him.

THREE INGREDIENTS OF MY HOTTEST SEX FANTASY: Naked men, dark corners and lots of lube

FAVORITE ITEM IN MY SEXUAL TOYBOX: Blindfold.

MOST PRIZED POSSESSION: My Medal of Bravery from my time in the Canadian Military

HOBBIES: Working out, travel, making money, having sex with hot men.

PETS: I have two Siamese cats and an Australian Cattle dog.

PET PEEVES: Smokers, and immigrants who think that we as North Americans need to accommodate them. They need to learn our way of life and start to respect it.

If someone were to come to you for advice about getting into the business what would you tell him?

Plan before you get in. Hire a good manager and create a good business plan.

What are the best and the worst parts about being a porn star?

Fame and fame.

So how is fame a double edged sword?

Good thing, for the most part you get special treatment in the gay community. The bad thing is the people who are jealous like to start rumors that for the most part are not true.

What sort of rumors do people usually tell about you being a porn star?

You must be HIV positive or get STDs regularly. Also that all porn stars are sluts.

How do you think this career choice has changed or affected you?

It has made me a better lover.

Can you give me some specifics on how being in porn has made you a better lover?

It teaches you control over your urge to blow your load and also how to extend the pleasure of the sexual experience, be it in a group or one on one.

Porn sets are often the scene of some odd, surreal, or hilarious incidents. Do you recall one you would care to share?

Due to the fact that I do not gossip, nothing to share that would not make someone feel like a dirt bag.

What is the most aroused you have ever been on screen?

Doing *Hot Firemen* I came three times in one position. Man, Johnny Hanson was good.

Have you ever developed a crush on any of your costars? Care to name names?

Chad Connors and Johnny Hanson

If we were making JT's Orgy who would you want as your four co-stars?

Chad Connors and Johnny Hanson, Brian Kidd, Drew Peterson … more if possible.

What things do you usually do to prepare for a XXX shoot?

Workout, good diet and plenty of sleep.

JT Sloan [PHOTO COURTESY SLOAN]

And how do you usually spend the evening after a day of filming?

Depending on my schedule for the coming days, I usually would go out with friends and then go home and have crazy sex with my man.

Is it educational, humorous, arousing, or unbearable to watch yourself in a movie?

I tend to be more critical with how I moved, held my abs and so on.

If you could change one thing about the way the industry is run what would it be?

I would definitely make it so that the featured actors get a portion of all sales of the videos.

Do you have some amazing fantasy you are just waiting for some director to ask you to film?

Yes. My ultimate fantasy is to be the bottom in a sex club gang bang, and my husband is the top controlling who fucks me and where and when they cum.

Do you think the adult film industry has an obligation or responsibility to portray safe sex practices?

The role of the porn industry is to create a fantasy world of possibilities and not preach about safe sex. I feel that those who watch should be old enough to make their own decisions with regards to their own health. We do not go to mainstream movies to learn how to live our daily lives, so why should we watch porn to learn how we should have sex.

Porn stars are often considered these ideal physical specimens, but if you could change one thing about yourself through cosmetic surgery what would it be?

Have all my hair removed. If only the general gay populous knew what it takes to look so damn hot they would have a whole lot more respect for what the porn stars do.

Looking back do you have any childhood or adolescent memory that you just shake your head and think, "Yep, that kid was destined to grow up to be a porn star"?

Yes I always fought to remain naked, even at school (pre-school.)

If you were offered a role in a fetish film how far would you go?

As far as possible except scat, urine pain or blood.

In your opinion does this career make dating easier or tougher?

Tougher as you get one of two things happening. 1) No one wants to date you because you are a slut; 2) You don't measure up to what they expect from the Super Porno Star.

When it comes to seducing a man I've found nothing works better than...

Being forward and blunt. "Let's Fuck!"

Where is the wildest place you've ever had sex?

Beside the Pacific Coast Highway in Malibu.

"I believe that if you fear anything it controls you."

Two sides of JT Sloan [PHOTOS COURTESY SLOAN]

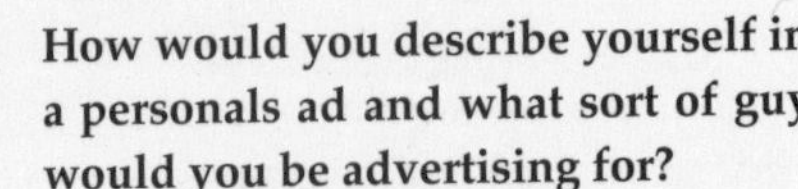

How would you describe yourself in a personals ad and what sort of guy would you be advertising for?

I would be short and sweet but basically say if you are real, truthful and honest about yourself and what you want let's talk. You must have an open mind and understand that there is a vast difference between love and sex.

If you had to make the choice between love and sex which would it be and what are your thoughts regarding fidelity?

The truth is that in a gay relationship, if anyone thinks that they are living a true monogamous relationship is either lying or cheating, both of which will eventually destroy their relationship(s). True love is the ultimate goal in life, but that can only be found by being honest with the one you love.

Speaking sexually very few guys are as skilled as me when it comes to ...

Control of my sphincter muscles.

So what is the JT key to such control over your sphincter muscles?

If I told you then everyone could work on the control and that would make my talent the norm.

When you pass a hot looking guy on the street what gets you to turn around and do a double take every time?

If he is cute and has a huge package.

Describe your ideal romantic evening?

Nice dinner out then get naked in a hot tub with my date and his best friends.

Describe your dream vacation.

With my husband on a nice tropical beach, naked and have ten other hot boys/men at our beck and call to fulfill any sexual fantasy myself or my husband has. And of course it would have to be filmed for posterity.

DIESEL **WASHINGTON**

How did you get started in the business?

Well, I did some soul searching first, but I knew porn was an avenue that I wanted to get into. I took some pics and sent them to TitanMen, got a response back and decided to give it a try and the rest is history! I've always been a fan of TitanMen because they use hot muscle guys and appreciate fetish and kink rather than just vanilla sex.

What were you looking for when you got into it?

At the time, I wanted to be taken seriously as a porn actor and show off my talents and abilities. At the same time, getting paid to fuck hot guys is like a dream. I also wanted to bring more men of color into this business, since I haven't seen many well-known black gay porn actors in this business and I want to change that. It's 2007 and you can count on one hand the instances where black models have crossed over into mainstream porn. Otherwise, it's all thug related, interracial or other specialty film. So I hope to change that!

What about making XXX movies surprised you?

I always thought like many people, it was easy work, that all you had to do was go on set and fuck and get your check. Most of the positions that look

STATS

BIRTH DATE: April 11, 1976

SIGN: Aries

HOMETOWN Staten Island, NY

HEIGHT: 6'6"

WEIGHT: 245 lbs

TWO BEST CHARACTER TRAITS: I'm open minded and blunt.

TWO WORST CHARACTER TRAITS: Impatient and too aggressive.

FAVORITE MUSIC: It's a tie between hip hop and R&B.

FAVORITE MOVIES: *A Clockwork Orange* and the *Matrix* series.

FAVORITE MOVIES I'VE BEEN IN: *Folsom Filth* and *Boiler*.

XXX COSTAR I'D DO AGAIN IN A MINUTE: CJ Knight.

IF I COULD MAKE ONE REQUEST ON A PORN SET IT WOULD BE: That people have fun and laugh because it breaks the tension.

AS A TEEN I ALWAYS FANTASIZED ABOUT SEX WITH: Vanessa Del Rio.

CURRENT FANTASY MAN: Ryan Reynolds.

SEXIEST PART OF A MAN: His butt.

THREE INGREDIENTS OF MY HOTTEST SEX FANTASY: Condoms, lube, and Ryan Reynolds.

FAVORITE ITEM IN MY SEXUAL TOY BOX: Paddles.

MOST PRIZED POSSESSION: My mind.

HOBBIES: Working out and people watching.

PET PEEVES: Liars, time wasters, people without goals.

Diesel Washington [PHOTO COURTESY TITANMEN.COM]

hot on screen are not easy to do especially when there's a camera in your face, and a crew, lights, etc. Most times you have to hold your body a certain way so that the camera man can get the best angle. It was more work than I thought, but overall I'm getting used to it and enjoy performing.

That's so true, porn is notorious for putting guys in less than comfortable positions for the sake of the camera ... what is the toughest one you've had to assume for the sake of the shot?

"You can count on one hand the instances where black models have crossed over into mainstream porn. Otherwise, it's all thug related, interracial or other specialty film."

Well, for me it's all about the shot. I've always tended to naturally put my body into different positions for the sake of a good fuck, but now I do it for the camera. The hardest one was the reverse cowboy for my scene in *Boiler*. I had my scene partner CJ Knight sitting with all of his weight on my lap; CJ's about 5'8" and I'm 6'6" so his feet didn't even touch the floor in that position. So I'm holding his weight in my lap and laying over the edge of the box standing on my arms with my feet on the floor fucking him at the same time. I was kind of tired a few minutes into it. But looking at the scene onscreen it looked hot and that's all that counts to me.

I first realized I was a porn star when ...

I first realized when people started using my stage name like it was my actual name. I created the character and the name, but to hear it spoken as a real name of a person that really exists was a shock to me at first.

What is the most aroused you have ever been on screen?

I'm the most aroused when I perform the fucking scenes. I like to get a good blow job and everything, but I really enjoy fucking, so when it's time to fuck I get the most turned on. When I tend to fuck my partners doggie style, I'm the most aroused I can be.

If you were putting together a movie called Diesel's Orgy who would you want for your 4 costars?

Mason Wyler, Erik Rhodes, Cole Ryan, and François Sagat

If someone were to come to you for advice about getting into the business what would you tell them?

First off, you have to be dedicated to the business and know all the effects of doing porn. If they could live with that, then they'll be fine. They have to be taught how to stay well-conditioned, coming to the set looking healthy and fit to perform to the best of their abilities. A lot of things go into being a porn star. You can either be a person that does porn, a porn star, or a porn superstar – it's your choice.

When fans meet Diesel Washington

they undoubtedly expect a certain person – how do you think you differ (or do you) from their what they expect and that XXX persona?

Well, I don't know what people expect from me really. I tend to be my own person and like to have a little bit of privacy. But I really express myself in my own blog that I write www.Dieselwashington.blogspot.com. I write about things that piss me off, sex and generally my take on life.

As a teen you fantasized about Vanessa Del Rio and now your current fantasy man is Ryan Reynolds ... when and how did that change come about?

Growing up I lived very macho. I had girlfriends (that I was fucking), played sports throughout high school and college. I was in the military for three years. As I matured, I developed an attraction for both men and women and accepted that I was bi. It grew from there and I guess my tastes have changed, which is always a good thing. I still love Vanessa Del Rio because she was very sexual and confident in her movies. The change to Ryan Reynolds was just because his body was so well-toned and muscular, I had to give him props.

People always think of porn stars as these perfect specimens ... but if you could change one thing about yourself through cosmetic surgery what would it be?

I wouldn't change a thing!

How would you describe your ideal romantic evening?

I can't describe it to you. All porn stars have to have their secrets, and that's one of mine.

One of your pet peeves are people with no goals ... can you name for us a few of yours?

A few short term goals are to film excellent movies, win best performer or actor, and try my hand at directing. A few long term goals are to go back to school, start my own business, buy a home and travel the world.

HARRY **WOLFE**

Harry, how did you get started in the business?

I started out doing webcam shows online for audiences on a particular site. The audience kept growing so I decided to broaden my horizons and try pictures, started my own website, www.blkhrywoof.com, added my own gallery of pics, was then found by a photographer for Black Inches Magazine. We did a set together and after they were published, I was approached to do video by Pantheon Productions. Since then, I've done a few more films, been featured in three calendars, and there's even a refrigerator magnet out there with my mug out there, along with a few other choice parts, (Laughing).

What are the biggest challenges to running your own site?

Basically when I designed my site, I wanted to just make sure that I put a bit of genuineness into it. Sure, there are plenty of pictures, but I wanted

STATS

BIRTH DATE: June 20, 1969

SIGN: Gemini

HOMETOWN: Atlanta, GA

HEIGHT: 5'9"

WEIGHT: 185 lbs

TWO BEST CHARACTER TRAITS: I'm very easy to get along with and I can listen.

TWO WORST CHARACTER TRAITS: I'm dangerously attracted to bright colors and shiny objects, (Laughing) and I tend to be a bit blunt when giving advice, especially if it's for someone's own good.

FAVORITE MUSIC: Anything Prince and definitely house music.

FAVORITE MOVIES: Anything Sci-Fi.

FAVORITE MOVIES I'VE BEEN IN: *Daddy Dreaming* (Pantheon Productions) and *Bears Will Be Bears* (Bearfilms.com).

XXX COSTAR I'D DO AGAIN IN A MINUTE: Clint Taylor

IF I COULD MAKE ONE REQUEST ON A PORN SET IT WOULD BE: Less direction, more action.

AS A TEEN I ALWAYS FANTASIZED ABOUT SEX WITH: John Travolta and Erik Estrada.

CURRENT FANTASY MAN: Classic Colt Star Pete Kusak.

SEXIEST PART OF A MAN: His ass, for sure, followed very closely by his calves.

THREE INGREDIENTS OF MY HOTTEST SEX FANTASY: Musclebears, Leather, and a camera.

FAVORITE ITEM IN MY SEXUAL TOY BOX: An extra thick Cyberskin black dildo I'm trying on for size.

MOST PRIZED POSSESSION: My Husbear of ten years and my closest friends. (You all know who you are).

HOBBIES: I run my own website, www.blkhrywoof.com, I am learning to play bass guitar (Anybody wanna play?), video editing, and photography.

PETS: My two cats, Mardi and Mimi.

PET PEEVES: Lateness of any kind when it comes to meeting up.

to make sure people saw my thought processes as well. It gives the visitor a sense that they are getting more than just a picture site, its also my blog. You get to also know the person behind the pics. I think that's important with what I wanted to portray and keep it true to myself. I think I've done a pretty good job so far with that concept, so I may as well keep on that path.

What were you looking for when you got into making XXX movies?

I wanted to see how far I could really go with it as long as I was getting the offers to do films. I only average about one a year so far, but it's not a full time career for me. I'm just having fun in this little journey of mine, met a few lifelong friends along the way and I haven't regretted a single thing about it.

Were the people who knew you surprised by this life development?

Oh, yes. My friends that know me now, and knew me a few years ago as the shy introverted type were really shocked. Most of them finally admit that it's something they also wanted to try but never could push through that barrier within themselves to just try it. I just had my twenty year reunion with my closest friends from college. They were the most shocked. They knew me as such the shy guy that was always the cautious voice of reason in every little wild thing they did. But they got a kick out of the whole idea that "Lil ol' me" had changed the most. Who knew I had a wild streak.

I'm interested in how you mention a lot of guys think about making porn, but they have a barrier that holds them back. What was the thing or things that pushed you through that barrier and allowed you to make that leap?

People have things in their lives that will either allow them or stop them from making porn or even taking personal pics of themselves. Either job, clergy (not that it seems like much of a stretch anymore), or family. People come up to me on occasion and reveal that they always wanted to do something in the same line as the things I've done. I just tell them, there's nothing stopping you but you. For me, when I started pursuing this, my line of work was usually spent on the phones as part of a tech support job. Nobody sees my face or really puts my voice together with what I've done.

Recently that changed, and I changed jobs and the job put me onsite in different locations where people come in contact with me everyday and do see me. You have to know at anytime, someone could recognize you and say just about anything. It has happened already, and yes, my boss knows now. He was the first to spill the beans and admit he knew. And no, it did not affect my getting the job in the first place.

I've gotta hear how one goes from being shy to a XXX guy. What was that transition like?

Well, that was a long process of self discovery on my part. I wanted to see how far I could go with doing something completely outside my comfort zone and also something that could kinda break that mold of always being the shy and introverted guy. Knowing what I wanted and going for it helped me see that I can do whatever I put my mind to. Porn for me was some-

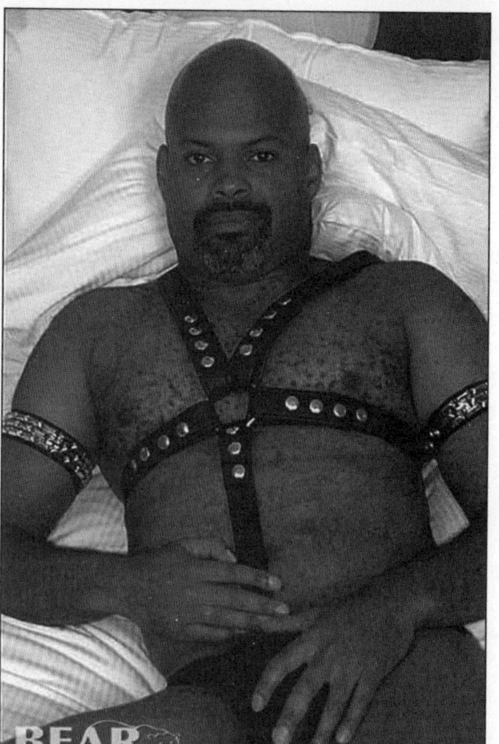

Harry Wolfe [PHOTO COURTESY BEARFILMS.COM]

What is the most aroused you have ever been on screen?

I'd have to say the scene with Clint Taylor. I was getting nailed on the kitchen counter, which was a fantasy I never got to do at home. After that scene, I was on a high all to myself, having completed my first scene on film.

So Harry, have you always been attracted to bears or did that develop at some point in your life?

It's kinda developed into its own monster as I've gotten older. Nothing turns me on now like a big, well put together, furry man.

What do you usually do to prepare for a film shoot?

Right before, I'll sit in a corner and just relax while the guys setup. If my scene partner is there, I'll play with him and get him worked up and he'll usually do the same with me. I've really lucked out and had some excellent choices made for me as far as who I'm paired up with.

what of an experiment to see how far I could go with that same shy person I was. He's still there from time to time, but he doesn't stop me from trying new things because of what other people might think anymore.

Do you recall the first movie you made and the first bit of direction you were given?

My first scene ever was with Clint Taylor in *Daddy Dreaming*. The director knew it was my first time and gave me some tips on where to stand, but for the most part, told me to relax, just do whatever comes to mind, and a lot of it, whatever it is. It turned out to be a phenomenal first time.

And how do you usually spend the evening after a long day on the set?

By that time, I'm usually starving, so I'll eat something light, then head out on the town and play some more. I did a sex club in San Francisco between shoots, but I won't cum if I can help it. I wanna save that for the set the next day. I love to get right to the edge.

Do you think the industry has a responsibility regarding the use of condoms and/or promoting safe sex?

I'll admit, I love watching condomless sex over any other, and let's face it, its kinda caught on popularity-wise over the past few years. As for responsibility, though, I feel like it's up to the individual to make educated decisions to what they choose and choose not to do in this field. There are risks you take in any sexual act. I choose to keep myself as safe as possible when doing them. The industry doesn't get to make that decision for me.

If you could change one thing about the way the industry is currently run what would it be?

I think that if I were asked that a few years ago when I was trying to get into doing porn, it would be, to get some new faces out there on the screen. For such a long time, the faces stayed the same no matter where you looked. Nowadays, I'm glad to say now that there is a niche for just about any type of porn you want out there. So in a sense, my one suggestion did come true. So at the current time, my answer is no. I know, that was a long way around saying no, but I wanted you to know why.

Do you have some best example of bad behavior on a XXX set you would care to share?

I have heard from a friend of mine, no set that I was ever on, but he was in a scene with a guy who couldn't top unless he was barebacking. It wasn't a barebacking set, but to get the guy hard, they cut the top half of his condom off so on film, he was wearing it, but on the inside, not so. It kinda makes you wonder how often that happens.

Porn sets are often the place of some surreal and hilarious incidents. Do you have any personal tale you would care to share?

During a porn shoot in the Bahamas on a tourist island, I was shooting a scene fairly out in the open which required the need for spotters on each end of the trail we were on as well as the beach we were shooting in front of in the distance. Between shoots, I was working on stroking myself up under a tree, when off in the not too far distance, I see one of the spotters who was to watch the beach area for tourists standing away from where he could see anyone coming. He got closer to talk with me and directly behind him was a group of ten kayakers, but they weren't rowing by, they were coming right up to the beach. I saw this and asked the guy standing in front of me to block their view so that I could pull my shorts up as they were coming closer much quicker than I was comfortable with. By this time they had completely come ashore and were looking directly at us as I stood up, pulled my shorts up, completely flashing this group of ten that I now refer to as the Kayakers from Christ, to stop our shoot.

As I made it back over to where the other guys in the film were resting, the producer was rolling shooting some candid footage for like a blooper reel. I wasn't aware of that since I had just flashed a family of ten and was mortified beyond belief. The producer, with the camera straight on me, asked me, "And do you know why we have to stop?" implying that we were wrapping up to get back on the cruise ship.

I in my infinite anger over what just happened, blew up and said, "Of course I know! It's because of those Kayakers from Christ came up and ruined our shoot! And I flashed them! I fucking flashed an entire family on the beach!"

He laughed at me, put down the camera and said, "No, it's because our time is up here on the beach. But I'd like to meet this family."

The footage of the beach, and the blooper reel turned up missing and never made it to the DVD. But there are five or six crew members that will be able to say they watched me have a meltdown on film and lived to tell about it.

"'Those Kayakers from Christ came up and ruined our shoot! And I flashed them! I fucking flashed an entire family on the beach!'"

Do you get recognized for your XXX work and if so what has been the most unusual circumstance of being recognized?

It's not like it happens every day, but it does happen more times lately when I'm out with my friends. One guy came up to me, pulled me to the side, and told me that he really appreciated what I had been doing and that he was one of his biggest fans, and as he's talking to me, a single tear rolled down his cheek, (not an exaggeration). I was floored for the rest of the night.

Sweet. So have you ever made a fan's fantasy cum true?

Twice, and both times, it was well worth it. I don't make it a habit of doing that, but the feeling was definitely mutual.

How do we get you in the sack and what do we do with you once we get you there?

My nipples are the keys to the kingdom as far as I'm concerned, but they have to be treated just right to unlock the rest of me. Too hard, which most people try first, and I instantly turn off. Stroke and tease them just right, tongue welcomed, I'll more than likely respond by jumping your bones right there.

How would you describe yourself in a personals ad?

Shy and mischievous cub type seeks a kitchen partner to cook up some fun. Can be slow to come to a boil, but when it gets hot, I like to simmer for a good while before finally declaring a good dish great. Guaranteed to melt in your mouth. Also great for leftovers.

Do you have some ultimate fantasy you would love some director to ask you to film?

Someway, somehow, I wanna have sex in the desert on a motorcycle. Leather would be a plus, but I'd definitely settle for the desert scene. That would be hot, literally.

Do you have any childhood or adolescent memory that you can look back upon and say, "Oh yeah, that kid was destined to grow up to be a porn star"?

I was more of a geeky kid growing

up all through high school. I didn't really see myself as an extrovert at all, but looking back, I wish I did tell at least someone I knew to keep an eye out for me. I'm going to shock them all.

What is the biggest misconception people have about you when you meet them?

I have heard people say that I look taller on film than when they meet me. (Laughing). I'm only 5'9, not that it's short by most standards, but its an interesting conversation starter that I've come across more than once. Also, people tend to think that I'm a lot more outgoing when in all actuality, I'm very shy. I can't tell you when the last time I ever walked up to a hot guy and introduced myself. Sure, I'll cruise the hell out of him, but it's usually the other guy that makes that all important first move.

If a guy came up to you and asked for advice about getting into the business what would you tell him?

Just be sure that it's something you are willing to chance family, or job, or whatever having possible access to the stuff you put out there. It's a pretty big step to take, but I say, if you do decide to do it, have fun, and don't take the whole thing too seriously. It's what you make of it.

If you were to make a movie called Harry's Orgy who would you want as your four costars?

Mario Ortiz, Hank Hightower, Anthony Gallo, and Peter North/Matt Ramsey.

Speaking sexually very few guys are as skilled as me when it comes to ...

I can spend hours eating a guy's furry butt. I really enjoy making a man squirm with my tongue. Nothing gets me off more than teasing a guy's ass with my tongue until he squirms and moans like he's going out of his mind.

So I want to hear more about calves. That's an interesting body part to choose. What makes them sexy to you?

The look of thick calves on a hot man just completes it for me. I just love to grab them and kiss them, and throw them on my shoulders and fuck the hell out of the man that owns them.

Where is the wildest place you've ever had sex?

On an island in the Bahamas for Bearfilms. Now that was a fantasy come true. We were on a somewhat secluded part of the island where the scenery was straight out of a romance novel. The ironic tragedy of that story is the footage of that island romp turned up missing by the time the movie was sent to the editors. So there is lost footage of us out there somewhere.

Do you think you are a typical Gemini and if so, how?

I really don't follow the whole astrology thing, never did, but from what I have been told about my personality, they say I do have the split personality they say Gemini's possess, along with a mean streak to go with it. But that doesn't come out too often.

Describe your ideal romantic evening.

I like it simple when it comes to romance. Wine, candles, maybe a whip or

Harry Wolfe [PHOTO COURTESY BEARFILMS.COM]

two, and no distractions from the outside world, snuggling up and watching a movie with my Husbear, then maybe we can just curl up in each other's arms and fall asleep wherever we are.

If you had to choose between sex and love which would you choose and what are your thoughts about fidelity?

Well, that's a tricky question which requires a few answers. Having been in a relationship for ten years now, and about seven of those years being open, which allows me to do porn in the first place, I have to say that I would choose love. I say that because I know where home is at the end of the day and we have a love bond that I have never had with another man, but I am well aware that I am also a creature of sex. I really don't think that the average male gay, straight, or otherwise is really content with just one mate. I love sex, sometimes more than I should, and more than my own good would allow me, and in that respect, I would have to choose sex.

If you had to compare yourself to an animal what species do you think best captures your essence and why?

Funny you mentioned that. When my husband and I met, he told me that I reminded him of a Bonobo, a type of monkey that spends most of its waking hours pursuing sex. Granted, I had every option to take the monkey thing as offensive, but I didn't and saw his point after I learned more about it. They truly will fuck anything that moves, male or female. If they aren't fucking each other, they are jacking off like crazy. To a small degree, I can agree with him. I have a very high sex drive and like to use it.

If your life had a theme song what would it be?

Prince, "Erotic City." One of my all time favorites ever.

Describe your dream vacation.

An island in the Caribbean, with no one for miles except me and my man, or men (hey, it's my fantasy). Just relaxing in the sun, or sunset, what have you. No cell phones, no cars, just the waves for as far as the eyes can see. Pretty tame, huh?

RYANN **WOOD**

How did you get started in the business?

I was actually spotted on my Manhunt.net profile through another actor Chad Leigh. Chad and I chatted a few times then when I was on a trip to Ft Lauderdale I met with Howard Andrew who was Chad's agent. Now, Howard Andrew is my agent as well. I told Howard I only want to do this if I can work with the big production companies, and about three seconds later he was on the phone with Michael Lucas setting up an interview.

What were you looking for when you got into it?

Honestly I didn't even know myself what I was looking for. Money wasn't really the issue. I was just looking to experience something new and totally different from the real me. As I may have said before I am a very shy person but when I am in front of the camera it's like I'm another person, so in a way doing porn has liberated me and broken me out of my shell a bit.

Since you're basically shy were the people who knew you surprised about you getting into this?

Some people were very surprised and others definitely know how sexual I am and said if anyone could do it

STATS

BIRTH DATE: December 21, 1981

SIGN: Sagittarius

HOMETOWN: Philadelphia

HEIGHT: 5'11"

WEIGHT: 165 lbs

TWO BEST CHARACTER TRAITS: I'm intelligent and affectionate.

TWO WORST CHARACTER TRAITS: I'm shy and rather quiet.

FAVORITE MUSIC: Everything – pop, R&B, jazz.

FAVORITE MOVIES: Romantic comedies.

FAVORITE MOVIES I'VE BEEN IN: *Ritual* by Falcon/Mustang and *Ranger* by Falcon/Mustang.

XXX COSTARS I'D DO AGAIN IN A MINUTE: Trey Casteel, Tim Towers.

IF I COULD MAKE ONE REQUEST ON A PORN SET IT WOULD BE: Some damn healthy food! It's always junk food on the set.

AS A TEEN I ALWAYS FANTASIZED ABOUT SEX WITH: Sadly, Luke Perry (*90210* was popular back then).

CURRENT FANTASY MAN: Jake Deckard.

SEXIEST PART OF A MAN: His legs.

THREE INGREDIENTS OF MY HOTTEST SEX FANTASY: Rain, lighting, and lube.

FAVORITE ITEM IN MY SEXUAL TOY BOX: A free standing sling.

MOST PRIZED POSSESSION: My man.

HOBBIES: Roller blading , working out, cooking, and reading.

PETS: Rocky my Beagle.

PET PEEVES: Ignorance.

I could! I'm very shy when I first meet people but once you get to know me personally you find that I am more out going and talkative and just need to break out of my shell.

And with being shy, does being in front of the camera liberate you? So what other differences are there between you and Ryann Wood the porn star?

"I was very curious though, about what is going on in [Jack Nicholson's] head as he drives by and sees a couple guys fucking so close to his property."

Well the biggest difference is the shy issue. I feel much more sexy now and also more at one with my body. I've learned a lot from other models about just being who you are and feeling good enough. Wow, this is so deep!

You didn't expect it in a XXX interview huh? Looking back on your life do you see anything which makes you think, "Yep, that kid is going to grow up to be a porn star"?

Oh, God no! Never in a million years did I think I would be a porn star. Growing up I was always overweight. My highest weight was 240 pounds when I was 16 years old. So I never even had the slightest thought that I someday could be a porn star. Of course who doesn't fantasize when they are young about doing it and about being that person on the TV feeling all that pleasure.

You weighed 240 at 16. How did you manage to lose the weight?

Well, when I was about 16 I saw some pictures from a wedding I was in and decided right then – how can I live like this? I was always a lineman playing football from age 5-16 so everyone always wanted me big. I finally said enough and started doing track and not really eating the healthiest way but cut down a lot on food. Now I follow a diet and fitness plan that is best for my body. The key is switching that switch in your brain that says working out is so much work to saying that working out is fun!

Following that dramatic weight loss do you think being so desired now carries a special sort of meaning for you?

It definitely does carry a special meaning. I still have that fat kid stuck in my head sometimes so when someone comes up to me or e-mails me saying how sexy, hot, and lean I am I sometimes think they are crazy! But I am getting better about it. It means a lot to have the effect that so many people say I have on them. Turning someone on and pleasing them is a huge turn on for me.

Do you recall your first film and the first bit of direction you were given?

Oh yes I can't imagine anyone not remembering their first film. It was a movie called *Manplay #25: Mansized* the director was Ray Dragon. I was very nervous. I think the first direction I received from Ray was to not be nervous and also "Do not look at the camera!"

What about making XXX films surprised you?

The craziest thing to me about XXX films is how nice everyone is. Of course there are a few arrogant people out there but other than that the other actors and crew and directors are just so friendly, nice, and out going. I was also very worried about coming across drugs. I have never done a drug and never intend to. So when I started porn I was just worried that it would be drug central and to this day I still have never seen a drug on a set.

Your fantasy includes rain, lightning, and lube. Why is sex always better during a thunderstorm?

Sex in a thunderstorm – I don't think it gets much better than that. There is just something about the smell in the air, the way the wind blows the curtains, and the noises that fill the air while having sex. It's just so sensual and erotic to me.

Where is the wildest place you've ever had sex?

Ryann Wood [PHOTO COURTESY LUCASENTERTAINMENT.COM]

Honestly, probably the wildest place to me was while I was shooting my scene for *Ritual* (Falcon/Mustang) I was on the top of a hill in Malibu, CA over looking the ocean. I remember in the middle of the scene I had to take a piss and walked a bit down the side of the hill to a tree (I was of course still totally naked) I looked out at the ocean and just thought to myself this is so wild and surreal. Then of course Jack Nicholson drove by. (He lived in the ranch next to the one we were shooting at).

So did you wave to Jack Nicholson when you were standing there naked?

Oh, no, I think at first I jumped behind the tree! I was very curious though, about what is going on in his head as he drives by and sees a couple guys fucking so close to his property.

Speaking sexually, very few people are as skilled as me when it comes to ...

Being a power bottom – at least that's what I am told. John Bruno the director of both my Falcon/Mustang movies told me he hasn't seen a bottom that can take it and enjoy it as much as I do in a long while. I take that as a huge compliment!

So is there some secret or key to being a power bottom?

Hmmm – I can't imagine there is a secret to being a power bottom. So many people ask me how I can enjoy getting fucked so much. I honestly think it has to do with the first time a person tries to get fucked. Not that I want to get too deep into my first time exploring anal sex, but for me it was a very good experience. The guy that I was exploring with new that it was my first time and he took things very slow, he even explained about condoms and lube and just was very gentle. Once my first experience was over I enjoyed it so much that I think there is something in my brain that just clicked on saying bring it on! So it allows me to relax and enjoy!

When you pass a hot looking guy on the street what gets you to turn around and do a double take every time?

Eyes. If an attractive guy is walking toward me down the street and he looks at me and makes a dead lock eye contact maybe a slight smile, that gets me every time.

So what are the joys of a freestanding sling?

What aren't the joys of a freestanding sling? You can bring it anywhere you want to bring it. If you have never been in a sling you need to try it out! It's a great experience to just be able to lay back and swing yourself into a nice big ...!

What are some things you always to do prepare for a movie shoot?

Definitely make sure a few weeks before that I stay strict to diet and exercise plan. The morning of a shoot I usually eat light maybe do a little cardio then just try to mellow out throw my iPod on and relax and save energy for the scene. They call it "Hurry up and wait". You are always in a hurry to get to the set get all prepared then you sit around waiting for everything else to be ready, lighting, cameras, other models. So to just mellow out to some music or spend time talking to other models and makeup crew is always fun and relaxing. I'd be lying if I said I don't get nervous before a shoot but I do I think most people do because like I said before, you are in a very vulnerable state when you are filming.

What is the most drama you have ever encountered on a film set or during a shoot?

Honestly, I haven't really encountered anything too dramatic on a set. During the shooting of these movies people are so go with the flow. A lot of them have to be since things can change from minute to minute depending on who has a hard on who doesn't, and who's ready to fuck or get fucked.

What is the first thing you do when you come home from shooting a movie?

Have sex! Whenever I am done

Ryann Wood [PHOTO COURTESY LUCASENTERTAINMENT.COM]

with a shoot I am always so horny. It's like I don't care if I had sex for 5-6 hours in that day it's not totally fulfilling since you are doing everything for the camera.

Have you ever developed a crush on any of your costars? Care to name names?

I don't know if I would call it a crush, maybe more of a connection. Being in porn and being naked for sometimes 4-6 hours or more you can feel very vulnerable. There are some porn stars out there (mainly the bi or gay for pay guys) who are very to the point and are just there for the money. Then there are others who actually make an experience out of it. The most I really connected with someone on a sexual and friendly level would be Tim Towers, Trey Casteel, and Cole Ryan. They were all very fun to be around and work with and of course our connection during the scene shows on the camera.

If you were making a movie called Ryann's Orgy who would you want as your four costars?

Hmmm. Such a tough question! Jake Deckard, Jason Ridge, Mason Wyler, and Chad Hunt. Of course I would be the only one bottoming!

Is it arousing, interesting, surreal, or painful to watch yourself on screen?

All of the above! First thing that hits me when I see myself in a movie is definite pain – you are your worst critic remember, so it's a constant – oh don't bend that way, oh that's something I need to work on – then I get interested in seeing how it was all edited together and if the chemistry is good. Then of course the whole surrealness of it -is that really me? Then sometimes arousing because it brings back the memory of shooting the scene.

Describe your ideal romantic evening.

My most romantic evening would include a four-course meal that I would cook for my partner. Candles all over the table, some Lizz Wright on the stereo, a nice bottle of white wine, and of course a thunderstorm.

How do we get you in the sack and what do we do with you once we get you there?

I'm a very shy person so it sometimes takes an out going guy to get my attention. Eyes are a very sexy feature on guys you can read so much into them and can tell sometimes their thoughts just by eye contact. Once you get me in bed I guess it all depends on what mood I am in, but kissing is a must to turn me on.

Describe your dream vacation.

I definitely love tropical places. Love to have walks on the beach especially at night. Then be able to go out and have a few drinks and dance all night long. Breakfast in bed with my man then head back to the beach to lay under the sun all day and jump in the ocean to cool off. Vacation is the time for no stress no worries and the sound of the ocean to me is something that just washes all the stress and worries away.

So now that you are in the business do you have any long term plans for your affiliation with the industry?

I do plan on working in the business as a model/star as long as people want to see me. I really enjoy doing this work and have a lot of fun on set and meeting all the other models. As for after my modeling career may end – I'm not sure if I would stay in the industry. Many models continue to be on set as PAs and directors, makeup artists. Not sure I would go that route but hey – never say never.

How would you describe yourself in a personals ad?

Ambitious, good-natured, shy, sexual GWM Always up for meeting new friends and occasional fun. But I am taken so not looking for more than friends. 5'11" 155 blond/blue 8" cut vers/bttm. Check me out at www.ryannwood.com

TRE **XAVIER**

How did you get started in the business?

I answered a modeling ad for a website in the back of one of the gay weekly magazines telling the gay-happenings in New York. I went there cautious because there was no website listed, and it turned out being for showguys.com, which was a Badpuppy website at the time.

What were you looking for when you got into it?

I was looking to become more sexually liberated, and show the reality of gay black men to undo the misconception that porn at the time helped make the American gay community believe – the thought that we're all buffed, bald, and always a top.

So has this XXX path been a liberating journey for you and if so in what ways?

Yes it has. I often tell people that porn is the way I found my voice, such as by way of my blog. Most of those thoughts on sexual fantasies and so-

STATS

BIRTH DATE: March 31, 1971

SIGN: Aries

HOMETOWN: Brooklyn

HEIGHT: 5'6"

WEIGHT: 145 lbs

TWO BEST CHARACTER TRAITS: Insightful & defensive for the underdog.

TWO WORST CHARACTER TRAITS: Procrastinating and an often misunderstood silent demeanor.

FAVORITE MUSIC: All kinds because I use a different type of music for every mood I'm in.

FAVORITE MOVIES: *It's A Mad Mad Mad Mad Mad World.*

FAVORITE MOVIES I'VE BEEN IN: *69 Fuck Street* and *Dillon: The One.*

XXX COSTAR I'D DO AGAIN IN A MINUTE: Jason Dean – and this time instead of only sixty-nining and being the bottoms for everyone else, we'd take turns being the bottom with each other.

IF I COULD MAKE ONE REQUEST ON A PORN SET IT WOULD BE: When my co-star is done, can I have all the cute guys in the crew gang-bang me?

AS A TEEN I ALWAYS FANTASIZED ABOUT SEX WITH: A different hot guy every other day.

CURRENT FANTASY MAN: Brent Everett.

SEXIEST PART OF A MAN: His butt.

THREE INGREDIENTS OF MY HOTTEST SEX FANTASY: Hot guys in a variety of nationalities, bodies drenched with sweat, and great asses on all my tops.

FAVORITE ITEM IN MY SEXUAL TOY BOX: Just lube. I don't really do toys.

MOST PRIZED POSSESSION: My brain.

HOBBIES: Writing, dancing, drawing, and clothing design.

PETS: I love all animals, but I currently have no pets.

PET PEEVES: Slow-walkers and people who drag their feet.

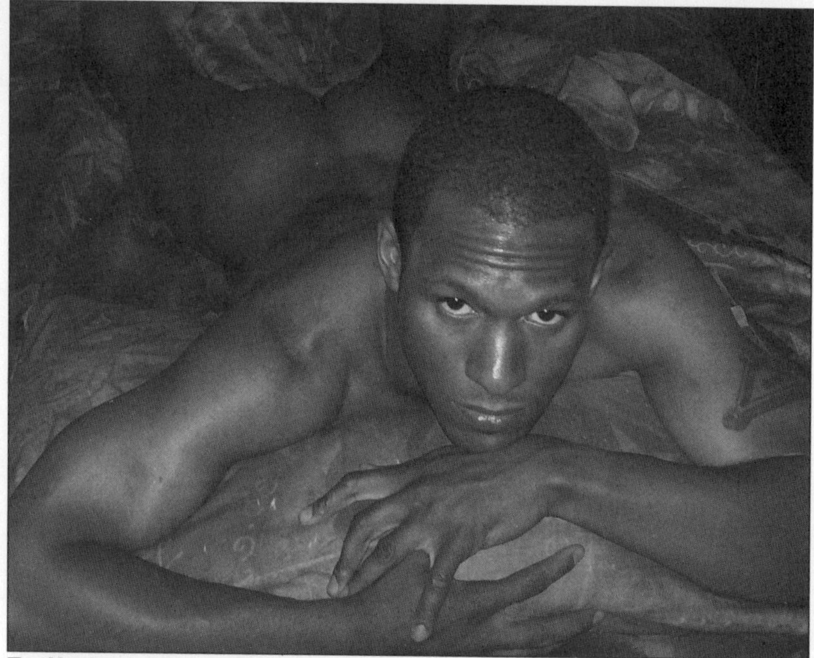

Tre Xavier [PHOTO COURTESY XAVIER]

cial issues would just stay inside me if it wasn't for my being in porn.

Where did your XXX name come from?

Before doing gay porn, I was in mainstream entertainment, and used Xavier as a middle name. I always liked the unusual nature of that name, so I kept it and made it my last name for porn. Tre comes from the nickname I gave myself (since my legal name starts with L), The L XTreme because every time I try something new, it's brought about by extreme measures. So I took the tre of XTreme and made it my first name, and put the accent on it to make it stand out even more.

Did you surprise yourself by making the plunge?

No. What surprised me is what I am becoming able to do with myself and for the gay community because of my name.

So what are some of the things you have been doing?

I've been a guest-caller at Will Clark's Porno Bingo which is held weekly at a NY bar. At this event, all money made from bingo card sales goes to a charity. The last time I was guest-caller, the beneficiary was AIDS Service Center NYC. One of the managers offered me a tour, and I took him up on his offer so instead of being the pretty little porn actor, I actually knew what services my appearance were helping to keep afloat. While there, I was invited to take part in AIDS Walk NY 2007 and be on their team, and I once again accepted. I'm glad I did it, and I'm very much considering doing it again. I may even try at some point try to follow in Will Clark's footsteps and create charity events.

Giving back is definitely important. Do you recall your first movie and

the first bit of direction you were given?

Yes, it was *Oh Boy Escorts 2*. I was told to take off my jewelry like my watch, yet my co-star was allowed to leave his on.

Hmm, curious. Did you ask why your jewelry had to go but the costar could keep his?

No, I didn't. I suppressed my annoyance towards it. Mainly because it was my first movie after most of the mainstream gay porn studios never showed any kind of interest in me.

What was the best advice you were given starting out in the business?

Will Clark told me to not let anyone take advantage of me. And I'm sure that has made me a few enemies, but at least my self-respect is in tact for being true to myself. So I can truly love the person I see in the mirror.

What is the most aroused you have ever been on camera?

My group scene from *69 Fuck Street* and watching Jason Dean's ass bounce from getting fucked by Jake Corwin.

If we were making a movie called Tre X's Orgy who would you want as your four costars?

Nickolay Petrov, Rafael Alencar, Mason Coxx, and a long-overdue Asian stud.

You've been in the business for a bit. What has been the best example of bad behavior (and not the good kind) on the XXX set?

The director being tactless enough to tell my co-star he's not a very good top. Tactless because he said it in front of me and a guest. And he still expects this guy to perform for him after taking a shot at his sexual ego.

If someone were to come to you for advice about getting into the business what would you tell them?

Actually, I've been answering questions already. I would say first and foremost make sure your sexual preferences in partners and actions are respected. If not, then they are scum and you shouldn't work for them.

What has been the most unusual or interesting thing a fan has requested of you?

The most interesting thing that's been requested of me is my phone number. I found it interesting because it showed that since the person knew I performed an intimate act (sex) on camera, he wanted to be more intimate with me on some level beyond the regular of performer to fan.

When guys who have seen your movies approach you in person how do they usually say their expectations differ from who you are? Does that make sense?

My blog has been a big help with that. They're a little weary because they think I'm just putting on a front about me being shy, and questioning my looks. But they meet me in person, and see how shy I really am when I'm complimented, and they like me more for that.

Going along with that what preconceived notions do you think people automatically have when they discover that you make porn movies?

They think it's easy to get me to

have sex of any kind with them, anal or oral. I've been to sexual parties and guys seem offended when I kindly say no. They forget porn actors are human, therefore they have a preference just like they do. We're just enough of an exhibitionist to show our preference in front of a camera.

"Stop spreading this bullshit belief that bigger is better. I've had guys with cocks that are probably 5x5 give me way more pleasure than guys who are probably 10x6 or bigger."

What things do you usually do to ready yourself for a day in front of the cameras?

I shave my chest and some body hair, and I abstain from any sexual activities for 3-5 days.

And how do you typically spend the evening after a day of filming?

If it's a weekend, go out dancing. But during the week, go home, prepare myself for my next day at my day job, jerk off to the thought of my co-star's dick in another scenario, then go to sleep.

Gay XXX is notorious for putting guys in some very uncomfortable positions for the sake of the camera. What is the most uncomfortable position you've had to assume for the sake of the shot?

When I did *Love of the Dick, Vol. 4,* I had just gotten over a back spasm I got just ten days before from the nervousness of my go-go debut, but still performed with. So any position was uncomfortable, but the worst was me holding myself up with my shoulders on the floor, ass in the air, and legs spread apart so Double R could dip his cock into my ass.

So tell me about the go-go experience. How is it unique? Was it the ultimate for an exhibitionist?

Its uniqueness depends on who you work for. I have done the standard of wearing underwear to the extreme of being totally naked with party-goers able to suck my dick and lick my ass out in the open. With that in mind, it is definitely the ultimate for an exhibitionist.

What are the best and the worst aspects of being in the business?

The best of this business comes from what you the individual do with it. Such as my getting involved in Will Clark's charity events, and my blog telling my personal stories to let other gays questioning themselves know that they are not alone with their inner-struggle. The worst of it is the limiting racial thinking of many studio heads. I see so many non-black actors who make it clear they would love to fuck me, yet when a Black and White come together for a scene, the studios market it as a big deal. And an even greater example is the lack of Asian actors in gay porn. With this being America, those things shouldn't be.

So do you think the XXX world is

making progress in the area of racial diversity or do things seem just as locked as ever? What do you think would be the best way to speed up the change?

There is progress, but it's happening so slowly you have to look real hard to notice it. What could speed up the change is for directors to learn how racially accepting their audience is, instead of catering to their own limited thinking.

If you could change one thing about the way the industry is currently run what would it be?

Besides the racism, I would have to say to stop spreading this bullshit belief that bigger is better. I've had guys with cocks that are probably 5x5 give me way more pleasure than guys who are probably 10x6 or bigger.

Do you think the industry has a responsibility regarding the use of condoms and/or promoting safe sex?

I think the industry has some responsibility. Because the fact is that if you do as an adult act (like sex), you should not have to have your hand held by being told what to do. However, since most scenarios in porn are of fantasy encounters, I think the industry does have a responsibility in promoting safe sex. Not to be a hypocrite, but there is a part of me that would love to be the bottom in a barebacking gangbang getting cumload after cumload put in my ass. But the reality is that HIV/AIDS is out there, so unless I know everyone's status and the movie has a disclaimer regarding that, I have no business participating in that kind of behavior, especially in a movie.

What is the biggest misconception people have about you when you meet them?

They are surprised at how shy I am.

I first realized I was a porn star when _

You asked to interview me.

Glad to help you with that awakening. If you were offered a role in a fetish film how far would you go?

Some spanking and water sports while wearing leather or latex clothing.

Porn sets are often the place of some surreal and hilarious incidents. Do you have any personal tale you would care to share?

During the shooting of *Oh Boy Escorts 2* my scene partner – Joseph Nash, was told by the director (Tyson Cane) that he needed some spit so the blowjob he was giving me would look better. So Tyson Cane gave him some water. The funny part is that the guy didn't drink the water, so when he resumed giving me a blowjob, all the water in his mouth (still cold) just splashed all over my dick and crotch.

Do you have any childhood or adolescent memory that you can look back upon and say, "Oh yeah, that kid was destined to grow up to be a porn star"?

Not anything anyone else would see. But to myself, I have always been sexually aware, and looking for new info about sex to better my knowledge of myself and others even before I was in my pre-teens. Maybe that's why I seem to know how to act and write in a way that gets people going?

Speaking sexually, very few guys are as skilled as me when it comes to ...

Dirty talking because a big dick can hurt so good, instead of whining like it hurts so bad.

I love dirty talk. Give me an example of your sweet talking filth.

I actually said this in real-life then used it to win in Will Clark's Porn Idol contest for his dirty dialogue section: Oh yeah, stick that tongue in my ass. Ooo Baby, your tongue feels like you're teasing my ass with the tip of your dick. Now give me the real thing. Go slow. Now stop. Yeah, I know it's teasing you, but I want to feel your cock throbbing in my ass. Oh it feels so good. Now – bang the fuck out of me. Yeah! Yeah! Yeah! Fuck yes!

You are nasty! Where is the wildest place you've ever had sex?

Straddling a slightly reclined passenger side in the front seat of a guy's car while he fucked me from behind, with the car parked directly across the street from Splash Bar in NYC while they were still open.

How would you describe yourself in a personals ad?

Smart, insightful, African/Native American/Venezuelan male (yes, I'm a mutt and love it) would love the company of someone who will cherish his good points, and he will do the same for you.

Describe your ideal romantic evening.

Any place on any night I can share my thoughts with him about the world with no interruptions.

If you had to choose between sex and love which would you choose and what are your thoughts about fidelity?

As much as I love sex, I choose love. I like to go for things that you have to work for, and love is something you have to work at building and maintaining. Sex, especially in this day and computer age, is very easy to get. My thoughts on fidelity is that if you have an agreement with your partner to have an open relationship, then being with others is fine. But to have sex outside of your relationship unbeknownst to your partner is trifling and cowardly. And if the other guy knows he's involving himself with someone who's spoken for, then he deserves every bit of bad karma he gets. I've been approached by guys who tell me upfront that they have a boyfriend, and as much as I would love to find out what his boyfriend feels when he's fucking him, I send the guy on his way to avoid that bad karma.

If you had to compare yourself to an animal what species do you think best captures your essence and why?

I would have to say the feline species. I'm territorial like a lion about anything that's mine especially anything with the prefix of self (like self-respect, self-esteem, etc.), and I become at first a verbally violent terror when that line is crossed. I'm like a cheetah because I am very fast both physically and more importantly, mentally in a good way. I'm like a panther because people try to read me, but they never get the full story. And lastly, a house cat because home is where I find my peace.

Describe your dream vacation.

Anywhere that has clean air, the love of my life, and no superficial judgments.

If your life had a theme song what would it be?

There are so many, but I'll pick one I'm sure many will overlook. "New Power Generation" by Prince.

Where do you hope this career takes you?

I never expected much when I got into it. But with the notoriety through my blog, I think I may use it to segue into writing.

Tre Xavier [PHOTO COURTESY XAVIER]

ABOUT THE **AUTHOR**

Owen Keehnen is the author of two previous books of gay male porn star interviews, *Starz* and *More Starz*. His stories, articles, and erotica have appeared in numerous periodicals and magazines worldwide such as *The Windy City Times, Christopher Stree, The New York Native, Honcho, Torso, Mandate, Inches, Hyphen, Ex Lover Weird Shit, Men's Style,* and *Out and Proud in Chicago*. Owen's work has also appeared in the anthologies *Best Gay Erotica of 1996, Butchboys, Happily Ever After: Erotic Fairy Tales for Menand 'Flesh and The Word 3*. He is a former nationally syndicated interviewer, a former columnist for *Penthouse Forum* magazine, and co-editor of the annual *Windy City Times Pride Literary Supplement*. He is currently the driving force behind the horror film website racksandrazors.com and has even appeared in a couple horror films such as *Birthday Bash* and *The Small Assassin*. At the moment he is finishing work on a humorous fictional autobiography called *I May Not Be Much But I'm All I Think About* as well as a gruesome horror novel entitled *Doorway Unto Darkness*. Owen resides in Chicago with his partner Carl, their two dogs Flannery and Fitzgerald, as well as a cat named Kitten.